I0595037

HIGHLANDER AT HEART

Moment In Time Series

Y M ZACHERY

In accordance with Australian copyright laws (1968) the scanning, uploading, and electronic sharing of any part of this book without the permission of the publisher constitute unlawful piracy and theft of the author's intellectual property and can incur legal action. If you would like to use material from the book (other than for review purposes), prior written permission must be obtained by the publisher who can be contacted at wild.dreams.publishing@gmail.com.

Thank you for your support of the author's rights. This book is a work of fiction. References to historical events, real people, or real locals are used fictitiously. Other names, characters, places and incidents are the product of the author's imagination, and any resemblance to actual events, locales or persons, living or dead, is entirely coincidental.

Wild Dreams Publishing
A publication of Wild Dreams Publishing
Traralgon, Vic
First published in 2016
© re-released 2017 by Y M Zachery
All rights reserved, including the right of reproduction in whole or in part in any form.
Wild Dreams Publishing is a registered trademark of Wild Dreams Publishing.
Manufactured in Australia.
All rights reserved.
Cover © Veronique Poirier

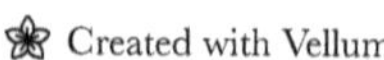 Created with Vellum

ACKNOWLEDGMENTS

I want to give a special thanks to my husband and children for their faith in my ability to accomplish my dreams and with whom I would not be where I am today. To my great friend Katie and her red pen and for keeping me motivated, without her I would not have been able to accomplish my goal. To Mel for being the best friend a girl could ever have. You are the inspiration for one of the characters in this book, I thank you for your friendship over the years and for always being there through the ups and downs of life. Without the support of these people I would not have achieved all I have.

To my partner in crime J B Joseph thank you for coming on this journey of re-release with me. And to Veronique Poirier, thank you once again for your outstanding covers, you have no idea how much I love this cover. It is unique and captures the essence of the story I was trying to portray.

Lastly to all my dedicated fans and readers I hope you love the new releases as much as the old versions.

PROLOGUE

The Highlands of Scotland 1250 A.D

It was bitterly cold and the rain, which had been threatening to fall all day, had finally broken through soaking them thoroughly. Looking up, Fearghas watched the clouds cloak the looming cliffs above in darkness, goose bumps spread over his skin as an eerie, ominous feeling settled in around him. Shaking the feeling off, he took a deep breath and kicked his horse into movement. As he rode on, the mist that hung heavily in the air thickened, making the path in front of him treacherously difficult to see. *Och, this was all he needed*! Kicking his horse, a little harder he sped up as the rain picked up its intensity. As it thundered down, the already perilous path became slick with mud and his horse stumbled losing its footing. Despite the danger, he urged his horse onward, keeping up his brutal pace; he had no choice, there was no time to waste.

The cliff wound towards the waterfall which acted as the entrance to Allna Calda Mhar cave, their destination. His body ached all over, the arduous two-day trek through the Assynt hills from the MacDonnell keep was taking its toll and he was exhausted. They'd had little rest since they had started out for the mountain; just enough to nourish them and give them what little strength they needed to reach the cave. Although MacDonnell was used to the cold winters that stormed the Highlands, the rain that pelted him, along with the knowledge of what he was about to do, sent a numbness through him like none he had ever known. He could no longer feel the leather reins between his fingers and the stinging, needle-like rain no longer bothered him as he raced on, adrenaline and desperation keeping him going. Time was running out, not only for their journey, but for each and every clan member in the Highlands.

Trouble had been brewing for quite some time and recently the devastation and killings that had racked the countryside had intensified. A dark evil was rising up like a curse, wrapping its toxic magic around everything and everyone, threatening the Highlands he called home. This was worse than any human war ever forged, this was dark magic's quest for complete control over the human world and there was only one way to defeat it. His eyes involuntarily flicked up towards the heavens and he shuddered as flashes of light skittered in unnatural paths through the dark mass above them. Even the clouds themselves were tinged with strange hues of purple and green, hovering like an ominous omen, demonstrating the power that was growing daily. Giving one last shudder, he urged his horse to a faster pace.

They kept going along the winding path, making sure not to slow down, and then he heard it, the sound he had longed to hear. The unmistakable crashing force of water cascading down the cliff face soon grew to a deafening crescendo as they approached. The water fall roared around him, mimicking the anger that was rolling within his body, he desperately wished there was another way, his body tensed as he thought about everything that he was about to lose. The bundle in his arm stirred and let out a cry that was lost to the ferocity of the roaring water as it silenced the world around him. He would love nothing better than to stop and comfort the bundle in his arms, but not yet, he would not rest until he was at the entrance of the cave.

He continued on, following the path until it brought him to the meeting place behind the waterfall. Here he was able to stop under an outcropping not far from the entrance; dismounting wearily he looked down at his beloved daughter and sighed.

"Doona worry lass, ya Da is here, all will be fine." He cooed trying to comfort her.

Now if only he could bring himself to believe that. Shaking the sober thoughts from his head, he slowly made his way over to a ledge nearby and gently placed her down; giving his tired arms a chance to regain feeling. He noticed that the druid wasn't here yet, that meant he had a few minutes to try and make her as comfortable as possible. He placed her on a ledge that jutted out from the wall, noting the reason for her restlessness; her plaid was coming undone and the rain had started to penetrate the inner folds, making her damp, cold and uncomfortable, poor lamb. Reaching down he tried to fix it clumsily, but he was so cold that his hands were shaking, making the task almost impossible. Eventually, despite his trembling fingers, he managed to rewrap the plaid so that the dryer parts could warm her cold shivering body. It was the best he could do. If only he could replace it with the dry blanket he had in his satchel, but he couldn't – she needed *this* particular plaid to go through with her; this plaid had her name stitched into its bright patterned textile next to her mother's brooch. Both would be her only tangible connection to her past, *to him.*

A noise coming from behind him gained his attention, and quickly he turned towards where the noise had emanated, sword drawn and ready to fight off whoever had found him. His eyes met with nothing. He couldn't just stand here waiting for them to ambush him. He picked up his daughter and made his way further up the path towards the entrance of the cave, staying close to the wall to avoid slipping in the oozing mud.

As he neared the entrance, he heard the distinct sound of a throat clearing, and renewed anxiety bubbled inside him. As he closed in on the entrance his eyes adjusted to the shadows that spilled out of the cave, it was then that he saw a figure. The man was six-foot-tall with jet-black hair. With mixed emotion, he recognised the dark plaid draped over his shoulder; it was the same plaid worn by all druids in the Highlands. The black was a symbol that that they belonged to no clan, yet controlled all. The druid stood there blocking the entrance to the cave; an imposing power emanated from him. MacDonnell prayed that this was 'Fer Doirich', the druid that was to help him with his mission.

The man moved slightly and, as he did, the torch that he had been holding in his right hand reflected off the inner walls of the cave, allowing Fearghas a glimpse of a jagged scar that ran diagonally across the man's left eye. Yes! Thankfully, this was Fer Doirich. The scar appeared to grow as the light danced and flickered, and the fierce presence of this man made Fearghas thankful that Fer Doirich was on their side. Fearghas knew that, even though the man had a reputation that could send any man quaking to his knees, the druid would never harm them. Fer Doirich was one of the few magic keepers left that believed in the good of the world. He was willing to fight the evil that the black magic had brought upon the Highlands and in this, they shared a common goal.

The druids were an ancient group of magic makers that protected the secrets of time and space. Every Highlander knew of them, but few knew the full extent of their powers. The druids originally tried to encourage this shroud of secrecy as it kept their enemies from gaining knowledge of their strengths and weaknesses. If it ended up in the wrong hands, knowledge like that would destroy them all. A fact made all too clear by the brewing trouble. Druids had always used their magic for good, until now.

Now, many of the druids had been swayed to the dark side by the promise of greater fortune, power and knowledge. There were only a handful of druids left that still believed in the old ways; that they were here to keep the balance between man and power. They were the only ones willing to stand between the evil that threatened The Highlanders. They were the Highlands' last hope. Them… and Ceana.

"Are ya sure ya wanna do this?"

The druid questioned Fearghas, no doubt testing his commitment to the cause. "The lass might no' survive the trip."

The druid's voice had him once again questioning the sanity of their decision, looking down, he found himself staring into his daughter's emerald green eyes, eyes that mirrored his own. She appeared to be watching him as if asking the same question. As much as he didn't want to send his daughter into the unknown, he had no other choice; this was the only path left for him to take in order to keep her safe. The plan may be dangerous, but he knew that staying here would guarantee her death and the end of many clans.

"Aye, Fer Doirich, I am sure. At this moment, nobody but us kens what the lassie is capable of. And you ken as well as I that if we do no' do this, then she will die. We have no other choice, the only way to save her and the Highlands is if we send her to another time."

"And ya ken that it will be some years before she can come home?" Fer Doirich prodded further.

"I am fully aware of the stakes here druid. I ken that she can only come home when she accepts and understands her gift." He snapped back.

The druid nodded with satisfaction. "Och come then, we must move quickly. I still have to perform the cloaking spell before I can send her through." Fer Doirich ordered, before he disappeared into the dark cave.

MacDonnell still wasn't sure how this spell was meant to keep her safe from those who would try to find her, but the Druid had assured him that the spell would hold for as long as they needed for her to grow and learn how to use her powers. Trusting in that, all he could do was follow the druid into the shadowy corridor that would lead them to a fate, a fate neither he nor his daughter had chosen. He sighed as he once again found himself wishing that he lived in a different time. But he didn't, and although he wanted to go through the portal with his daughter, he knew he couldn't. He needed to be here for his clan and his people and no amount of wishing was going to change what was about to happen, there was no other way for them to defeat the dark magic.

The deeper into the cave they went the more nervous he became, it was all happening too fast, he needed more time. Slowing down his steps, he glanced at the bundle in his arms. She had fallen back asleep, peacefully unaware of what was about to happen. Then it hit him hard, this would be the last time he would lay eyes on his lass until she had grown. And he would not be there to see her grow. A sharp pain of regret sliced through him as he wondered what she would grow up to be like. Would she have her mother's quiet disposition or his hot temper? Would she be the first lass in the MacDonnell clan to resemble the MacDonnells or would she be the spitting image of her mother? A tear rolled down his cheek and, as it dripped from the end of his chin onto her little hand, question after question hammered him. It was in that moment that he vowed, one way or another, he would move Heaven and Earth to bring her home. Leaning down he placed a kiss on her forehead and whispered. "Always remember who ya are lass." He knew that she was too young to understand him, but if he knew anything, it was to trust in the magic and, in a world where magic was everything, he had faith that his words would somehow guide her home again.

Looking up, he noticed that the druid had disappeared out of sight and his footsteps seemed to be fading. The druid was quite a way in front and his torch was getting dimmer.

"Come on MacDonnell!" The druid abruptly shouted from within the darkness. His tone sharp, "we are running out of time".

The druid was right; picking up his pace, it didn't take long before he matched the man's wide steps. The sound of the waterfall grew more distant the further into the cave they travelled. The trickling of the water over moss covered walls and insects scurrying away from their echoing footsteps to find a dark haven now replaced the roaring of the water. Anxiety and adrenaline had set in again and he no longer felt the weariness that had engulfed him a short while ago. His daughter stirred slightly, he pulled her tighter into the folds of his embrace, hoping he would get to hold her again one day.

The deeper into the cave they ventured, the quieter it became, and alongside the noises of the cave, he could hear the sleepy murmurs of his daughter and he only hoped that one day he would have the chance to explain to her the reasons behind what he was about to do. But for now, he'd placed his faith in the druid's plan.

"We're here." Fer Doirich's raspy voice stated moments before they broke through the darkness into a brightly lit chamber.

They were no longer in the dark corridor; instead they appeared to be in an antechamber of some kind. It was bathed in a light so bright that they no longer needed their torches. But the cave was fully enclosed, so where was the brightness coming from? MacDonnell noticed that the light was glistening down from the roof, the rays so intense that it appeared as though the night sky was radiating from the rocks, casting moonbeams over the walls and floor, illuminating the cave around him. *More magic.* He shouldn't be surprised; he had heard that caves such as these existed, but he had always thought they were nothing but myth. Blinking rapidly, his eyes finally adjusted to the sudden brightness and the room came into focus. The first thing he saw were eight stones that sat in the dusty floor in the middle of the room. They were spaced evenly in a circle and were deeply embedded in the floor. Looking closer he saw that, in line with each of the stones and further to the edge of the cave, stood eight stone columns, each as tall as the druid, starting thick at the bottom and thinning out at the top to form a point. And he was standing right in the middle of it all, turning in a full circle, trying to take it all in.

"Put the lass right where ya standin' and then get out of the circle!" The druid barked.

Fearghas couldn't believe it was already time to do this. He'd only just had time to catch his breath from the journey and now he had to let his daughter go. This had to work; if it didn't it would be another six months before another opportunity arose. By then everyone, including his daughter, would be dead. The druid had explained that the portal would only open in line with each equinox. During that month, the portal could be opened each night at midnight, but, at the end of the month the portal closed for good until the next equinox, when the cycle started again. And, tonight was the final night of this cycle. The druid had chosen this night deliberately so that once she was through no one could follow her. Well, not for another six months at least and, by then, hopefully the other druid would have hidden her well.

He could see the druid was starting to lose his patience, time was running out fast. He only had a few seconds left to say his final goodbye before he placed his wee bairn's life into the hands of another. Lifting her up, a waft of lavender that was uniquely her drifted up to greet him. The coolness of her cheek greeted his lips as he gave her one last kiss. "I hope one-day ya will be able to understand why I had to do this. Ya just too important. You're our only hope for survival lass." He whispered into her ear. A heavy feeling filled his chest as he looked at her one last time before placing her in the inner circle. As he laid her onto the cold ground, she let out a frightful scream. It was then that a horrible notion entered his mind.

"Are ya sure the druid will be waiting for her on the other side?" He asked turning to Fer Doirich fighting the rising urge he had to grab his bairn and just go home.

"Aye. She will be safe with him. Now stop your blathering and let me concentrate," he replied impatiently. He drew a symbol on the first column. "These symbols are right." He mumbled as he made his way from column to column.

Slowly backing out of the circle, Fearghas stood at the edge of the ring watching on in silence as the druid made his way around to each of the eight columns, marking each one with a different symbol. His eyes followed the druid as he tried to figure out what each of the symbols meant. The only one he recognised was the eternity sign. Eternity, that sign alone worried him; it sounded so infinite. And once again he was gripped with an overwhelming feeling of hopelessness and fear. He prayed once more that he would not have to wait long before he had his daughter back in his arms.

As more of the signs were etched, an unnatural wind started rushing and swirling around him. It pulled at his hair and tousled his plaid, a shiver ran up his spine as immense power surrounded him. It appeared to pulsate within the walls of the chamber.

He flinched as a loud crack of thunder sounded overhead and he watched on, helpless, as the cries of his daughter became screams of terror. His heart felt torn and a lump formed in his throat, the demand for the druid to put an end to it all lodged there. He wanted to sweep his daughter up and take her away from this magic. But he knew that for her sake and that of the Highlands, he couldn't. Her life and the lives of their clans were more important than his own selfish needs. He knew he had to let her go, but doing so was killing him.

By now the wind had picked up with more ferocity, it was howling as it tore loose rocks from the floor of the cave and tossed them around. He could no longer hear his daughter's screams through the roaring of the vortex that appeared to surround her. The cave was vibrating from the force of the wind and he was sure that any minute now the roof would be ripped apart from the force. Surely the cave could not take much more of this punishment. Turning his gaze back to the druid he noticed that was only two more symbols to go. This was it. He closed his eyes praying for his daughter's survival.

"Laird!" Came an abrupt shout from the darkened corridor.

Both of them stopped and turned towards the entrance as his son burst into the antechamber. The lad was dripping wet and his breath came in shallow waves. The wind was still raging around them and the lad had to hold onto the wall as he slowly made his way over to him.

"What is it lad?" He snapped, grabbing him by the shoulders so that he wouldn't be blown away by the force of the wind. He had stationed his son with a few men in the trees below to watch for any trouble.

"They're coming Da!" It was all the lad could get out before he bent over at the waist in a coughing fit, trying to recover his breath. That was all the information he needed, he knew what his son was talking about. *Damn! It was too soon! How did they find him so fast?*

Turning to face the druid he saw the same fear and adrenaline that he felt coursing through his own blood visible in his eyes.

"Finish it NOW!" He screamed at the druid above the howling of the wind, finally releasing some of the pressure that had been building up in his throat. The druid rushed forward to the final stones and etched in the last two symbols, the wind howled louder as a vortex grew in size like a monster descending from the ceiling, swirling angrily around his daughter, waiting for the opportune moment to snatch her in its claws.

He couldn't do this.

Releasing his son, he rushed forward just as a loud boom of thunder rent the air, and he could only watch as she vanished before his eyes. He stood there staring at the space where she had been moments before, feeling nothing but emptiness; it was too late to do anything. She was gone.

Falling to his knees his heart sank. His baby was gone. He felt numb and all he could do was just sit there, staring at the space she had just occupied, in stunned silence. She was gone. He closed his eyes and then opened them again hoping that it had all been a bad dream, but she was still gone. He didn't think the emptiness inside of him could get any worse, until the druid's softly spoken words reached his ears, words that would haunt him forever.

"Och what have I done?" He heard as the druid mumbled them over and over again.

Lifting his head, he looked to where the druid had been standing and dread filled his heart. The druid's face was pale, his eyes were closed and he was facing the heavens as if to be saying a prayer.

"What?" Fearghas choked out. The emotion that he had been feeling since this all started boiled to the surface. The druid turned and looked at him and the look of pure desperation he saw in the druid's eyes made his skin crawl. Even though he knew something was horribly wrong, he needed to hear it.

"WHAT!" He screamed. The haunted look on the druid's face was replaced with one of fear. He could only imagine what was escaping through his own eyes. Even his son shied away from the intensity of the roar.

"I'm sorry Fearghas, I doona ken…"

"Where is my daughter?" He interrupted in a low, forceful, menacing tone as he slowly rose from his knees. It almost sounded as if he had growled it. Walking slowly towards the druid, he repeated his question. The druid backed away from him. It was well known that when a Highlander was calm they were extremely dangerous, and right now Fearghas was the epitome of calm. The rage that had replaced his emptiness was dangerously close to surfacing and, if the man didn't answer him in the next few seconds, he would likely snap his neck with no regard for how powerful he was.

"That's just it. I doona ken." The druid whispered.

The gravity of what had just happened finally hit him, hard. His daughter was gone, and they didn't know to where or when the lass had been sent. Not only had he doomed her but he had also doomed the Highlands. Letting out a roar that could be heard from miles away, he sunk to his knees once more. *How could this be happening? What had he done?*

CHAPTER 1

Gold Coast, Australia. Present Day.

This assignment was giving her a headache; referencing was a bitch. No matter how many essays she had done, the referencing never got any easier. This one was due at the end of the day and she still needed about two hundred words to finish it. But for now, she was working on the footnotes and bibliography while she waited for today's guests. Staring at the screen, she wondered where to go; each professor favoured a different style of referencing to her last and trying to figure out which would please Professor Pemblebrook was driving her insane. All his students knew that he was a real Nazi when it came to referencing. He would nit-pick the smallest of mistakes and many students had failed, simply because they had put in a space where there wasn't meant to be one. Looking back at her screen she realised that she had reverted to the old style. "Damn it!" She cursed, hitting the back-space key repeatedly with great force. She would have to delete it and start from the beginning. Turning back to her referencing guide she endeavoured to understand the mind of her professor. Yep, it was going to be a long day.

When deciding to become an archaeologist, the idea of delving into subjects like Scottish mythology had been intriguing. After all, how hard could it be to find some artefacts and discover where they had come from? The history of it had already been written, she'd assumed naively. How wrong that was. Her studies had since taught her that historians had their own take on events and, with new finds being discovered every day, supposed 'history' continued to change. Added to this, the methods and systems used by archaeologists, which all contained bits of science and statistics, two subjects she hated; you had what was currently her life. She sighed in frustration as she once again made a mistake. This was doing her head in, and for the hundredth time this semester, she wondered why she kept doing this to herself. *Ahh that's right, it was because she loved history so much.*

She just had to keep telling herself that all of this would soon be over and she would be a full-blown archaeologist and all the late-night study sessions and assignment worry would all have been worth it. But as she sat staring back at her computer, the words seemed to blur together. *That was it!* She had done enough for now. It was definitely time for chocolate, a cup of tea and a break. Throwing her pen on the desk, she pushed her chair back, stretched her arms above her head and groaned as her back cracked in complaint. Feeling a little more human, she stood up and began to turn towards the kitchen when the phone rang, startling her. So typical, just as she needed a break, the joint got busy.

Ceana ran the popular Firefly Hideaway with her brother and sister. It was located in the heart of the Springbrook Mountains in the Gold Coast hinterlands. Timber cabins were built into the rainforest, each sitting on the edge of the creek that ran through the heart of it all. She'd always thought it was like being lost in a fairy tale and, to illuminate that theme, each cabin was named after mythical creatures, many of them from ancient times. Every one of the cabins contained wood fireplaces that guests took full advantage of once the cool air hit in the evenings. At that time of night, the forest around them filled with the smell of wood smoke, a smell that she had always loved. For some reason it filled her with a sense of calm and it felt as though there was a memory that belonged with the smell, a memory that she never seemed to be able to grasp.

The fires filled the cabins with the smell of cedar, permeating all aspect of the lives of its guests. Her guests had often told her that touches such as these brought them back time and again. Each cabin also housed a spa in front of a full-length glass wall that framed the rainforest and, at night, the rainforest would light up with fireflies dancing from one tree to another. It lit the forest up and you would often see children trying to catch them or whispering to each other about how the forest appeared to come alive. It was this phenomenon that had inspired the name for the popular romantic getaway that was her father's concept. Like her, he had loved history and his passion had ignited her own. He had wanted to create a place that embraced all the joys of the modern world while creating the sense that their visitors had been transported to another realm, a realm where the names on the cabins could truly exist. And he had accomplished it. For three years running, the Firefly Hideaway had won the award for *Most Popular Honeymoon Destination* in Queensland. She smiled at the memory of her father as she reached for the ringing phone and all at once the door swung open and guests started arriving. She quickly fell into the familiar rhythm of bookings and questions; groaning internally, she realised her chocolate would have to wait.

It was 3:00p.m. before she got the chance to sit back down at her computer and look at her assignment again. Where had the day gone? Luckily, she still had some time to do the last of the referencing and the final two hundred words before her deadline. She was stressed about the mark she was going to get and had to keep telling herself that this was only her minor assignment. The major part was due in four weeks' time. But the reassurance wasn't working, she needed every mark she could get. If her grades fell she would not be able to get the job she

wanted, and that was not an option. She clicked on the file to open it again and read over her last paragraph, willing inspiration to come. She knew she had to get back to it, yet no matter how hard she tried, her brain wouldn't focus. The weather wasn't helping. The rain, which had begun to fall in a steady flow about half an hour ago, drummed against the tin roof and, coupled with the

warmth from the fireplace, her desire to curl up in the corner chair and read a trashy romance novel intensified. Highlander stories were her favourite. They took her away to a place she longed to be. Ever since she could remember she had had a passion for anything Scottish, from their language to their history. She hoped to go there

one day and explore the many castles that were in ruins and… deep down, she fantasised that perhaps she would find her own Highlander. For now though, she had to finish university and if she didn't get this assignment done, she would have no hope of graduating at the end of the year. With longing, she glanced down at the book sitting beside her on the desk, sighing she turned back to

her assignment. "Damn Professor Pemblebrook," she swore as she started where she'd left off.

⁂

Ceana had finally gotten her assignment in at 11:45p.m, with fifteen minutes to spare. She'd worked through dinner, eating a sandwich while typing. Now it was 12:45a.m, and even though she was tired, sleep evaded her. She'd been looking at the ceiling for over an hour, willing herself to fall asleep. She'd even gotten up at one stage and made herself a hot chocolate; normally it would have worked, but not tonight. She'd even been desperate enough to try the old counting sheep cliché but, after seventy-eight of them, all it did was make her hate the white, fluffy balls of taunting hell. No matter what she tried, she still managed to return to the thoughts that kept her awake.

Every year, on this day, she faced a similar battle. No matter how worn out she made herself, or how busy she had been during the day, she still found herself here on this night thinking about her past, wondering just who she was. It was on this day, twenty years ago, her parents found her on the path leading down to one of the cabins. There had only been five cabins back then. Ceana had known from an early age that she was adopted, no one else knew of course; her parents had loved her as equally as much as her siblings, Tristan and Katie. But her parents believed that she'd had a right to know in case she decided to find her real parents one day. She loved her adopted parents as much as a child could. To her they *were* her real parents, even if the blood that ran in her veins did not match theirs. Their love was what made her who she was, it was what made them a family. Despite the questions it raised, Ceana had loved hearing the story they'd told her when she was too young to understand the implications, and, as a child she would make her mother tell her every night until she fell asleep. The story radiated love and pride and eased any negative thoughts away. She closed her eyes, letting the memory surface, letting her mother's voice tell her about the night a stork had left them the most precious gift, one that changed their lives forever.

The Firefly Hideaway *had just opened and already the five cabins were booked. The guests were set to start arriving tomorrow, as long as the storm eased up. She looked out the window at the sound of rain falling hard, the storm had come out of no-where. The wind was starting to pick up, so much so that she could see some of the trees bending and swaying dangerously from the force. Just then a loud crack of thunder rumbled through the air close by and the crashing sound that followed signalling a potential disaster.*

"Jason," she called out to her husband in the next room. "Do you think that tree falling could have hit one of the cabins?" She heard his footsteps as he entered the room coming to stand behind her. He wrapped his arms around her and placed his head on top of hers.

"I don't think so Kris. But just for you I'll go and check." He placed a kiss on her cheek and walked out the door, shrugging on his jacket.

She smiled fondly, watching him as he strode out the front door. She wondered how she'd gotten so lucky. Jason was her high school sweetheart and ever since she could remember they'd had this dream to open up a romantic getaway together. Now after years of planning, it was finally coming true. Turning back towards the window to watch him, she realised that he had forgotten his torch. He was not going to be able to see anything out there without it. Quickly donning her raincoat, she headed out into the storm in search of her husband.

Making her way along the wet path, which was made from timber and was lifted just off the rainforest floor, she hit a slick patch and almost slipped. The wood in this area hadn't had sand lacquered into it. She would have to remember to let Jason know. He would have to go around and check all the other paths as well. The sand made the surface rough enough to walk on when it rained; it was a must for the safety of their guests. Slowing her pace, she made her way carefully along the slippery path. The last thing she needed was to break something. She had just rounded the corner, towards the Loch Ness Monster cabin, when she'd heard a faint crying over the sound of the rain. It almost sounded like an injured animal. The closer she got to it, the louder the cries became and then she saw it. It was just lying in the middle of the path and it wasn't an animal. It was a baby! Forgetting about the slippery pathway, she ran to the child while screaming for Jason.

It only took her a few seconds to reach the little bundle and when she did she knelt down beside it. She could feel the water from the wet pathway seeping into her pants but she didn't care. The baby had been left out here in this storm, wrapped only in a plaid blanket. Who could do such a thing? What kind of person could just leave a precious baby in a storm like this? A million questions were rushing through her mind.

Finally, she could hear her husband's footsteps as he came running up behind her. "What's wrong?" He asked, panting. Rain was trickling down his face but he didn't seem to even notice. Looking up at him she moved slightly to the left, showing him the bundle, his face changed from concern to shock. "Where did it come from? None of our guests have arrived. Why would someone leave a baby here?"

He was throwing so many questions at her. For each one she only had one answer, "I don't know Jason but we have to do something." She pleaded. Picking the baby up she cradled it in her arms, the blanket moving as the baby continued to cry, the poor thing was drenched, they had to get her out of the rain and warm before she became sick. It was then Kris noticed a name etched in the corner of the plaid, "Ceana." She breathed.

"What did you say?" Jason asked.

Looking up at her husband, tears filled her eyes. "The blanket says Ceana." She replied through her tears.

Jason took the baby from her with one hand and wrapped the other around her shoulder. He kissed her head and then whispered, "Well let's get Ceana home and out of this damned rain." She noticed the compassion in his voice and her heart filled with pride for the man she had married.

With both girls wrapped in his strong embrace, they headed back to the warmth of the cabin.

FOR MONTHS her parents had tried to find her biological parents, to no avail, and then they were allowed to adopt her at six months of age and she had officially become their daughter. However, they never stopped searching for answers and then two years later, Tristan and Katie, or 'double trouble' as she had named them, were born. Then the fun began. Once Ceana started asking her own questions, they started searching again, but just like before, nothing came of their attempts. It was as if her birth parents had never existed in the first place. At first Ceana had been angry that they had been unsuccessful in their search for answers. She had wanted to find them so badly. There were so many questions she needed the answers to, like who she was and why they had just left her. She was angry with them for abandoning her as they had – who just left a baby out in a rain storm? – and, as the years passed with no answers, her anger towards them mounted.

Yet, despite her anger, a piece of her still believed that one day she would find all her answers. The historian in her longed to know the truth about her past, which was the only reason she wanted to find them. She had never wanted a relationship with them, she had the perfect parents already. From the day her parents had found her, they had given her all the love and support she needed. They never denied her the chance to find her biological parents and through all the disappointments they had been there lifting her back up. She would never have gotten through it without them.

Apart from the matter of her real parents, her life had been almost perfect, until about six months ago. It was a day much like today. Ceana had been running the Hideaway for the weekend. Her brother and sister were off with friends and her parents had gone away to a conference for the weekend. It was around six in the evening, on Sunday, and the rain had begun to fall, yet again defying Queensland's reputation as the Sunshine State. Her parents should have been home and she was trying to ignore the niggling concern building up inside her. Upon hearing a car pull up later that night, she rushed to the door in relief, ready to give them hell for not calling. It was a joke she liked to play on them, showing them what it was like to be in her shoes on the nights she had come home later than her curfew. Swinging open the door, her smile froze. It was not her parents, but two police officers standing there, their faces saying it all.

The next hour had been a blur of emotion, numbness and denial. Katie had rushed home from her friend's place and together they tried to brace for the impact of losing their folks. They hadn't told Tristan straight away, he was away up the Sunshine Coast on a surf tour and she'd not wanted to tell him over the phone. He didn't find out about the accident until he returned two days later. The police had informed her that her parents had died in a car accident on the Pacific Motorway and in that moment, their lives had changed forever. They explained that it had been a freak accident. There had been a pile up due to the wet conditions, and a truck, which didn't see the accident in time, slammed on his brakes causing his rig to career into the other lane, smashing right into their car. The speed and force of the impact had killed them instantly. It took months for any of them to function properly again; Tristan put his tour on hold, Katie took time off work, Ceana had time off from university and they shut the Firefly Hideaway while they found a way to cope with the loss of their parents.

Their regular guests had been so generous and caring that, when they reopened a couple of months later, they were the first to book in and help make sure everything ran smoothly. So here she was six months on, running the business with her brother and sister, keeping the dream of their parents alive. The pain hadn't gone away, they had just learnt to deal with it, and all three of them lived their lives to the fullest. *'Every day is a gift,'* her mother used to remind her when she'd be feeling down. Now that she was gone Ceana tried her best to live by those words. Laying there, remembering her mother and father brought back the emptiness that she felt in their absence, the pain and fear she had felt on the day of their accident washed over her so intensely it took her breath away. Her heart ached to have her mother back. She was the one she'd discussed her hopes of the future with. And her father, the one person who understood and shared her love of ancient things, would have known how to perfect her essay, but they were gone. She thanked God each day that she had her brother and sister, otherwise she would have been alone in the world again. Giving in to the pain, she cried herself to sleep.

Ceana looked at the alarm clock beside her bed. Crap, that couldn't be right, but looking again the time didn't change. It was 10:00a.m already. *Someone should have woken me up by now,* she thought. Jumping out of bed, she rushed to get ready. It was her day to work on the reception desk again and she was late. While she was getting ready, a niggling thought in the back of her mind kept on telling her that something was not right, someone should have woken her. She had a quick shower and dressed in her traditional long pants and white shirt. Then, pulling on her jumper, she rushed out to the front counter.

The minute she entered the reception area the niggling thought became a roar, everything was unusually quiet. Normally, at this time of the day, Katie would be in the house somewhere making noise and the reception area would have been full of guests checking in and out. Even on their slowest day it was never this quiet.

"Hey Bata, where is everyone?" She called to an empty room and received no response.

Frowning, an uneasy feeling began to settle in her stomach. Something was definitely not right. Her palms began to sweat and her heart began to pound with alarm. Turning around, she went to go in search of her sister. She hadn't taken two steps when the bell above the door chimed, a normal, familiar sound. *Thank God*, she thought to herself as her heartbeat slowed down and her body began to relax. Shrugging off her unease she turned to face her guests with a bright smile. But the smile died on her lips; her heartbeat quickened once again, as she stared, frozen on the spot.

In front of her stood the most amazing male specimen she had ever seen. He was over six-feet tall, wearing nothing but a plaid. His jet-black hair reached his shoulders, and his body, oh there weren't words for it. His presence alone intimidated her, which was strange, it wasn't often a man *could* intimidate her and he had yet to speak a word. He just stood there watching her as intently as she was watching him.

"C-can I help you?" She managed to get out, embarrassed over her lack of eloquence and composure.

"Aye lass, ya can." He replied in a deep Scottish accent.

Oh God his voice, it was pure heaven. She grabbed the side of the desk as her legs turned to jelly. She could not stop looking at him as he started towards her. Her breath caught in her throat, his steps were so fluid and purposeful it was almost like he was a panther on the prowl. That was all she could compare it to. He didn't just walk, he looked as though he was stalking her, luring her in to a false sense of security, before moving in for the kill.

It didn't take him long to reach her, now he just stood inches in front of her. She could feel the heat radiating from his body and she could see his pulse beating at the base of his throat. She stared and couldn't take her eyes off that point. She could only watch in stunned fascination as he brought his hand up and placed a finger underneath her chin, tilting her head back so she was looking directly into his eyes. She lost her breath again. His eyes were magnificent. The colour of the clearest ocean, so lusciously blue that, as she stood there staring into them, she felt as though she was drowning.

Turning her head abruptly, she broke the contact. She had to. His eyes were mesmerising her to the point that she felt herself leaning into his hold. Moving her eyes lower, she thought she could find a safer spot to look at. She was *so* wrong. Her eyes settled on his mouth instead. A mouth so full, with lips so luscious, all she wanted to do was kiss them. A small smile formed at the edge of it. The smile didn't help; it only made his mouth more tantalising. She let out a small breath as she continued to stare at his mouth, then without warning, he kissed her so deeply that a searing heat instantly spread to her core. It was as if he had read her thoughts. All her senses were heightened; she could feel his breath mingling with hers, becoming one. He smelt of the forest, fresh and musty all at the same time and, and like her hideaway, it reminded her of a memory she could not grasp.

As his tongue mingled with hers, she tasted scotch and honey, then, finally, she could hear his panting breath entwined with hers as their passion rose in intensity. She was so completely lost in the sensation that it took her a while to realise her feet were no longer touching the ground. Suddenly she knew that she had to get away from this man, he was dangerous, and if she didn't break the kiss now, it wouldn't be long before she begged him to take her here on the floor.

"W-what are you doing? Please put me down." She managed to gasp out as she pulled her lips away from his.

"Nay lass I will not do that," he whispered into her ear, as he kissed his way down her neck.

"Why?" She choked out with a tremble, as goose bumps spread over every inch of her body at his touch. She knew she should be terrified, but oddly, the longer he held her, the safer she felt. She didn't understand the pull this man had on her, he was a stranger, but it was as if she was somehow meant to be in his arms.

"Doona be afraid, lass, I am not here to hurt ya." He said, lifting her head up so that he was again staring into her eyes.

"Then why are you here?" She boldly ventured almost afraid of the answer.

"I'm here to take ya home, lass. It's time to remember who ya are." He stated, smiling down at her.

❦

CEANA WOKE up in a cold sweat, heart pounding, looking over at the window she could see it was still dark outside. Turning to the clock, she noticed that it was only 2:00a.m. It was that Goddamn dream again! It was back, but why? It had been so long since she'd had it, in fact the last time she remembered having it was around two years ago, when they had suddenly stopped. She had been so happy when they had; she wasn't sure why, but for some reason, the dream always shook her to her core. They had started when she was about fourteen years old and every six months she would have the same dream, it never changed. Each detail of it was exactly the same, right down the clothes she wore. It wasn't so much the dream that scared her, but his statement at the end of the dream that left her shaken. For some reason, the statement that she had to remember who she was felt a little too real for her liking. Sighing, she laid back down and tried to go back to sleep. The dream kept playing over in her head as she tried to figure why it was back. Trying to calm her brain, she decided to pick up a novel and before she knew it, it was 5:00a.m. *This is ridiculous,* she thought. There was no way she was going to get back to sleep. Tossing her blankets aside she got dressed and went for a run instead.

After her run, a shower and some breakfast, Ceana entered the reception area ready for work. She normally loved working on reception but she knew today was going to be a long day. Not only was she lacking sleep, but it was one of their busiest days of the year.

They had five cabins checking out and five new batches of guests checking in. The phone was going crazy with people still hoping to get in over the winter break. The Australian winter was the most popular time for guests to come and experience their little part of heaven. The weather was perfect for the fires at night, but still warm enough to enjoy the many rainforest walks available, during the day. For the next few hours, Ceana focused on her job, ensuring that everything was ready for her guests and answering the phone. But the memory of the dream and its sudden return remained stuck in her mind and she felt unsettled for the rest of the day. *Why was it back now?* Though the question was driving her crazy, she knew she wasn't going to get an answer today so she focused on her duties and, for the hundredth time, she answered the phone, pushing the question into the back of her mind.

"Good morning, Firefly Hideaway, Ceana speaking."

"Hi dear. We just wanted to confirm that everything was okay for our arrival. We're hoping to arrive tomorrow, but they are predicting that Cyclone Oswald will be hitting the coast early in the morning, so we will let you know if plans change." Came a familiar, elderly woman's voice through the receiver.

Ceana smiled as she recognised Mrs Samson. Mrs Samson and

her husband came up here every year for their wedding anniversary. They had married each other, twenty years ago, after both of them were left widowed and had been her parents' first ever guests. They still managed to come up to the hideaway, even though they were well into their eighties now. She reassured Mrs Samson that everything was ready for their stay and that she would wait to hear from them tomorrow. She reassured them that, if they couldn't get through because of the storm then, she would re-book them at a later date, she then said goodbye before Mrs Samson could get going with one of her stories. Normally, she would have loved to stay on the phone to chat, but, in her current mood, she knew that she would not be a good listener, she was having a hard time peopling today. Placing the receiver back on the cradle, she leaned back in her chair, when suddenly an arm shot past her face followed by a loud, "Here!"

Ceana jumped with a yelp. She hadn't heard her sister come up behind her while she was on the phone. Swinging her chair around to face Katie, she playfully kicked her. "Bata, would you quit sneaking up on me. You scared ten years off my life!"

Katie laughed. "I was hardly sneaking. Maybe if you weren't so busy trying to get poor old Mrs Samson off the phone you would have heard me coming."

Pretending to be offended, she gave Katie her most outraged look. "I will have you know; I would never try and rush Mrs Samson off the phone. I love nothing better than gasbagging with that sweet old lady."

"Aha." Katie replied while standing there giving her one of her famous 'I don't believe a word you're saying' looks.

Turning back around to the desk, intending to ignore her sister, she looked down to see what she had brought. *Thank God, it was lunch.* It had been hours since she'd had breakfast and Ceana didn't realise how hungry she was until just now.

"Thanks sis, you're a gem." She declared as she turned back around to face her sister. "I guess now I can keep you around for a little longer," she said with a wink.

Katie laughed. "Any preferences for dinner?" She asked as she walked back towards the kitchen.

"Nope, as long as it's edible, I'll be happy."

"Can't promise that." Katie yelled back as she continued down the hall.

Ceana watched her sister leave with fondness. Every day she thanked her lucky stars that she had ended up with such an amazing family. Katie was a petite ash blonde and was only about four-foot nine, with large hazel eyes. She was the calm one in the family, she rarely got angry about anything and more often than not, she was the voice of reason. No matter what was going on or how angry someone was, she could just come in and defuse almost any argument. Come to think of it, she couldn't ever remember her sister raising her voice in anger. She would simply say or do something sarcastic, making the other person feel like a complete twat. Tristan and herself were usually Katie's main target. But more than that, the one thing Ceana admired most about her, was that Katie lived her life without fear. She was always up for an adventure and was just happy to go where life led her, enjoying every opportunity that was given to her. Ceana envied Katie's ability to be fearless. Nothing terrified her more than not having plan as she was afraid she would miss something important.

The bell above the door chimed, bringing her out of her musing. She swung her chair around just as the other half of the 'double trouble' came strolling through the door, with his best friend Marcus in tow. Marcus was six-feet-tall, give or take a few inches, with blond hair and green eyes, describing him, you would imagine that he was the typical, cliché surfer type that you found all over the Gold Coast. And the fact that he was also a player and had women tripping all over themselves to get a date with him only enhanced the image. However, he wasn't just good looking, he was intelligent too, something that people were stunned to learn as they got to know him. In fact, not *just* merely intelligent, Marcus was what most people would call a genius. It was how Tristan and he had met. They had both been in the advance programs at school and had graduated two years ahead of their peers. You wouldn't know it though by the way they acted. They were both quite talented at hiding their smarts.

Taking a good look at the pair, she noticed that today, they looked like they'd been tossed around in a washing machine – their hair was standing up in all directions, their clothing crushed and crumpled. She could only guess that they had spent the day down at the beach surfing, again. This was crazy in her opinion; not long ago the weather bureau had warned that cyclone Oswald was making its way down the coast and most of the beaches were closed due to rough waves, debris and high swells. When she had voiced her concerns to her brother this morning, he had informed her that a puny little storm would not stop them from riding the best waves they'd had in years. Well, that was their excuse anyway. They had then headed out looking for an open beach and from the looks of them, they had obviously found one.

"Well, I'm glad to see you two made it back alive. I didn't think we would see you for days." She said as Tristan leaned against the reception desk.

Grinning at her he replied, "Sorry to disappoint you sis, but they ended up closing down all the beaches. Not before we got a few waves in though," he said smirking at her. "I tell you what, the weather is really picking up out there. It was a good thing we left when we did. Marcus is going to stay here a few days by the way; it's going to hit pretty bad down his way." This was nothing unusual. Often when the weather turned bad or just because, Marcus would spend a few days up here. She didn't mind of course; it meant more hands on deck to help out, which was particularly useful when a storm like this hit.

"Well I'm glad to see you do have a brain after all." She shot back at them.

Tristan just laughed and moved around the counter to give her a hug while Marcus took his spot. Leaning his elbows on the bench he looked her in the eyes and smiled. Ceana knew what was coming and she tried to hold in the laughter that was brewing up inside her.

"I think, during this storm, an angel fell from heaven cos I'm damn sure I'm looking at one right now." He said smoothly. She snorted. She couldn't help it. His face was contorted into an expression he clearly thought alluring, which actually just looked plain ridiculous from where she was sitting.

"Does that line work on anyone?" She commented. Her question registered on his face in a mix of feigned hurt and rejection, then he burst out laughing. She grinned, that was what she admired most about her brother and Marcus. They both had a great sense of humour. For most women, a sense of humour coupled with a rocking body, a deep, rich voice and a heart of gold made for one delectable, eligible bachelor. But she just didn't see Marcus that way. Being Tristan's best friend and an honorary member of the family, he was more like a younger brother to her and she would always love him as such. Even though it was clear he wished it wasn't like that, she just wasn't attracted to him. Ceana had known Marcus as long as she could remember, and when they were younger, they had treated her like one of the boys. Until she had grown boobs and his testosterone had kicked in. Now, every time he saw her, he attempted to make her one of his lovesick groupies, which would *never* happen.

Her deflection did not deter him either, which didn't surprise her one bit.

"Ok then how about this one? Have dinner with me Saturday night. You never know, you might be surprised to learn a thing or two about magnetism, something you never learnt at school."

And there it was the familiar routine. Marcus always tried a new pick up line on her right before asking her to dinner and he always asked with that same smile, the one that he thought was seductive, yet only reminded her of a cute little child trying to get his way. Most of his pickup lines were corny and this one wasn't any different. In fact, it had to have been one of his most ridiculous yet. They never worked, of course

She shook her head, smiling and replied with tongue in cheek. "Marcus, as much as I appreciate the offer of a physics lesson, when are you going to realise that I am so out of your league you would have to travel twenty thousand of them under the ocean to even have a chance? You think with the amount of times I have said no that you'd have given up by now. Here I was thinking you were smart. Besides I am too old and too wise for you."

Tristan chuckled. "Marcus, I agree with her, aren't you sick of having your balls handed to you on a platter?" Tristan ribbed him.

"She is well worth the pain and one of these days I just might get lucky." He replied puckering his lips and making kissing sounds in her direction.

Rolling her eyes at him, she reached for the bookings diary. With a pout Marcus acknowledged defeat and they said their goodbyes, leaving her to get back to work, promising that they would catch up at dinner. It wasn't long before more guests started to arrive and by late afternoon they were almost to capacity with only the *Loch Ness* cabin empty. The rest of the afternoon was spent settling in guests and organising the books before heading to dinner.

CEANA TURNED over in her bed and looked at the clock; it had just ticked over to 1:05a.m. Dinner had been over for hours and it appeared as if another restless night was upon her as her mind wandered, free from the distractions of work. *How had her life gotten to be so dull and boring?* She wondered. Here she was on a Saturday night and instead of being out with her girlfriends at a club, she was lying in her room wondering where her life was heading. To top things off, she was still a virgin at the age of twenty. Of course, it was something she could change quite easily, but unfortunately, it was not that simple. She wanted passion and she had yet to find that with any man, well except for one, and he wasn't even real. It wasn't as though she hadn't tried. Ceana had dated her fair share of men, from surfers to scientists, but they had somehow pushed her further away from finding the man of her dreams. Her last boyfriend had been the nail in the coffin. Thinking about Adrian sent a shiver down her spine. She had come close to giving him not only her heart, but also her body and it had nearly cost her, her life. She was just lucky that he'd revealed what kind of toad really hid beneath the veneer of a prince before it was too late.

Ceana wondered if she really would have given him her virginity if he hadn't turned out to be a monster. She wasn't so sure. No matter how much she tried to tell herself that he was the perfect man, she just never felt the passion that her dream man had conjured up. Maybe that was her problem? Maybe part of her had been comparing every guy she dated against the guy from her dreams. She knew he wasn't real but still, she couldn't help it. He really was the perfect guy. Not only did he have the looks, he had the wide shoulders and rock-hard abs that would put any model to shame. He also had the height, which was important to her. She loved the fact that she had to tilt her head back to look into his eyes. His massive biceps and skin that looked like it had been brushed lightly with warm chocolate, also helped his cause. Ceana had often dreamt about running her tongue all over that hot body and she could not forget his voice. When he spoke, it was as if someone had poured a whole bottle of whisky down her throat, her whole body warmed from her head to the tips of her toes turning her muscles to marshmallows. But, the most important aspect that her dream guy brought to the table was the passion that he made her feel.

He always made her body tremble and her heart race when he touched her. She knew instinctively, from the way he held her, that he would never hurt her. He somehow always managed to make her feel safe and secure like nothing in the world could hurt her. That was why the dream was so frustrating. More often than not, it left her wondering if she would ever find a man in real life that could induce that same reaction. Turning over and groaning into her pillow, she realised that she needed to stop being so picky if she was ever going to get laid. Otherwise, with the way her life was heading, she was going to end up living alone, a crazy old cat lady, and she really hated cats.

THE NEXT MORNING, Ceana was woken by a loud crack of thunder. The rain was falling heavily, and the wind had picked up. Judging by the noise that was coming from outside, the storm was finally here. Getting out of bed, she didn't worry about putting a robe over her PJs she simply hurried to the office and began the task of ringing all the cabins to make sure that everyone was ok. As she got off the phone, she remembered that Mr and Mrs Samson were heading up early and they would be here soon. She just hoped the weather calmed down enough to let them get safely up the range.

Thinking about the Samsons brought a smile to her face. They were a funny old couple who had seen so much in life. They spent their time travelling and seeing as much of the world as they could. The stories they told were amazing. That was the beauty of this job. The Samsons were not the only people to come through here with stories of wonder, the guests often included international ones who came to view the beauty of the rainforests that surrounded them. These people were the reason she loved working in the reception area, she never knew who would walk into her life. And sadly, between work and university, it was the only excitement in an otherwise dull existence.

"*The storm is getting stronger, as we come to you live from downtown Surfers Paradise. The wind has picked up and reports say that Springbrook Mountain appears to be bearing the brunt of it. This area has not seen a storm like this in twenty years. Officials are urging all residents to stay off the roads where possible. Residents are also advised to stay inside and check that all loose items are secure. We will keep you updated on the storms progress throughout the day.*"

Ceana was just about to ring the Samsons when the report came over the radio. She could hear the wind blowing fiercely. Ha, *'Beautiful one-day Perfect the next,'* my arse, Ceana thought thinking about the tourist slogan for Queensland. More like *'Beautiful one-day fucked the next.'* She would have to remember to get Tristan on to making sure everything was secure. The more the wind howled, the more she worried for the elderly couple. She really hoped they'd had the sense to stay put or to stop until the rain and wind eased up. Worrying, she picked up the receiver to call them when the bell over the door in the reception area jingled, signalling their arrival. "Thank God!" She whispered as she replaced the receiver. They must have gotten on the road well before the storm intensified.

Turning around she reached for the spare towels that they had in the office just for such emergencies. She then moved out into the main reception area to greet them.

"Hello Mr and Mrs Samson, welcome back to the Firefly Hideaway. I hope that your journey here was not too bad...

The sentence died on her lips and she stopped dead in her tracks as she finally saw who had entered. It wasn't the Samsons, but she wished it was. *This couldn't be happening. It just couldn't.* She closed her eyes hoping it was just her imagination yet, when she reopened them, he was still there. Her heart picked up speed, *how could this be happening? Had she fallen asleep?* "BATA!" She shouted, as she walked over to the reception desk grabbing it for support. She was afraid her legs were going to crumble underneath her.

Katie, who had been in the next room, came running into the reception area. "What, Cee, what is it?" She asked a note of worry in her voice. *Thank God,* she thought, hearing her sister's voice. Okay so Katie was here. She was afraid to take her eyes off him, but she had to know if she had finally lost her mind. She turned to her sister and, grabbing her arms, she asked what she thought must have appeared to be the dumbest question in history, but she had to know. "Please tell me you see him and that I have not lost my mind?"

Ceana could see that she had startled Katie and, for a split second, the concern in her eyes made her sorry for worrying her sister.

"Cee, are you alright?" Katie asked with a frown.

"Yes, yes I'm fine. Can you just answer me? Do you see him?" She asked once more.

"I'm not sure of the *'him'* you are referring to, but if you mean one of the two soaking wet gentlemen standing in our reception area, then of course I see them. If you are referring to anything else then I'm afraid the answer is yes, you have lost your mind."

At any other time she would have laughed at her sister's response, but right now she just couldn't manage it. Her sister had done it again. Katie had managed to make her realise how idiotic the question had sounded.

"Ok I think you should go have some tea or perhaps a Valium and calm down. We know how afraid of storms you are. But first, you might want to get the phone. It is ringing off the hook."

Ceana could barely stand, let alone get the phone.

"Can you get it, Bata?" She asked pleadingly.

"Sure, but could you at least help the poor guys standing there dripping all over our floor? All that water is an accident just wanting to happen" Her sister said as she walked past her to get the phone.

Damn, why had she done that? She should have answered the phone, now she had to deal with *him*.

It was fine, she told herself, she just had to pull herself together long enough to find out what they needed then she could send them on their way. Her legs were shaking madly; taking deep breaths she tried calming her nerves before turning around to look at her new guests. Once she had though, her legs started trembling anew. *Nope, it was not going to work*, she thought wildly. She could feel her heart pounding in her chest and she felt faint. Her breath was coming in short sharp bursts and she swore that she was about to hyperventilate. This could not be happening. It was a coincidence that's all it was.

If Katie wasn't standing right there, staring at her as if she'd gone mad, she would have thought that she had fallen and hit her head, or perhaps dozed off. It was the only logical explanation, because standing right here in her reception area was the same man that had invaded her dreams for most of her life. Tearing her eyes away from the mysterious stranger, she focused on his companion. It was only then that she realised that this couldn't be her dream as there had never been anyone else with him. Forcing herself to focus on his companion, she was finally able to start getting a grip on reality.

His companion's hair was a different colour, more a reddish mahogany, yet his eyes and facial features were almost identical to the gentlemen standing beside him, suggesting that they were related somehow. They both stood over six-feet in height and were wearing the best made pair of leather pants she had ever seen. There were no seams or zippers in sight and they fit their bodies like a glove. Yet, he did not hold the same magnetism as the first gentleman. Thinking of her dream figure caused her eyes to wander back to him and, of their own accord, they travelled slowly up his body. *Why couldn't she stop looking at him?* There was no way that this was the man from her dreams, she knew it was impossible, men did not just materialise from dreams.

Conflicting and tantalising images from her dream flashed through her mind. That was the final straw. Falling back into the chair, she tried to control her rambling thoughts and get her mind straight. The same question kept playing over in her head. *Could it be? If it was, how?* Things like this just weren't possible, *were they?* How could this particular man be standing here looking at her? How could she have visualised him standing here, before she had even met him? He was staring at her just as intently as she had him, concern and amusement etched on his face. She was sure he was trying to figure out if she was mad or not and, even though it had only been minutes since they walked in, it had felt like time had stopped.

Katie finally finished the phone call; she walked around the desk towards the men, grabbing the towels from Ceana, giving her an extremely pointed look that meant she would be explaining herself later for leaving the two men dripping wet in the reception area.

"Hello gentlemen and welcome to the Firefly Hideaway. I am Miss Thorne, and this is my sister, how may we be of service?" Katie asked with all the professionalism that Ceana normally possessed, as she handed them a towel each.

"Good Morning lass I am Laird McKinnon, and this is my brother Caelan. We were wondering if ya family would be so kind as to spare us lodgings for the night?" He asked.

Ceana's heart began racing again. *My God,* she thought, *the man was actually Scottish.* As if this day wasn't weird enough he had to go and be Scottish. Okay, she just had to think. She knew instinctively that he was the one guy on this planet that could break her heart. She was not sure how she knew that, she just knew that she was not ready for that. If she was lucky, once she had him booked into his room, she might be able to avoid seeing him. She could get her brother and sister to look after them, ensuring that the chances of running in to him were slim. *Yes, that would work.*

Numbly nodding her head at that plan, she looked down at the list of cabins and realised with a jolt of joy, that they were at full occupancy. The last cabin was reserved for the Samsons. She breathed in a sigh of relief, now she could send them away to somewhere else, somewhere where she wouldn't have to mentally pull herself together when she ran into him and she would not have to feel guilty about doing so.

Looking up at them again, whilst avoiding eye contact, she answered, "I'm sorry gentlemen but we are currently at maximum capacity, however you can stay at the Manor across the road. I would be happy to ring ahead for you."

She was just about to pick up the phone and dial Katrina across the road when Katie stopped her.

"Don't bother Cee, a cabin just opened up. That was Mr and Mrs Samson that called. They can't make it up the range in this storm. Apparently, the road they are on is flooded and they can't get through. They ended up checking into Vanessa's Lodge. I told them I would get them back in when they get through. So the Loch Ness Cabin *is* free."

The universe was against her, it had to be. The storm just had to hit, causing a vacancy just when *he* shows up needing it. Well, there was nothing she could do. She would just have to book them in. She would have to remember to kill her sister later for not letting them go; she had almost succeeded in getting them out of here.

"Well gentlemen, it seems to be your lucky day." She replied forcing a smile to her lips. A smile that she in no way felt. Turning back to the computer, she started booking them in. They checked in as Kessan and Caelan McKinnon, *yep bloody Scottish.*

"It may be your lucky day but it sure as hell isn't mine." She mumbled under her breath as she entered their details.

Out of the corner of her eye she saw Caelan bring his fist up to his mouth and cough. It sounded like he was masking a laugh and when she looked up at him, his head was slightly lowered and his hair had fallen forward concealing his face. His shoulders were shaking slightly and only a few short coughing sounds were coming out as if he was clearing his throat. *Surely they hadn't heard the last part? She had whispered it under her breath, hadn't she?* Looking at Kessan, she noticed that he still looked the same, legs slightly apart and arms crossed at his chest, regarding her with a bored look on his face. Looking back to the computer, face flushed with embarrassment, she completed their booking. She had to get them out of here as fast as possible before she managed to make an even bigger fool of herself. Why didn't she just stay in bed this morning?

Moments later, the door opened again; looking up from the computer eagerly, she hoped that somehow the Samsons had made it. But no such luck, it was only her brother. She deflated.

"Cee, is there anything else you want me to do before I head over to Mr Brown's?" He asked, glancing curiously at their new guests. He had told her yesterday that he was going to go and check on each of the cabins during the storm.

"Yeah I do, can you just hang about for a minute while I organise this?" She didn't wait to acknowledge his answer. Looking back at the computer, she printed out their paperwork, while Tristan introduced himself to the men.

As Tristan entertained the newcomers, who stood awkwardly in the reception room, Katie came up behind her. "Oh my. They are so gorgeous. Have you ever seen anything like it Cee?" She whispered breathlessly into her ear.

"Perhaps we should invite them for dinner and maybe if I'm lucky one of them will ask me out on a date." She laughed.

Then, before she turned around, Katie threw in one more comment, the icing on the cake of an already humiliating ordeal. "By the way, I'm glad you decided to wear your *nice* PJ's to work this morning."

Ceana cringed; she could not believe she'd forgotten that she was still in her sleepwear! Thank God they weren't too revealing, normally she would have been in a sheer camisole; however, due to the cold weather, she was wearing her white and black satin kami and long pants ensemble. Still, it was not the outfit you wanted to greet good looking men in, but it was definitely better than her other choice. Her cheeks pinkened as she wondered what the men must think of her. The idea of them accepting Katie's offer was horrifying. She wasn't sure how she'd respond to seeing him again so soon. She looked down at her PJ's and wished that someone would just put her out of her misery already.

"Don't you dare Bata!" She hissed back furiously. But, her reply went unheard as Katie turned to the men and started up a conversation about their dinner plans.

Hopefully they would be happy with just the room and would kindly turn her sister's offer down, providing Katie got up the nerve to even ask. Ceana knew that was a lost wish though, as Katie may be the quiet type, but she was never shy. She had no problem chatting with anyone and when she put her mind to something, not much could stop her from following through. There was nothing Ceana could do but wait with dread to find out how her night was going to turn out. It could go two ways; she would have to put up with being close to him all night, or she could spend the next couple of days avoiding him. Neither way seemed pleasing to her present state.

CHAPTER 2

What else would bloody go wrong this week? Kessan wondered how his life had gotten so complicated. As he walked into the keep, the feeling of trepidation increased as he wondered what the MacDonnell Laird and the druid wanted from him. Kessan knew they had come seeking his help, and he couldn't refuse, Kessan owed the bastard his life. Reluctantly he had agreed to listen to what he had to say, but he knew it was meddling in things he didn't want to meddle in. He walked into the great hall where the old man sat waiting for him to arrive.

As he sat down at the table, Kessan signalled the maid to fetch them something to eat and drink, then he turned to the elder Scotsman.

"Ok. Get on with it. I have matters to be aboot." Kessan commanded impatiently.

"I need ya aid lad and, before ya think of saying nay, keep in mind that I am calling in the favour ya owe me." He replied, apparently unfazed by Kessan's sharp tone.

That was one thing he respected about the old goat, the fact that he always got straight to the point.

"Do ya ken the tales of my daughter's disappearance?" The old man asked.

Kessan nodded, a little confused as to why the old man would be bringing that up. He remembered them well, he had grown up on the stories of the crazed old man who had killed his only daughter. "Aye. I do but what has that to do with me?" He asked.

"Well, laddie, I need ya to go and find my lass and bring her home."

Kessan sat up straighter in his chair. He couldn't believe what he was hearing and questioned the man's plea. "What are ya on about ya old fool? What do ya mean bring her home?" How do ya suppose' I bring a dead lass home?" He asked, unable to hide the disbelief in his voice. The old man must be going crazy. Surely he had to be out of his mind!

"Nay, son I assure ye my lass is not dead. Merely in another time – the tales were merely rumours started to protect her and hide her from those that would wish her dead. I would go myself, but McKenzie has his men watching me, he has suspected I ken something more than I'm tellin'. If I went through they would follow me and I would not only be jeopardising her life but it would also endanger all the Highlanders here and the world where Ceana was sent. You are the last person that the bastard would expect to help me. Therefore, it makes ya the perfect choice for the quest." He explained simply, his old eyes searching Kessan's.

It made sense that McKenzie would be watching the Highlander, especially if he had any inclination that his daughter had been in hiding. In all the years since the day of her disappearance, there had been speculation of why he had killed his daughter in addition to rising rumours amongst the divided druids who knew of a powerful weapon against the dark magic.

He had only been five the day MacDonnell's wife and – or so they had been led to believe – child had been killed. Many said it had been an accident, but MacDonnell swore that it was at the hands of Laird McKenzie, Kendrick's father, for the family's power. When the bairn also disappeared, everyone had assumed that the MacDonnell had killed his daughter to save her from the same fate and he had done little to discourage the rumours, though there was no evidence to charge him.

Once leader of a struggling clan, the elder McKenzie had started turning to dark magic to gain more power and respect, or fear, from his opponents. Kendrick and Kessan shared their troubled childhood together, choosing to spend the days hunting, training and chasing women as they grew to age. But for Kendrick in particular, life wasn't so blissful as the dark magic took control over his father, who would lash out at the lad, releasing his stresses and paranoia in beatings. One day, after a longer than usual hunt, in which Kendrick had disappeared for a time, they'd arrived back to McKenzie's keep and found his father in a fit of rage. Kessan remembered Kendrick's screams and pleas as the Laird beat down on him after finding out that he did not have some kind of news about a weapon that had the power to destroy him.

The beatings only stopped when the laird suddenly turned up dead, after a particularly violent accident. Kessan had always suspected Kendrick's involvement in his death, but once again, no proof could be found. His suspicions only grew as Kendrick gleefully took over his father's place where greed and power turned his former friend into something unrecognisable. Knowing what his friend was probably capable of, Kessan had tried to keep his head down during the brewing trouble; he avoided taking sides, he had seen many good men fall, and he would not put his clan in danger by choosing sides. But that was what the old man was requesting of him right now.

It would seem that the weapon *was* the child. MacDonnell hadn't killed her, he had hidden her. But how could *she* destroy the dark power that had become the sole focus of the McKenzie clan?

Frustrated, he slammed his fist down on the table.

"What do I have to do?" Kessan asked, knowing instinctively that he was not going to like the answer.

"I need ya to travel to another time and land. Ya see, twenty years ago we sent Ceana through a portal with a cloaking spell. However, something went wrong, she was no' sent to the time she was meant to go to, she was sent somewhere else. It is only now that the cloaking spell has waned that we have been able to track her. But the problem ya ken is, that if we can track the lass, so can McKenzie."

"Och what ya tellin' me old man is that ya want me to go through a magic portal to a time ya know nothing about, in order to bring back a lass that ya do no' ken how to find."

"Aye" was all the Laird said.

"Do ya ken what ya ask of me old man?" He snapped. "If McKenzie ever found out that I was even considering helping ya, he would kill my clan and me faster than ya could blink!" he continued, hoping he could talk some sense into the old goat.

The Laird put his hand on Kessan's shoulder. "Aye and I am

truly sorry lad, but you're the only one I trust with this task. Ya owe me this." He pleaded.

The bloody bastard. He knew that Kessan would not be able to deny him. Sighing, he nodded his agreement. He always paid his debts. It was the one thing that made him who he was. *Damn him and his honour.* Kessan's honour meant everything to him. He was nothing without it. His brother had always said that one day it would get him killed and he just might be right this time.

HE COULD STILL REMEMBER the day as if it were yesterday. He had been but a boy of ten when the Laird had saved him from falling to his death. He was on the edge of a cliff when his horse had reared up and thrown him over. Kessan remembered hanging from a branch that he'd managed to cling to on the way over. It had felt as though he'd hung there for hours, even though the Laird said it had only been one. His hands were cut up and bleeding from where he had tried to pull himself onto a ledge and, by the time the Laird found him, his hands had become weak. It was all he could do to hold on. His voice was hoarse from yelling. Just at the moment he'd decided to give up, MacDonnell had come upon him. He'd happened to be on his way to see Kessan's father and, without a thought to his own safety, he'd lowered himself down the ledge and lifted Kessan to safety. After cleaning him up, the Laird brought him home, without mentioning to anyone what had happened. And he had never asked for anything in return, until now.

God damn the old man to hell! He had no choice but to agree. He owed him that. "Aye, I will do this for ya old man, but tell me, how I will find the lass in the place ya plan to send me. She was a mere babe when she went through the portal, she would be a lass of twenty now. She would no' look the same as she did then."

Kessan hoped that, by laying the facts out at the old man's feet, he would change his mind. But he didn't.

"Och, that is for ya to figure out when ya get there lad. I'm sure ya will be fine. Surely the times will no' have changed so much."

"Damn ya to hell," Kessan spat. "Why now? Why is it so important that she come home now? Ya don't even have a keep for the lass to come home to."

The old man's face coloured. Kessan hadn't meant to embarrass the Laird, he did not agree with what McKenzie had done to his home. However, he needed to know and understand everything. And he knew there was more to this tale than the lines they were feeding him. He had a feeling that he wasn't going to get the whole story until the old goat was ready to give it to him. Crossing his arms over his chest, he sat there waiting for MacDonnell to tell him the entire story. The Laird took a sip of his ale and looked over at the druid, who gave him a slight nod; at last, they were going to tell him something.

The man was out of his mind if he thought Kessan would just turn up in another time and find the lass. A lass that would have no memory of where she come from. Kessan shook his head this mess was all because of the damn magic. It always came back to magic. He had never trusted magic. Each time something went wrong, or someone got killed it was because of magic. The very Highlands he loved were in danger of being destroyed because of it. Ever since he could remember, Highlanders believed and trusted in the magic yet all he could see was that it gave power to men who abused it and it always came at a high price, usually the cost of human life. In his opinion, people should just learn to leave it alone. Here he was about to go and find a woman, who should have grown up in the Highlands with her family, and instead was sent away with no memory of who she was – to another time no less. He then had to convince her of who she was and bring her back to a place and time she would know nothing of, without making himself sound crazy. There was no way out. His honour wouldn't let him refuse the Laird. He only hoped that Fer Doirich and MacDonnell were telling the truth and that this lass would be able to stop this madness for good.

There was no way he was going on this journey without getting something from the old man. "Aye, alright I will go and retrieve the lass, but then we are even, ya hear me? I do no' ever want to see ya on my land again, or I will kill ya myself." He warned. "And ya will tell me everything ya ken or the deal is off, honour be damned." He was starting to get angry now. Just thinking of what was going to happen was putting him on edge. "I will not be going into this blind. Do no' leave any details out and if ya donna like my terms ya can just leave." He was hoping that his tone and demands would be enough to make them rethink their choice of sending him, but they didn't. Instead, the druid nodded his approval and the old man began his tale.

Kessan should have just walked away, told them to find someone else, but the honour in him cemented him to his chair. For the second time today, he found himself cursing his honour.

THEY HAD ALREADY BEEN in the meeting for well over an hour and MacDonnell had filled him in on as much as he could. Finally, after being silent for most of the time, in his low voice the druid began explaining the error that had occurred in the calculations and its implications. Instead of going to the druid that was to prepare her for her fight ahead, this glitch had sent the lass further into the future than expected and, to make matters worse, they had not been sure exactly where in this time the lass was and whether she would have even been in Scotland, until recently. MacDonnell explained how they had searched for years for her and finally Fer Doirich had been able to narrow down her location to within a certain time and area.

"Ya see lad, that is why it has taken us so long, otherwise we would have been here sooner."

Just when he didn't think his life could get any worse, this journey went from being a pain in his arse to a nightmare. Not only could they not guarantee where he would end up, they also could not provide him any details of what the world was like or what he would find when he arrived. Basically, once he was through that portal, he was on his own. Leaning back in his chair he rested his arms on the edge, threaded his fingers together and placed them on his chin, deep in thought. *Was he was really going to do this? Was he really going to go to a place he had no idea about, by magic no less, and search for a lass that may or may not still be alive and all the while leaving his family here in danger?* They wanted him to leave tonight at midnight, for the two-day journey. They had done that on purpose, he realised; he did not have time enough to change his mind. *Good thing too,* he knew he would have if he had been given much time to ponder the outcome of this little journey.

And all too soon, the deal was done, all that was left to do now was finalise everything here. He would do this one thing and then he would come home – hopefully it would still be intact – never to be bothered by magic again. If, for some reason, he didn't make it home, however, he had to make sure that his family knew what to do in his absence. He would not go before making sure that his family had some kind of protection and MacDonnell would be providing it; he was the reason that they were in danger in the first place. Standing up, placing his hands on the table, leaning towards the man, he sealed his fate.

"Ok old man, ya have my word. I will go and find your lass and bring her home. But while I am gone, you're to aid my brother and my men in keeping this place safe and if anything happens to one of my clansmen, I will hold ya personally responsible." He stated in a cold, hard voice. A voice that promised vengeance and pain if harm came to his family.

Most Highlanders would have been smart enough to feel some fear at his words, but not MacDonnell. Instead he studied him, a mixture of emotion on his face, but fear was not one of them, rather, he saw admiration and respect. "Aye lad, ya have my word that I will do all I can to keep ya kin safe. Just bring my lassie back."

After shaking hands to seal the contract the two elders left, old man MacDonnell walking stiffly out the door and into the keep. It was then Kessan realised how much of a toll this war and events of the past years had taken on the Laird. Even though he resented the man for making him do this, he also respected MacDonnell for moving heaven and earth to protect his kin, something he would do himself. He finally knew what side of the war he wanted to be on, he wanted to be on the side that valued life over magic. Pouring himself another ale he went over what they'd told him. *Bloody magic, there was no avoiding it.* And now, his life and the life of the lass were deep in its clutches. Slamming down his drink, he thought deeply about the week ahead and what he would tell his brother, Caelan, when he arrived. No matter how he worded it, it still sounded crazy, even to him. He had sent one of his men to bring his brother up to the keep. This was not a conversation he was looking forward to. Not only did he have to let his brother know he was leaving but he also had to let Caelan know that he would be in charge of the clan in his absence. A pressure he knew his brother didn't want to bear.

Like the rest of his life, his brother would become another thorn in his side. His week started to plummet even further into the Loch when he tried to explain to his brother what he had been asked to do. It had not taken his men long to find his brother, he had been in his usual place, the study, working on the household accounts. He had taken over this responsibility a year ago, which suited Kessan just fine and he trusted Caelan with the task. Caelan loved it, he had always been more of a scholar type than a warrior. His brother and sister were the two most important people in his life, even though he was Laird, he never treated them as if they were any different than himself.

Sighing deeply, he reached for his glass. It was empty. *Damn.* He was going to need a stiffer drink to get through this. He signalled the maid that was walking past the doorway.

"Bring me another." He ordered.

"Something troubling ya brother?" Caelan asked as the maid rushed past him and out the door.

"Aye," he replied as the maid re-entered the room with his drink. Grabbing it, he drunk it in one mouthful.

"Another!" He requested as his brother sat down across from him.

"Must be bad." Caelan replied looking at the now empty glass in his hand.

Kessan nodded. "Aye brother, ya can say that." He answered. Caelan raised a questioning eyebrow at him. There was nothing more to do but fill his brother in on what was happening. Kessan filled him in on the conversation that he'd had with the Laird and he was not surprised at all by Caelan's reaction. He couldn't blame him really, Kessan was still having trouble accepting the story himself.

"Ya can't be serious Kessan. The old bastard is mad!" Caelan replied incredulously as he stood up and started pacing.

Kessan watched his brother pace back and forth. He knew exactly how he was feeling. Not twenty minutes ago he had questioned the old man's sanity himself, "I have to, Caelan, I owe him, I need ya to stay here and look after the clan while I am gone." He ordered.

"Ya outta ya mind if ya think I am gonna stay here while ya go to some strange land on ya own!" Caelan shouted at him.

"And ya outta ya own mind if ya think I'm gonna let ya come!" Kessan shouted back.

Caelan had stopped pacing and now they were both standing at the table with their hands pressed firmly down against it glaring at each other, both mad as hell. The maid scuttled into the room with the second drink, neither man paid her any attention. Placing the drink on the table she left the room as quickly and quietly as she had entered.

"Well ya either let me come, or I will follow ya through after!" Caelan warned in a low, direct voice.

Slamming his fists down on the table, Kessan roared. "This is not a game, Caelan, I doona ken what I will be walking into and I …"

"That is exactly why ya need me, Kessan. It is not safe to go on ya own!" Caelan roared back.

"Och tell me this than brother, who will protect the clan *and* Thora if we both go?" He shot back at him.

Kessan was hoping that the mention of their sister would convince Caelan to back down, but he should have known better.

"Brodie can protect the clan and Thora as well as, if not better than I." Caelan said bluntly.

Kessan swore. "Bloody hell! So much for being Laird. What good is it to have power and influence when nobody listens to me anyway?" He grumbled to himself.

"Come on brother, ya will be glad to have me with ya." Caelan said more calmly now knowing that he had won the battle.

Kessan shook his head, *bloody hell, there was no way out of thi*s. He knew his brother was right, but it didn't make it any easier to accept. He didn't like the idea that his brother was now risking his life as well. Sitting back down he shot Caelan a look that showed he was not pleased.

"We will see." He replied.

Realising the futility of trying to get his brother to back down, he decided to put him to some use. Downing the drink that was sitting on the table they started planning. They had to figure out how were they going to get to the cave unnoticed by their enemies, no doubt there would be someone watching him, waiting to see if he betrayed his oath to stay neutral. They also planned precautionary measures for when they arrived in the new land. They packed some gold for bartering, but they would only use it if they absolutely had to. Once they had plotted out every detail, they parted ways.

Kessan decided to see Thora, Caelan went back to the study to finalise the financials before they left. Striding out of the room, intent on finding his sister, he rounded the corner and ran into yet another problem. Freya McKenzie. *Damn. When had his life become so complicated?*

As PART of an earlier arrangement with Kendrick, Freya and Kessan had been betrothed not long before the trouble had started. She had come to stay with him for a while so

that they could get to know each other before the wedding. However, the longer she stayed, the more he knew that he did *not* want to spend the rest of his life with her. The longer she stayed, the more her true nature came out, and he learnt that she was just as mean spirited as her brother. He did not want that in his life. On top of that, she was never kind to Thora, his sister, and she was especially cruel to animals, an attribute he despised in people. Kessan eventually wanted a family to keep the name and bloodline of the McKinnon clan going. But he didn't just want a mother in name for them, he wanted one that would be kind and gentle, just as his mother was, a woman who would demonstrate the kindness that still existed in the world. He quickly came to realise that Freya was not that woman, instead she was controlling and manipulative and when he announced that there was not going to be a wedding, her true colours shone through for *everyone* to see.

She'd started screaming at him, smashing anything she could get her hands on, all the while insisting that he was making the biggest mistake of his life and it wasn't until he'd threatened to send her home that she calmed down and begged him to let her stay. She'd sworn that if she went home a failure, unable to secure a union with him, her brother would just as likely kill her. Kessan had no trouble believing that, after all, McKenzie was at the very centre of the current trouble in the Highlands. Kessan knew that he wanted him under his power, and he thought that a marriage to his sister would accomplish this. So, without a marriage, McKenzie would have no need for his sister. It was only on that basis that Kessan had allowed her to stay. He had made her fully aware that he wouldn't marry her, or give her children and that if she stayed here it would be as an unattached woman, making her a disgrace in her family's eyes. She had agreed and was now living in one of the empty cabins just inside the walls and all the men knew that she was not to be bothered, unless she wanted it. Most of the men were happy to leave her alone. She was known to be quite a shrew, of course that didn't deter some, and she openly accepted them into her bed.

"Kessan, I dinna ken ya were still up." She purred as she placed herself closer to him.

"Freya." He nodded wearily as he took a step back from her pointed advance.

"I heard you shouting when I came down the stairs. I hope it is nothing too serious?" She asked, her voice like liquid steel. It felt cold and emotionless, to match her personality. He didn't trust her. He knew that if she found out what they were planning, she'd use the information to regain her brother's trust as well as a position within her family. She wouldn't hesitate to repay Kessan for the shame and exile his choices had caused her.

"Nay, just some news that a few reivers had reached our land. Brodie will deal with it tomorrow so there is nothing to worry aboot." He answered.

He could see questions in her eyes as she tried to figure out whether she trusted him or not. Then it occurred to him that she should have been home by now. *What was she up to? Why was she in the main part of the keep at this time of the day?* He wondered.

"Why are you not at home Freya?" He demanded.

She flushed, "Um, I was on my way there now. I was just coming back from the kitchens. Cook has been helping me learn the way in which a kitchen should be run." She smiled sweetly.

But he knew she was lying. She would not look at him directly and she was clearly agitated. She had her hands balled into fists within the folds of her skirt. There was no way that Freya would ever demean herself by working in a kitchen. *Aye she was up to something.* He thought, but right now, he had bigger things to worry about. He would rather be spending this time with his sister before he left, than talking to this woman.

"Well ya had better head there now." He ordered.

He didn't wait to see what her response was. He just walked past her and headed up the stairs to find his sister. He still hadn't come up with a decent lie to tell Thora about their leaving, he had opted not to tell her the truth as it would only put her in danger. The less she knew, the less chance she had of being used for leverage.

❧

KESSAN WAITED 'til most of the keep had retired before meeting Caelan in the stables. They had left at a time when there would be no one around, apart from a few of his most trusted men who were on duty, and they would never assume to question the Laird as to his coming and goings. Then they had gathered their packs, which were lightly packed for the two-day journey, and left the keep. Now here they were, a couple of days later, standing in a cave he had never been in before, waiting to be sent through to God knows where. Looking around he noticed that the cave did not appear like any other cave, he could practically feel the magic running through it. God, he hated magic.

"Och MacDonnell get on with it. We are ready." he snapped. It was a lie of course, how the hell did someone prepare for this? He just wanted to get it done, the quicker they completed the journey, the quicker he could come home to his highlands.

"Aye laddie, but remember, ya only have one month to make it back through the portal before it closes for another six months!"

"Aye. I remember old man, you just remember what ya promised me." He shot back.

"Aye lad. I will watch over ya kin myself while ye are gone." MacDonnell promised.

"Aye, make sure ya do." He commanded the old man. After all, it was the least he could do.

Stepping into the ring of stones at the centre of the cave, Kessan waited with his brother to be sent through to a time and place, which could very well be far different from the world they now lived in. His only hope was that it was not too different. He watched with dread as the druid began etching symbols onto the columns and an increasing heaviness settled in his stomach. As the symbols were drawn on each stone, a strong wind surrounded them. By the time the last symbol was etched it was blowing so fiercely that his hair was whipping his face and the dust matched the vortex of wind that surrounded him. His heartbeat raced as the reality of what was happening hit him. It suddenly became all too real. *What had he been thinking placing their life in the hands of magic, what would happen to them, would they be ripped apart?* It almost felt like they would as the force of the wind increased and tugged wildly at their clothes and hair. He felt a pang of pity as he thought of the little bairn making this journey, she would have been too young to understand all this, making the terror she felt all that much worse, and then to be sent where no one was waiting for her

Just when he thought it couldn't get any worse, the cave filled with a roar so unnatural he could not hold back a cry of alarm –, it was a sound that would

haunt his dreams – then there was nothing but blackness. He could not see anything but darkness around him, if it wasn't for the sounds and smells that were surrounding him he might have thought he had died. His fear was eased somewhat as he heard the laboured breathing of his brother next to him and it was in that moment that he was glad that Caelan had ignored his wishes. He could still smell the heather of the Highlands and the smoke from the lit lanterns in the cave. Opening his mouth, he tried to call Caelan, to find out if he was experiencing the same sensations as he, but no sound came out, his voice lodged in his throat. The smells and sounds of the cave faded further and further away, then everything changed.

His eyesight had yet to return so, as his other senses came back, the first thing he noticed were the smells that surrounded them. It smelt like deep forest, unlike the forests he had grown up in. It was different to the forests back home; there were smells that he had never encountered before. Mixed together, they were kind of sweet and minty. He could also hear birds. Even though they had birds at home, none sounded like this. They sounded as if they were laughing at him.

Then, just like in the cave back in the Highlands, a loud crack of thunder sounded overhead, it was as if there was a storm right on top of them.

Slowly his eyesight started to return. Blinking rapidly, he tried to clear the blurriness. He looked over to where his brother was and saw him leaning against the wall trying to gather himself.

"Och are ya alright?" His voice sounded raspy to his own ears. At his brother's nod he too tried to gather himself. Och Christ that was the worst thing he had ever been through. Goddamn magic! He would rather take on an army full of Sassenachs than do that again. Taking in depth breaths he tried to steady his breathing. Once he had himself under control he took in his surroundings. They needed to determine where they were.

The first thing he noticed was that they were standing underneath what appeared to be a rock cave that was open at each end, with a path that ran right through it, the rain was pouring through the opening drenching them where they stood.

The wind was still howling, and trees all around them bent against its force. The light that was trying to break through the dark clouds alerted him to the fact that they must have arrived just as dawn was breaking.

The druid had warned him that they would not arrive at the same time they left. He also warned that they would not be in the exact location, but it would be close. It was up to him to find out where the lass was now. The druid had informed him that, once a week at midnight, he would open the portal to this location just in case he had found the lass.

The vortex of swirling dust had disappeared, yet the wind was still howling, and the rain was coming down so hard and fast that it was penetrating the top of the stone arch and in no time at all they were drenched, even the rain here was different to that at home. The cave surrounding them looked different, but he knew that his feet had never left the ground; if he didn't know better, he would think he was still back in the Highlands, however, one look around proved to him that he was not.

Trying to figure out where to go next, he noticed that the path in front of the rock cave forked into three possible directions. Only one way had a sign, and thankfully it was in English. So that was one clue, he had to be in a Sassenach place; *well, a place in England was better than any other*, he thought to himself. Thankfully, his father had made them learn English as children to prepare them for a future working with the Sassenach. The sign appeared to point to the top of what looked like

a mountain and written on it were the words *'Firefly Hideaway.'* Hopefully that was somewhere they could get food and lodgings for the night and perhaps some information from the locals regarding the area and people living here. With any luck it would only take a couple of days to find the lass and then head home, after all even after all this time, he imagined most people would remember a baby showing up unexpectedly in the area.

He thought fleetingly of his home. He was counting on Brodie and MacDonnell to keep his movements a secret. If they failed it didn't bear thinking about what would happen, this place seemed vastly unprotected. He sighed. Well there was nothing for it.

Following the sign, they set off on the next leg of their journey, one that would change his life forever.

Back at the cave, the Laird and the druid looked at each other.

"If this fails, Fer Doirich, the Highlands will fall and there will be nothing we can do to save it." Fearghas said gravely.

"Aye, MacDonnell," he agreed. "Let's just hope they find the lass afore the dark one finds out what we are planning. McKenzie is one of few who suspects the truth of her importance and it must stay that way." He replied solemnly.

"God speed to them." He whispered. Turning around he headed towards the entrance. "We must prepare the men for battle, one way or another after this month, the Highlands will be changed forever."

Heading out of the cave the pair made their way back to camp, discussing the preparations that needed to be made.

She had known Kessan had been up to something! And now she had proof. Oh, Kendrick was going to love this. Kessan had pledged to be to remain neutral. Perhaps she could use this to her advantage. Kendrick could kill the lass and then he could blackmail Kessan into marrying her. *This was her chance.* Ever since she could remember she had wanted Kessan as her husband. The love she had for him had started when she was a lass of six, she remembered how sweet he had been to her after she had fallen from her horse, and in her entire life, he was the only man who'd ever shown her any sympathy or care.

Her father and brother had been so cold. They always went out of their way to make sure the people around them knew what the meaning of pain was. Her brother had not always been like this. He was once as kind and gentle as Kessan, but years of torture and degradation at their father's hands had turned him into what he was now. A *monster*. She'd gladly watch the Highlands fall to her brother just to have the one man who showed her any compassion in her life for herself. When she was done, Kessan would be hers. Nothing or no-one was going to stand in her way. And as an added bonus she would unite the two clans and then their families would be unstoppable in the Highlands. Maybe she could even convince Kessan to take the power for himself and then *she* would be the powerful one, not her brother.

Now she had finally found a way to make him hers, and when she was through she would have him on his knees begging her for forgiveness. She smiled a chilling smile of glee and anticipation. As an added bonus, the boys had left Thora at the keep, the perfect leverage against McKinnon. She would tell Kendrick that Thora was on her own, a vulnerable pawn. This would not only gain her the leverage they needed to blackmail the Laird, but it would finally gain her back the respect of her brother. Thinking about what her life would be like with Kessan filled her with hope, hope that her life would finally work out, she was certain that one day he would love her as much as she loved him, and then he would forgive her for selling him out to Kendrick.

She watched and waited for the highlanders to leave, bunkering down in the stables, making sure to stay out of sight. That was where she was sitting now watching for the men. She hoped it would be soon, she was starting to get cold and the smell of manure and horses was starting to permeate her hair. Earlier on, she had stolen some riding clothes earlier from one of the stable boys. It would make it easier for her to follow them on horseback if she wasn't worried about a skirt. Finally, the door opened, sliding quietly over to the edge of the stable and she peeked through the slats of wood as the McKinnon brothers entered. She knew they wouldn't be able to see her, their stables were further to the front and, to her relief, they had only brought in one lamp She made sure to stay low, just in case. Thankfully, it didn't take them long to saddle their horses and leave.

Making her way out of the back of the barn, she grabbed the horse that she had tethered in the forest, away from prying eyes, and started following them. She followed them at a safe distance in the shadows making sure to keep off the road. She was not worried about the bandits, everyone in the Highlands knew who her brother was.

After several hours, they reached a cave and she noticed that MacDonnell and an old druid, with a distinct scar on his face, were already there. She watched as they all made their way up to the cave at the top. There was no use in following. She only wanted to know where they went after this, so she waited down the bottom for what seemed like hours, waiting to see if he came home with the lass. She wondered briefly how they had kept the child hidden in this cave for so long. Surely her brother would have checked her the day of her disappearance.

But, when only MacDonnell and the druid came back, Freya grew furious as she realised her mistake. They stopped by their horses. Instead of mounting up, she overheard them discussing what would happen when Kessan came back with the lass. At least all was not lost. She had been able to hear the entire plan! Now she just had to get to Kendrick and tell him about what she had seen and heard, he would never believe what she had to tell him. She waited a short while longer before they finally left, and once they were gone, she mounted up and started riding to her brother, like the devil himself was chasing her.

<h1 style="text-align:center">CHAPTER 3</h1>

As they walked to the top of the mountain, Kessan thought about how he was going to find the lass. The forest surrounding them almost made him feel like he was back home; almost! The wind and rain that pummelled him reminded him of the storms back home, however the trees and strange materials jutting out of the rocks did not remind him of the cliffs back home. Not to mention how different the creatures were, numerous times they had been startled by birds that were too big to be chickens seeking shelter from the raging weather. It looked like a bird that would make a good dinner back home. Then they had numerous close calls from snakes, which came up out of nowhere at their feet. The first one, they had to strike down with their swords as it reared its head and attacked, hissing angrily and meaning business as the men interrupted its dash to get out of the storm. They had snakes at home but nowhere as big or aggressive as the ones here. *Could magic be at work in this realm as well?*

The path that they followed provided them with its own challenges as it continued to wind around the mountain, crossing back on itself repeatedly. They had to stay close to the wall to avoid losing their footing in the muddy track and the edges of the path were treacherous and slippery. At one stage, their path detoured, and they were forced to walk around a roaring waterfall. Like the one back home, the torrent flowed over the edge with such speed and ferocity with the downpour from the storm that, if they had fallen, they would have had no hope of surviving. As they continued on, the storm raged without letting up, thunder and lightning cracked around them with such force it shook through the ground they were walking on.

Suddenly, an enormous bang echoed through the forest, signalling that the lighting had struck a tree somewhere near and the noise it made, when it crashed down into the rainforest before coming to its final resting place, displayed the wrath of Mother Nature in all its splendour. It was another good twenty minutes before they neared the top. Once there, they came upon a grey, sturdy-looking staircase that had been moulded into the mountain with some kind of netting lining the edge of the path. Kessan assumed it was there to make it difficult for someone to tumble to their death. Aye, this place was definitely different to his homelands where such measures were not taken and men simply died if they were careless enough to get close to the edge. He wondered what kind of weaklings lived here.

Not far after the stairs, a wooden path materialised out of the rainforest floor and, in the distance, there were twinkling lights of homes. They stopped dead in their tracks and looked at each other curiously. The lights were dazzlingly bright in the shadows of the angry and darkened sky, far brighter than that of candlelight – this world must have magic! But, be that as it may, it seemed as though they'd finally found a village. Hopefully someone there could help them with food, shelter and information.

Watchful and alert now that they were nearing civilisation, they made their way along the wooden path, preparing for trouble; the guards of this village can't have been too far away. Curiously enough, as they neared the huts, he noted the lights were definitely not produced from candles and the closer to the cabin he got the weirdness of this land continued. Inside, there was a strange, tiny image moving on the wall, it flashed brightly. *How could that be?* He could see the cabin's occupants moving around but the ones on the wall never moved further than the edge of the black square. On top of this he could see right through the clear frames that encased the window and right there in front of him was a faint image of himself staring back. Placing his hand upon the opening, he was not shocked to see that it didn't go straight through.

The rain also could not permeate the building this way, instead it ran in streams down the clear material that covered what should be a window, it was nothing like the cloths that covered the openings back home. And where were the guards? They'd managed to walk right up to the village without being stopped and questioned. There was no wall surrounding the keep and no-one was protecting it from invaders. Where had the druid sent them?

He half wondered whether this had been some kind of trick to get them out of the Highlands, so they could use his keep and his people for their cause. So, help them if that was the plan, but for now, he had to trust that the old man and the druid were not playing them for fools.

"What do ye ken brother?" asked Caelan in a low, nervous whisper. "This is some mighty strange village. Where do ya think the main keep is?' He continued while scanning the darkened forest. "I hope that the druid got it right and has not sent us off on a goose chase."

Caelan had voiced his own thoughts as if he knew what he'd been thinking. Kessan looked over at his brother, who looked as out of place and as confused as he felt. He could sense that Caelan was anxious in the way he was spitting out questions faster than Kessan could answer. Putting his hand on his younger brother's shoulder, he tried to offer as much reassurance as he could muster.

"I ken it is a strange land Caelan, but we have a job to do. I only hope that the old man knows what he is doing. I doona think he would've asked us to do this had it no' been necessary."

His brother nodded a silent response and Kessan hoped his speech was as convincing as it sounded but a part of him was glad that he was not the only one having doubts about the trustworthiness of the druid. This was indeed a strange place. Nevertheless, they were here now; the only thing to do was to head to the main keep and inquire with the residents if they could stay the night. From there, they could gain their bearings and find out as much as they could about this time. He'd give it a week. If they had no news on the lass, he was heading home and to hell with the druid and MacDonnell. They would have to find another way to solve their problem.

Continuing on, they eventually reached a gate that opened up into a main area. It could not be a paddock; there was no grass, only a firm, hard strange surface that led directly to the main building. Walking through the gate, Kessan stopped dead in his tracks, his eyes widening as he noticed the various carriages sitting in the paddock. But they were not like the carriages he was used to at home, these were made out of metal and they had a weird, clear coating, much like the ones that were on the houses, where the windows should have been. There were no curtains covering the windows either, you could see straight into them! *Where was the privacy?* They also varied in size, shape and crazy colours marred each one – a far cry to what they were used to at home.

"What is it?" Caelan asked, wide eyed.

Suddenly, Kessan was brought out of his stupor by a large growl that reverberated through his body, and then, carriage much like the ones in the paddock roared down what looked like their own roads, only it was black and rough, not dirt. Before Kessan could blink again, the carriage was gone, but not before he had realised something strange. The carriage had moved on its own! And to top it all off the person sitting inside appeared to be unafraid. *How was that possible? Where were the horses? Where on God's green Earth were they?* Question after question ran through his head. He had no answers for any of them. Taking a deep breath, he felt for the first time that they were way out of their depth. This time was clearly nothing like home and he had never felt this out of place before. The feeling was extremely unsettling. He glanced quickly at his brother to gauge his reaction. Caelan had gone stock-still and had lost some colour in his face. He did not blame his brother for his reaction, not many things could frighten a seasoned Highlander but even Kessan was unsure about this world.

Hiding his own shock and fear from his brother he said, encouragingly, "come Caelan let us see if these brew folks will give us a bed for the night and, in the morn, we will begin our hunt to find the Laird's bairn so that we may quit this place as soon as possible."

His brother closed his eyes, shook his head as if to clear the images he'd seen and turned back towards the building without a word. They walked the last one hundred yards with great caution. He kept an eye out ahead of them, while Caelan watched their backs. There was no one more that Kessan trusted at his back than his brother. He found himself once again thankful that Caelan had ignored his pleas to stay and was grateful for his familiar presence in such a strange place.

At one and nine Caelan was already on his way to being a great Highlander. He was devoted to his family and Kessan knew that in any crisis, Caelan would take a sword in honour of Kessan, just as *he* would do for his family.

With a sigh of relief, no other strange things occurred as they finally made it to the main building of the keep and, when they entered the great hall, Kessan was astounded by the cosiness it offered. Even though it was essentially a small room, the fire burning in the hearth reminded both men of being back in the Highlands in their own homes. It was comforting and a relief after the freezing rain and the strangeness they had encountered. *Surely if a place could feel like this then it couldn't be too dangerous,* he thought to himself. However, the minute he turned away from the fire the familiarity ended, and his brief moment of relief washed away. Looking around in wonder he noted all the strange objects in the room. Right in front of him there appeared to be a bookshelf but there were not only books lining its shelves. There were strange objects in all different shapes and sizes, some were long and rectangular in shape and had weird names written on them. *"Monopoly"* was one and then there was one called *"Trouble."* Along the top of the bookshelves, there appeared to be books of some kind, but they were so thin that Kessan did not know how they could get any information worth knowing inside of them. The label underneath them read DVD's. *What were these DVD's?* He wondered. Turning towards the desk, he noticed there was some kind of map of the area stuck to the front. He made note of it. That might come in handy later for scouring the lands to figure out where they were.

Moving his eyes from the map, he searched the room further, behind the desk there was a large white rectangular box that had a big red button in the middle of it. It had the word *'Power.'* written under it. Just above that power button was two tiny rectangular openings next to each other and a larger thinner one just above it.

Studying it further he noticed the words HP written on the bottom underneath the power button. *What was HP?* Kessan wondered if this was how the people in this time controlled power, what else could it mean? On the desk itself there was another large white box, he could not see what was in the box as it was facing towards the open inner doorway behind the desk.

With nothing familiar to attach himself too, each new object only offered more questions. He took in more of the room and he noticed that his brother was staring at the ceiling.

Following his brother's gaze, he saw what had his attention.

Right there, in the middle of the roof were those strange, magical too-bright-to-be-natural candles again. *Mo clreach* he couldn't wait to get home.

Suddenly, the device on the ledge in front of them let out a deafening shrill. Kessan eyes shot to the desk and he took an involuntary step away from it, eyeing it warily. It didn't appear to do much but complain with an unnatural clanging which set his ears ringing. Instantly on alert, he was afraid that it was part of the dark magic they had just seen outside.

With magic, anything was possible, and caution was necessary. Another twinge of home sickness hit him in the pit of his stomach. He missed his simpler life, without the strange gadgets and things he didn't recognise. He hadn't even met a human being in this new time and already he was sick of having to deal with things he did not understand. *What if the people and their customs were as bad as he imagined?* Both men looked at each other as the shrill noise continued.

Kessan began to wonder whether there was anyone here. As his ears slowly became used to the shrill, it suddenly stopped, then more sounds emerged from the room beyond them and a mixture of relief and trepidation washed over him as he made out the sound of someone talking in the back room. *Friend or foe?*

His eyes queried Caelan as the voice they had heard out the back came into the main area. "Welcome to the Firefly..." the voice said. The rest of the sentence faded away. The moment he laid eyes on the owner of the voice, he felt as though he had taken a blow to his midsection that left him winded. Before him stood the most beautiful maiden he had ever seen. She was not overly tall, but she was not short either, and she had a figure that would make any man hard with desire. Her brownish/blonde hair reached all the way down to her waist and a few waves rippled its surface. Her lips were just plump enough for kissing and, by the Gods; Kessan had never seen clothes like the ones she was wearing. Unlike the clothes that the women in the Scottish Highlands wore, this woman wore trews so shiny and tight that when she walked, they stuck to her body and accentuated each luscious curve; her top was not much better, it was also a shiny black edged with white lace. Her arms and shoulders were bare, and the neckline came down into a V right to the top of her breasts. As he watched her, he wondered how the men in this century survived all the temptation she offered. There must have been battles waged over this woman. *Who was her keeper and how could he let her dress in such a provocative way that would bring trouble to their keep?*

"Mine." He growled just low enough so that his brother could hear him. Out of the corner of his eyes he caught the slight smile on Caelan's lips. He hadn't meant to say it out loud, but now they were out he was not taking them back. His brother now knew that this wench was off limits. It was then that he realised that a newcomer, a petite, blonde-haired woman, had entered the room and was speaking to her. She had also reached across the desk and grabbed the contraption that had started shrilling again. Looking over at his brother, Caelan mouthed the word 'mine' in response, accompanied with a grin and a wink; it seemed as though Caelan was suffering the same affliction that had affected him. Following his brother's gaze back to the blonde woman his lips twitched into a barely noticeable smile, yes she was a bonnie lass. It didn't take long before the second woman turned to them, introducing herself.

"Hello Gentlemen. Sorry to keep you waiting. Welcome to the Firefly Hideaway, I am Miss Thorne, and this is my sister, how may we be of service?" A loaded question, he thought wickedly, imagining what kind of services he'd like from the pretty lass standing behind her sister. Kessan had a few ideas about what he would like to do with her. But first they had a job to complete and the sooner the better, by the looks of it. The last thing he needed now was to be mixed up with females from this time.

"Good day lass, I am Laird McKinnon, and this is my brother. We have travelled a great distance and are quite weary; we were wonderin' if ya family would be so kind as to spare us lodgings for the night?"

The older lass studied the front of the silent white box intently. It didn't take long before she turned to them with a smile, replying:

"I'm sorry Gentlemen but we are currently at maximum capacity, however you can stay at the Manor across the road. I would be happy to ring ahead for you." She sounded a little too happy for his liking. *Why was this lass so keen to get rid of them? Perhaps she was as shaken by their presence as he was hers.*

The younger Miss Thorne turned to the elder, bending down to whisper something to her, just as she put the contraption that she had been holding down. He thought had heard her call it a *'phone.'* He filed that information away for later. Apparently, she had just informed her sister that a cabin had just become available as the couple who were meant to be staying in it could not make it. Relief washed over him, the last thing he wanted to do was to travel anywhere else in this strange land without first learning more about it.

He was aware that the older sister was not happy about the change in plans. His exceptional ears had picked up her cursing the universe under her breath. It was unlucky for her that both he and his brother had good hearing. However, unlike himself, Caelan was not as adapt at hiding his emotions and he had to cover up his laugh with a cough. She looked up at him in surprise, a flicker of embarrassment flashed across her face and he could see the suspicion in her eyes. It wasn't until she had turned her back to them that he let the smile he had been holding in come forth, it more amused rather than offended him. Perhaps he was going to have some fun here after all. Really, how different could the women here be compared to the ones back home? He just had to remember that the task came first. But, there was no reason he couldn't have some fun in the meantime.

"Aye, that will be just fine, Lass. Any place will do as long as it is out of the weather." He replied. He was not sure if he would be able to get to sleep knowing the lass was so close. He was under her spell and yet could do nothing about his lust. Time was running out and he had to keep his mind on the job they were sent to do. 'Avoid temptation,' he repeated to himself.

"How would you like to pay for your room tonight, Mr McKinnon?" The young lass kindly asked.

How could he have forgotten that they would expect some kind of payment for their stay? He had no idea what kind of currency they used in this time, time for Plan B. He addressed the lass again, trying to sound apologetic "Unfortunately we have lost most our possessions during this wild storm, all we have to pay ya with are a few gold coins. We are more than willin' to do tasks around the keep in order to make up the difference, as we are no' sure how long we will be staying, perhaps we could tend to the horse?" He said, hoping they had some horses. Both the lasses looked at them in utter shock and sympathy. Thankfully, it didn't take them long to accept his lies.

"Well it's lucky you've come here then. With the weather as crazy as it is, there's no way we could toss you out. And we cannot take what little money you have left, I'm sure we can work something out." The younger sister replied with a smile on her face.

The chiming of a bell above the door indicated that someone else had arrived. They turned to the door as a young man entered the establishment. Kessan assumed that this was another relation as he held a remarkable resemblance to the younger Thorne sister. The older one, he thought, held no resemblance at all to the two younger siblings, save the hair colour, although hers was darker. She must have taken after the other side of the family. The young man was asking the elder Thorne if she needed him for any further work. He noted with renewed interest that he had also addressed her as 'Cee.' He now had her name!

"Actually Tris," Cee responded, "before you go, can you make sure that there is enough firewood in Nessy? These two gentlemen will be staying there for a couple of days." He noticed that, while she was talking, she made eye contact with everyone else except him. *Yes, he had definitely shaken her.* He had been right, the newcomer was the girl's brother and Kessan grinned, maintaining a non-threatening stance as the brother sized the two of them up before sticking his hand out in greeting. The brother was unperturbed, he didn't appear nervous in the Highlanders' presence and Kessan noted that he was more welcoming than he would have suspected a man in charge to be. He'd apparently decided that the two clansmen weren't a threat upon sight alone. He'd never before been seen as harmless and it unnerved him. At his keep, Kessan held absolute power over the clan, and all would jump to do his bidding, in fear of his wrath. It was strange, the people in this century seemed overly trusting and unfazed by newcomers. It was a new feeling and Kessan was not sure he liked it.

Kessan had to pull his thoughts back to the present as Tristan queried their purpose. "What brings you blokes so far from home?" He asked.

Blokes? Kessan had to pause a minute to translate the unfamiliar word before addressing the brother. "We are looking for a long-lost relative. We have been informed that the lass is in this area somewhere but we donna ken her exact whereabouts." He answered, keeping the story as close to the truth as he could. He knew that if he kept close enough to the truth it would be easier to gain their help, without having to tell them the whole truth. Out of the corner of his eye he could see the two lasses having a quiet conversation behind the counter. The younger sister had obviously said something Cee did not like as she had spun around in her funny chair so fast that she was but a blur of colour. She'd tried to say something in response, a frown clearly displaying her disapproval, but had given up when she noticed her sister was no longer paying attention. Instead, the sister had ignored Cee and was heading towards them.

"Almost like a quest." She said brightly, catching the last of their conversation. "That sounds really interesting. You should join us for dinner and tell us all about it and your trip. After all, you've had a long journey. The last thing you would want to do is make dinner." She said brightly.

"Yes." Tristan agreed. "And perhaps we may be able to assist you in finding your relative, after all we have lived here all our lives."

Kessan could see alarm register on Cee's face as she heard her sister invite them to dinner. *What was that all about?* He wondered.

"Thank ya lass. We would be honoured to join ya, as long as your cook doesn't mind?" He asked. The siblings looked at each other with identical looks of confusion.

"Um I think you are mistaken Mr McKinnon. We don't have a cook." Katie informed them "Actually it is my turn to cook tonight." Piped in Cee, "and we are having chicken risotto if that's alright with you?"

She spat the last part out, almost challenging him to argue with her. Maybe she was even hoping they would cancel. Well tonight was not her night, what the little vixen didn't know, was that he never ran from a challenge. He had never heard of, let alone tried 'risotto' before but he was going to call her bluff. He was more determined now than ever to find out the reason behind Cee's obvious opposition to his presence.

"Dinner it is then!" He agreed, giving her a satisfied smile.

He watched on as Cee turned around and went back to finishing their booking with a little bit more force than before. But it wasn't long before she turned back āround smiling at them as she addressed her brother, "Tristan, would you please show these gentlemen to their cabin?"

"Sorry sis, but I only have time to check the wood pile, I'm sure you can handle it." Tristan replied as he left, nodding to the men as he went.

Kessan waited patiently while Cee turned in her chair,

apparently seeking out her sister, but she had already disappeared. The look on her face was priceless when she realised that she had been left alone with them. That suited him just fine. Kessan smiled as she stood up and ushered them through the door. Walking behind Cee on the way to their room was fantastic he was getting a magnificent view; her arse was not perfectly rounded but that didn't bother him. He could watch the way it moved all day! He could feel himself becoming hard with desire; he hoped they got there soon.

As they walked down the wooden ramp through the rainforest, he watched the rain fall of the parasol she was carrying, again he marvelled at the softness of the people here. She had offered them one but, considering their current state, he'd declined, besides a little rain never hurt anyone. She filled him and Caelan in on the history of the cottages. Caelan seemed to take it all in, asking several questions and listening intently to what she was saying, yet Kessan could not concentrate on the conversation. He would have to remember to ask him about the details later. They were alone now, just the three of them and if it wasn't for his brother's presence, he would have grabbed her and kissed her just to see what kind of reaction he got. *Soon,* he promised himself. He couldn't wait to see how much fire was lurking beneath that façade.

They reached their destination in no time at all and the first thing he noticed about the cabin was that it was at the far end of the holdings. If he hadn't known that this was the last cabin left, he would have thought that she had done it on purpose. Kessan smiled to himself. This trip was going to be an interesting one after all and, if it took them a few days to find the Laird's missing bairn, at least it would be an interesting couple of days. Perhaps if he was nice he might even be able to convince this little minx to aid him in his search, thus killing two birds with one stone. But, as Miss Thorne opened the door to the cabin, Kessan lost that thought and for the third time today, he was once again reminded that they were in a completely different century. Because there, hanging on the wall right in front of him, was the current date, and it was telling him that they had travelled over nine hundred years into the future. '*Galla.*'

CHAPTER 4

This *was going to be a great night,* Ceana thought with sarcastic irritation as she opened the door to Loch Ness. This cabin, along with the Tuathe De' Danann cabin, was her favourite. Not only had they been named after Scottish mythological creatures but they were also the biggest. Nessy had two main bedrooms, and where the other cabins had ladders built into the wall to access the upper room, this one had a winding staircase. As a child, she had often imagined herself as a princess descending those stairs. While their mother cleaned, she and Katie would often play in the cabins, pretending that they were in a faraway land. Oh, the fun they'd had. It was also one of three cabins that had an open fireplace which stretched across one half of a wall. The rest had potbelly fireplaces as they were more compact and took up less room.

Stepping aside, she allowed the men to enter the cabin before her. As she did, she caught a glance of herself in the glass door and cringed. She was still in her PJ's and her hair was a fright! The rain had only added to the effect. Now she would have to go the extra mile tonight at dinner, to make up for first impressions, a new dress, shoes, and make up – the works. She needed to show him that she wasn't so frumpy. It should not matter of course, but, for some reason, to her it did. The man was the spitting image of the man in her dreams, but in the dreams she was at her best, not this train wreck! She knew that the real-life version would never find her attractive like this. Her cheeks warmed as memories of her dream filled her mind, she decided that she had to get this tour over with as soon as possible so she could go and hide in her bedroom for the rest of the day. Perhaps she would stay there until their guests left. Now that sounded like a plan.

"Here we go gentlemen. I hope everything is to your liking. Please do not hesitate to phone the reception desk if you need any extra blankets or pillows." She recited the usual spiel, just with a little more speed than usual as she tried to hurry the process. *'Please need me.'* Her treacherous mind invaded her thoughts and she quickly shook her head, blocking the images from her mind.

"If you need us for anything you just dial 9 and we will assist you, day or night." She continued hastily. Ceana was just about to make her escape when she caught sight of their expressions. They looked like a pair of stunned mullets. It was as if they had never heard of a telephone. *Surely not?* Maybe they lived high up in the Highlands where certain technology had yet to reach. She supposed that *could* be possible as Mr McKinnon took in his surroundings with that same curious expression on his face as that of a two-year-old discovering wrapping paper for the first time. She watched as his keen dark eyes darted across each object in the room. She could not help notice how observant this man was. *He was definitely one that she should stay far away from,* she decided. Thanks to her little sister, that was going to be much harder now. She had a feeling that Bata was trying to play matchmaker, and if she was, she was she going to pay big time. In fact, she had the perfect pay back for her. She would make her take care of the Donaldsons next week, she thought, grinning to herself. They were their least favourite regulars who, despite being frequent customers, complained about everything. Yep, Bata was definitely going to be looking after them.

As she plotted her sister's downfall she kept an eye on Mr McKinnon. It was as if he was waiting for something to come out and bite him. A smile slipped past her lips. It couldn't be helped. She was going to warn them about the native animals that could come in at night but thought better of it. She didn't want to freak them out any more than they appeared to be. Just then he turned to her as if sensing her amusement, as he did he appeared to grow even taller. She had met some commanding men in her life but this one gave them all a run for their money. Finally, he gave a short bow and thanked her for her assistance.

"If ye dinna mind lass, can ye show us how ye would be usin' the um, telephone? The one ye have here is a wee bit different to our one." He asked.

There was that voice again. And just like in her dream, it was as if she had taken a large gulp of scotch; and the warmth slowly penetrated her entire body, starting at the base of her skull and spreading its fingers down the length of her body until it reached the tips of her toes. He always spoke with an even tone and yet it still had an edge to it. She could almost guarantee that, if he were in medieval times, he would have no trouble controlling an army of Highlanders. His voice was one that commanded obedience, yet at the same time, it promised seduction like nothing ever experienced. *How was she going to make it through dinner?* Ceana worried that she was going to make a fool of herself again, especially if she had to listen to that voice all night. *Perhaps she could fake an illness?* She thought quickly, and then dismissed it. Yeah like that would work. As if her sister would fall for that one. There was no way Bata would ever let her get out of this. She would have to come up with something better later, but first things first, she needed to focus on getting through *this* moment right now.

"Sure, no worries, Mr McKinnon." She answered.

"Please lass, call me Kessan," he informed her. "I am sure we are goin' to be great friends, ye and I." He smiled at her. His eyes crinkling around the edges.

God damn it. That smile could make a nun turn bad, she thought. All she wanted to do was get out of here. There was no way she was going to be friends with this man. *Lovers maybe,* she suddenly thought wickedly, *but not friends.* She caught herself, *again with the treacherous thoughts!* She had to stop thinking like this. It was going to get her into trouble. Right now though, she had to finish showing them how to use the telephone. Pulling herself together mentally, she admonished herself. She would be dammed if her hormones would wreck the reputation her family has built for this place. She could just imagine the headlines now, *'popular hideaway offers a new kind of fun for their guests.'* Walking over to the telephone, she picked it up and demonstrated how to use it. He had come up behind her to get a better look and her face heated and her heartbeat intensified. He wasn't making it any easier to push unwanted thoughts and images away by standing so close to her. He smelled of the fresh forest. A smell she had loved all her life. All she wanted to do was lean over and take a big whiff of him, that way she could remember what he smelt like when she dreamt of him tonight and dream of him she would. She knew that the dream was bound to come back again tonight, especially after today's events. But she didn't think going up and openly sniffing him as if she were a dog would add to the impression they already had of her. *Man*, she needed to get out of here.

"Is there anything else that I may help you gentlemen with before I leave?" Ceana asked, hoping that they were right for now. She needed some fresh air.

"Would ye be able to have someone bring us a washtub? We would like to clean up afore dinner." The younger McKinnon brother ventured.

Ceana stared at them dumbfounded and thought to herself, "Damn they really must have lived in a cave in Scotland."

Caelan burst out laughing and she felt her cheeks heat up as if they were on fire. She couldn't believe that she had just said that out loud. *What was wrong with her?* If their first impression of her went down well, this sure as hell wouldn't. *Oh yeah, your first impressions just keep getting better, Cee!* She scolded herself. But why was she complaining? Maybe if they thought her uncouth, they would decide not to have dinner with them after all. Then pride kicked in and she realised she didn't want them thinking of her like that. Afraid to look at Kessan again, even to gauge his reaction, she decided to hightail it out of there before she dug herself a much deeper hole. Rather than be completely rude though, she turned around to say goodbye, and she caught sight of him. He was standing there with his arms across his chest, one eyebrow raised as if waiting for her to explain. He was not angry at her slip up, if anything he looked slightly shocked and amused. They were waiting for something and then, on seeing the bathroom behind him she remembered their request. *Oh, right, the washtub.*

"The bathroom is over there, and another one is upstairs, so you do not need to share. I hope you enjoy the rest of your day, I look forward to seeing you at dinner." She lied, and with the final set of instructions administered, Ceana fled from the room as fast as she could. She didn't think her cheeks could get any hotter. *How could she have said that out loud?* She really was losing her mind.

On her way back up to the main house Ceana kept on going over her last conversation with Kessan and felt humiliated. This was nothing like how her dream was supposed to go, she had made a right fool of herself. *Could this really be the man from her dreams or was it just a coincidence?* The more she went over it, the crazier it drove her – there was no possible explanation, well any that made any sense… then suddenly it hit her like a bug hitting the windscreen. She knew *exactly* what was happening. It had to be some kind of joke! That was it. Perhaps he was an actor who had come here to play a prank on her. But, then, if that was the case, who could have set it up? Running through a list of people in her head, she tried to figure out who would have had the knowledge and power to pull off something this bi… Bingo! She came to a name on the list that instantly rang an alarm bell – her best friend Mel. After all she was the only one who knew about her dream man, the only person she'd ever told in detail. It had to be! Ceana began to relax as she continued back towards the main house. This made more sense than her dream becoming a reality. She snorted at herself for being such a fool. *Right! two can play this game,* she thought as she picked up speed. Running the rest of the way back to the main house she felt lighter and happier than she had all day. It was time to set these wheels in motion. Mel was in for a rude shock.

Mel and Ceana had been best friends since primary school and they did everything together. She was always there for Ceana and, no matter what time of day, they knew that they could ring each other if there was trouble. In fact, Mel was there when her last boyfriend had attacked her. She had arrived just in time, rushing Cee to the emergency room. If it wasn't for her, Cee would have been dead. Instead, she only had a few tiny scars left from the injuries he had caused. The most damaging scars could not be seen. They were the psychological ones.

The downside to Mel was that she had a bad habit of playing practical jokes. Once, in high school, she'd put a whoopee cushion on the science teacher's chair. It had backfired on her of course, the science teacher was sick that day and the Deputy Principal had filled in until a substitute could make it. Mel had received three days' detention for that one. Of course that didn't stop her; she had also got them banned from doing experiments, in science, after she began to mix the wrong chemicals together on purpose. Once she set their lab desk on fire, by accident that time, but it was still hilarious. Most of the time she loved Mel's pranks, except when they were directed at her; she much preferred when she was aiming them towards someone else, especially when that someone else was her brother. Thinking about all the fun they had Ceana's mood lightened a little. Tonight might just be fun after all. It might be a nice change of pace to have one of Mel's pranks backfire on her which, despite the whoopee cushion incident, didn't happen all that often. Ceana smiled. Yep, this was going to be fun!

As Ceana entered the main house she heard Katie in the kitchen. Heading that way, she decided to let her in on part of her plan. She noticed that Katie had already started on dinner, walking over to her she picked up a carrot and started to munch on it.

"Bata, there will be one more person coming for dinner tonight okay. Do we have enough food to go around or do I need to go to the shop?" She queried.

Katie turned to her and smacked her hand as she reached for one more carrot.

"Na Cee, I'm pretty sure we'll make do, as long as you stop eating the food." She reprimanded. "I know it was your turn to cook but I felt like doing it." She offered as way of explaining what she was doing.

Ceana didn't mind, it saved her from cooking. It was one thing that she couldn't say she was good at, not that she didn't try. At least their guests' meal would be edible tonight.

"By the way who else is coming, and what has you smiling like a mouse that caught the cheese?" Katie asked.

Nothing got past her sister. "Mel's coming. Well I'm sure she will come once I invite her and tell her all about the testosterone that rocked up on our doorstep. I also wanted some support, thanks to you, dumping me into the proverbial frying pan. I thought I could use some help making sure I didn't make a fool of myself any more than I already have." Ceana replied, hoping it sounded convincing.

Katie looked at Ceana suspiciously, "should I be worried? Since when have you needed her support around men?" She asked. "When one of you plan something against the other it usually means trouble. Should I start running for the hills now, or can I wait for dessert?"

Ceana burst out laughing at her sister's prediction. Oh, there was going to be some trouble alright, just not for her. "Don't worry

Bata this is going to be entertaining. Trust me you have nothing to worry about." She said with a wink.

"Ok," she laughed, "should I warn the boys or should I let them be surprised?"

Ceana thought about that for a minute. "No, let them be surprised." She responded with a wicked gleam in her eyes. She left her sister to finish dinner and set off to ring Mel. If anything, it would teach Tris a lesson for taking sides with Bata. Next time he might reconsider which sister to back. Walking back down the hall to the reception desk, she felt a little devious and she couldn't wait to set her plan in motion. Then she was going to go and finally have that long hot shower she had been wanting all morning.

Sitting down she picked up the phone and dialled Mel at work. Normally, she wouldn't call her friends at work but since Mel owned her own accounting firm on the Gold Coast, there was no need to worry about getting her in trouble with the boss. Ceana thought about the view from her office window, during this storm it would have been magnificent. Ceana loved that view, she would often go and meet her for lunch just so she could sit there and watch the ocean waves roll in. Situated on the twenty-sixth floor it overlooked the beach on one side, and the Hinterlands on the other. Her office was only one of a few that had this view in her building. To top it off, her building had the best revolving restaurant on the top floor, giving its diners a 360° view of the coast. The best part of the restaurant however, was that it served all you could eat seafood, fresh from the trawlers. They tried to get together for lunch at least once a fortnight – that way their busy lives never came between their friendship.

As she waited for her friend to answer the phone, she thought about their friendship. Everyone always commented on how different they were, and they weren't wrong. Mel and Ceana could not have been more opposite if they'd tried. The most obvious difference came in their chosen career paths. Ceana had never gotten how Mel could love maths and numbers; so much so, that she had opted to become an accountant. The most boring job in the world if you asked her and Mel had the exact same sentiment about Ceana's love of Ancient History or – as she put it – old dusty things. Regardless of their differences, this never affected their friendship. In truth, it is probably the reason they got on so well. They never fought about anything as their tastes were so completely opposite that there was never any reason to argue over something or someone.

"Good afternoon. Gold Accounting Firm. This is Melissa."

Ceana heard her friend relay the familiar greeting and smiled, she sounded so professional, if only her clients knew the real her. "Well Melissa speaking, I was wondering if I could make an appointment to come in and have my books looked at. You see, I've heard there is a great accountant there that can smudge my books for me. I need her to hide my pimping money."

At the other end of the phone Mel laughed. "Well I am afraid you are going to have to wait since it's tax time again. I am up to my eyeballs in BAS Returns. Unfortunately, I have many other people to make rich before you, but then again, they have waited this long, so a few more minutes won't hurt."

"Well I will be happy to distract you from your boring number problems for a bit." Ceana snorted.

"So, to what do I owe the pleasure of this call? Did we have a lunch date this week that I forgot about?" Mel asked. This reply did not surprise Ceana one bit, Mel was always forgetting things. It was common knowledge that if you had an appointment with Mel you had to text her the night before to remind her about it.

"No we didn't." Ceana laughed. "I was just thinking that it has been such a long time since we caught up, that you should come to dinner tonight." Ceana said.

Mel chuckled. "Cee you are such a dope, we only saw each other two nights ago. I'm not sure I can. I have a lot of paperwork to get through. At this rate I would probably need a boat to get there, the rain has been intense all morning." Mel answered. Ceana knew that it wouldn't take much to get her to change her mind. She had just the thing that would get her attention.

"You have to. I have a surprise for you." She baited.

"That sounds a bit dubious." Mel said. Cee knew that she wouldn't be able to resist. Mel hated mysteries as much as she did. It didn't take long for her to change her mind, "What the hell, I'm up for anything you can throw at me, what time do you want me there?"

It was Ceana's time to laugh. Mel was in for a surprise all right, perhaps after the joke was over she could date Mr Dreamy actor. "Around seven is fine, and Mel? Drive safely, the roads on your side of town are still open, but just to be sure, bring some clothes in case you have to stay, oh and dress to impress." She said before hanging up on her friend so she couldn't rethink her acceptance. She knew her last comment would guarantee Melissa's appearance tonight. She was just too curious a person not to.

"That wasn't really nice Cee, you could have given her a little clue." Bata clucked. "Please tell me you at least are going to tell her before the guys show up?"

"Nope!" She answered wickedly, winking at her sister as she headed to her bedroom. She no longer dreaded tonight. In fact, now she couldn't wait for it to begin.

❦

As she let the hot water flow over her body in the shower, she thought about tonight and was glad that Katie had settled on a nice big roast tarragon chicken instead of the risotto. A roast was *perfect* for stormy weather. She spent a good thirty minutes in the shower letting its warmth relax her tight muscles. After the morning she'd had, the time to herself was bliss. If only the hot water could rinse away her embarrassments from this morning. After she stepped out and got dressed, she wasted no time heading to the kitchen to help Katie prepare dinner. She couldn't let her do it all on her own, especially since technically speaking, it was her turn to cook. Perhaps she could organise a nice dessert. Now that was something she could do well!

As she rummaged through the kitchen checking the stocks for dessert, a niggling feeling kept on in the back of her mind, questioning her plan and her reasoning. Even though she was sure this was one of Mel's devious plans, the tiny voice in the back of her mind kept asking her, *what if this was not a joke?* She quickly dismissed it from her mind. It had to be Mel, the alternative scared her too much to contemplate. *There was no way it could be real, could it?* The doubts clouded her enthusiasm with uncertainty and suddenly she wasn't sure now that she wanted to go ahead with tonight after all. *What if he turned out to be the real deal?*

CHAPTER 5

Kessan stood in front of more see-through walls, this place liked see-through walls. He looked at the tiny room with hesitation. Not only was it small but if someone came in to the room they would be able to see him in all his glory. Looking at the wall he noticed metal branches sticking out with red and blue dots that appeared to be indicators for something. What, he didn't know. *How the hell did he work this contraption?* Turning the left handle slowly, he was surprised when water started coming out from the apparatus at the top. Cold water crashed down over him at first, startling him with its bitter sting, and then, by God's teeth! It warmed before he had time to recover from his surprise and almost burnt the hairs off his body! He cursed, turning it off quickly. He decided to try the other one. Thankfully, this one stayed cold. In the Highlands, you either had a cold bath, a swim in the Loch or you heated water up over the fireplace. He stared at the knobs in front of him. Perhaps if he turned the other one on slowly while the cold water ran it might warm up a bit. He tried it and soon had a beautiful and more tolerable temperature. He sighed as the water cleansed his weary body. He could definitely get used to having fresh water on hand like this, he thought blissfully.

Kessan could not remember ever feeling so clean after stepping out of a washtub. Having a bath in the Loch came close but most of the time it was freezing cold, so cold that it stole one's breath the moment they entered. Often he would dive straight in to ease the shock. The icy water felt like needles all over his body and if one spent too long in its embrace, they could die from the chill. This did not allow a person to stay in long, a quick wash where necessary and you had to be out to dry off in front of a fire. This, however, was amazing. He thought about standing in the stream of water all night, but the temptation to see the little minx with fire in her emerald eyes held more appeal.

The wench baffled him. He had never before met someone with whom he felt such an overwhelming burst of desire upon first sight. Not only did he lust after her, but for some strange reason he felt an overpowering need to protect her. An unbridled image of her with rumpled clothes, a wild look and simmering smile entered his mind. Oh, there was no way he was going to leave this place without sampling a taste of the fire that lie beneath the surface. But, before he could enjoy her, they were going to have to find Laird MacDonnell's bairn. They did not have much to go on. After many years of searching, the druid had only been able to find the area of where Ceana had been sent. To add to the frustration, the only piece of evidence they had to go on was the plaid the bairn had been wrapped in. God's teeth, he hoped she still had it.

He was also told that she had a tiny birthmark at the base of her neck, just below her hair line. It was unique, only a true MacDonnell heir would possess the mark. It was said to look like a small heart with an arrow piercing the centre. This information presented a whole set of problems within itself. Would she know if she had the mark? It was in an area that not many people had ever seen themselves before so asking her may be pointless. Now he had to come up with a plan to catch a glimpse of the lass's neck without scaring her off and this was on top of actually finding the lass. His only hope was that there might be a family resemblance, however they were not holding out hope as most of the women in the MacDonnell clan, looked nothing like the males. Raising his eyes to the heavens he wondered what he had ever done in his life to deserve this. Closing his eyes, he took a deep breath and readied himself for the task ahead.

"Kessan, are ya almost ready to go? We do no' want ta be late. They might really think us barbarians." Caelan said on his way to the other bathroom.

Kessan smiled to himself as he remembered the little minx's slip up this afternoon. He didn't think her cheeks could have gotten any redder and damn, if that didn't add to her appeal.

"Aye brother, I am ready when ye are, but before we go, remember no' to give away too much of our purpose. After all we doona ken who we can trust in this time yet."

"Aye, let's just hope that we can trust these wee lasses. I would sure like to get to ken the younger one more intimately." Caelan replied to his brother as he walked up the stairs.

DAMN, it was almost time for dinner and Ceana could not calm the butterflies that had started in her stomach. They had appeared there the moment she set eyes on her guests and they had not quietened one bit. If they didn't stop soon she was sure she was going to be sick. Oh, she knew that vomiting all over his shoes would add to her appeal, especially after this morning's graceful introduction! She supposed it couldn't get much worse. She had already made a fool of herself in front of the sexy Highlander, not once but twice. Thinking of him again started her stomach rolling. Just the thought of facing the imposing Scotsman was both exhilarating and terrifying. She could not remember ever feeling this conflicted with herself before. She looked around the kitchen for something that would calm her nerves. Aha! There was a bottle of wine sitting on the kitchen bench. Just what the doctor ordered, a pre-dinner drink. *What harm could it do?*

After pouring herself a glass, she went to the oven and opened the door to check that the roast vegetables were not drying out or cooking too fast. Everything, well everything food-wise, was going smashingly and it smelled heavenly. *At least one thing was going right today*, she thought, thankful that her sister was an amazing cook. Closing the oven door, she leaned against the bench, trying to remember if she had broken any mirrors or crossed the path of any black cats recently. Nothing came to mind. So why was the universe and her friends plotting against her?

Katie entered the kitchen as Ceana filled her glass a second time, her eyes travelled to the wine glass.

"What?" Ceana asked, sounding defensive.

"Nothing at all… It's just that you only have a glass of wine before dinner when you are stressed or have something major on your mind, like an assignment. As far as I'm aware you finished your assignment yesterday and your next one is not due for weeks, so I am wondering what has you turning to alcohol this time?"

"Bite me Bata!" The minute the words were out of her mouth she knew she shouldn't have reacted, that only made her sister even more curious.

Katie sniggered at Ceana's reply. "Wow, he really has got you riled, hasn't he? What makes me curious though, is why? You've never reacted this way before. So come on, spill the beans. What's up?"

"You know what they say Bata, curiosity killed the cat. Perhaps you really should take note of that." She snapped.

Changing the subject wouldn't work. When Katie wanted to know something, she was like a dog with a bone. Her sister leant against the bench across from her and folded her arms across her chest. Ceana braced herself for the onslaught.

"Come *on* Cee, you know that changing topics doesn't work with me, so spill!"

A knock on the door saved her from replying and when Mel entered without waiting for an invite, Ceana breathed a sigh of relief. She was starting to think her plan hadn't worked and that maybe she wouldn't show. But then again, the storm outside wouldn't have made it a pleasant drive, the worst of it was over, though there was still plenty of rain about, coming in scattered bursts.

As if she could read Ceana's thoughts Mel got straight to the point without even a hello. "Come on Cee. What *is* this big bloody surprise you have for me? And I would just like to point out that the little stunt of yours today was not overly nice. Do you know I could not focus for the rest of the day? I was too busy worrying about what the bloody hell was going to happen tonight. So much so that by about two this arvo I gave up trying and went home early so that I could figure out what to wear, and then I stupidly drove up here in this storm; thankfully most of the roads were still open, but only just there were trees down everywhere on the side of the road."

This was gold, Mel was clearly on edge. Perhaps she would think twice about playing a prank on her next time. Ceana gave her a sweet smile and replied. "You will have to wait a little longer I'm afraid."

"We have to wait for the rest of our guests to arrive but trust me, it will be well worth the wait!" Katie added.

As she walked past Mel to the living room, her best friend's eyes light up with excitement. She put her hands together in front of her, waggling her fingers like an evil murderer from a horror film. "This does sound more interesting by the minute!" She cackled. Her facial expression changed all of a sudden and her smiling enthusiasm was replaced with a look that accompanied a person who had just eaten something sour. It was quite comical to watch. "You had better not be trying to set me up with Marcus?" She snapped. "I'm sorry Cee, I love you and would do anything for you, *except* dating Marcus just so that he will leave you alone. That's where I draw the line!"

"Come on Mel, best friends are meant to help each other out in tight spot. If I can't count on you to be my wingman. Who can I count on?" She asked sweetly.

The look Mel gave her was one of such disgust. "Ceana Thorne, so help me God if this is your big surprise, you will regret the day you ever met me!" She declared.

"You can relax Mel, I would never try and set you up with Marcus. I like him too much to do that to him. You would eat him alive and leave the poor boy wondering what happened." Ceana said through her chuckles.

Mel poked her tongue out which only increased Ceana's amusement. She was trying to recover her composure but then she remembered the horror on her best friend's face at the thought of dating Marcus and the laughter bubbled up again. That was one of the reasons she loved her so much; she helped remind Cee to allow a little fun into her life and made even the gravest of situations bearable.

Just then, the boys entered the room in time to catch the end of their conversation and noticing the look on Marcus' face set her off again. The poor man had heard what they had said, and he was standing there looking as though he wanted to strangle Mel.

"I'm sorry Marcus." She managed to get out. "I did try to get her to go out with you, but you know how stubborn she can be."

Marcus now looked embarrassed. This made her laugh even harder.

Tristan took sympathy on him, "Trust me man, you should be thankful that neither of them want you. They are both as loony as each other!"

Out of the corner of her eye Ceana saw Mel grab a cushion off the chair and aim it for his head. Tristan caught it and, with a one flick of the wrist, tossed it back at her. His aim was better than hers though and the pillow connected solidly with her ear.

"Now, Mel that is no way for a lady to behave in front of gentlemen." Tristan said in a mock hurt voice.

Ceana snorted, "Oh that's a bit rich. I wouldn't call you a gentleman."

Her brother turned to her and winked. "Oh but sister dearest, I wasn't referring to myself. I was referring to our guests."

It was then that she finally noticed that they were not alone. All four men were now standing in the living room watching Ceana with a variant of different expressions. All probably trying to determine just how crazy she was. Her eyes fell on Kessan and stayed there. She could not get over how handsome he was. She shook herself out of her reverie as Tristan broke her trance by introducing him to Mel. Kessan smiled. It was the same smile that he had used on her earlier, it changed his whole demeanour, making him even more appealing and making her weak at the knees. Ceana's entire body was hit with a pure bolt of lust like none she had ever experienced before. Glancing at Mel, she saw that her best friend was as star struck as she was and for the first time today, she began to believe that Mel might have had nothing to do with this after all. Her shock was just too real. It didn't take her as long to recover however and once she came out of her daze she returned to her normal self. As was her usual habit, she ran up and jumped on Tristan, giving him a hug.

The teasing started up again. "Hey short fry, I swear that you get shorter each time I see you." Tristan teased her.

"I do not, you butthead, you just get taller. Soon I will have to drop a brick on your head to stop you from growing." She threatened with a smile.

As the bantering continued, Ceana looked around the room and noticed that Kessan was watching her. She saw amusement in his eyes, along with something else, something she could not pinpoint. But then again for all she knew it could have been pure boredom or even disgust at her childlike behaviour. Before she could dwell on it further, she was lifted off her feet and grasped in a huge bear hug.

"Marcus, put me down you great oaf!"

A rumble of laughter greeted her in response, "not until you give me a welcome kiss." He told her as he puckered up his lips. She couldn't help but laugh. She knew he was only mucking around but she also knew that if she gave him a kiss he would not knock her back.

"The only thing you are going to get Mr Slade is a fat lip if you don't put me down."

"You can't blame a man for trying." He continued with a wink. "Maybe I would have better luck with Mel, I hear that she digs me." Ceana, Mel and Katie took one look at each other and all three of them burst out laughing.

Walking away from Marcus she headed over to Tristan who had joined the two guests. "Hey, how was your day?" She asked giving him a hug.

"Not bad, there wasn't much to do at Mr Brown's place so we were able to get it all done before the worst of the storm hit. Oh, I made a quick run to the store and picked up some drinks for tonight. I got you some Jack Daniels and I thought our guests might appreciate a good Scotch to drink with dinner."

With that statement, all eyes turn towards Kessan and his brother. "Aye we would indeed." Caelan replied. Kessan was still watching her and when her eyes met the dark blue of his, the breath left all her body and the butterflies started again. This night was going to be a long night if she couldn't control herself. It was hard. He was so damn fine. *Was it possible for a person to get more attractive in such a short time?* She would swear that all cleaned up he was even more desirable than he had been this afternoon. Tristan had been able to find them some spare clothes of his that fit, and while she thought that his black pants had done him justice it was nothing compared to him in the pair of denim jeans and black shirt he was now wearing.

All sorts of images were floating through her mind, but the most prominent was of the two of them naked in bed. She had to do something quick to dispel them – dinner, go and set up dinner she told herself. She left the others in the living room drinking and talking. They were all curious about their guests and their travels. That accent of his followed her out and down the hallway to the dining room as he started to explain how they had lost their belongings. *God help her.*

It didn't take her long to set the table and dish up dinner. Before she knew it, it was time to face him again. There was nothing else to do now but eat.

"Ok guys dinner is ready." She called out from the dining room.

"Smells good Cee, but then again Katie's cooking is always awesome. Maybe you should take notes." Marcus said as he walked passed her, slapping her butt as he went. Ceana punched him on the arm and told him to stop being an idiot. What she didn't see was the reaction of the man who was following them, and it was probably a good thing, because if she had seen the look on the Highlander's face she would have run for the hills. He looked as though he was ready to kill.

⁂

Kessan was unprepared for the murderous feeling that washed over him and it was all focused on the young man walking in front of him. The moment his hand had touched Cee's arse, Kessan had wanted to draw his sword to cut him down where he stood.

"Easy brother, he dinna' mean anything by it." Said a voice in his ear. Only Caelan was aware of the slight change in Kessan's demeanour and he could only guess at what had caused it. But he'd know his brother well enough to pick up on his moods. Kessan gave a short nod in understanding and reached for the glass his brother held out. *That drink of scotch was not such a bad idea after all.* He followed the rest of the party in to dinner. It was going to be a long night. *Aoife* save him.

CHAPTER 6

Looking at the clock on the cabin wall, Ceana was surprised to see that time had been flying by. They were almost finished their main meal and it hadn't been as uncomfortable as she'd imaged it would be. However, that was mainly thanks to Tristan and Marcus who had kept up a steady stream of conversation and jokes. They had spent the entire time hounding the men for information on Scotland as they were planning a trip there next year. The men responded in turn, happy to offer the boys information on the Highlands. She noticed that they tended to give aloof answers about where the best places were to visit. Ceana couldn't complain though; she loved hearing about Scotland. The one place that she had always dreamed about going. In fact, she was quite jealous that the boys *were* going.

The only thing better than learning more about Scotland, was that she got to listen to Kessan and Caelan describe it in their authentic, heavily accentuated accents.

The smoothness of their voice made it sound even more magical and mythical.

Despite the comfortable setting, the nagging feeling in her stomach returned. She looked at her best friend with fading hope that she would provide any indication of what she was planning, Mel was not giving anything away. To top it off, she seemed as intrigued with Kessan's stories as anyone else. She never thought Mel had that much talent with acting or pulling such a good poker face. The other puzzling factor was the way in which Kessan described the Highlands in such detail as if he'd lived there all his life. It sounded like every history book she'd ever read. This only added to the voice in her head telling her that this was real and no prank. She had to be sure. She had to devise a way to get a reaction out of Mel. One that would show that these two knew each other. So far they had acted as though they were complete strangers.

"Hey Mel. I was just wondering if you had met any new people this week or spoke to anyone with an interesting job, say like an actor?" Ok so she could have been a bit subtler, but enough was enough. The longer this went on, the crazier she was becoming. Mel had been talking to Katie when Ceana threw that comment at her and now she was staring at her as though she had lost the plot.

"Um, trust me Cee, if I had spoken to any actors this week you would have been the first to know." Mel replied, staring at Ceana with a mixture of confusion and concern.

'*Ok, that was too sincere,*' she thought feeling panicked. She knew Mel well enough to spot her tells when she was lying and she could see Mel was telling the truth. Which meant that this was no prank. *Could it be that the man sitting at the end of the table really was, quite literally, the man of her dreams?* She felt faint.

A feeling of panic rose over her and she knew that she needed to get out of the room now. She was starting to feel dizzy, and nauseated. Not wanting to draw attention to herself, she decided she would go and check on the next course. "Bata, could you please come and help check on dessert?" She asked her sister. Katie raised an eyebrow but did not question her and relief flooded her when she simply nodded, stood and followed her into the kitchen without so much as a word.

Walking down to the kitchen, away from the noise of the dinner table, her nerves started to calm down. Ok, she thought to herself desperately, she would give it one more shot to see if she could crack Mel. If that fell through, then she would have to find a way to deal with the fact that there really was a Highlander from her dreams staying in one of the cabins. They finally reached the kitchen.

"Ok, what gives Cee? You could have checked the dessert without help." Katie stated.

"Alright, so I didn't really need you to help with dessert."

"Well duh!" Katie replied sarcastically.

Ceana gave her a look that told her she did not appreciate her sarcasm.

"I needed you to help me devise a plan in order to get Mel to fess up to what she has done. And since you are more devious than the two of us put together I thought you could help."

"Ok, now I don't know if I should be offended or not, but I think I will take it as a compliment and help you. Now could you please explain to me *what* you think Mel has done? Otherwise I can't really help you."

She really didn't want to explain this to her sister but she knew she had to,

"Oh, alright."

Ceana then explained to Katie what she thought Mel was up to. Her sister of course thought she was out of her mind, but decided to help anyway. They stood there by the kitchen bench for about five minutes. Ceana was so focused on finding a solution that when her sister spoke, it startled her.

"I've got it! If you offer to help Kessan find this long-lost relative, then they will be forced to admit that there really is no relative and that it was all part of a plan."

Ceana had to admit it had merit but what if they did turn out to be legit? She would be stuck escorting the Scotsman around, placing her in his company more often than she wanted. Her heartbeat picked up and a spark of excitement exploded within her at the thought of being near him for long periods, possibly even alone. Her cheeks burst into flames as she thought about what she would like to do his body. She was thankful that her sister could not read her thoughts.

"Have I told you recently Bata how lucky I am to have a sister like you? Especially when you're not using that devious mind against me?" Katie just laughed.

"Ok you head back on in to dinner and I will finish up here." Ceana offered.

With that Katie headed back to the dining room, not before she poked her tongue out at her sister who rolled her eyes back with a grin. Ceana was glad that she now had some time alone to calm her nerves as she put the

final touches on the Pavlova. Once it was done, she headed back to the dining room to finish eating.

Kessan was just leaving the bathroom when she stepped out of the kitchen and she walked straight into him. She yelped in surprise and stumbled. He instinctively grabbed her arms just below the shoulder and a bolt of electricity shot straight through his body. She raised her head towards him and started to thank him, stuttering the words in an embarrassed panic. But once she looked up into his eyes, he was lost. He wanted to kiss her, and he could see she wanted it too. Lowering his head towards her slowly, he gave her time to stop him and when she didn't, he knew that she wanted this kiss as much as he did.

This knowledge fuelled his blood even more. The moment his lips touched hers he was lost, it was a tentative kiss at first but, as she melted into him, he increased the pressure.

He lifted her chin up with his

thumb so that he could deepen the kiss. She tasted like pure heaven, cream and vanilla, and the smell of lavender floated up and engulfed him. He had to stop this soon or otherwise he would be lost. Slowly, he pulled away from her and was pleased to see that her eyes were hazed and her lips looked as though they had been thoroughly kissed.

He ran the pad of his thumb over her bottom lip, his body hardening even more when her tongue darted out and tasted his skin. He couldn't help having one more taste of her, but this one was softer than the last. He watched as her eyes closed and a soft moan escaped her lips.

This sent a masculine pride through him and at that moment, his mind repeated *'Mine'* once more. She would be his all right. He vowed that he would have this minx in his bed before he went home. Darting his tongue out he ran it where his thumb had been moments ago before pulling back. He tilted her head up to look at him.

"Ailleagan meinn, what have ya done to me?" Releasing her abruptly, he turned and walked away, leaving her standing there in the hallway.

❧

Ceana was stunned. She could not move from where she stood, her heart was racing a mile a minute and she had to lean against the wall to support herself. She had not been concentrating when she'd came out of the kitchen. Ceana had been too busy thinking about *him* and as if her mind had conjured him up, she had practically stepped right into his arms. A bolt of pure lust engulfed her body when he grabbed her.

Never before in her life had she experienced such pure desire. She knew now why she was still a virgin. There had never been any spark like that at all, with anyone. She had gone to thank him for preventing her fall but she knew, in that moment when she looked into his deep blue eyes, she was gone.

She felt like she was drowning in the ocean. She knew looking into those mesmerizing eyes had been a mistake, they had hypnotised her like a snake's. It was as if they were magnets drawing her gaze up to his. She saw in his eyes the exact moment he had decided to kiss her and, God help her, she could not stop him and it only took her a moment to realise that she didn't want to.

Ceana *wanted* to taste this man, a man that looked uncannily like the one in her dream, even if only once. Ceana had eagerly met him and she was not disappointed, he had tasted of scotch and honey and, to top it off, he smelled of pure unadulterated male. She'd almost stopped breathing when he deepened the kiss. The only thought that had been racing through her head was a plea, *'please, do not let him stop!'*

Oh, the man could kiss. She had been kissed before but never like this. He made her feel as though they were the only two people in the world and that he was preparing to devour her for dessert and, by all that was holy, she wanted him to. The kiss had ended all too soon and Ceana felt like weeping but before she had the chance to beg him to continue, he leaned in and kissed her again. A softer kiss this time. Before he pulled away, his tongue darted out and ran along her lower lip. Then as if nothing had happened he stopped, straightened and just walked around her and headed back to the dining room without a word, no, wait, he had said something. He had called her something unfamiliar right before he had asked her what she'd done to him. She couldn't believe his nerve, *what*

she'd done to him? He was the one that left her stunned in her current position. Most importantly, she would have to remember to look up what he had called her. She would have to remember not to be alone with this man again,

because the next time she would not be able to stop herself from begging him to take her. On the up side, if this did turn out to be a prank, she had at least gotten her fantasy kiss from her dream guy, and it hadn't disappointed.

⚜

KESSAN COULD NOT HELP the satisfaction he felt when the little minx re-entered the dining hall five minutes later. She looked flushed and embarrassed and she would not look directly at him. He wondered how long it would take before she gathered up the nerve to look at him again. He stared at her, willing her to look at him and it didn't take long before she turned those emerald green eyes of hers on him. He was still amazed at how green her eyes were. They reminded him of the heather covered fields of his wonderful Highlands. He could see a spark of fire within them and he could just imagine what she'd be saying to him if they were alone. He raised one eyebrow daring her to say what was on her mind, he was not disappointed.

"Mr McKinnon, since you have not had any luck in locating this missing relative of yours, I would like to help you find her if you don't mind. I happen to know the lady who runs the office of Births, Deaths and Marriages which would be the best place to start your search."

He watched as she gave him a sickly-sweet smile at the end of her speech.

He stared, the chit was offering to put herself in his company on a regular basis. The Gods were definitely playing with him. *What was the little minx up to?* He knew she didn't want to be in his company, she had inferred it herself a few times today. She had practically choked on the last part of her statement before she had raised her near full glass of wine and drunk it in one gulp.

Something inside his head screamed at him to reject her offer. He knew she would be a distraction and yet, before he could stop himself, the words, "aye, thank ya lass, we would be much obliged to ya." Spilled from his lips. *What was the matter with him?* His brother began to choke on his mouthful of food – Caelan was obviously thinking the same thing. Instinctively Kessan knew she was up to something and he was going to find out what it was. He watched with amused fascination as her eyes widened and she sucked in her breath, he couldn't believe it, the wench had expected him to say no. Aye, this was getting more and more interesting he was going to have some fun here and the chit in front of him, with her green as grass eyes, was going to provide it. She just didn't know it yet. He would eventually go back to his Highlands with the MacDonnell lass and defeat the magic that was trying to destroy all he loved. But in the meantime, he would get the most out of the situation.

Ceana couldn't believe it. Bata's plan had backfired. The lout was meant to refuse her offer, at which point she would call Mel's bluff. But no, he had accepted it! What did that mean? She glanced at Mel to gauge her reaction, but she was deep in a conversation with Tristan. This was getting ridiculous. She didn't have time for games anymore. She stared at Mel, as if willing her to look at her, but she kept on talking. After five minutes of trying to get Mel's attention without drawing everyone else's she gave up and opted for something less subtle. Grabbing a carrot from her plate, she pegged it with the intention of hitting Mel's head. She watched it sail through the air, horrified as it went straight past its intended victim and hit her brother right in the eye. He stopped talking and stared at her, stunned. Groaning, she dropped her head to the table, she could not believe it. Lifting her head up she watched as he, with deliberate slowness, picked up some potato on his fork and took aim.

"Cee," he said in an even voice. "I thought you would have learnt your lesson from the 2012 food fight saga. It is not wise to throw food at me."

He got just the reaction he wanted, the entire table turned their way to watch the scene unfold.

"Don't you dare, Jackass! I was merely trying to get Mel's attention, but as usual your big fat head got in the way!" She snapped.

Tristan just laughed at her, which only enraged her further.

"I would think really carefully before you throw that Tristan. Do I have to remind you about the last time you threw something at ME?" She was reminding him of the last food fight he had started. The battle had not stopped at the dinner table. They spent a week trying to outdo each other. Their antics ranged from frogs in the bed, *her bed*, to itching powder in his wet suit. Not appreciating someone messing with his surfing, Tristan had called it quits after that and usually threatening him with similar consequences made him think twice. This time it wasn't working, and she could see the glint of amusement in his eye as he pulled the fork further back.

"You wouldn't dare." She hissed at him. *Not in front of the Scotsman*, she silently begged him. Her carrot was bad enough.

"Oh, wouldn't I?" He waggled the fork, closing one eye to aim and exaggerating the moment.

Man, he was such a child, she thought as she stood up and placed her hands on the table. She leaned forward. "No, you wouldn't." She ground out through clenched teeth.

On that note, Tristan stood up and leaned in closer to her face, making sure that his projectile was right in line with her nose.

Both of them stood there staring each other down, neither one prepared to back off. It was not until she heard her sister's voice that she came back to her senses.

"Well, I bet you guys were not expecting dinner and a show." Katie said evenly, glaring at her siblings.

Sitting back down reluctantly she dared her brother to continue. Thankfully, he followed suit and slowly eased himself down again. He smirked at her as he ate the potato on his fork. She hated that he thought he had won. "You know Tris, sometimes you're such a Neanderthal!"

"I love it when you speak ancient to me Cee." Tristan laughed.

She just smiled at him sweetly and replied, "if you don't stop that mouth of yours, I am going to use my knowledge of the Egyptian burial methods and bury you alive!"

The whole table but the two dinner guests, who were smiling in polite bewilderment, had started to laugh. Katie, forever the peacemaker, was the first to speak up once they calmed down. "Now come on you two, act like family members and grow up a bit or you may give our guests the wrong idea."

"They *are* brothers, Bata. I am sure on more than one occasion Caelan has wanted to toss a carrot at his own brother's head. God I've only known him a day and I've had the urge." She said pointedly. She couldn't help it, after all of today's events, her temper was wearing thin and she just couldn't hold in her frustration any longer.

Caelan gave a deep booming laugh in agreement. Smiling innocently at Kessan, Ceana continued to watch him as she put a fork full of roast in her mouth. He was doing that annoying thing where he lifted one eyebrow as if to question her. All she wanted to do was walk up to him and yank it back down. Well she had already made a fool of herself, so she may as well keep it up, pushing her chair out she looked straight at her best friend. "I need to speak with you. In private!" She stated pointedly.

"What did I do?" She heard Mel ask behind her as she strode determinedly towards the kitchen. She was ready to put an end to this prank. *It had to be a prank.* Mel followed her into the kitchen, calling out to Tristan as she trailed behind her.

"Tristan, if you hear me screaming, will you come and save me?"

"Not on your life, short fry, you're on your own. I still owe you for filling my surf board bag with sand!" Tristan's voice sounded behind them.

"You know, your sister's right, you are a jerk! Next time, I'll make sure it's something that isn't so easy to clean!" Mel yelled back to the dining room.

She waited by the bench until Mel entered. "What's up Cee? You seem a bit frazzled tonight."

Turning to her best friend she pleaded "Mel, please tell me that this is one of your practical jokes! Tell me that the man out there is someone you hired to get back at me for setting you up on a blind date!"

"Cee what are you on about?" Mel asked, clearly confused.

She was starting to sound desperate, even to her own ears. "Come on. That man out there is exactly like the man from my dreams and you are the only one who knows that much about them. You set it up, didn't you? Tell me I'm not crazy!"

Her face fell as she took in Mel's expression. It was all the answer she needed, and the sinking feeling was back in her stomach again. This was not good. She leaned back against the bench defeated.

Mel stared at her. "Are you bloody insane? No I did not hire him, but you know what? I'm kicking myself that I didn't think of it!"

Her legs suddenly gave out and she had to sit down, lifting herself up on to the bench, she let her head fall into her palms. Her mind raced, this guy was for real. How could she have dreamt of him so perfectly when she had never met him before? It was not only the way that he looked but also the way that he made her feel, the way he spoke, and the way he sounded. Everything about this man matched her dreams and, remembering what his purpose was, she didn't want any part of it. Now she had promised to help him! What was she going to do? Ok, she would just have to find this lass as soon as possible and then send them back to wherever they came from. Somehow, though, she knew in her heart that it was never going to be that simple. Mel sat down beside her.

"Cee, tell me what's going on. What do you mean he's the man in your dream?"

KESSAN AND CAELAN had been watching the antics of the siblings curiously. Never had they seen a family act like this. Kessan loved his family. He was the Laird, and everyone had to treat him with respect, even his siblings. Their childhood was full of rules and lessons, for him they all built up to becoming a Laird of the Highlands. It was the same for most Highlanders, they were either training for the battlefield, learning how to run a keep or training to become a Laird.

Caelan turned to him, "I must admit to ye brother, the lass was right. There have been many a time where I have wanted to throw something at ya head!"

Kessan laughed. "As me with you."

When Cee had asked his brother that question, Kessan had thought it was just her way of making a point. He had not been prepared for her declaration that she had wanted to throw something at *him*! He could not have been more intrigued and pleased, knowing now that he had affected her more than she liked. He was going to use this to his advantage. He had the minx right where he wanted her and boy, did he want her. Remembering their kiss and the fire that shot between them, he had to reposition himself in his chair. His cock had become so hard that it was straining against the inside of his trews. If he did not change the path of his thoughts soon he was not going to be able to walk out of here. He wished he were wearing his kilt! These modern-day trews left no room for a man to grow. Of course, if he wanted, he was sure he could have the chit now, but he was not in the Highlands and here he had to act as they did. He didn't want to draw any unnecessary trouble whilst they were here. He was not some Sassenach noble. He would bide his time for now and focus on the task he had been sent to do. When the time came, he would have her and she would know that she was his. He was going to make her so crazy with desire that when the time came, there would be no doubt in her mind what was happening. He could not wait for tomorrow.

CHAPTER 7

"Where did ye hide the lass, old man?" He threw the goblet into the fire and screamed in frustration.

Some of his maids stopped and stared at him.

"What are ye looking at, get back to your chores!" He snapped at them angrily.

He had been sitting by the hearth for hours staring into the fire trying to put himself in the mind of his enemies.

"Would someone bring me a damn scotch?" He shouted. He needed a stiff drink.

He could not believe that MacDonnell had gotten away from him. The man was forever a thorn in his side.

MacDonnell was recruiting anyone who would listen. It was clear he was planning something. To start a war was his guess. Bah! As if any of them could defeat the magic that he possessed! Nothing could defeat the power that was bubbling inside of him. The magic was dark and powerful, so powerful in fact, that sometimes it scared even him.

Even he could feel his humanity slowly slipping away with each passing day. But he didn't care, if it meant power. Soon there would be no pesky feelings getting in the way of what had to be done. Soon the magic would consume him so completely that he would be the master of the Highlands and anyone who defied him would die. With that thought, the darkness inside of him moved and pulsated as if impatient, he felt as though he had a hundred, fiery, hot hands rolling around inside of him and he felt indestructible. He could hear dark voices in his head reassuring him that, if he conquered the Highlands, all the power of the unknown could be his.

He could remember the day when he had taken gained the power for himself after taking his father's life. The old man had been on one of his rants again, telling Kendrick how disappointed he was in the man that he had become. It had all started when Kendrick had been unable to find out what had happened to the MacDonnell lass. There had been whispers that the Laird had hidden her.

Little did his father know that he should have looked closer to home for his undoing. On that day, the first voice whispered through Kendrick's mind, coaxing him to take his father's life and the power that resided inside of him. The voice showed him what he would become if he did this. All he could think about was becoming the most powerful Laird in the Highlands. His father had spent his days telling him how worthless a Laird he was going to be, and just to make matters worse, all the other clans around him only became more wealthy and powerful while his suffered and struggled. He wanted not only his father to fear him but also the clans, and the one clan that he wanted to suffer the most was the one that stood in his way, the family that was protecting the magic, the MacDonnell clan.

It would be a bittersweet victory for him, after he'd run his sword through his father and watched the life blood seep from his eyes. But nothing changed, no-one had respect for clan McKenzie. They all looked down their nose at him just as they had his father and frowned on the dark magic. He had become so bitter that even his best friend had turned against him. Not that it mattered, the man had had no drive for power and had decided he did not want a part of it. Kessan had pleaded for him to reconsider but Kendrick had made up his mind. The power was the only thing that mattered, power and respect.

His trouble had not ended there. During his search for the prophesised MacDonnell lass Kendrick had discovered that the lass possessed the same power as her mother. With this power, she was the only one who could stop him. He'd known the old man wouldn't have killed his daughter as others were so quick to blame, But MacDonnell *had* placed her in hiding and once the Laird had heard of his father's death he and the blasted druid went into hiding themselves.

In a fit of rage and desperation Kendrick had exiled the entire

MacDonnell clan and destroyed the keep. He had hoped this would bring the old man out of hiding, along with the lass. When that failed, he had then set about exiling and destroying anyone who aided the bastard unless someone came forward with information, but nobody knew where the infant was. If they did, they were protecting her. His only hope now was that someday she would emerge from hiding and he would be ready. For now, as he waited, he forced the other clans into joining his cause to build a powerful army. Eventually all the clans would bow to him. No-one would ever call him worthless again.

His thoughts were interrupted by his sister, Freya, as she came rushing into the room. Her hair was wild, her clothes ripped and rumpled and her face dirty. She looked as though she had been travelling for days.

"What happened to ya?" He asked, surprised at the dishevelled intrusion.

"Och brother, I have been travelling non-stop all night to bring ya some news and that's all ya can say? Nay ya doona even care that ya sister has been out there alone. The only thing you care about it this stupid war! Perhaps I should keep the news I have on the MacDonnell lass to myself. At least until you start showing ya care!" She fumed.

Kendrick had tuned out at Freya's dramatics. She irritated him immensely with her self-absorbance and her desire for attention. He had been happy for her to stay at the McKinnon keep. It kept her and her incessant whining away from him. He was about to dismiss her when his mind processed what she had said. "What did ya just say? What do ya ken about the lass? Are the rumours true!" He demanded eagerly.

"See, I told ya, all ya care about is your stupid revenge on the MacDonnell clan! Maybe I might just take my information with me and go somewhere where I'll be appreciated!" She whined.

He saw red and felt the magic in him boil. She had pushed him too far. Kendrick had her around the neck before she could utter another word. "Sister dearest," he hissed, eyes flashing. "I suggest you tell me what information you have right now, before I snap your pretty little neck!" She blinked, eyes wide with fear and surprise but no words came out. "And may I offer ya a word of warning" he continued in a steely voice. "Ya had better tell me all of it! I am in no mood for ya games!"

Kendrick's breath came out in rasps. He needed to know badly and needed to know now! He could feel the magic well up in him as he thought about finding the lass and killing her. Finally, after so many years he was going to have the information he needed. If his sister was lying to him, there would be no place on Earth she could hide from his wrath! He pressed his fingers into her throat a little harder.

He felt her throat working beneath his fingers as she tried to speak but all that came out was a squeak and a gurgle. He released his hold just enough so that she could get the words out. "Before I tell you," she panted, "ya have to promise me that ya will no' harm Kessan! I want him for myself. Ya can do what you like to the lass, but he must remain unharmed." Her eyes pleaded with his.

"Freya, ya in no position to bargain with me lass, I donna give a damn about Kessan, what has he got to do with this?" He said coldly.

Her face had gone pale at his reply and she had started to squirm in his grasp.

"Halt and tell me now Freya what ya know before I kill ya!" He roared.

"Aye, ok, but please just let me go. Ya are starting to hurt me!" She began to cry.

He pulled her close to his face so that she could see that he meant what he said next. "Aye, but I'm warning ya. If you try and leave, I *will* kill ya with my bare hands. Are we clear?" He waited until she nodded upon which he opened his grip. She fell coughing to the floor, hands protectively clasped at her throat. He glared at her without feeling. He knew the human side of him should feel some kind of compassion, but it just did not come.

"Out with it now, Freya!" He hissed.

She gulped in air and faced him, eyes filled with tears and fright. "I ken where the lass is," she declared. His eyes bore into her with such hatred that she knew she had to tell him all of it. He took a menacing step towards her. She backed away from him, the rest rushing out of her. "MacDonnell sent her through a portal to another time."

"What else." He snapped.

Freya quailed at his tone, "Kessan has gone through to retrieve her. They plan to use her to defeat ya." She whispered.

Kendrick let out a roar. *How could he betray him like this?* Kessan was going to pay. He walked over to his sister and grabbed her by the neck again lifting her until her feet were no longer touching the ground. "Ya better no' be lying to me lass!" He hissed.

She squirmed and coughed and tried to shake her head in his grasp.

"Do ya ken where the cave is?"

"Aye." She rasped.

"Good. You will tell us all you know. Tavis get in here now!" He ordered his commander. Tavis was a mean bastard. He enjoyed watching people suffer, as much as Kendrick did. He had red hair that reached his shoulders and a beard to match. A scar ran the length of his jaw in a jagged line, he was missing an eye and he wore an eye-patch and this, coupled with his thick build, made him the perfect candidate for the role of his commander. Tavis was not afraid to get his hands bloody.

Looking at his sister, his anger started to rise again. Her pleading sickened him, he could not spend another minute in her worthless presence. Dropping her to the ground, a purple outline of his hand forming around her neck, he glared coldly at her. She scooted back towards the wall burying her head in her knees. "Go and get yaself cleaned up and do not come back into my presence until ya have!" He snarled.

He watched as she left with rapid speed, head bowed, avoiding his gaze. He needed to think. This changed everything! Time Travel? Druid magic? No wonder no one could tell him about the lass. If Freya was telling the truth, he would stop at nothing! He would soon have the lass. He would kill her! He grinned, suddenly feeling much better. The first thing he had to do was find a druid that could help him figure out how to work the damn portal and then try and figure out where they had gone. He was finally going to kill the lass. Kessan, he wanted alive, he was going to make the traitor pay for betraying him. It was a shame really. He thought his best friend would eventually join him, even if only to protect his own clan. Instead he had joined forces with MacDonnell. Now he was going to have to kill him, but not before torturing him for his betrayal. He would start by killing his family.

CHAPTER 8

She was about ready to scream, she was so frustrated. After discovering that Mel did not have any part in Kessan's appearance, she resigned herself to the fact that her dream guy was for real. He was a real, honest to God Scottish Highlander! The knowledge of this had brought on a rollercoaster ride of emotions and she still hadn't been able to decide how she felt. The fantasies and images from her dreams, coupled with the confusion and fear of what it all meant, caused her to have little sleep at all, and now she was helping Kessan track down their relative.

At the beginning of the week, part of her was excited and intrigued, especially after that kiss, that she was going to get to spend some time with the hunk of a man. But, as the week wore on, she became more and more confused and the lack of success their search was getting was exasperating. The first frustrating encounter occurred when she took them to the Births, Deaths and Marriages Registry. She had organised for the highlanders to meet her friend KC in the mall at Surfers and had asked her friend to do her a favour. She had assumed that the men would give her the information they'd had, and she would then email KC and go into her office the following day to see if she could find any information. Ceana told them that this was the best place to start when looking for someone.

She had hoped that she would not have to go into town herself but the boys were being oddly tight-lipped about the whole situation. They refused to give them much detail to go on. They had told her that they wanted to keep it quiet until a point came when they could no longer get by without her needing to know more. The cloak and dagger antics were confusing her and she tried to tell herself that it was simply because they were strangers and since they didn't have a clue where they were going, she was going to have to go to Surfers after all. It had all gone downhill from there. It had started from the moment they met in the car park where they had seemed fine, until she had opened her car door and told them to hop in. They responded by acting strangely nervous and they began conversing in their native tongue. She assumed they had been discussing what they were going to do and she tried not to let it bother her, instead focussing on their Scottish accents. Then they had both ceased talking and stopped dead in their tracks, just staring at her. They were looking at her brand-new Outlander as if it had grown horns.

It had taken her twenty minutes of convincing to get them into the car. Anyone would swear by the way they were acting that they had never seen a car before. She'd never had this much trouble getting her old dog to sit in the back. Eventually she had convinced them it was ok. She did this by getting into the car herself and smiling at them, like a crazy person. *Where the hell did these guys come from?* She climbed into the driver's seat and, after a moment's hesitation, Kessan hopped in beside her. He sat in silence, staring at the radio and all the gadgets on the dash with amazement. She stared at him. *Ok this had gone far enough.*

"Come on, don't tell me you two have never seen a car before. How far up in the Highlands do you live?"

She waited for a reply and it was a full minute before Kessan answered her.

"Och aye, we have seen a…. car, before lass, it's just we do not get ones like this where we come from." He had paused at the word car as if trying it on for the first time.

Part of her knew he was lying, but she let it go, she didn't really want to know. From there her day only got weirder. Kessan had gripped the seat tightly and sat frozen the entire way to Surfers. She had looked into the rear-view mirror and noticed that Caelan was not faring much better. Whenever a car or truck would go speeding by them with a roar that shook the Outlander gently, the boys would flinch and close their eyes. At one point she swore that she could hear them reciting a prayer. Both men were a nervous wreck by the time they got to their destination. She parked the car and took them to McDonald's where KC was meeting them for breakfast. KC loved her Micky D breakfast, as she liked to call it. KC's uniqueness was what Ceana loved most about her, and so breakfast was part of the agreement. She left the boys in her capable hands.

"When you are finished just meet me back at the car, ok?"

They both nodded their understanding. Finally free to think for herself, she decided to go and have a look at the damage that had been done by the storm and she headed down Cavil Avenue. It was going to take weeks for the city to clean this mess up. There were windows smashed in almost all the buildings along the strip, and fallen trees and debris were strewn all over the place. As she made her way back around to the main strip on the beach, she could see that some of the apartment blocks had been smashed with seawater, others had lost their awnings and there was still debris on the beach itself, thankfully Mel's building had been far enough back from the beach that it had escaped with only minute damage. Looking back at the beach, Ceana felt depressed to see such a pretty spot so damaged and it did nothing to help her mood. Opening the hatch, she lowered the tailgate so she could sit and watch the waves rolling onto the shore.

As she sat there contemplating the strangeness of her life, her brother pulled up on his motorbike bringing her out of her musing. This was one of Tristan and Marcus's favourite spots. It wasn't that surprising to see him there. *Perhaps she would ride his bike home,* she thought to herself. *He* could drive their neurotic guests' home instead. She always kept her own riding gear in the back of the car just in case.

He removed all his gear and joined her.

"Don't tell me you're thinking of going for a surf?" She asked.

"Ha ha ha, no Sis, you can relax, I just thought I would come and see what damage had been done." He sighed as he looked out over the water.

She watched his expression go to one of longing as he looked out at the waves, waves that were still washing debris onto the battered beach.

"Damn! It's going to be ages before I can go for another surf." He sounded as if he was going to cry.

She was starting to feel a little better about her crappy day as she sat, staring at the waves with her brother beside her, until something made her look up and she noticed her ex walking towards them.

"Could this day get any worse?" She groaned.

Tristan turned to where she'd been looking. He looked over at her and smiled mischievously.

"Cheer up Cee, this could be fun!"

Pushing off the back of the car, she braced herself for the fight that she knew was coming.

❧

ADRIAN MARTIN HAD BEEN her boyfriend for one year. She had thought herself so lucky when she started dating him. Adrian was thought to be one of the most charismatic men around. He was six feet tall and had jet-black hair. His eyes were a deep chocolate brown. Many thought he was from an Italian background, but he wasn't. He always dressed in expensive clothes and he drove a BMW. When he smiled, he made you feel as though you could trust him with your life, he made everyone around him feel amazing and he came across as a real-life gentleman. They met in a local club and from the beginning, it was the epitome of a perfect relationship, he had played the doting boyfriend, always taking her out and buying her gifts.

But it hadn't taken her long to learn that looks can be deceiving, and it was a lesson that she would remember for the rest of her life.

Everything had been going great until, about ten months into it, she noticed signs of his manipulation and control as he'd begun to respond with outbursts of anger when he didn't get his own way. She lasted another two months telling herself that he'd change, that each incident was a one-off thing, he was just having a bad day. The final straw came when she found out that he was dealing drugs to the local school kids.

When she found out, she realised he'd never change and she had decided to meet him at the spit, in a public place to call it quits. It was around five in the afternoon on a summer's day; Mel was going to meet her there at five-thirty as they had organised to go out after. The afternoon didn't go as planned. She knew that she should have just walked away and told him over the phone when he showed up already in a bad mood, but it only enforced how much she'd needed this to end. He needed to hear it from her face to face. What she wasn't planning on was how badly he was going to take it and she remembered the angry look on his face as he screamed at her.

"How dare you! What gives you the right to think you can leave me? You're mine." His eyes had that dangerous, angry glint that always made her blood run cold.

"Adrian, don't be ridiculous. I am not a thing for you to possess and that is precisely one of the reasons I can't do this anymore!" She had said with a shaky voice. She had known the minute she had called him ridiculous that it was a bad move, but she couldn't help it. He made her so angry. How dare he think that he owned her.

"Goodbye, Adrian!"

With that, she had turned to walk away, and that's when her night had turned to hell.

"How dare you walk away from me!" He had shouted at her and then he had unleashed the true extent of his fury. He had grabbed her arm, spun her to face him and punched her right in the jaw. The force of it and the shock of the assault sent her stumbling to the ground. He didn't stop there, she couldn't remember exactly what happened after that first punch, the shock and pain was too much. Before the night was out, he had put her in hospital with four broken ribs, a fractured jaw, a broken arm and a concussion. He had beaten her until she had blacked out. Thank God she'd had the sense to organise a night out with Mel, who'd found her in a bloody slump on the ground. She'd rushed her to hospital. Recovery had been painful but something inside her had changed from that moment on. She'd sworn then and there that no man would ever have the power to leave her helpless again.

Ceana had been engrossed in the memory that she became distracted that he was right in front of her when she looked back up, a self-assured sneer on his face.

"Well fancy meeting *you* here. Hey, listen Cee, I was just wondering if we could go somewhere and talk? I think I deserve a chance to explain myself." He asked.

She stared at him. *Was he for real?* She looked back at Tristan just to make sure that he was still there. She did not need him of course but she felt safer knowing that he *was* there. Tristan may have looked relaxed to any passer-by, but she knew that he was ready to step in if it was needed. He'd wanted to kill Adrian the day after it had happened, but she wanted to get her own revenge on him.

"No Adrian, we can't." She stated firmly.

"Please Cee, I have changed, everyone deserves a second chance." He pleaded.

She snorted, *so he thought he had changed? Unlikely.*

"Decent people who make normal mistakes deserve a second chance, stupid misogynistic animals such as you, who prey on the weak, deserve to go to jail." She felt a mixture of fear and anger boil up inside her as she spat the words out, wondering what he'd say.

He stared at her as a flash of rage danced across his face. His eyes narrowed. Yep, there it was, the reaction she had been waiting for. *Changed my arse*, she thought and fought the urge to shrink back as Adrian took a menacing step towards her. This was it. This was the moment she had waited for. She had to remind herself to breathe. That was easier said than done, and when his hand shot out and gripped her arm tightly, for a split second she was back there, that terrified, naive little girl she had been two years ago. Then his next words shook her out of her stupor.

"I see you still have a smart mouth," he hissed at her, "You obviously didn't learn from the last time. Maybe it's time I taught you another lesson." He was still sneering at her. He had grabbed hold of her, bringing his face so close to hers that their noses were practically touching, and she could smell the alcohol on his breath.

His grip on her arm tightened painfully and she knew it was going to bruise. She also knew that he had whispered the last words so as not to raise Tristan's anger. What he didn't know was that she didn't need her brother to protect her. After Adrian had left her for dead, beaten and bloody on the footpath, she had vowed it would be the last time anyone would be able to do that to her again. Once she recovered from her injuries, she took up martial arts to learn how to protect herself. She could see Tristan move to stand behind her, but she could take him on herself. "Well I have news for you, dirt bag, *nobody* owns me."

With that, she kneed him right in his groin. "Arsehole!" She spat at him. He doubled over and she laid a roundhouse kick on him that lifted him right off his feet and flung him away from her where he landed on his back. She walked over to where he lay groaning. His nose was bleeding profusely and was probably broken and he was still holding his damaged manhood in his hands. She then placed her foot right on top of his hand pushing down so hard that his hand pressed into his already aching groin.

"I am only giving you this warning once. Stay the hell away from me!" She spat. She didn't really expect an answer from him with the pain that he was in, but she wanted to make sure he understood her.

She pressed a little harder until he answered her in a high-pitched voice.

"Alright fine, you crazy bitch. I will stay away from you." He screeched.

Happy and hopeful that, for now he would leave her alone, she removed her foot but before she did, she made sure to give it one last painful twist just for good measure. She turned around to Tristan who had the biggest grin of pride on his face. "Oh, Cee the look on his face when you kneed him was priceless!"

She was trembling from the adrenaline at finally confronting the other man who had haunted her dreams at night. She couldn't laugh yet though she knew she would find this funny later, but right now she was still shaken. Tristan put his arms around her and she gratefully accepted his comfort.

"It's ok Cee, the bastard will think twice about coming for you again." He chuckled. "In fact, I think I'll think twice before messing with you."

She looked up and gave him a grateful smile and she noticed Kessan and Caelan had been coming back to them. They must have seen the argument. They were standing there just staring at her with shocked looks on their faces. *Oh great.* She groaned. Just what she needed, more testosterone. That was it! She was riding the bike home! She'd had enough of men for one day and right now she just needed time to herself to think.

"Hey Tris, you can drive home, I'm taking the bike!" She said, knowing he'd be okay with it.

He nodded and she was grateful that she did not need to explain herself.

She gave the boys one last look, put her gear on, mounted the bike and took off.

❦

THE REST of the week wasn't much better. For the next two days, they would head down to Surfers to see if they could find out any more information, and the pair would still act as though she was trying to kill them. On Thursday she'd had enough. Ceana decided that it would be much faster and easier if she showed them how to find the information they needed on the computer.

They were relieved and seemed to like this idea, especially since they did not have to get into the death trap, as Caelan had labelled it. She was also snowed under with university commitments that were due at the end of next week, plus the running of the cabins. All of these things were frustrating, but nothing was frustrating her more than Kessan himself. She could not get him out of her head. She looked up from her research and over at him.

He was sitting beside his brother as they searched the web for any information on their relative and, judging from the look on his face, they were not getting anywhere. She sat there and studied him for a little while longer, admiring the way his jaw flexed as they came to another dead end. God, he had driven her so mad with desire all week that even just watching the way his jaw moved was starting to turn her on. This week had been hell to start with and then he added to it by making her crazy – the kiss replaying in her mind over and over again.

Whenever he got the chance, he would touch her which made her body sing. There had been a couple of times where she'd thought he was going to kiss her again, but he never did. He would stand so close to her that the heat radiating from him could be felt through her clothes. Then he would lean in close to ask her a question. But once he had the answer, he would move away and go and help his brother.

She swore he was doing it on purpose. Although the only satisfaction she got from this was the fact that his little games were also having an effect on him as well. She could tell that he was getting tenser as the week went on, she could see it in his eyes.

Yet, for some reason he was refusing to make a move.

She knew too, that he was becoming increasingly frustrated that their search had so far yielded no results, no matter how many questions they asked or where they searched.

Right now though, that was the last thing on her mind. The only thing that would make her feel any better was the one thing that she could not have! She dropped her head onto her notebook. God, she hoped they found something soon because if they did not find what they were looking for and go home she was either going to go out of her mind or give in and make the first move.

❧

KESSAN COULD NOT BELIEVE the rotten luck they were having. They had been searching for four days now and nothing, not one single trace. There was no record of any bairn named Ceana having been adopted in this area around twenty years ago. Miss Thorne's friend was in the process of getting them a list of the adoption that had occurred during that time but she said that it could take up to five days. All other avenues were coming up empty.

They had been searching this Goddamn computer all day and nothing! It didn't matter how many sites they went to they came up empty handed. They had even gone to see some of the locals who had been here around that time but no one knew of a lass who'd been adopted twenty years ago from Scotland. Cee had told them that even if they had moved away, their records would still have been listed in the Births, Deaths and Marriages registry and with that they would probably be able to find her current location. MacDonnell had told him that her name had been printed on the blanket so there was no reason for him to have guessed that her name could have been changed. To top it off, not only was he frustrated with the lack of information, he was also sexually frustrated.

At the beginning of the week, he had set out to seduce the lovely Miss Thorne. He had planned to get her so worked up with lust that by the end of the week she would be begging him to take her but his plan was backfiring. He knew he was getting to her, he had caught her staring at him on numerous occasions and even now she could not take her eyes off him. It was making it hard to concentrate on the task that was in front of them. He could sense her wanting and, when he walked away from her, the disappointment was so palpable that it was becoming harder and harder for him to do so. The little vixen was even invading his dreams.

What he needed was to go out into the field and do some kind of hard training to take his mind off of her. He needed to tire out his body to the point that the only thing he would want to do was to sleep. He would do so first thing tomorrow morning, he was going to take his brother deep into the forest. He had the perfect spot. In fact, it was not far from the portal. He would train until his body hurt, then he would train some more.

Kessan had just received another blow to his torso from Caelan.

"If ya keep this up Kessan, I am going to win this battle!" His brother wheezed.

Kessan snorted, stood up and charged at his brother, knocking the younger McKinnon to the ground. Nobody had gotten the better of him since he was a young lad who had barely begun training. After a life time of training and discipline, he had become one of the most feared Lairds in the Highlands.

"Do not get too complacent dear brother; I can still wipe the floor with ya, aye." He let out a mighty war cry and charged his brother, again knocking him down with a thud.

Caelan fell to the ground. "Alright, I concede, ya still the most fearsome Highlander, now can we go back to bed?"

"Get up and stop being a lass, if I didn't ken any better I would have thought I had two sisters, not one!" Kessan taunted.

Caelan burst out laughing; "Now come brother, I have yet to have enough sleep." Caelan got up and moved back into position. But Kessan had stopped paying attention. There was someone coming down the track. He signalled Caelan to be quiet. They had been practicing behind a waterfall as this had seemed the most inconspicuous place for them to bring out the swords without someone coming upon them by chance. It also gave them a good view of the trail on both sides, a feature that Kessan was glad for now as he caught sight of Cee coming around the corner and down the trail.

"Ok Caelan you can go back to bed now, but use the other path will ya." He whispered urgently.

"Aye." Caelan answered. However, as he was preparing to leave he, turned to Kessan and taunted. "Maybe I should warn her that ya are not in top form today? The lass might like to ken that she could best ya today."

"Just go would ya and be quiet aboot it." He shot at his brother. He couldn't have his brother spoiling his fun. "I've been waiting for this battle with the little minx for far too long." He whispered to himself.

Caelan did not hear the last part; he'd already headed up the opposite path, chuckling to himself. Kessan walked over to two large rocks next to the waterfall's pool and he placed his sword behind them. He then turned around and waited for her. And that was how she found him, leaning casually against the rock, arms crossed over his chest, watching her. He was just sitting, watching and waiting.

CHAPTER 9

Another dream had woken her up at 5:30a.m. This one had affected her more than usual. It felt much too real now with Kessan only metres away from her. She decided to go for a run through the rainforest. Running had always aided her in sorting out her feelings and emotions. Whenever something was troubling her, she'd lace up her shoes and run. She threw off her covers and got dressed. Ceana headed out past the cabins to the track that led into the rainforest. As she walked past the Scotsmen's cabin, she noted that all the lights were off, and she could picture a certain man asleep in bed. *The jerk!* She bet that his sleep was not interrupted by stupid dreams.

This brought her mind to his sleeping habits and she wondered if he slept naked, she wagered he did. She let out a frustrated sigh, oh how easy it would be to go and slide into a warm bed with him! It was the thought of a warm bed that made her realise that the cold had started to seep into her bones. She had come to a complete stop outside of his cabin.

This man was going to be the death of her. She had to start moving. Her body was starting to shiver. She needed to get her blood pumping. It was coming into winter so although the sun was just starting to rise, its warmth would not reach the forest until about 10:00a.m. and the forest was still shrouded in a faded darkness as the light slowly tried to penetrate its depths. She had run this path so many times that she knew it like the back of her hand and the lack of light was no obstacle. With her body cooling in the chilly morning air, she put her earphones in and started her run into the rainforest.

She had been running for half an hour now, her body was well and truly warm, but she still could not get the damn Scotsman out of her head. She was coming up to her favourite part of her run where the path split into two and she could either go in front of the waterfall or behind.

Usually in winter she would stick to the front path as the spray that came off the water was quite chilly. However today she had the urge to go behind it. The waterfall acted as a curtain and one could sit behind there without being seen by the world. It was where she came to think about life or even just to take a break from life. Everything seemed better when you were sitting behind a waterfall, watching the colours dance through the water as it cascaded in front of you on its journey down to the pool below. The fall was in full force today due to all the water they had gotten from the storm. That was why she didn't see him until she had run behind the curtain of water.

There he was sitting on *her* rock, in the one place that she came to for solace. He had his legs crossed at the ankle and his bare arms were crossed over his extremely masculine, naked glistening chest. That was the first thing she noticed. He was not wearing a shirt and those black leather pants hugged his body so tightly that it outlined every delicious male feature he possessed. It had to be a crime for one man to look so Goddamn lickable.

"Fuck me!" The statement was out of her mouth even before she could stop it. She knew it was not at all lady-like but right now she was feeling anything but. Her temper was rising and his next comment did not help calm it any.

"Well lass, if that is ya wish I would be happy to oblige. After all I was just thinking the same thing."

She was speechless. *Was he for real?*

"That is *not* what I meant you dolt, that's what we call sarcasm. Look it up!" She snapped.

She turned to leave, just wanting to get out of here and then the past week came rushing back to her, like hell she was leaving. This was her place and if anyone was going to leave, it was going to be him. After all, he had become so good at walking away. She knew that she was overreacting but couldn't help it.

All week this man had been playing with her emotions to the

point that she was ready to jump his bones. To top things off this morning she had that stupid dream and now all she wanted was come and sit at her waterfall so that she could get some clarity back into her life, but he just had to be there. As if intruding on her dreams was not bad enough here he was standing right in front of her, intruding on her haven, and that just felt like the last straw.

"What the hell are you doing here? I thought a man such as yourself would not be able to pull himself out of bed before the sun." She knew that she was walking on thin ice insulting him but she could not help herself.

"Ya best remember lass, I am no' your brother and I will not smile sweetly at ya while ya insult me, so I hope you're ready to say ya sorry or pay the consequence. Aye, a kiss should do it." He threatened as he took a step closer.

She couldn't breathe. He was that close to her that she could smell his sweaty scent. He was intimidating her, yet the husky tone he was using implied that the consequence he was talking about might not be so bad. Here he went again making her so crazy with desire and then he would just walk away. Not this time. "Now listen here buster do not threaten me, and if you even so much as try to kiss me, I am going to bite your tongue off!"

She was hoping that he didn't call her bluff. She wanted him more than anything but didn't want to be the first to show weakness. Her pride and stubbornness was on full alert.

"Well we shall have to test that then won't we lass?" He reached out, grabbed her upper arm, and lowered his head towards her.

She froze, confused. If he kissed her one more time she would be begging him to make love to her. Stepping to the side she tried to outmanoeuvre him in a way that would loosen his hold, hoping she might be able to wriggle her arm free, but he only tightened his hand on her arm. She panicked and reefed her arm back with force, she screamed at him, "Let me go!"

But she needn't have said that; he had already let her go. She was closer to the edge of the walking trail than she thought and right then she instinctively knew that she was going into the pool. Bracing herself for the onslaught of cold water, she prepared herself to freeze. She knew it was not going to be pleasant. Her family and friends had always swum in this pond under the waterfall when they were children, and even in summer, it was cold. Within seconds she felt her body slam into the pond below. The water felt like a thousand tiny needles hitting her body. Thankfully the waterfall was still a couple of metres forward from the cliff face. The tiny outcropping above her head was forcing the water over it, forming a small pool behind the waterfall. Much like a private oasis. Even though they'd had the storm a week ago, the force was still intense, if it had been a couple of months earlier she would have had to deal with the waterfall pushing her under. Once she'd caught her breath, she planted her feet on the bottom of the pool and stood up, water streaming down her face. She was furious.

"Y…y…you j…j…jerk!" She stammered, shivering profusely.

Now she was so cold that anger was the only way she had of keeping her blood boiling enough to keep her warm. It didn't seem to be helping though, she could feel goose bumps all over her body, her teeth would not stop chattering and she was sure that her knees were knocking together under the water. She had hoped to see some kind of remorse on his face, but when she looked at him she only saw amusement. *That low down rotten barbarian!* She fumed.

⚜

KESSAN COULD TELL from the moment when she stood in front of him that she was itching for a fight. He had known the minute she saw him that she was not happy. That little statement of hers however conjured up images of what he would like to do to her, images that would make the little Miss run away and hide. To top it off she had deliberately insulted him, probably hoping that he would get angry and leave.

Well he had news for her. He was not some *Sassenach* who would cower away from some slip of a woman! If it was a fight she wanted then a fight she would have. He had not meant to send her toppling over the edge, in fact he was about to dive in after her when she had resurfaced spluttering and practically foaming at the mouth. It was then that amusement replaced the moment of worry, he was certain that this was the first time the lass had gotten a taste of just desserts.

Leaning back against the rock, he widened his smile, just because he knew it annoyed her. His amusement grew with each name that she hurled at him and, at this precise moment, she reminded him of a wild cat. Despite the stream of words coming out of her mouth, he still found himself charmed by her and he had to admit, she had a vast vocabulary. Consumed by his thoughts, he had stopped paying attention and it was only just now that he realised she had been wading into shallow water. She had been moving so subtly not to draw attention to herself.

His amusement died a short death the moment he got a good look at her. Her hair was wet and hanging in a straight line down her back, her eyelashes glinted with drops of water and the way she was looking at him made him instantly hard, her mouth, which was so full and kissable, also had droplets of water precariously perched on the edge.

It was as if they were begging him to come down there and taste her. However, the most enticing part about her present state, the thing that made his cock strain harder against his trews, were her wet clothes. They stuck to her, displaying all the curves of her body. He could see the areola of her breasts as they strained against her shirt and the patch of dark hair in the v of her hips could be seen through her pants which had now become practically transparent.

There was no way that they would be leaving this waterfall until he had tasted every inch of that luscious body.

CEANA SAW the change in him instantly. She had been ranting at him hoping that he would be a gentleman and take the hint, leaving her alone, but he just stood there laughing at her. The lout! She had been calling him every name she could think of which only increased his humour. That was it. She was not going to stand here any longer freezing. She still had to make her way home. Ceana just prayed to God that she didn't catch pneumonia before then.

She could not even steal his jacket; he hadn't been wearing one. Making her way over to the bank, she noticed that he had stopped laughing, looking up at him, she discovered why. Oh stupid, stupid, stupid, how could she have forgotten that she had worn her white running gear, she stopped in awkward horror, trying to decide if she should go back into the water, or continue with her original plan.

Once she got a glimpse of his eyes, however, her feet felt glued to the bottom of the pond. She could only watch in fascination as he lowered himself down the rocks, into the water, right in front of her. Even though goose bumps spread all over his body, there was such an intense heat radiating off him, it made her want to crawl into his skin in order to warm her own body.

She was brought back from her thoughts when he reached out and gently, possessively grabbed fistfuls of hair on either side of her head, tilting her head back as he did and then it came, he kissed her. It was so much better than the kiss they had shared the other night. This one was harder, deeper, more purposeful and it made her feel like it was the first time she had ever been kissed. The rhythmic way that his tongue kept darting around in her mouth and the intense pressure of his lips on hers made her feel as though he was making love to her mouth. His tongue tasted each corner of it. God this was the best kiss she had ever had. There was no way it could get any better. But as if he could read her mind, he tilted her head back a little more and kissed her even deeper.

It felt like only seconds when he started to slow the kiss. He gave a few more nibbles and soft kisses before pulling away.

"How is it you always taste like vanilla and cream?" He whispered.

She did not want him to stop. If he stopped it gave her enough time to come to her senses and she did not want to be sensible today. Today the only thing she wanted was him. Once and for all she wanted this man like she had never wanted anything else in her life. "Kessan please." She knew she was begging but at this point she didn't care. She only hoped that he knew what she wanted, and thank God, he did, because those words were the only permission he needed to continue.

"Wrap your legs around me lass." He instructed her. As he spoke, she felt him lift her out of the water. She obeyed and, as she felt the v of her hips encounter his manhood, they both groaned in unison. Slowly, he began to walk her backwards, and when he moved, his cock would rub against her, driving her crazy until her backside finally came into contact with the rocks behind her. He gently laid her back as the waterfall fell in a cascade behind them. He looked down at her, "are ya sure lass?" She did not know how this man had gotten through her defences, but the one thing she was sure about was this moment right here.

"Aye." She mimicked.

Her attempt at his accent seemed to calm him a bit and when he laughed, it brought their bodies back into contact. The laughter soon died from his lips and was replaced with a hiss of pure pleasure. She could no longer think. The things he was doing to her body were already unbelievable. She grabbed on to his arms, which he had placed on either side of her head. They were so thick that her small hands only made it halfway around them. He felt so solid.

She wondered if the rest of him was as hard as his biceps. Her breath started coming in short pants and she swore she was about to hyperventilate. 'Focus Cee.' She kept telling herself. Ceana did not want to miss a moment of this. Her first time could not have been any more romantic, yeah it was different to the way she'd always pictured it and even dreamed of it, but this was so much better. She was going to make love to a Scottish hunk under a waterfall, could she be any luckier? She could feel him lifting up her shirt; her body was that taught with lust that even the material of her shirt being pushed up her body with his big hands was turning her on.

"Oh. My. God!" She breathed.

That was all she could think when he started kissing the same path that the shirt had taken. When he reached her bra, he wrapped his mouth around her breast and used his tongue in contrast with the lace to send her to the stars. It was as if a thousand butterflies had just been released inside her stomach and a warm sensation started in her groin. Once he had finished with her left one, he kissed a path over the right one, which he lavished with the same amount of attention. She started to squirm, she couldn't help it. She needed him now. He seemed to sense her frustration, because the next thing she knew he was ripping off her bra with his bare hands.

"Sorry lass, I ken I should go slower, but I am too impatient, I need to feel ya breasts against me, NOW!"

He lowered himself down so that his chest hairs rubbed against her breasts, and she was fulfilled once more with pure ecstasy. She could not wait any longer. She wanted to feel him inside her. She wanted to feel him all the way to the depths of her soul, but it didn't matter how much she begged and pleaded, he was determined to go slowly.

He started kissing a path back down her body until he reached her plump breasts once more. He placed his palms on them and started to palm them. He placed the areola between his thumb and forefinger and squeezed it just enough. Oh, she had never felt anything like this. *How could it hurt but feel good at the same time?* It was then, in her ecstasy, that she noticed that her breasts fit into his palms perfectly; as if they had been made especially for his touch, she thought giddily.

Groaning she laid her head back down, now was not the time to get all fantastical she thought to herself, and then she couldn't think at all, he had pushed them together and started sucking on them hard and then soft. He showered each breast with just the right amount of pressure to make her wild. Grabbing handfuls of his hair she wrapped her legs around his body hoping to keep him there yet wishing for something else at the same time.

He gently removed her hands from his hair.

"Please." She begged him.

"Shhhh, *ailleagan meinn.*"

"What is that you keep calling me?" She asked, trying to focus on anything other than what he was making her feel.

She never got her answer though. He only chuckled and continued to make his way down her body, every nerve felt like it was on edge. He would only kiss her sparingly, but his mouth was that close that she could feel his hot breath against her body and every time his lips touched a piece of her skin, a longing deep within her screamed out. He continued this torment for what felt like eternity until she thought she was going to go crazy with desire. He had finally reached her belly ring, which, after a slight pause, he sucked into his mouth running his tongue around the rim of her belly button.

She never imagined that it could feel like this, she was hot and cold all at the same time. He nipped her on the hip, lavishing it with kisses afterwards. Her mind had been so focused on what he was doing that she hadn't even realised that he had skilfully removed her pants and underwear without ever breaking contact with her body.

It was not until his lips were on the inside of her thighs making their way to the centre of her body that she realised she was now completely naked. She should have been embarrassed, but her body was too wired to feel anything other than undulated lust for the man who was doing this to her.

At that moment, he lifted her higher on the rocks and placed her legs over his shoulders opening the core of her up to his eyes. Her breathing became more rapid and she felt exposed lying there, spread out on the moss-covered rocks under the waterfall. But, rather than the chill of the morning and the iciness of the water, she felt heat and fire.

Reaching for her clothes, she tried to cover herself up, but he had other thoughts in mind and he started nibbling on the tender flesh of her thigh, working his way up until he reached her core, and then he stopped and looked up at her.

She was staring straight into eyes that were as blue as the Caspian Sea, as he took her into his mouth. His tongue made love to her. He tasted every inch of her and continued until she had reached her first peak. He kept licking and sucking until she climaxed but he did not let up until he had lapped up the very last drop. She blushed a deep, crimson red as he maintained eye contact. She could not take her eyes off him. She whispered his name and his nostrils flared as his tongue seemed to drive deeper into her. She couldn't keep her eyes open any longer. Her head fell back and her legs tightened keeping his head there. Her body felt like it was going to snap. Then her body did snap! She let out a scream so loud that it echoed through the rainforest. She could not move as her body went rigid.

In an instant moment, her world felt like it had shattered and she saw a thousand stars. How could it get any better than this? Surely there was no way in the world anything could feel any better than she did right now? Then Kessan slowly made his way back up her body and when he reached her mouth he kissed her until she was ready for more. How could he not be finished? How was she going to go again? But just as quickly as the thought entered her mind, her body dismissed it as it warmed and responded to his kisses. This man was magnificent. She only wished she could keep him. With a quick move, he picked her up and turned her around so that she was facing the rock wall, her knees were spread apart on the lower rocks just level with his hips.

The space between the two rocks meant she had no choice but to keep her legs apart otherwise she would land right back in the water. He then placed her hands level with her head. She felt so exposed sitting like this, and yet she was not scared, she waited eagerly. With that he slowly stepped in between the two boulders, placing himself square between her legs. He grabbed her hair pulled her head

back and kissed her deeply right as he inserted two fingers inside her. She whimpered into his mouth. She could not take much more of this. "Please Kessan, I want you inside me. I need to feel you."

KESSAN WAS UNDONE by the words, he wanted nothing more than to drive himself right up to the hilt, but he had to take it slow. Kessan had to remember that she was still a virgin. That was a shock he was not expecting. The women of this time were not like the ones back home. It had appeared as though their views on sex and marriage had changed since his time. Yet, when he placed his fingers inside of her, he discovered that not all women were free with their body, he was filled with animalistic satisfaction when he found her maidenhead still intact. No other man had touched this woman before him and that awoke in him a protective need and a sense of ownership and, if he had anything to do with it, he would be the only man to *ever* know her like this.

He wouldn't be able to hold out much longer, but he needed her ready, the last thing he wanted to do was hurt her. It was going to hurt, there was no way around it; he just hoped her pain didn't last long. He could feel her nearing the peak again as his fingers drove in and out of her. Placing his thumb on the sweet spot that he knew would drive her crazy, he circled it around and around her nub. In no time at all she was ready she tilted her head onto his shoulder and once again screamed out, her juices coating his fingers.

That was all the enticement he needed, and he couldn't wait any longer. This woman had been tormenting him all week and now it was time. Withdrawing his fingers, and with great care, he slowly pushed his way into her until he reached her maidenhead. Pausing he gave her one last chance to stop.

"Lass, ya need to focus for a minute. If ya want to stop ya need to do it now. If we go any further it cannot be undone."

Ceana kissed him long and hard in response.

"Kessan, this moment in time with you is all that I have dreamed about, in ways you couldn't possibly imagine or believe, now please make love to me." She pushed her hips back against him, telling him not only with her words but also with her body. Cee wanted this as much as he did. *Thank the heavens*; he was not sure he would have been able to stop if she had refused. He thrust into her in one swift movement until it felt like he was at the entry to her womb. There he stopped holding her tightly against his hips. It couldn't be helped, she whimpered and he knew he had hurt her when he broke through. He tried to give her body time to adjust to the size of him, but she pressed back against him eagerly.

"Lass, ya have to stop moving, ya need time to adjust."

"I've adjusted already, now please move." She begged.

He chuckled, her temperament was just as fiery during sex as it had ever been. He started moving, but slowly, though she would have none of that. She placed her hands lower down the wall and matched him stroke for stroke.

He was losing his mind. If he did not slow her down, he was going to reach his climax before she did. Leaning forward he started rubbing the spot that he knew drove women insane; he moved hard and fast within her, making her as wild as he was. He could not have slowed now if he had wanted to.

Then, with animalistic strength, she clenched her body around his cock and she climaxed; his world exploded and, with one final thrust, one final roar, he too reached his own climax, spilling his seed within her. It felt like infinity before either of them came back down to earth. Kessan slowly pulled out of her then laid back on the rocks, cradling her in his arms. He knew they should probably get dressed soon before the rest of the world woke up and intruded on their haven, but he wanted to savour this moment for as long as possible.

They both lay there quietly, each lost in their own thoughts. Her hand was gently stroking his chest, reawakening the animal inside him. If he didn't stop her, he would be making love to her again. But it was too soon, she needed time to heal, the best thing for him and her to do was to take a cold bath. And that was precisely what they were going to do. Gently lifting her off the rock, he wrapped her legs around his waist once again, and carried her away from the rock until they were under the waterfall so they could wash off and cool down at the same time. The cold water did its job but they still could not keep their hands from exploring the other's body. They kissed and touched each other, which was fine by him. He felt a rush of disappointment as she finally moved away from him.

"Well, this was certainly an interesting morning." Ceana said. "If I had known that insulting you would have led to this, I would have done it days ago." She joked.

Kessan laughed. "Sassy little minx, if ya keep talking like that we will no' make it home."

They waded deeper into the water and remained there a little longer, enjoying each other's company in silence, before reluctantly dressing to go back to the cabins. It would not be long before someone realised that she had not come back from her run at the usual time.

Cee had just informed him that they were on one of the well-worn tourist paths and anytime now, someone could come walking along and catch them swimming naked. Getting dressed turned out to be a little more difficult than Kessan first thought, their clothes were sodden and made it challenging getting them back on, they were both freezing now that their fire had died down and Cee would not stop running her hands over his body. He might have to send her on her way and go for another quick dip by himself if she kept it up.

"Lass, if ya doona stop that, we are no' goona make it home. Ya are too tender to do it again so soon. But I promise ya, we *will* do it again." He whispered as he kissed her neck.

That seemed to placate her for now and mercifully she finished getting dressed. They slowly walked back to the cabins in silence just enjoying each other's company. Kessan walked her to her door, "thank ya lass, for the gift." He then kissed her, but he had to pull himself away from her before he forgot himself and made love to her right there on her doorstep. It was difficult to leave her, especially when he looked at her the way she was.

Her lips were swollen from his kiss, her eyes were filled with desire and he could see the pulse beating at the base of her throat. He took one last look, shook himself out of his torment and then turned on his heel sprinting back to his cabin, putting some much-needed distance between them. Now the only thing he had to do was try and remember his place the next time they met.

CHAPTER 10

After dropping Cee back at her room, Kessan realised that he had forgotten to pick up his sword. *Damn it!* All he wanted to do was have a nice hot shower and crawl back into bed for a couple of hours, but that would have to wait. He left to jog back to the waterfall. It took him no time at all to reach the place where they had been moments before. He had shoved his sword in behind two boulders the minute he had seen her rounding the bend. Wouldn't that have been a fun conversation, trying to explain why he and his brother had been out in the early morning fighting with swords? He collected his weapon and headed back towards the cabin. He had already wasted too much time this morning.

The end of the month was getting closer and, if he did not find the lass soon, he would have to go back to Scotland empty handed and wait another six months before they tried again. Be damned if he was spending six months here while they waited for the next equinox. He would love to have more time with Cee, but duty came first. Kessan had to get back to his clan. A lot could happen in six months and he needed to be home in order to protect his people. He would just have to figure out another way to keep Cee.

He was just passing the portal when, without warning, the wind picked up and leaves and dirt started to fly around him. He felt a sudden ominous feeling as the air around him changed. The wind seemed unnatural, reminding him of the time he had arrived here. Surely, MacDonnell wasn't stupid enough to come and find the lass himself? After all he hadn't been gone *that* long. Then, before he had time to think, a loud earth-shattering boom rent the air right before two of McKenzie's clansmen came through the portal.

He stared in horror, frozen. This was bad. If he had not come back to get his sword, Kessan would never have known about them until it was too late. Worse still, what if they had come through earlier when he and Cee had been exposed and unguarded? *What where they doing here?* But, deep down he knew that this meant only one thing, *Kendrick knew!* Something must have gone wrong back home. His mind raced. *Had MacDonnell been captured?* Did that mean he was already dead? As far as Kessan knew, MacDonnell and the druid were the only people who knew where they were.

Kessan watched the two Highlanders. Mercifully, they had not yet noticed him. He still had the element of surprise. He remembered how disorientating the trip had been and hoped to use that at his advantage. They would still be getting their senses back and they would still be confused. Now was the perfect time to act. Stalking forward stealthily, he grabbed one of the men and lined up his sword against his throat before either of them had time to react.

"Ya had better drop ya weapon Coll," he addressed the other Highlander in a quiet voice, "or I will slit his throat."

He hoped that Coll would not force him to kill them just yet. He needed to find out what was going on.

"Where is the lass, McKinnon?" Coll sneered.

He was right, that was why they were here. They assumed he had found the lass.

"What lass?" Kessan asked feigning innocence, letting the man talk.

"Doona play daft with us Kessan, we ken you came here for the lass. Now, either tell us where she is or we will go and find her ourselves. And we *will* find her." He mocked.

"I doona ken lad, I have no' found her yet. So I canno' see how ya will." He informed them.

"Doona be lying to us, Kessan," Coll roared.

"Are ya questioning my honour Coll?" Kessan asked in a quiet, calm tone. "Cause if ya are, I will have no other option but to kill ya here and now. I will tell ya one more time, I doona ken where the lass is."

He was hoping that both men would accept his response, but in true Highlander spirit, he knew deep down they were here to accomplish a task, and they would be determined.

"Well, we will just have to take ya back to Kendrick and ya can tell him yourself. After all, the portal is almost closed. And, by the time it reopens, you and all the other traitors will be dead. The lass will be of no matter then." Coll sneered.

Kendrick had clearly found out that he was aiding MacDonnell. It was urgent now that he find the lass. His entire clan was in danger. Angry, he decided that he'd had enough of dealing with these two. Who were they to think that they could defeat him? He had beat men twice their size in battle. They didn't stand a chance.

Drawing his sword back he ran it across Liam's throat, slicing open the main artery.

He stood without feeling as the man slumped to the ground, his lifeblood pouring out of him and running through the crevices on the forest floor. Coll froze there in shock for the briefest moment. The delay gave Kessan time to prepare for his attack. With a roar, Coll came at him and engaged him in a fierce fight, but his anger and emotions worked against him and he was no match for the experienced Laird. Kessan was able to get the upper hand quickly and it was not long before Coll met the same fate as Liam. He hid the bodies back in the cave before he headed back to the cabin. He had hidden the bodies inside the cave, in hope that when the portal opened tonight they would be sucked back home.

He did not understand how the men that sided with Kendrick had turned out so differently from the rest of them; they were all about destroying the Highlands with no remorse or second thoughts. He hated having to kill them for that. However, war was war, and during war people picked sides and died. Well this was it. Now he had been forced to finally pick a side and Kendrick clearly knew about it. *How*? He wondered, worrying about his clan. He knew that he could no longer sit on the sidelines hoping that somehow Kendrick would give up this thirst

for power. This just proved that he was beyond all redemption. His only hope lay in the MacDonnell lass. A lass he had yet to find. With any luck he would be able to find her soon and get home before Kendrick figured out that his men had been killed, he knew that, enraged, Kendrick *would* go after his family and Thora was still in the Highlands alone. A panic overtook him like none he had felt before. He started running towards the cabins. Kessan had to find Caelan, time was up. They had to find the lass now!

CEANA LOOKED AT THE CLOCK. *Damn, it was only nine.* It was her day to staff the front desk again and, while the place was not as busy, she was trying to finish off the final touches of her report. It was proving to be a difficult task. Every other minute she looked at the door wondering where Kessan was. Then her mind would replay the wonderful morning she'd had with the Scotsman, making writing her report near impossible. She sighed, a permanent, content smile on her face, the only visible sign of the moment they had shared.

Something he said had puzzled her though. What had he been referring to when he thanked her for the gift? She also realised he had never answered her question about the name he had called her. She would have to remember to ask him about it again. Her report was not helping the situation, it pertained to medieval Scotland 1150-1180 AD. This was the area that she loved the most and she was doing her thesis on this period.

It fascinated her how, during this time, more clans were wiped out by one war than any other period of time in history and no-one was certain who had started the war or what made this war so different to cause so many deaths.

Not much research had been found on the era due to the lack of scholarly literature available, much of the writings that had been uncovered by archaeologists appeared to be the ramblings of men who were either ill with fever or had simply lost their mind.

Such accounts would often talk about a black magic that destroyed them. Perhaps she could ask her Scottish guests. They would know more about their history, after all McKinnon *was* one of the original clan names. In fact, they were mentioned in the writings a lot. She had discovered this not long after her guests had arrived. Why not ask them? Why couldn't she use live resources if they were available? She looked up, Kessan may not have been there, but Caelan was. He had been working on finding their relative when she had come in this morning. She had enquired as to Kessan's whereabouts when she had entered; he didn't even look up from the computer as he'd answered her.

"He is still abed Miss Thorne. He was worn out. Must have had a rough night."

She could swear there was amusement in his voice, but surely she was mistaken. There was no way he could know about their encounter this morning. Unless Kessan had told him. Looking over at him, she noticed that he was no longer looking at her, instead he was looking around the room as if searching for something, or someone.

"Missing something?" Ceana asked him.

"Och, um, no, I thought I heard someone come in with ya lass that is all?"

Ceana noticed a slight colour rise in his cheeks. That was strange, she had only been teasing him.

"Nope just me." She reassured him.

"So ya sister will no' be joining you on the reception desk today then?" He asked.

"No, she had to other stuff to do today. She said she had to get ready for tonight. I guess she's going out with friends or something. Why? Did you need something?"

"Nay lass, I was just wondering." With that Caelan turned back to the computer, but a small smile played at the edge of his mouth. Ceana wanted to pry more into that smile, but she had bigger fish to fry. She needed to find out as much about their history and background as she could while they were here. This stuff was going to be gold for her assignment and, since Kessan wasn't here to pick his brains, Caelan's would have to do and she intended to pick it as much as possible. "Hey Caelan, do you know much about your family history?" She queried.

His head snapped up so quickly and sharply that the curious feeling that had been niggling her all week rose up again. It was an odd reaction to her simple question. She also noticed that he seemed a bit hesitant when he answered her.

"Why do you ask lass?" He said finally.

What were these boys hiding? They had been mysterious right from the beginning; their behaviour was often weird and they still had yet to tell anyone, but KC, any details about this long-lost relative of theirs. Now, to top it off, Caelan seemed on edge just because she had asked him about his family. Perhaps there was some dark criminal history behind this relative? She would have to remember to see if she could get some details off Kessan later, perhaps whilst they were in the middle of making love and his guard was down. It always worked in the movies.

"Well, it's just that I am completing an assignment on a war that occurred in Scottish history and, during this time, the McKinnon clan was one of the clans who had lost all of their people and land in this particular war. There hasn't been much literature from that time found and many speculate that it was the war that killed so many, while others say it was more likely the plague. I just thought that, since your ancestors were a part of this war, you may have been told their history."

She looked over at him to gauge his reaction to her question, only to note that his face appeared to have gone as white as a ghost. He must have known something otherwise he would not have reacted so dramatically. She supposed it could have been a sore topic, they were Highlanders after all. During her studies, she had discovered that many Scottish people, the men particularly, were proud of their clan's history and perhaps, unbeknownst to her she had insulted him somehow. But. Nevertheless, she needed to know this information, so she pretended that she hadn't noticed his reaction and continued with her questions.

"Even though there is not a lot of literary evidence, some has survived." She explained, "Unfortunately they are not at all insightful. You see, many scholars deem them as nothing but a madman's scribbling's. For instance, there is a particular piece of writing done by a man named MacDonnell, who talks about a dark magic destroying the land. He describes their fight in graphic detail. He even mentions a few clans that fought with him. I believe the McKinnon's were one of them. He also mentions a lost hope that has to be found."

Ceana continued reading for a little while longer, to see if she missed anything.

"See, you can understand why many scholars of this time are dubious in using these writings." She said. "I was just hoping that you might be able to shed some light on this. I hope I did not offend you." She finished, looking up.

It was only at this point that she realised Caelan still had not said anything. She had also failed to notice that, in the middle of her readings, Kessan had entered the room; he had obviously woken from his sleep. Looking at him, she noticed that he looked as shocked as Caelan. *What was with these two?*

❧

KESSAN HEADED towards the reception area in the hopes of catching

Caelan alone. He knew it was going to be a long shot, but just maybe he might get lucky. Not so; he heard Cee talking even as he opened the door. Her voice was like soft silk and for a moment he was lost in the sound of it that he had not noticed what they were discussing. If he hadn't seen his brother's face, he probably wouldn't have paid attention at all. But he had seen it, his brother sitting at the computer desk staring at her, his mouth agape and he looked

as though he were in pain. Kessan made no sound. He just waited to see if his brother would notice him, he didn't want to interrupt Cee. Finally, Caelan caught sight of Kessan, and when he looked at him, his eyes held a look of fear, sadness and relief. A mixture he had never seen in his brother's eyes before. *Had they found something on the lass? Was it bad news?* There was only one way to find out. He signalled his brother to remain silent as he listened in on her story. It was then that he caught the name MacDonnell. He was stunned, but then realised she was talking about their history told in this time. What she was saying *couldn't* be true. If it was, and, if they didn't find the lass, this was what was going to happen to their home. *His* home. Destroyed by Kendrick? He remembered the two bodies that he'd left in the cave. Whatever this war was, it was escalating back home

He could not let that happen, they had to find her, even it meant searching every corner of this God forsaken place. He turned his attention back to Cee, who assaulted his brother with question after question, not knowing what she was doing.

"Doesn't that just sound so fantastical?" She asked his horrified brother. "Do the Scottish men of today still believe in the magic that the Highlanders back then did? Are you still all raised practicing the traditions and beliefs of your ancestors?"

When Caelan didn't answer, she raised her head from her book and finally realised that Kessan was standing there. She smiled an innocent smile at him and it melted some of the tightness away that he had been feeling, she didn't understand the gravity of her revelations, but it didn't change what he had heard.

"What were you just reading lass?" He asked her. His voice had an edge to it that even he could hear, but under the circumstances he could not help it. He had a feeling it was going to get much worse before it got better. She gave him a curious look, but thankfully did not ask any more questions. He did not think he was up to lying to her right now; he hoped that his brother hadn't given too much away.

"Nothing. I was just reading Caelan some of the Ancient texts I was using in my research. I am doing a report on the war that almost destroyed the Highlands sometime around the 12th century. I was providing him with a bit of background in hopes of getting a Scottish perspective about the events."

Kessan made himself relax, he did not realise how tense he had been. He was relieved that Caelan hadn't told her anything and that she had only been curious about history.

"Och lass ya should not believe everything you read. Especially when it comes to tales of Highland battles. Obviously it dinna wipe out the clans such as the McKinnon's otherwise we would no' be here now." He said. What he didn't tell her was that if he did not find the lass they were looking for and get home soon, the stories that she was reading would, in fact, become alarmingly real and the McKinnon clan, and many more alongside it, would cease to exist.

It all rested on him finding the MacDonnell lass and taking her home. If he didn't, according to her readings, he would not have a home to go home to. To make matters worse, Kendrick now knew where the lass was and once he figured out that his men would not be returning, he would send more men to replace them. He sat down beside Caelan "Have ya found anything yet?" He asked.

Caelan looked at him and, without speaking, he let his brother know that something had happened and they needed to hurry. "Nay." Caelan nodded at him, indicating that he understood. "But the list that the lass KC was compiling for us came through this morning so we can go through the names tonight. With any luck, we will find her there."

"Good, well let's keep searching anyway." Looking back at the computer, he prayed that somehow today they would find her, but by the afternoon, despite their efforts, they had come up empty handed, again. Their only hope now lay in the list of lasses who had been officially adopted about twenty years ago. Kessan was starting to get frustrated all over again, it had been a long, wasted day of nothing and finally, they had retired to their room for the night. Caelan had just sat down and started to go through the papers.

"Ya ken brother, perhaps it is time we tell the lass some more information. She may be able to help us, after all she did grow up here and she also attended school here. It is quite possible that she is acquainted with the lass herself." Caelan suggested.

"Aye brother I think ya may be right." Kessan agreed. "I guess it's time we tell her more. We're running out of options. I trust her, and she kens more about our lives than we do it seems."

He thought of his clan and Kendrick back home.

"I'll go and talk to her now." Kessan said getting up from the table.

Leaving his brother to look through the papers, Kessan headed to Cee's room. It was only partly why he wanted to go there. Right now, all he wanted to do was hold her and, perhaps after they talked, he could make love to her. He knew he should give her a couple of days to heal, but after the day he'd had, he just needed to be a part of something good. He needed to remove the feeling of death that surrounded him. The door opened and he stared as she stood in the doorway wearing nothing but a black see-through slip and all his plans for waiting went right out the window. There was no way there would be any talking first, right now he just needed her.

❧

CEANA OPENED THE DOOR. "Hey Bata, are these the shoes you wanted for tonight? I wasn't sure which of the red ones you wanted." It took a moment for her to realise that her sister wasn't standing at the door. Instead Kessan stood there looking at her as though he wanted to devour her. Her heart started going a mile a minute and those goddamn butterflies were back, making her feel nauseas

and excited all at once. Finally, she was going to get some more alone time with him.

"Hi. Is there a problem with your cabin?" She inquired, hoping that was not why he was here.

"Nay lass, I came here to ask for help, but I think that that can wait."

Her excitement grew as he walked into the room and picked her up. She wrapped her legs around his waist, feeling the heat of anticipation reawakening inside her. Walking her backwards, he whispered in her ear, "I have waited all day to do this, lass."

She felt her back against cold wood and they moved with the

door as it closed gently behind her. Then it came, the moment she had wanted all day; he kissed her just as deeply and passionately as he had this morning. She heard a slight click and realised vaguely that Kessan had thoughtfully locked the door, but she didn't care. Wanting to feel his skin on hers, she slipped her hands in between them and tried pulling his shirt off over his head but it wouldn't budge, it got stuck. Growling in frustration she tried to tell him between kisses what she wanted.

"Kessan I need your help here, I want to feel your skin. Please!"

With one smooth motion, he pressed his hips against her, pinning her to the wall and leant back, away from her. With one foul swoop, she yanked his shirt off and she hungrily ran her hands over his shoulders, down his arms and back up over his abs and chest. She loved the feel of him, he felt like silk stretched tight over steel. She leant forward and ran her tongue around his nipple, loving the sound that he emitted at her touch. It empowered her. Perhaps she could be a little more daring. She wondered briefly what he would think of her, in this moment, and then she realised that she didn't care. She just knew that right now she wanted to explore this newfound power and passion.

"Kessan you need to help me. I have to feel your skin against me, and we have too many clothes on." She said sounding frustrated, even to her own ears.

She could feel his manhood swell against her straining against his pants. She loved the way her words could stir that amount of emotion in him. She wanted them off now. She wanted to feel that power against her naked skin.

"Aye lass we do." He growled in her ear.

She noted that his voice had gone deep and had a husky sound to it. He sounded as though he had just gotten over the flu and all the coughing had left him with a raspy voice. Coupled with his gorgeous accent, nothing sounded sexier to her right this minute. He started lowering her, and it wasn't long before her feet touched the ground, a pang of disappointment shot through her at the loss of contact. Slipping out from under his arms, she moved behind him. This was it, her heart raced with anticipation, fear and excitement. It was time that she took control of her fantasy. It was her turn to make him squirm, before she lost her nerve.

"Kessan, do you trust me?" She asked leaning into him. He was now leaning against the door. Her question had taken him by surprise. She felt him pause for a second, and, unused to being so forward with men, anxiety gnawed away at her. She would bet her bottom dollar that the man standing in front of her did not trust many people in his life, and when he did, it would be wholly and completely. But, did he trust *her*?

"Aye lass I do." He finally answered.

She was both surprised and elated with the answer. She pulled away and searched his eyes; she could see that he meant it. It was an exhilarating feeling knowing that she had tamed this magnificent, masculine man and that he let her into his circle of people he trusted in this world.

She smiled at him. "Then could you please close your eyes and place your arms down by your side." His eyes widened with surprise but he never once questioned her, instead he did as she asked, silently, maintaining eye contact with her. Now she was going to find out just how far his trust went.

"Before I go any further, I need you to promise me that you will not touch me until I am finished, no matter what happens?"

He took a little longer to answer that one, his eyebrows raised curiously, his eyes boring into her hungrily. "Aye lass, I promise I will endeavour to try."

Not exactly what she was after but good enough. Ok here went nothing. She took a breath to gain her composure. She was still uncertain where her sudden daring came from. Inexperienced in such matters, she never did anything that was out of her comfort zone and here she was about to do the most daring thing she had ever done in her life. With him though it was different, and she knew that she wanted to taste him the way he had tasted her. She wanted to see if she could make him as mindless with passion as he had done to her. She did not want him watching her simply because she didn't think she could handle having those blue eyes studying her as she attempted this for the first time.

"Kessan close your eyes." She waited until he obeyed. Then she started getting to know his body, skin on skin, touch on touch, breath on breath. Her lips met his for a fleeting kiss but when he tried to deepen it, she moved away and continued to kiss her way down over his chest. Once there she made her way to his nipples and ran her tongue around them over and over again. Kessan squirmed beneath her.

Kessan could not believe what the lass was doing. When she had first asked him if he trusted her, he surprised himself when he answered her with an 'aye,' realising that he did indeed trust her. Then the lass had asked him to make that ridiculous promise, a promise that was becoming more and more difficult to keep. He balled his hands into fists and pushed them hard into the door to stop himself from reaching out and grabbing her. He tensed once more when her breath skimmed over his chest, and the lower she went, the harder it became to keep his promise. At the moment, she was kissing her way over his abs. When she got to his navel, she swirled her tongue around and around, driving him crazy. He had slept with many women before but never had he felt like this.

His rigid body protested and the further down she went, the more control he had to muster in order to stop himself from taking her the way he wanted. The Highlander in him was screaming out, telling him to just turn her over and ride her until she knew what it was like to be had by a true Highlander. He would ride her hard and fast until she screamed out his name for all the heavens to hear. Even as his body screamed out to end it, he had not made a move to stop her. He braced himself on the door as she continued her torture. He was determined to let her take her time with him, to experience this new level of trust, to soar to new heights. He had promised her and she trusted him.

His honourable intentions almost flew out the window when she finally reached the core of his manhood. He felt like he was a green boy of ten and four, when he had experienced sex for the first time, as her breath floated over his shaft. He kept his eyes squeezed tight and suppressed a moan. He was not sure how much more of this he could handle. It was increasingly hard to focus, to man the control he needed to avoid spilling his seed before he even got inside her. He was vaguely aware that she was kissing him again, making her way closer and closer to his cock. Kessan's head fell back against the door and he started thinking of what he had to do back home, anything to take his mind off how good her warm breath felt against his inner thigh. Then his whole world shattered as she took him into her mouth. Kessan's eyes flew open and he looked down to where she was kneeling in front of him with his cock in her mouth. He stared, his mind numbing as she worked her mouth up and down with such love and attention. He could not believe how innocent and erotic this was. Supressing a groan, he could feel himself reaching his climax and, if he didn't stop her soon, he would explode into her mouth.

"Lass, ya have to slow down otherwise I am gonna' come before we even have a chance to make love." He stammered.

She did not slow down. Instead his words only seemed to urge her on. Moaning, he closed his eyes and laid his head back against the door as the gentle onslaught continued. This lass was amazing and one way or another he was taking her home, he conceded in his hazy mind. The little minx started making her movements slower and deeper while rubbing his sack. It was driving him mad. Finally, something splintered and Kessan could not handle the sweet torture any longer. He grabbed her head and he thrust himself deep into her mouth one last time, throwing his head back emitting a growl from the depths of him, carrying with it her name as his juices pumped into her warm mouth. When he had finished, he dropped to his knees in front of her and kissed her passionately. Never before had Kessan felt the likes of this! He had given many women oral pleasure, but he had never received it back. He kept kissing her trying to gain some composure; he was sure that if he tried to stand right now he would end up right back where he was.

"W...w...was that ok?" He heard her ask tentatively between kisses.

Was she out of her freaking mind? If it got any better, she would have killed him.

"Aye lass, it was more than ok." He answered her shakily.

They sat like that for a moment as his legs finally gained some strength back then, standing, he picked her up and carried her to bed. There he treated her to the same torture she had given him. He had not let up until she reached her climax twice. He entered her in one movement and proceeded to show her the stars again. When they had decidedly finished with the bed they both made their way to the magic of the 21st century bath, where they proceeded to make love again as the warm water heated their fiery passion.

CHAPTER 11

Lying on her bed with their legs entwined she listened to his heartbeat return to normal. She had never felt so content or safe. As she laid there, her eyes closed, she was exhausted from their escapades and was just about asleep when someone knocked on the door, startling her awake. *Bloody hell* she had forgotten that Katie had been coming her way to borrow a pair of shoes. She sat up and looked over at Kessan. She wasn't sure she was ready to let her sister know about their relationship and she certainly didn't want her to find out like this! She had to hide him.

"Kessan, Get up! You need to hide. The bathroom will do!" She hissed urgently at him.

To her frustration he didn't move, instead Kessan just gave her a lazy smile, placed his arms behind his head and asked, "now lass, do not tell me you're embarrassed for ya sister to find me in ya bed?"

"Of course I am you dolt. I do not need my little sister discovering that you have turned me into a raging bag of hormones!" She snapped, trying to keep her voice down.

Kessan laughed at that, and her attempts to get him off her bed and into the bathroom only added to his amusement. "Ya ken lass I am goin' to have to break ya of this affinity ya have for calling me names."

"Yeah, yeah fine you can do that later, but for now would you just get in the bathroom?" She begged as the knocking grew more insistent. She knew that if she did not open the door soon, Katie would not hesitate to break it down. She grabbed Kessan's arm and pulled him towards the door. Kessan was trying to stifle his laughter by the time she got him into the bathroom.

"Oh would you shut up already. It won't help hiding you if she can hear you."

As she closed the door, he made himself comfortable. He was leaning against the bathroom sink with his arms crossed at his chest. Completely naked. Man, was he magnificent. She was about to pull the door all the way closed when she heard her sister call out.

"Ceana Thorne if you do not open this door soon, I am going to presume that you are ignoring me or something has happened and I will be forced to break down your door, again. I know you are in there, I can hear your voice."

"Hang on Bata I'm just getting out of the shower!" She called, hoping she sounded convincing. Ceana turned around to grab a towel that was behind him to make the lie more believable. "Right, remember what I said..." She never got to finish, the look on his face stopped her dead in her tracks.

"What's wrong?"

"I thought your name was Cee?" He asked, choking the words out.

It stunned her, not only was the question so out of the blue, but the intense look on his face, like her answer could change everything between them, suddenly made her feel uneasy as she remembered the more unsettling parts of her dream.

"Cee is a nickname, I didn't see the point in correcting you. Besides, you normally call me lass. Not that it matters, now move and we will discuss the merits of my name when I get rid of Bata." With that, she gave him one final glance before she closed the door on him.

Ceana opened the door and there her sister stood, dressed up to the nines.

"Here are these the ones you wanted?" Ceana asked as she thrust the shoes at her, hoping that she would take them and leave without questioning her further.

"Yep those are the ones. Who were you talking to just now?" Katie questioned casually, looking at Ceana curiously.

"Myself." Ceana said innocently, hoping to dissuade her sister from prying too much.

"Why are you so dressed up?" She threw back at her sister.

"No reason at all, just felt like looking nice." She smiled sweetly and the vague answer Katie gave only made Ceana more suspicious. "Anyway, gotta run," she said hurriedly turning away when she saw Ceana's look.

Closing the door behind Katie, Ceana was thankful for small favours. Although it did leave her with a few questions. Ceana would have to remember to look into it further tomorrow, but for now she was just glad she had left, the last thing she wanted was for her sister to find out that she had been sleeping with Kessan. Ceana knew that one day she would have to tell her, but not right at this minute. She wanted to enjoy the secrecy of their romance just a little bit longer before she told the world about it. She felt as if telling people about the relationship would take some of the magic away. Then she would have to face the prospect that if it was real it could end, no, she corrected, *would* end. She wasn't ready to face the fact that this romance could not go anywhere. He was Scottish for Christ's sake. Once he found his cousin, he would head home, and she would never see him again. Tears pricked her eyes. How was she going to let him go? Perhaps it was time to end it now before she fell in love, and then it hit her with the force of a ton of bricks falling from the sky.

"Holy shit," she whispered to herself. *How could she have been so stupid?* She had already fallen in love with him. She was so caught up in her emotions that she didn't hear Kessan come up behind her.

"Lass ya ken she will find out sooner or later?" He said almost right beside her ear.

She jumped a foot in the air, hitting her head against his chin. "Man. Warn someone before you sneak up on them. You scared me!" She scolded.

She knew she was snapping at him, but she couldn't help it, after all, it was his fault that she had fallen in love with him. She noticed that he was still staring at her with the same odd expression on his face. She opted to answer him before he started asking her what was wrong again, because in all honesty she did not know if she could explain it.

"Well we don't even know where this is heading so why do we need to say anything to any one?" She asked him. "After all it won't be long before you head home, and all of this will be like a dream. For now, I just want to have you to myself, and enjoy it while I have the chance."

The look he gave her could have melted her on the spot, he was angry with her for some reason, she could see it in his face and when he spoke his voice was cold and determined. It scared her, and she backed instinctively up against the door. This did not deter him, and he matched her movement and placed both his hands on either side of her head, grabbing two handfuls of hair he held her there. His grip did not hurt her, but it let her know that she was not going anywhere until he allowed it.

"Let's get one thing clear *ailleagan meinn,* you and I are far from done and you are mine make no mistake of that." He bent down and kissed her so passionately that she felt it all the way to her toes, giving her no chance to argue the point. She knew she should have been angry with him, she had promised herself that no one would ever try to own her again. She was no man's possession, but she could not help being thrilled to her core with the knowledge that *this* man wanted her. But it was hard to maintain that same level of excitement and lust that had spurred their earlier relationship because the reality of their situation started to creep back in. He must have felt her reluctance as he stopped kissing her and pulled away, but he did not let her go. She felt her tears threatening to fall again. How was she ever going to let him go?

Trying to forget about it for now, she racked her brain with a way to move the topic away from anything that had to do with their future. "That name that you keep calling me, what does it mean?" She asked.

He gave her a sexy, lazy smile and his bluer than blue eyes were eating her up again. He lowered his head and kissed her slowly this time, his words finally ended up depleting the rest of her brain cells, leaving her at his mercy.

"Come lass, I want to lie with you for a wee bit afore I have to go back."

The next couple of hours were spent talking and snuggling in bed. She told him about her life when she was younger, reminiscing about the antics that her and her siblings had gotten up to. She also told him about her parents and their dreams, and about the night her parents died. About the hole that their deaths had left. She had never really told anyone how much their death had affected her. Mel had an idea but whenever she'd tried to get Cee to talk about it; she changed the subject or just blatantly told Mel that the subject was off limits. The problem was that she could never express how much they'd meant to her. If it wasn't for them her life may have turned out completely different. Who knows what would have happened to her if someone else had found her. She could have even ended up in the system and God knows where that would have gone. With the way she had just been left in the middle of nowhere, in a storm no less, the most likely scenario was that she most probably would have ended up dead. The thing that she loved the most about her parents, was what she missed the most. Never once in her life had they made her feel like she was not one of their own. All three of the Thorne children had grown up knowing that they were loved equally. Of course, she did not tell this to Kessan. She was not ready to share the details surrounding her adoption. It was not like it would make any difference to his life.

☙❧

CEANA WOKE WITH A STRANGE FEELING. She felt as if she was being pinned to her bed, warmth surrounding her. None of this made sense. Had she turned her electric blanket on and forgotten about it? Her sleep-addled brain was trying to make sense of what she was feeling. It was odd, she did not usually sleep with it on; she'd had a fear of fire ever since she could remember and it was then that she realised the heat was coming from above her not below her. *Huh?* She slowly opened her eyes and went to stretch her arms above her head, but they hit something warm and large. Her eyes snapped wide and it was then that her brain finally kicked into gear and she realised someone was in her bed lying beside her. How could she have forgotten? She had never liked anyone sharing her bed, normally it took her ages to fall asleep if anyone was in there, but it had been so easy with him. They had spent nearly the entire night talking and, without even realising it, she must have fallen asleep with him right beside her. Thank God she had locked her door after Bata left last night. Ceana could just imagine having to explain the scene to whoever walked in.

Ceana wondered if he was still asleep. She would just have a quick peek to find out. She slowly rolled over to face him but once she got a look at him the breath left her body. He was awe-inspiring, even in his sleep. His hair had fallen onto his face so that it sprawled across his eyes, he had a slight morning shadow and his long eyelashes flowed over his face almost reaching the top of his cheekbones. She would kill for lashes like that. From her angle below him, she could see the top of his chest and she watched mesmerised as it rose and fell with each breath he took. His top arm was outside of the blanket and lying on top of her, which explained the weight. Moving her leg slightly, she discovered quickly that he was as naked as he had been last night. She could not stop looking at him, he looked so peaceful lying there and the hardness that she had sometimes seen in him was gone. She smiled, he looked almost boyish and that made her wonder what he would have been like as a child.

During their evening together, Kessan had told her bits and pieces of his childhood. From what she could make out, even though his parents had expected a lot from him they were still loving and nurturing. He had talked about his brother and the mischief they had gotten up to and she had gained the impression that back in his youth he had been a bit of a rogue. It was only now though that she realised he had never actually told her from where in Scotland he came from. On top of that, his descriptions of how he grew up were a bit odd. If she did not know any better, he could be one of the Highland Lairds that she often read about in her studies. Of course, she knew how ridiculous that seemed, but there was something different about him, something she could not put her finger on. There was one thing that last night's conversation had embedded for her and that was that the toughness she saw in him was not for show, he commanded respect and he got it. If only *she* could learn how to do that. Looking at him now she could see the softer side of him. The side that had saved his brother from a runaway horse, the boy who had taught his little sister to ride and the man who had made love to her so passionately. Yep, there was no help for it she was head over heels in L.O.V.E, love.

"Good morn'n lass."

She startled when she heard his voice. She looked up from his glorious chest, into his sapphire blue eyes and felt herself melting. Looking over at him again, she noticed the clock on the bedside table read 9:00a.m. Crap, she was going to be late for work. She had better get up before someone came looking for her. She pulled herself up to lean on one elbow as she pushed his arm off.

"Good morning sleepyhead. I was just wondering how long it was going to be before I had to wake you. Do you realise how hot you are making me?"

She cringed inwardly at herself. She had not meant it the way it sounded but clearly, he had taken it as an invitation. His eyes darkened with desire and she sucked in her breath waiting with anticipation for what was to follow.

KESSAN KNEW that she had not meant her comment to be an invitation but he was not ready to face reality.

"I'd be only too pleased to help ya with that affliction, lass." He said cheerfully.

Before she had time to answer either way, he had her on her back and had entered her in one movement. He was pleased to see that she was already ready for him. Their lovemaking was slow and leisurely this morning and he knew the moment it ended he would have to go back to the task of searching for the MacDonnell lass instead of spending time with her.

After they'd finished and had lain there entwined for a while, she was the first to move, "I have to have a shower and get ready, I am staffing the desk again today as the other two have plans. And I'm already late. Come on lazybones, get out of bed!"

He groaned, he did not want to get up but she was right, there was too much to do and it would not be long before Kendrick sent more men through the portal in search of him and the lass, they had to find her.

Ceana went into her bathroom only to yell back at him, "can you pass me a clean towel out of the top drawer?"

Kessan reluctantly got up from the bed and walked over to the dresser. He was not really paying attention to what he was doing. Instead he was lost in thought, trying to think of a way to tell Ceana who he really was. He couldn't bear to leave her behind. He planned to ask her to go back with him to his highlands otherwise, he would have to face a life without her. He sighed. But how do you tell a 21st century lass about magic and time travel? She had scoffed at the idea of magic as she read from her history books. He opened the drawers until he found one full of towels. He pulled out a cream coloured towel and, as he shut the drawer, something bright and colourful underneath the pile of towels caught his eyes. A slither of material had come into view and the only reason it had even drawn his attention was because the colours of the material were so familiar. If he wasn't mistaken, he would swear it was tartan.

Surely not! He sucked in his breath. He knew the lass loved Scottish things but why would she have a towel made out of tartan? He moved the top layer of towels out of the road and pulled the material free of the drawer. He stood staring at it, stunned. He had seen those colours his whole life, he could not breathe at the thought of what this could mean. Dropping the towel he was holding in his other hand, he opened the material up further just to make certain. There, in the corner was Ceana's name, just like Laird MacDonnell had said it would be. Her mother's brooch with the MacDonnell crest was still sitting on the plaid, right where MacDonnell had said it would be. Ceana, *his* Ceana was the lass they had been looking for all along, but how was that even possible? How was he going to explain this to her? There were so many questions he needed to ask. Did she even know that she was not a Thorne? If so did she know how she really came to be here? First thing was first though, he had to know if it was definitely her and for that he would have to check for the birthmark that would cement her identity. With a pounding heart, he quickly stowed the tartan back in the draw, he would get it later when he had more time. He took the towel to Ceana.

"Here lass, I've brought ya towel."

She was just getting out of the shower as he handed it to her.

"Thanks, I was starting to think I was going to have to use the handtowel to dry myself." She said sassily.

He smiled at her, he was trying hard not to just spin her around and rip her hair up to see if the mark was there or not. That would not work, the lass would think him crazy.

"Listen I have to go. Caelan will be waiting for me but I will see ya later on lass." He said distractedly.

"Oh, okay." She said.

He could hear the disappointment in her voice but right now, he wanted to go and check out their list of adoptions to see if her name and the name of her parents were on there. Leaning forward he grabbed her and pulled her into a hug as he kissed her on the neck, Discreetly, he moved her hair gently aside under the guise of the gesture, and there it was, the mark that confirmed this was the lass they had been searching for all along. A thousand thoughts and emotions hit him all at once. Kessan did not know how he felt about this. On the one hand, he now had a reason to take her home with him, their journey together was far

from over, but then on the flip side, half of the Highlands

wanted her dead, he reminded himself grimly. Turning on his heal he marched over to his clothes and got dressed, then with a quick glance to see that Ceana was not looking his way, he pulled the tartan out of her drawer and stormed out of her room banging the door shut as he went. What was he going to do? Goddamn it, he knew he shouldn't have touched her!

❧

Caelan was astounded at the news. "How is it even possible? The lass doesn't even look like MacDonnell!" Kessan sat down heavily and put his head in his hands, "I doona ken Caelan, but I am tellin' ya, the tartan was in her drawer and she had the birthmark right where the Laird said it would be!" Kessan walked into the cabin and all but threw the plaid at his brother.

"The search is over brother." He fumed. Sitting down at the table he started going through the list of adoption papers. It didn't take him long to find the one he was after. Staring down at the papers, his heart sped up. There it was in black and white, right under their noses. This had to be a nightmare. Ceana was the lass they were looking for. The proof was right there in his hands. Twenty years ago, she had been adopted, by the Thornes.

Caelan sat down opposite him. "Och brother what are we goin' to do?" He queried.

He sat silently, staring at the words on the paper in front of him and then looked up at his brother, "first I am going to find out why the lass dinna tell me that she was adopted, and then I'll have to try and convince her to come back with us." He said, not relishing Ceana's reaction.

"And if the lass won't?" Caelan asked, voicing his own concerns.

"She will no' have a choice. Either she comes willingly or we make her. Ya ken what MacDonnell said, the Highlands depend on her, and she is in danger if we leave her here." He said sullenly.

"Well brother I wish you all the luck of the Gods. Ya gonna be needing it."

Kessan sat back, a frown forming on his face, just how was he going to explain to her that she came from 12th century Scotland and that he was here to take her back? He could see it now. Ceana was going to think he had gone mad. She would put up a fight if he forced her against her will. She was going to be like a spitting hellcat. Why had the lass never told him about the adoption? After he had learned of her true name, they had discussed every aspect of her life in detail last night and yet there was no hint of her adoption. He was praying to all the Gods that she knew about it. The last thing Kessan wanted to tell someone was that they were adopted. Especially someone who had been close to their parents, parents that were now lost to her. What he already had to tell her was going to be shock enough.

Kessan spent the rest of the day preparing for the fight ahead and preparing to go home. He was worried. He was not sure what they would be walking into now that Kendrick clearly knew where they had gone. Kessan had finally been able to tell Caelan about all that had transpired at the portal and about what Coll had blurted out right before he died. His brother had been horrified at the thought that they had been discovered. Kessan could not dismiss the possibility of an ambush once they reached home. He hoped that their journey and the risks they were taking weren't to be in vain. How was the lass going to save his home especially when she didn't even know where home was? She certainly had the cunning and the ability to fight though, he surmised.

He allowed himself a smile as he remembered the day at the waterfall. He could not wait to see the look on the old Laird's face when he finally met his daughter, who was so different from anyone else in the Highlands. He had to laugh, even after decades apart in a different time and place, she had still turned out to be as stubborn as the old goat and his fight and passion had somehow ended up in her. Aye she would be fine, if she managed to survive the onslaught that was coming. She was definitely not what they were expecting. His smile broadened as he remembered the day she had taken out her ex with little effort. the Highlands were in for a surprise all right. Perhaps this was not going to be a bad thing after all. That night the brothers did not bother going to dinner, instead they went over the plans for their return.

The night was getting late and he had just finished having a shower – the warmth of the 21st century showers were something he was definitely going to miss once he arrived home. He and Caelan had finally come up with a plan on how to convince her to go with them. They were going to tell her once they had reached the Highlands. Showing her would be the only way for her to truly comprehend what was happening. Once there the lass would have plenty of time to adjust to the truth. He was getting dressed in his room and considering finding Ceana and asking her about the tartan. They had decided that honesty and bluntness was the way to handle Ceana, but they would hold off telling her about time travel. They were going to tell her that she was the lost relative, but they knew she'd need time to come to terms with the idea of magic being real. He braced himself, before opening the door to seek out the lass, when he was struck in the chest by a fist. Well it seemed the little minx had come to him. Kessan did not have a chance to ask her why she had come as she hurled herself at him, wrapping her legs around his waist, kissing him.

He could get used to being greeted like this, chuckling he asked her. "Have ya missed me lass?"

"Aye." She replied mimicking his brogue. This made him laugh harder. He would like nothing more than to take her to his bed and make love to her. But right now, they had more important things to discuss.

Walking out into the kitchen, he placed her on the kitchen bench. He had to unwrap her legs so he could position her better. She was not being overly cooperative.

"Lass I need to talk to ya first afore we go any further."

She let out a sigh. "Ok, but can we make it fast?"

Aye, he was going to like having her with him in the Highlands. Once his life was back to normal, he would be able to take her to bed whenever he liked. She would be his and no one could stop him. But, in order to get to that point, they had to first deal with the problem facing them right now. Time was running out. He knew that once he was home and that everything was okay there, he could finally claim her as his own forever.

"So, what did you want to talk to me about?" She asked.

Looking into her eyes so he could gauge her reaction, he reached down under the bench and pulled out the tartan. It had not been a coincidence that he'd placed her on the bench. He had hidden the plaid there earlier. "This." He said, holding up the plaid and brooch. He saw a flash of fear cross her face, right before she shoved him so hard and so unexpectedly that he stumbled back. She jumped off the counter and before he could stop her, she ran out of the cabin slamming the door behind her. He had his answer!

CHAPTER 12

S he ran until she could run no more, she knew exactly where she was going. Ever since she was a little girl, whenever she had a problem she would go and sit beside the waterfall. Thorne Waterfall had a much bigger pool, filled with fish and other creatures. Her father used to take the three of them fishing and swimming there as well and, after his death, she often came to this quiet, out of the way spot to clear her head. It was similar to the one her and Kessan had made love under, however this one offered more privacy.

Unlike the other waterfall in their rainforest, not many people outside of her family knew of it. It was about five kilometres into the seventeen-kilometre trail, and the trail itself became harder to navigate after about two kilometres. Once at the pond, she sat on a rock and buried her head in her lap, inhaling deeply after her run. She could hear the crickets and other night animals in the rainforest and felt calmer. She was not afraid to be here at night; unbeknown to her parents, she, Katie and Tristan would sneak down here when they were younger to swim in the pond on the hot nights during summer when they could not sleep. The place was familiar and the only place she felt completely safe.

"What am I going to do?" She asked the rainforest surrounding her. She did not understand why the feeling of dread had come upon her when Kessan had shown her plaid. Then Ceana's thoughts were racing as she remembered the words at the end of her dream, "I have come to take ya home." She shuddered. The only thing she did know unequivocally was that this man was about to change her life forever. Perhaps she was just being silly, maybe all he wanted to do was ask her about her family history. After all, he was a Scotsman and perhaps he wanted to share some details of his only family with her. There was just one problem; she did not know who her real family was and, on top of that, the look in his eyes told her that it was more than just about sharing family stories. Her dream had suddenly started to be all too real.

A voice suddenly shattered the comforting silence "Cee, where are you?" She gave a startled scream of shock before she realised that it was only Tristan. She had not realised that anyone had followed her.

"Over here, Tris." She replied with relief, she could not face Kessan at this moment. "What are you doing out here?" She asked.

"I could ask you the same question," Tristan replied, "I saw you running past the house as I was coming in from stocking up the wood pile in one of the cabins. I noticed where you were heading so being the man of the house, I thought I would come and make sure there were no bogey men in the forest that could eat you." He winked at her and puffed out his chest beating on it like a Neanderthal. She laughed. He always knew how to make her feel better.

"Thanks Tris, I needed that and you don't have to worry, it's nothing really, I just needed some space to think. I have been missing Mum and Dad a lot lately and sometimes I wish they were still here to talk to."

Tristan came over and gave her a hug. "I know Sis, I feel the same way sometimes. They always knew the right thing to say. I'm not much of an advice giver, but if you don't want to tell me, I can just sit here with you until you are ready to go back, if you like."

She was grateful to have her brother with her; she didn't know what she would do without her siblings, and at times like this, she was glad that she had someone she could lean on, quite literally. She would have loved to have been able to tell her brother what was going on and ask his advice despite his claims, but she could barely sort through the mess of confused feelings as it was. Putting them into words that her brother could understand without looking at her as if she were crazy was near impossible.

So, she just sat there looking out over the pond into the rainforest and tried to wrap her head around the events of the day.

Finally, as time passed by, she had concluded that no matter what Kessan had to say, she had to see this thing out. It was time to tell him about her family and the history of her adoption and that was not going to be easy. She nudged Tristan to let him know she was ready. She noticed that he had been quiet the whole time as if lost in his own thoughts, perhaps, she mused, they should start coming out here more often.

They walked back to the cabins in silence and on arriving she turned to her brother, "You go Tris, there is something I have to do. I will catch up with you in the morning."

"Ok Cee but promise me you will tell someone next time before you run off by yourself."

"Deal." She said, fondly, appreciating his concern.

She watched him jog back to the house. Waiting a few seconds longer until she could hold it off no more, she slowly made her way to her fate. It could have waited until morning, but she could not wait that long and she knew that she'd never be able to sleep until she'd heard what he had to say. Something was telling her that she had to go and see Kessan, so she turned towards the Loch Ness cabin instead. The closer to Kessan's cabin she got the more nervous she became, she felt as if she was walking towards a fate that would forever be out of her hands.

KESSAN WAS GOING out of his mind, it had been an hour since Ceana had run out on him and he had gone up to the main house looking for her only to find Katie, who hadn't seen her since last night. So he had gone back to his cabin to wait to see if she would return. If she did not come back in the next hour, he was going to go and find her even if he had to scour every inch of the damn rainforest himself. He knew that she had not left the mountain; her car was still in the lot.

"Brother if ya do not quit pacing, ya will fall through the floor." Caelan said eyeing him with concern as he entered the main room of the cabin.

Kessan shrugged and kept on pacing. He could not help it. The one person their lives depended on had disappeared and he had no way of knowing when she was coming back. He hated not having control of a situation, he hated feeling helpless.

"That's it; I'm goin' ta go look for the lass!" He stopped suddenly and strode to the door.

"Kessan just give the lass some time, she will be back. She is way too curious for her own good." Caelan, always the more logical, reasoned with him.

He deflated, "Aye I ken you're right Caelan. I just feel so frustrated. What if something happens to her?"

He began pacing again and his brother sighed. At the back of his mind, the notion of the ever-decreasing time frame before the portal closed kept on playing. They only had a couple of weeks left to get her back to the Highlands. Thankfully, they had found out about the lass so that was part of the problem solved. How was he going to get her to the Highlands without explaining where exactly they were going? His pacing sped up as he became more agitated, thinking about the Highlands, not knowing what was happening to his home.

Just as his patience was wearing thin, he heard footsteps outside and he opened the door sighing with relief at the sight of a tired and confused Ceana. His brother had been right. She was standing there on the landing. He could see that she had been crying. Kessan was not sure why, he had yet to tell her anything and the worst was yet to come. He went to her and wrapped her in his arms, "lass ya need to talk to me, why are ya so upset?" He asked.

"Why did you come here?" She appealed to him.

That question startled him, "ya ken why we came here lass." He said quietly.

She looked at him quizzically, her face shifting strangely with emotions and then she surprised him by stating "I'm the lass you are looking for, aren't I?" Her voice was flat and defeated.

She was a smart lass alright. "Aye ya are." Kessan said gently, waiting for her reaction.

❧

CEANA HELD her breath as she waited for him to answer her. Her dream forever playing in her mind now, even while she was awake. She suspected that she knew the answer already but she wanted him to say it; she had to hear it for herself. When he confirmed what she already knew, she moved out of his embrace to lean on the railing, needing space and time to sort out the thoughts flying through her mind as the world tilted around her. She was watching the fireflies dancing around in the rainforest, wishing she could take off and dance with them, leaving all the problems of this world behind just for a short time. She had known that one day she would find out about her real family, but it did not make it any easier to find out like this. She was not sure now whether she wanted to know why they left her. *Why had they come looking for her now?*

"Did you know all along that it was me? Was that why you were so keen to get close to me?" She whispered out into the darkness. Before he could answer, a thought turned her blood cold. "Please tell me we are not related." She asked turning to face him. She studied his face so that she could see his reaction. Her father had always told her that you could tell when someone was lying to you just by watching the way they reacted.

Right now though, she could not read anything in his face. Like always the man was a blank page, she gave up and turned around to watch the fireflies again.

"Nay lass, first of all we are not related and second of all I did not ken it was you until tonight. I had begun to suspect once I learned of your name but I did not ken for sure until I found the plaid. The adoption papers only confirmed it. You also have a birthmark on your neck that I saw this morning confirming it for sure."

She mulled over his words unsure of how to feel.

"So you know my family?" She finally asked.

"Aye."

She could see that he was wanting to tell her more and she was grateful for his patience and willingness to let her ask the questions. She lifted herself on to the railing and stared in silence for a while and then she made up her mind. "Can you tell me about them?" She asked tentatively, still not sure whether she was ready.

"Aye lass, I can but first can you tell me how you ended up here?"

She took a deep breath and then went on to fill Kessan in on the night that her family had found her.

"But why did no one around here mention ye when we asked?" He questioned her when she had finished.

She explained how her parents did not feel the need to let anyone know that she was not their daughter, because in their eyes she was.

"So that's the whole of it, now can you tell me about who my real family is and why they left me for dead?" She said bitterly.

He had not said much during her retelling, only stopping her occasionally to ask the odd question, and she waited anxiously for him to answer her.

He stared at her thoughtfully, "nay lass, they did not leave ye for dead. Your family loves ye and they did what they did to protect ya. I can tell ya as much as I can about them, but then I need to explain some things to ya."

And there it was, she was finally going to learn about her past, about who she was and how she came to be left in the forest on that fateful night. She spent the next couple of hours listening to Kessan tell her about her father, her mother and about her mother's death. She learnt many things, including the fact that she had an older brother, but even though Kessan was telling her about her family, it still seemed to her as though he was hiding something. Each new detail that came out was as if he were reading it from a story. There was no depth to it and she noticed that he only gave her the basic amount of information, just enough to keep most people happy.

They had been silent for about ten minutes now. Ceana assumed he was letting her digest the information.

"Thank you, Kessan, for telling me this, but I'm guessing you did not come all this way just so that you could fill me in on my family history." She said, with just a hint of annoyance, she knew that he was not telling her the whole truth. For much of the conversation, she had been sitting on the steps of the cabin looking out to the rainforest, while Kessan had been sitting behind her on one of the railings. Turning around to face him completely, she just caught the edge of a smile before he covered it. Trying to read him was like trying to squeeze water from a stone, useless. He only let you see what he wanted you to see.

"Well I am right, aren't I? You are here for something else, right?" She said.

"You're smart lass. Yes I am here for another reason. I have come here to take ya home."

Her blood froze as icicles danced across her skin. Her heart was racing a mile a minute and for once she didn't know how to respond. There they were. The very words from her dream. The words she didn't want to hear, the words that kept her awake at night. She pinched herself repeatedly.

"What are ya doing lass?" He asked her curiously.

"Making sure I'm awake. I did just hear you correctly, right? You want to take me where?" She wanted to scream the words at him, but she went for steely, rational calm instead.

"Home." He said simply.

Yep she had heard him right.

"You do realise how absurd this all sounds to me right? I am home. All of this here is my home!" She said waving her hands, to show him she meant where they were standing. "And I am with my family." She paused and looked at him. "Let's just say for pity's sake, that I go with you. How long am I expected to be gone for?" She asked.

He stared back at her for a moment and she could see him struggle to find the right words, finally he said, "I am not sure exactly lass, ye are needed in Scotland and I do not know how long it will be for."

That was it! She'd had enough, she stood up to go.

He made no effort to stop her but he did let her know he was not going to let this go "I need an answer, Lass." He said quietly. She stopped and faced him.

"You're out of your freaking mind! You know that right? You come here and expect me to just drop everything and come with you for God knows how long to help a family that abandoned me." She raged at him. "Please tell me if I have forgotten anything."

His expression was one of stone and she still couldn't read his emotions. Surely he didn't just expect her to want this? Her mind was racing with the consequences.

He shook his head. "Nay lass, you have not forgotten anything. Unfortunately, this is no joke, one way or another you will be coming with me, but you have my word that when you are finished helping ya Da, if ya wish to return I will bring ya back here myself!"

He was out of his ever-loving mind! She thought furiously stomping back up the stairs. She placed herself right in between his legs. Leaning forward she placed her face right near his and fumed.

"Let's get one thing clear right now MR MCKINNON!" She said slowly and carefully. "If you ever threaten me again I will personally rip off your balls and feed them to you. Are we clear? I will come with you if I choose to. And, if I choose to, it will be on my terms. Not yours." He blinked at her, unfazed by her response.

Turning away from him again she was just about to storm off when he grabbed her by the arm.

"Ok lass you have made ya point. Now let me make mine. That was no threat, I have come here to take you home one way or another." He said with a voice of steel. "I would prefer you to come on ya own terms but if I have to I will take ya on mine. We will be leaving tomorrow night one way or another so I suggest ya go home and organise anything ya need to and resign yourself to the fact. Oh, and one more thing lass, ye ever threaten my manhood again, unless it is pleasurable, ya will see a side of me ya will not like." He let go of her arm "Oh and doona even consider runnin' lass. I will find ya and I will not be happy when I do!" He stood there glaring at her until she turned away. He then stalked over to the door and stormed inside, slamming it shut on her.

❧

Ceana spent the rest of the night in a numb daze. She tried to think up a way out of the situation, but nothing came to mind. Oddly she found that a part of her didn't want a way out. She had spent her whole life wanting to know where she was from and wanting to go to Scotland and now she had the chance to do both with the man she loved. She had tried to use her anger to convince herself that she was not in love with him anymore but that was lie. She knew by the urgency in his voice that there was no alternative, he didn't seem happy about the situation either. She didn't know what she could do to help, but apparently, there was no other choice for her family in Scotland. She inhaled deeply, her mind confused, just this morning she was working on the reception desk and, now it seems it would be the last time she would do it for a while. She was resorting herself to the idea when the door opened and Caelan came walking in.

"Good morning lass, how are ya?" He asked a little too brightly.

"I've had better days, but I'm guessing you are not here to inquire about my feelings now, are you?" She snapped. His cheery attitude was pissing her off even more.

He smiled at her. Normally she liked Kessan's brother. He was much like Katie. Nothing seemed to faze him and he was always trying to make people feel better.

"Nay lass I am not. I have been sent up here to deliver a message. Do ya ken the cave about five kilometres into the rainforest? The one that splits the path into three directions?" He asked.

She was taken aback for a minute. That was not what she was expecting at all.

"Yes, I do. Why?" She asked hesitantly.

"Can you meet us there just before midnight?" He continued.

"Midnight. Why the hell do we need to go into the rainforest just before Midnight? I thought Kessan said we were leaving tonight?" She questioned.

"Kessan will explain it all to ye then, but for now, can ya just meet us there please? Oh, and Kessan said to warn ya that if ya make him come and get you, there will be trouble."

"Oh did he? Well you can tell your darling brother to go to hell!" She spat.

Caelan laughed, "I look forward to seeing ye at midnight lass; I hope ya have a good day."

And with that, he left. A good day? Was he kidding? This was one of the most miserable days of her life. She was leaving her family for God knows how long, travelling to God knows which part of Scotland, and she had no say in the matter and to top it off she was going to meet the people she had wondered about her whole life. Her day was going to be anything but good, it was going to be hell.

❦

As she packed her clothes, Ceana went over the afternoon in her mind. She had spent it with her siblings explaining everything to them and at first, they were shocked and surprised but ultimately, they were happy for her. She was finally going to find out who her real parents were. They trusted her, loved her, and knew that the bond they had

could never be replaced by anything. They even suggested inviting them here to stay once she found them.

It was hard saying goodbye. Mel had also come and said goodbye and she had promised to ring all of them as soon as she landed. Once she had finished packing, she looked at her clock. It was almost 11:45p.m. She supposed she had better go and find out what was going on.

Walking past the boy's cabin, she noticed that it was dark. They must already be down there. She picked up her pace a little, she did not want to be late. She knew that once she reached the cave, one way or another, her life was going to change forever. She rounded the corner and her torch found Kessan. He was just up ahead. Two rocks loomed in the sky, forming an open-ended cave. The rocks appeared like hands reaching out to take hold of something, and at night, the image was particularly eerie. She stopped dead in her tracks as realisation hit her and fear trembled through her body, she did not know if she could go through with this anymore. Perhaps she could turn around and just go home, forget any of this had ever happened. But deep down, she knew that the time for flight had long passed, it was too late.

A voice pierced her thoughts "Doona even consider runnin' lass I will catch ya before ye even reach the path." It was not a threat, just a simple statement.

"Well I guess I have no choice then do I? Why are we even here and where is your brother?" She asked defeated.

He took her bag from her, "I am still waiting for Caelan to show, but as to the why of things you will find out soon enough *ailleagan meinn.*" He said mysteriously.

She screamed at him as anxiety and fear reared its head, "Goddamn it, will you stop calling me that unless you plan on telling me what it means and would you give me a decent answer, the only reason I am going along with this cockamamie idea is because you have said I have no choice in the matter! At least have the decency to answer me, I deserve that much!"

He walked up to her.

"In time lass ya will ken all ya need to, but right now I need ya to trust me. Come with me I have to show ya something." He took her hand and pulled her gently towards the cave.

Walking with him into the cave the sensation that something was not right hit her. She needed something else to focus on.

"Fine if you can't tell me about where we are going, can you at least tell me what it is that you keep calling me?"

It looked like Kessan was actually about to answer her when they both heard running. Someone was coming their way. She tried to move out of his hold but he would not release her arm, instead he shifted his position and in no time at all was hugging her protectively. The defensive stand he took had Ceana alarmed. What wasn't he telling her? The footsteps they had heard were now slowing and within minutes, someone entered the cave. Ceana turned to face the newcomer and was shocked to see Caelan enter the cave with her sister on his shoulders. Kessan relaxed his hold, but only slightly, when he realised it was his brother but she was stunned and confused. Kessan looked as though he wanted to say something to Caelan and the silent look they shared told her that eventually he would. But still he said nothing, simply pulled her closer to him. This was not making any sense at all. Why would Caelan bring her sister here? Kessan knew something, perhaps Caelan had shared something with him. She turned back to ask Kessan what was going on, when the wind suddenly picked up, it was so strong that it was creating a vortex around them.

Ceana started to panic, she continued to stare at Kessan, hoping he would tell her what was going on.

"Simply lass, it means *'you are mine'*."

"What?" She questioned as her eyes moved from his face to the vortex and back again. Ceana was trying to figure out what the hell he was talking about.

"You asked me what the phrase means. Simply it means you belong to me." He said with a wink.

"For the last time I do not belong to anyone!" She growled at him.

"Ya do now." He stated.

And before she could muster up a reply, he leaned down and kissed her. The wind continued to pick up around them, swirling, howling, ripping at her clothes, he finished kissing her, and looking up at him, she knew that he was right, her heart was his now and forever.

"Are ya ready lass?" He asked.

She knew she should not ask, but she did anyway. "Ready for what?"

"To meet ya destiny!" It was a simple statement, and yet it held so much power that it took her breath away but before she had time to answer her world went black. She could still feel Kessan holding her, she felt his heartbeat where her hands pressed against his chest and could hear his breathing but when she tried to talk to him, nothing came out. She tried to scream but still nothing. She could smell the rainforest getting fainter and fainter until it was no longer there. A panic like none she had ever felt started to well up inside her, she wanted whatever was happening to stop.

Then like magic, everything changed. She could hear again. The first sound she could hear was the sound of a waterfall. *Oh thank God, they were still in the forest.* She thought, disorientated. *How did they end up near the waterfall?* Her eyesight and voice still had not returned and she was starting to fear they never would. Then out of nowhere, a loud boom tore through the air and the ground under her feet trembled violently and, as if by magic, the wind died down just as quickly as it had appeared. Her eyesight and voice came back within seconds of the wind disappearing. Blinking twice she noticed that she was standing in the centre of what appeared to be a cave, but it was not like the cave they had been in only minutes before. This one was fully enclosed and a circle of light seemed to shine down on them, but there was no hole in the roof.

"Katie!" How could she have forgotten about her sister? If anything had happened to her she was going to kill Caelan first and then his brother.

"I'm okay Ceana." She replied from the other side of the circle.

Turning towards the sound of her sister's voice, she was relieved to see that she was okay.

"You're lucky." She snapped at Caelan, who was standing next to her, but he just winked at her.

Furious, she wanted answers and she wanted them now, she whirled around and faced Kessan.

"Ok Mister, start talking and you had better tell me the entire story, do not even think of leaving anything out. But first of all where in the hell are we?"

"We are in the Highlands lass. In 12th century Scotland. Welcome home!"

Did she just hear him right? *12th century Scotland?* Time travel? All she could do was stand there and look around her. It was all too much. This was not possible. But somehow deep down she knew that he was telling her the truth.

"Kessan, I would like to go home now." She pleaded, overwhelmed as she struggled to process what had just happened.

"Ok lass." He whispered, reaching out for her. Then for a second time today, everything went black.

The mark of a Scot is that he remembers and cherishes the memory of his forbearers, good or bad. And there burns alive in him a sense of identity.
Robert Louis Stevenson

CHAPTER 13

Kessan caught Ceana just before she hit the ground, he had not expected her to faint, and as for Caelan, he turned and faced his brother angrily.

"What the hell were ya thinking brother?" He scolded.

Caelan looked at him with a devilish smile, right now Kessan wanted to knock that smile off his face. Now Katie was another body that they had to worry about, to keep safe. Having Ceana here was going to be difficult enough. Now there were two of them.

Caelan pleaded his case, "think aboot it Kessan, like I said last night, having Katie here will help Ceana adjust, consider how much easier it was for ya with me there." He said reasonably.

He had to admit that Caelan had a point, but he wondered how much of his brother's plan really came down to Ceana's needs or his own desires. He knew how Caelan felt for the younger sister, they had fought about it the night before, when Caelan had first suggested he bring her back to the Highlands. Even though Caelan had worded it under the guise of helping Ceana, he knew his brother had had an ulterior motive. Kessan had seen the relationship between the two growing in the past few weeks, often Caelan would disappear at night for a few hours. His guess was that he'd been with the lass. And while his brother had a point, it was still a huge risk. He cursed in Gaelic as he walked over to his brother.

"All right, fine, but she goes back when Ceana does!" He ordered.

His brother's expression told him he was not happy about the decision, but right now, he did not care. He turned away from where his brother and Katie had been standing. They needed to get moving soon, he was not sure how much time they had before someone realised they were there. That was if they hadn't already, the loud boom was hard to ignore.

"What was…?" Katie started to say.

Kessan and Caelan had heard the noise at the same time. Caelan's hand shot across her mouth cutting her off mid-sentence. Kessan signalled the occupants of the cave to be quiet. He silently made his way to the front of the cave to find out what was going on. Reaching the entrance, he stayed in the shadows making sure to stay hidden from detection. From his vantage point he could see right down the pathway that led to where they were. It was the only way into the cave so if there was any danger present it would come from that direction. Looking out into the darkness he could not make out anything at first, but then he could clearly see figures approaching the cave silently and swiftly. The mist of the waterfall was aiding them and, at first, they appeared as ghostly figures, he knew all too well that it wasn't ghosts. There it was again. The noise they had faintly heard before, it was a whistle. He knew that whistle. He had heard it all his life. It was the signal of the McKenzies. He had grown up alongside Kendrick and their signals hadn't changed. His blood ran cold. Och, he hoped MacDonnell was nearby, he was a seasoned warrior, but even this was too many men for just him and his brother to defeat. Not that they wouldn't try. Quietly moving back from the entrance, he made his way swiftly back to the others, they had to get ready for the fight that was coming.

His mind was racing trying to figure out a way they could get the lasses out of here alive but nothing was coming to mind. He was going to try and keep the women out of it as long as possible; it wasn't their fight, not yet. He could see the antechamber up ahead. Letting out his own sharp short whistle, he signalled his brother that danger was near and to get ready. When he entered the chamber a few moments later his brother was already moving, but Ceana was still out cold.

He needed to wake her up now! Kessan could not fight the enemy if he had to worry about her waking up in the middle of the fight. There was no time to be nice, picking Ceana up he carried her to the other side of the room where there was a shallow pool of water. He manoeuvred her until he could dunk her head into it. As expected, it did not take long for her to come around and, within seconds, she came up spluttering. He could not help but smile, she looked like a drowned rat. She was sitting on the ground between his legs with water streaming down her face, vigorously trying to wipe the freezing water out of her eyes. She opened her eyes and noticed all the water pooled around her. It was then that her eyes met his and narrowed. Seconds later, she lunged for him, beating against him with her fists.

"You bastard! Do you get some kind of pleasure out of trying to drown me?" She roared.

He knew she was angry but there was no time to placate her, "sorry lass, it had to be done and ya will have to put off killing me, right now I need ye and Katie to get out of sight." He commanded.

Not giving her a chance to respond he rose from his crouched position and walked back towards the entrance.

"Caelan come with me." He ordered.

He did not need to make sure that his brother was following his orders. Back here in the Highlands he was Laird, and when he spoke his people obeyed without question. It had to be that way. It was the difference between life and death. He was just about to leave the antechamber when a thought crossed his mind. Ceana was not like his people. He knew that she would not follow his orders. He had to make sure that she stayed safe. Stopping he faced her, "promise me, no matter what ya hear, ya will no' come out of this cave." He ordered.

Saying nothing, she stared at him with a defiant look on her face. Making his way back over to her, he grabbed her chin making sure she knew what was going to happen.

"If you think to disobey me on this, lass, you will pay for it later. Ya are no longer in your time and if you so much as get a scratch because you dinna listen to me, you will see a side of me ya will not like. Am I clear?"

She looked at him. He could see that she wanted to argue but she was a smart lass and knew better than to push him right now. But, she did not let him go without letting him know what she thought about his directive.

"Yes I understand. I am not stupid, but don't expect it all the time." She spat.

Kessan could live with that for now. She would quickly learn that this was his home not hers and here, his word was law. She would follow his orders when her life depended on it. A short yell came from outside the cave. Kessan could not waste another minute here. He back to his brother and then they headed out to the entrance. They had to be in position to fight the oncoming army. They'd decided that they would rather meet the enemy in the open where they had a better opportunity to fight than, in the cave, where it was easy to be cornered.

The army that was ascending the cliff had its own challenges to face, the cave only had one entrance and the path that led up to it was narrow with a steep slope that fell about twenty-two feet into a ravine full of sharp, jagged rocks at the bottom of the waterfall.

The enemy would have to come up single file if they wanted to make it. At the top of the path it opened into a small clearing in front of the cave, and there was only enough room for a handful of men at the most, he presumed.

These problems may have been a disadvantage to Kendrick's men but for himself and Caelan they became assets and they planned to use all of them to gain the upper hand against his enemy. They positioned themselves on either side of the cave's entrance, bracing for the onslaught.

"Och brother, ya ready for a fight?" Kessan looked over at Caelan and could see the adrenaline play out on his face. Kessan was also feeling the excitement that accompanied a battle. It had been a while since he had the chance, or reason, to engage in a decent battle and now all they had to do was wait. They didn't have to wait long before the first clansman appeared before them. Letting out an almighty war cry, Kessan raced forward and engaged the McKenzie warrior, their swords clashing in contact, and moments later he felt his sword pierce the flesh of his enemy. Placing his boot against the man's chest, he pushed the soldier from his sword and over the edge of the cliff before turning to face his next enemy.

They were coming thick and fast and even though only a few could fight them at a time, more were coming up the hill.

If help did not arrive soon they might be in some trouble.

Kessan had not gone unscathed during the fight, he could feel the warm blood trickling down his skin from where his enemies had made contact. They had to continue to fight for as long as possible. They had to keep them from finding the women. He thought of Ceana and renewed strength fired through his body. He would not let them win. Charging the oncoming enemy, the battle began.

CEANA DID NOT KNOW how much more she could take, it had been over an hour and the noise that was coming from outside had only picked up. The cry that she had heard when it first started had shaken her to the core.

"Ceana will you please stop pacing! You're making me dizzy. It's like watching a tennis game." She heard her sister whisper.

She couldn't help it. Sitting still was driving her crazy. She ignored Katie and kept on pacing when all of a sudden, a loud scream pierced the air. That was it! She could not stay here any longer. She had to go and find out what was going on.

"Stay here Bata, I will be back." She ordered.

"Cee, you can't go, we were told to stay put." Katie hissed at her.

"Come on Bata, when have I ever done what I was told." She tried to joke, masking the terror she felt.

Katie laughed a quiet chuckle. Ceana was happy to see her smile again. She really hated seeing the worry on her sister's face. Ceana paused. During this whole ordeal, Katie had not once seemed worried that some lunatic had stolen her right out of her bed and brought her to God knows where. The only thing she seemed worried about, was their disobedience.

"Bata, what the hell is going on with you and Caelan?" She queried.

Two red flags appeared on her sister's cheeks. Bata lowered her head and quietly declared, "I'm in love with him."

All she could do was stare at her sister open mouthed. It all made sense. "*That's* why you have not complained about being here." She accused.

Her sister shook her head, "No, I was so upset last night when he told me that he had to go home. The thought of never seeing him again broke my heart. So when I woke up here I didn't even question the how or the why of it. I was just thankful to be with him, even if it's only for a little while longer." She sighed.

Ceana was stunned. How she could have missed the budding romance that was happening between her sister and Caelan? Well, she did had had her own Highlander to occupy her thoughts with, she mused. She could not blame her sister for wanting a little extra time with her man. That was after all the main reason she had decided to come to Scotland herself. Her musings were interrupted when more loud cries, and the sound of metal against metal, rent the air louder than before. If this did not stop soon she was going to go crazy. She felt an overwhelming urge to scream and then as if nothing happened it suddenly went quiet. Looking over at her sister she signalled her to hush and stay put. Katie shook her head trying to let her know that whatever she had in mind was a bad idea. She was probably right. But Ceana had to know what was going on, and she ignored her sister's warning.

Slowly making her way along the wall she inched herself closer to the entrance of the hall; this side of the cave had hardly any light and the closer she got to the corridor the darker it got. She could feel the moss at her hands and the water trickling over her fingers. It was cold and slippery but she was determined to stay on her path and she knew it was the place to offer her protection. If anyone entered the cave hopefully, she would see them first.

The darker it got the harder it was to calm herself. She tried focusing on breathing in and out slowly. She only hoped there were no snakes or nasty critters living in the crevasses of the wall. That was all she needed, a spider crawling up her arm. Finally, her hand came up against thin air; she must have reached the opening to the tunnel!

Turning, she slowly peered around the corner to see if she could see anything. There was nothing but complete darkness. She could not even see the light at the end. Ceana paused for a second and considered her options. Did she really want to go down that creepy path? Who knew what would be hiding in the darkness, waiting for her.

"Cee, I really don't think this is a good idea." Katie said right behind her. She gave a muffled yelp of surprise and spun to face the place where the sound of her sister's voice had come from. Katie had whispered her comment, but in the silence, it sounded as loud as a gunshot and had scared ten years off her life.

"Bata! Don't do that!" She whispered back furiously. "Will you quit worrying. I will be fine. I was just going to creep to the entrance to see if I can find out what the hell is going on."

She was not sure who she was trying to convince; herself or Katie. She was so focused on her sister that she did not hear the figure coming up behind her. Before she knew what was happening, a hand shot out from behind her and landed with force over her mouth.

Ceana tried to scream but, as she sucked in a breath to release it, another arm snaked around her stomach squeezing the breath from her lungs. Suddenly she was taken back two years, when she felt defenceless. She hated this feeling and the fact that her sister was also here made it worse. Katie! Was she okay? It felt as though time was standing still. She had to try and get out of the hold this mountain of a man had her in, she knew he was tall because she could feel his chin on top of her head, but his height did not bother her. Like her trainer always said, the bigger they are the harder they fall.

This was it. If she was going to do anything about it the time was now. Ceana grabbed the hand around her mouth and tried to twist it so that she could throw her attacker over her shoulder, just as her trainer had taught her. But it didn't work. It was as though he had been expecting it.

Before she knew what was happening she had been spun around so fast that she stumbled forward right into the Highlander. Her hands were firmly pressed against his vast chest, his arms pinning her to him. This was not the best position to be in but she would not give her captor the pleasure of seeing her fear so she kept her head down, looking at the ground. When she wouldn't meet her captor's gaze, a hand placed itself under her chin and forced her to look up into his eyes. This was even worse than she thought, it could have been anyone else, but no it had to have been him.

Kessan's eyes were so full of fury that she felt as if she were being fried on the spot. She knew she was in big trouble. She had two choices; she could cower and apologise or she could fight and the first was not in her nature.

"Ya had better have a good reason for being over here wench." He snarled.

Racking her brain, she tried to come up with a plausible explanation for being where she was. How much of her conversation to Katie had they heard? She shot her sister a look to see if she could help, but she was hugging Caelan and he was kissing her with adoration. When did Katie grow up so fast? She would never get used to seeing her as a woman. She still did not have a plausible answer for Kessan and she knew he was waiting. She was just about to plea the fifth when it dawned on her what he'd called her.

"Well lass, I am waiting." Kessan's stern voice demanded.

She fumed, oh, he was going to get an answer all right. Reefing her chin out of his hold, she pushed back on his arms to gain her release.

Ceana got what she wanted, he let her go, but that was his first mistake. Ceana pulled her arm back and punched him square in the midsection with all her strength, but was dismayed to see that all it achieved was an aching fist, as if she'd punched the wall of the cave instead. He didn't even flinch. He just raised one eyebrow and folded his arms over his chest. Her blood began to boil, how dare he! Lunging forward, she was determined to make him feel it this time but she was not quick enough. He grabbed her arm and spun her around until her backside was pressed firmly against his groin. She did not want to be in this position. She was angry, but her treacherous body was already responding to his touch which infuriated her even more. She should be angry with him for the way he controlled her, so why did her body desire him? She had to free herself.

"Let me go, Kessan." She said in a steely, quiet tone. Almost immediately, his arms released her, taking her by surprise, and at the sudden loss of support she stumbled. The next thing she knew she was sprawled on the ground at his feet. Looking over her shoulder at him, she gave him a *'fuck you'* gesture. She knew it was childish but, in her current mood, she didn't care.

Of course, it didn't faze him, he just stood there shaking his head.

"Now lass, that is not at all ladylike, perhaps it is time I taught you how to behave."

Was he for real? Standing up, she turned around, dusted her pants off and took a step backwards, making sure that she was out of reach, and then she exploded.

"Look here, you chest-beating Neanderthal, I have news for you. You sir, are not my father and you cannot tell me what to do." She inhaled and continued. "And if you ever call me a wench or threaten my person again, I will make you sorry you were born a man, *capiche*?"

Nothing. The man was infuriating. He was not giving her any reaction at all. In fact, he was just standing in his usual stance staring at her. She was just about to give him what for when she heard coughing coming from behind him. Damn it to hell.

"Who the hell are you?" She asked the man standing directly behind Kessan.

She knew she was being rude but after the day she'd had she didn't really care. The man did not answer her, so turning towards Kessan she asked him instead.

"Can you tell me who they are? Or is that just another thing you won't tell me." She snapped.

"Who they are lass is of no importance to ya, the only thing ye need to remember or know is that ya will listen to my orders the next time I give them?"

This was getting ridiculous; surely, he didn't think she was going to listen to this. "Ok Kessan I think it's time you tell me what the hell is going on. Then, I think I would like to go home, away from you and here..."

As she spoke, she had thrown her hands around indicating exactly where she was talking about, then it dawned on her, she still didn't know what the hell had just happened. Ok it was time to get some answers, what was going on?

"Um Kessan?"

"Aye, lass."

"Where the hell are we? And why are you bleeding?"

CHAPTER 14

Kessan knew that she had a right to know the entire story, but after the fight and then finding her putting herself in danger, he needed time to calm down. Her curiosity was going to get her killed one day and just the thought made him furious. She might not care about her safety but there were some who did. He decided to ignore her for the time being, focusing instead on his men. He needed to find out what had been happening while he was away. They also needed to figure out what to do next and quickly even though they had defeated the men outside he knew that it would not be long before McKenzie sent more.

"Brodie?" Kessan knew his Commander would know what he wanted and waited for his reply.

"I'm glad to see I'm not the only one you bark orders at." Ceana said as she glared at him.

He ignored her. He was not facing her but he knew she had made some kind of gesture behind his back. His men all had slight smiles on their lips and were looking at the pair curiously. Hell this woman was infuriating. He gave a slight nod to Brodie letting him know that he was ready to hear his report. Brodie gave Kessan his report on what had occurred since they left. Kessan paced the floor as he listened to what had been happening. All of a sudden, Brodie stopped talking but he had still to hear about his home.

"What of our keep?" He pressed.

Brodie cleared his throat.

"Well after Kendrick found out that ya had aided MacDonnell, the clan was exiled and Kendrick's men overtook the keep."

This was not good news, but at least it was still standing, so there was some hope of getting his ancestral home back at the end. Many were not so lucky with entire keeps destroyed. "How many were lost?" He asked.

"Fifty men, women and children in total." Brodie said solemnly.

Kessan sighed and said silent blessings for those he had lost. He started pacing again; even one death was too many. He stopped pacing suddenly realising that there had been no mention of his sister. He was facing Ceana and he stayed there.

"What about Thora?" He asked quietly.

Ceana's head whipped up at the name, he knew she was curious and a little angry. Kessan could see the tic forming in her jaw as she bit back a remark. Then it dawned on him, something was wrong, it was taking his man too long to answer. Still standing frozen as dread crept through his body, he readdressed the Commander, "Brodie, answer me now." A chill entered his tone and his eyes narrowed. He noticed Ceana drew in a breath and took a step back. He could only image what she was seeing in his eyes, his voice held the promise of pain if they did not answer. She was finally seeing the Laird that he was known to be.

Brodie cleared his throat again; there was a hint of nervousness and fear in his tone.

"I'm sorry Kessan, McKenzie has her," he bowed his head.

A cry of pure rage ripped out of Kessan before he could stop it, he swung around to face his men.

"We leave immediately." He ordered before storming from the cave.

❧

CEANA WOULD NEVER FORGET the look on Kessan's face or his reaction when his men had told him about Thora. She finally understood that underneath the man she had fallen in love with was one capable of killing; and she wouldn't want to be in the shoes of the man who had taken Thora. This woman obviously meant a lot to him. She could feel her temper rising again as a stab of jealousy reared its ugly green head. Was she really becoming this type of person? Never in her life had she been jealous of anyone, and she didn't want to be jealous now, but she couldn't help it. Kessan was hers and she would be damned if she would let him go without a fight. Ceana would have to remember to ask him about her when she got the chance. But not right now, the sound of rocks plummeting to the depths below brought her back to the task at hand, one she was trying hard to forget.

Right after Kessan had given them the order to leave, they left the cave, passing the aftermath of the battle – she had tried to avoid the bloodshed – and now they were currently making their way down the long narrow path that had led up to the cave.

Ceana's body was full of tension, all of the men were on edge, and after the battle they had just waged she could understand why.

Looking ahead, all she could see was a line of men, she knew that if she looked behind her, the image would be the same.

Brodie had been given the task of leading and Kessan, of course, was bringing up the rear.

Ceana and her sister had been placed right smack in the middle of them all, this was so that anyone trying to get to them would have to go through a wall of Scottish warriors first. She stared at her sister's back as she walked behind her, she could see Caelan just in front of Katie and she saw that he had his hand behind his back so that she could grab hold of it. She closed her fist as her palm itched; she wished she had Kessan's hand to hold especially since the path they were walking didn't seem all that safe to her, and was littered with the bodies of dead men. There was nothing like the protective pathways they had erected at home. She could see the muddy soft ground beneath her feet and for the umpteenth time more rocks and mud tumbled over the edge as someone in front of her put their feet a little too close to the edge.

Every now and then one of the men tossed a body blocking the path over the side, watching it bounce lifelessly down the cliff and listening to the noise it made as it crashed on the rocks below sent shivers up Ceana's spine and she tried not to imagine what would happen if she were to fall. Ceana's heart sunk a little more, would this ever end?

She tried focusing on the line in front of her, but she couldn't stop the uneasy feeling she was getting. She placed her hand on the rock cliff beside her and closed her eyes briefly trying to steady her stomach.

Ceana was terrified of heights and the sheer edge of the cliff they were making their way down was making her feel queasy.

Ever since she could remember, heights freaked her out, especially if there was nothing there to stop you from falling, no, she was sure nothing could be as bad as this.

Finally, they reached the bottom of the cliff. Her nerves had just started to settle down and her shaking legs had almost returned to normal when Kessan suddenly ordered them all to mount up. *Horses?* After all that? He had to be kidding. She sighed, first heights and now horses, could the day get any worse? She *hated* horses. She had fallen off her Aunt's horse when she was younger which resulted in a broken leg and eight weeks in plaster.

She had never forgotten the pain she'd felt that day and had never been able to get on another one since. She turned around to face the men and came face to face with Kessan's horse. The thing was huge; she had to tip her head back just to see the top of its head. It was truly magnificent with a jet-black coat that shone in the light.

Its mane was just as black as its coat, except for one streak of white that ran just behind its ear. The white strip of hair matched the white diamond in the centre of its forehead. The beast snorted and lifted its head showing its impatience. Her hands began to sweat.

Oh *hell* no. There was no way she was getting on that horse.

"I will walk, thanks." She said timidly. She could hear the fear in her own voice but she did not care, there was no way she was getting on that thing, not only did it look huge but if she fell it was a long way to the ground.

He stared back at her in amazement.

A voice beside her scoffed. "Doona be ridiculous lass, the camp is a two-day's ride from here, ya will never make it on foot." One of the men, she couldn't remember his name, said.

"Look…" She faltered, not sure of whom she was addressing.

"Duncan." He offered helpfully.

She nodded to him and continued, "look, Duncan, I really do not care how far the camp is; I will not be getting on any horse, ever."

She stubbornly turned around and started walking off. Hopefully they got the idea and would just let her walk. Wishful thinking on her part, she hadn't even taken a second step when she was lifted off her feet and placed on the horse in front of Kessan. She froze as her fears took over her body, she couldn't even scream or cry. She grabbed hold of the horse's mane, closed her eyes and held on for dear life. She was so stiff, she knew that she would soon be sore if she kept it up, but she couldn't seem to relax. She felt Kessan tighten his arms around her then his breath was right next to her ears.

"Relax lass, I willna let ya fall." He whispered.

She appreciated the support his strong arms gave her and, realising she had no other option, she willed herself to relax as much as she could allow herself to, and leaned against him shutting her eyes as tightly as she could. Instantly a myriad of senses hit her at once as his familiar, comforting warmth engulfed her, she could feel the hairs of his arms and chest rubbing against her own skin, electrifying her own. She could hear the soft hoof beats of the horses around her, coupled with the breathing of their companions and occasionally an animal's call from somewhere in the forest.

Then there was the smell. Oh God, she would never get tired of his smell.

It was the smell of pure male.

He somehow managed to smell of fresh air and the woods around them, with a hit of saltiness you got from sweat, without actually being sweaty.

It was a purely masculine smell, and it was nothing like the cologne-drowned men back home.

His arms were wrapped around her and she could feel his heartbeat pulsing in his wrist where she had a death grip on his arm, but for the life of her she could not ease it or open her eyes. She stayed like this for the next couple of hours, unable to fully surrender to the rhythm of the ride, just waiting for the moment when she would hit the ground.

Then, sometime around sunrise, curiosity finally overcame her fear and she finally dared to open her eyes. She was quite taken back by the surroundings, which were utterly beautiful.

Purple dotted green, which blanketed the hills and valleys below them.

The smell was absolutely amazing! She inhaled and breathed in the smell of truly fresh air, untouched by the day to day living of her own home.

There were green rolling hills all around her with glens all through them. This was what she had been dreaming of for years, she was finally in Scotland; well, she assumed she was in Scotland. It was time she had some answers.

"Kessan?" She ventured.

He obviously was not in the mood to talk as he didn't so much as answer her. She tried again, "Kessan?" This time she turned slightly in her seat to face him but he looked down at her and shook his head, letting her know that now was not the time to talk. She turned back to her position, feeling a little miffed. Fine, if that was how he was going to be, she would just enjoy the view. Perhaps she would ignore him when he decided it *was* time, see how he liked it. She knew she was being childish but didn't care. Her and Kessan were bringing up the rear again and Caelan and Katie were just in front of them. Katie, she noticed, had fallen asleep, her head lolling against Caelan's chest. She decided that she would try the same. God knows when she would next have the chance and she was exhausted. Leaning back against Kessan, she closed her eyes and let her mind wander off.

She was just about asleep when a loud whistle pierced the air right beside her ear. Turning in her saddle, she punched him square in the shoulder and glared at him but the jerk just smiled and then, without warning, leapt off the horse to the ground.

She was not expecting the move and, now that she was on her own, without the support, she could feel herself starting to fall, she slid and tipped sideways. *This was it. She was going to hit the ground again.* She closed her eyes and waited for the pain that never came. Two strong hands grabbed her and lowered her gently down. Once her feet found the ground, she was so relieved that she didn't realise he was still holding her, after a minute or two it finally dawned on her, "you can let me go now." She whispered.

"Are ya sure lass?" He replied, eyes twinkling.

"Yes of course I'm sure, you dolt." She snapped, she was not ready to forgive him for ignoring her.

Man, he could be infuriating, she thought with annoyance as he studied her without saying anything until finally, he let her go. Her legs buckled and, once again she found herself landing ungracefully in the dirt. Kessan had tried to grab her but he had not been quick enough. He reached down for her but she ignored his stretched-out hand. She did not want to get back up just yet, her backside, lower back and legs were cramping something fierce and she feared she would cry if he touched her right now.

"Don't touch me please," she whimpered, she hated how vulnerable she sounded but she could not help it. "I don't suppose you have any painkillers on you, do you?" She asked wistfully.

She knew the question was a dumb one, hell, they probably didn't even know what painkillers were. One look at Kessan's face confirmed her theory. But as usual the stubborn mule paid no attention to her plea and, with one swift movement, she had been transferred to his arms like a useless damsel in distress and he was walking away from camp, along a path surrounded by forest on either side. She could smell the heather of the Highlands and a faint mist was starting to form on the ground. It was only then that she noticed the sun had dropped lower in the sky. They had been riding for quite some time and the day had just slipped away. She didn't have her watch on her, so it was hard to tell what the time would have been at home, but by the looks of the sky it was late afternoon here, which meant that soon darkness would start its slow descent.

Normally she would have loved her surroundings and she would have spent hours marvelling in its beauty, right now though she could think of nothing more than the pain radiating up her back. The pain was getting unbearable. If he did not stop soon she was sure she was going to scream.

"Kessan, please, you have to stop I cannot take it anymore." Ceana whimpered.

"Shh lass we are almost there." He soothed.

She rested her head down on his shoulder as they walked and let out a moan, wondering where he was taking her. She noticed that he had left the path. Lifting her head to view her new surroundings, she realised that they were entering a clearing. In the middle of the clearing was a small pond where two rivers converged on each other. It was beautiful, tall trees formed a circle around the outside of the clearing and acted like a curtain, giving the glen a small amount of privacy, in that moment she could have kissed Kessan then for bringing her here. She was reminded once again why she loved this man.

"Ok lass, I am going to lower ya to the ground slowly and ya have to walk around. But do not worry I will not let go of ya until ye feel like ya can walk on ya own." He encouraged, as he slowly lowered his arms.

"Please don't Kessan, it hurts so bad, and I am not sure I could stand even if I wanted to." She pleaded.

"Ya, have to lass, ya cramping up due to spending too many hours in the saddle." He explained.

Ceana knew he was right but just the thought of the pain that was going to follow was enough to make her hold him tighter. Ok, she admonished herself, she had to stop acting like a baby, she had been in worse pain than this in her life.

"Fine then, let's just get this over and done with." She snapped, bracing herself.

She knew she shouldn't be snapping at him, and it wasn't the first time today she had done so, in fact she was acting like a dragon lady. This was not his fault; hang on, yes it was! He made her get on that damn horse. He was the one who insisted they travel for hours on end without taking a decent break. And he was the one that had brought her to this God forsaken place! Oh this was his fault all right!

"You can let me go now, I am fine to walk on my own." She once again snapped at him, her anger was coming back. Anger was good – while she was angry she wasn't thinking about the pain she was feeling, all she was thinking about was the pain she would like to inflict on him! She started to pace around the clearing, stumbling and stretching out her tired, cramping muscles. At first it was painful but the more she moved, the looser she got. She needed something to take her mind off the pain. They were alone and now it was time this man explained what was going on.

"Alright buster," she ordered, "it's time you started talking! Explain to me what the hell is going on, and who the hell is Thora?" She asked him, silently daring him to ignore her this time.

KESSAN WAS NOT surprised by her outrage. He had known that, from the moment he put her on *Bhaltair*, she had been seething. He could feel it in every muscle of her body. The grip she had on his arm was so tight that he could feel the tension radiating from her body. Each time she had tried to talk to him, he had stopped her – he had to pay attention to their surroundings. This only added to her anger. It took her hours before she relaxed, but by then it was too late.

Her body had already endured hours of riding. There were so

many things that he needed to explain, but first he needed to get them to safety and this was the first time that they had not been on enemy-laden ground. They had finally reached somewhere that they could rest for the night.

He knew of the clearing here and he had picked the spot so that the women could have some privacy, but also so that he could use the opportunity to get her on her own in order to explain some things away from his men.

"This was the first time today that we have not been on enemy land, lass." He explained.

"Oh, so that was why you were staying silent? I was wondering why you were ignoring me." She said with a little less heat. He could see her start to relax a little.

Kessan chuckled, "I was not ignoring ya lass, I was listenin' out for the enemy. This land is no longer safe and I had to be on alert for danger."

Ceana shook her head and opened her mouth to argue, but before she could say anything he added, "once you've had time to work out the knots in ya body, I will explain a few things," he promised.

He was expecting her to argue with him, but to his surprise, she nodded and continued slowly around the clearing, stopping occasionally to stretch, or to admire the glen. He could tell the feeling was coming back to her legs and the more she walked, the stronger her gait became.

Kessan leaned back against a tree and just watched her, she was beautiful and seeing her in his highlands brought a heavy feeling to his chest. What was he going to do with her if she wanted to go home?

He had already decided that he could never give this woman up, possibly even if it meant losing his highlands.

He looked around him; this place was his world. the Highlands were not just his home, they were a part of his soul, it was all he did and all he was.

Quite simply it was home, but for her he would give it up, he knew nowhere could be home without her. Perhaps he was getting ahead of himself. After all, if Ceana's history books were right and they did not stop McKenzie, there would not be much of his highlands left anyway.

Anger so powerful roared through him. There was no way he

would let that happen, he vowed that even if he was not here to enjoy it, he would not let the Highlands be destroyed by McKenzie and the dark magic. He had already lost many of his clansmen and now his sister was missing. What if McKenzie had killed her already? He could not imagine never seeing her sweet face again. He had seen many men killed by Kendrick, it was always brutal and the thought of his sister facing that alone made him sick to his stomach. God he hoped he was in time to save her. Kessan shook his head, trying to dispel the horrific image of his sister in pain. He would deal with her death when and if it happened, right now, he had to believe that she was alive. He had to figure out how he was going to save her from the clutches of evil.

The thought of her being in the hands of that monster was just as unbearable as her death at his hands. Thora had only been ten and three years when their parents had passed away, so he had raised her and taught her all that she needed to know. He had always been there to protect her, except this time, when she had needed it most.

He felt as though he had not only let her down, but his parents as well. He had promised them that he would always protect and care for his siblings above all else. He still remembered the day his father and mother had died. It was at the beginning when McKenzie had taken control of the power, he was trying to recruit Kessan's father to join him in taking control of the Highlands. His father had refused, made it clear that he did not want anything to do with the dark magic and had vowed that he would not take sides. Kessan's father was a well-respected and feared Laird. His mother was well-advised in the art of healing and both were loved throughout the Highlands.

Kessan would never forget the day of the so-called 'accident.' It had just started to cool down and winter was setting into the Highlands.

His mother had been called out to the Randall clan as their youngest daughter was running a high fever.

Kessan had seen them leave from the practice field and had waved them off; it was common for his father to go along with his mother on her trips lately, especially since Kessan had taken over the running of the clan.

However, on their way, a small band of exiled Highlanders had attacked them just outside of their land. They had brutally ripped both of them off their horses; raped his mother and then slit her throat. All while his father watched on helplessly. Initially, his father had fought them but he had received fatal wounds trying to fend off the bandits. His father had been unable to move with the extent of his injuries. He could only watch as his love was murdered before him. She lay beside him, blood running out of an ugly gash in her throat. The outlaws left him for dead.

He had lain there like that until his men had found them after coming back from a routine raid. They brought both his father, now weak from blood loss, and his mother's body home. Kessan would never forget the sight of his beautiful mother's lifeless body draped over the horse. Her hair was matted with her blood and her clothes were torn, leaving her exposed. He had run up to the horse with a cry, he couldn't believe she was gone, she had never done anything to hurt anyone. Her whole life she only ever helped people. He stood next to her, head bowed, and then he heard his father's weak voice crying out to him. He was barely alive.

Kessan ordered his men to take his father to his chambers. A healer was called, but the wounds were too great and he died days later from infection. Kessan spent those last hours sitting beside his father's bed listening to the man croak out the events and promised his father vengeance to honour his memory. He also promised to take care of his brother and sister.

Now McKenzie had her and he only hoped that, because of their past, Kendrick would not hurt Thora. After all, she had been like a sister to him. He knew deep down though the chances of that were slim. The more power Kendrick got the more he lost any sense of honour.

The more Kessan thought about it the angrier he got. He should never have left her alone.

☙❧

CEANA LOOKED up and noticed that Kessan appeared to be lost in thought. There was such a haunted look on his face and in that moment, all her anger disappeared. All she wanted to do was take away whatever was haunting him. She knew that she shouldn't interrupt his thoughts but the look on his face almost made her rethink her decision. She needed to know what was going on. It was time that she knew everything. She didn't want to approach him directly, that would only get her more vague responses. She looked around for Caelan, perhaps he would tell her what was going on. It was then that she realised they were alone, and there was not another soul around.

"Kessan, where is everyone. I thought we were stopping for the night?" She asked.

Her question brought him out of his musing and he pushed himself off the tree he was leaning against and strode towards her. She would never get enough of watching this man's body in action. He was powerful, like a tiger, and she noticed that even though he looked relaxed he was always ready to pounce into action.

He shook his head, "nay lass, we are not staying here the night. The others are just beyond the clearing. I thought you might like time to yourself."

She was pleasantly surprised, how did he keep doing this to her?

Walking up to Kessan she kissed him, "thank you for thinking of me. Once again you have shown me how much of a softy you are." She said slyly.

His face changed and his eyes narrowed, "I am far from soft lass, do no' forget that!"

She burst out laughing. She couldn't help it when she caught the serious look on his face. He really was affronted by her comment. "Don't worry my barbarian. Your secret is safe with me." She loved teasing him and from his frown, he had taken her bait, hook, line and sinker.

He stared at her with those narrowed eyes and then he grinned, "well lass now that ya have your sass back, we had better join the others. It will be getting dark soon, and we still have about an hour to go before we reach the camp."

She suddenly realised what that might mean, "oh, will my father be there?" She asked, uncertainly. She was not sure if she could face him now, not after everything that had happened to her today.

"Aye lass he will." He answered.

She paled, how could she have forgotten that she was about to meet her father? What was she going to say to the man who'd given her up? She could not be too mad for the life she had led, she had loved her mother and father dearly, and her siblings meant everything to her.

But, it did not change the fact that her real parents had not wanted her. What if he rejected her a second time? A distinct possibility with her 21st Century upbringing. Shaking her thoughts from her head, she reminded herself that she shouldn't care one iota about the man's opinion. After all, she didn't need some stranger's approval.

When all this was over she was going home to her brother and sister, who she knew loved her. But, part of her knew it did matter, she needed to know the reason why this man rejected her so that she could finally put it to rest and get on with her life. She would finally have the answers to all her questions. Was she ready to know the truth?

She stormed past Kessan, her anger and confusion returning. "Come on then, let's get this over with." She snapped trying to hide her vulnerabilities from him. Kessan followed and quickly caught up to her. Just before they stepped back onto the path that would lead them to the others, Kessan let out another of those piercing whistles and she flinched at the sudden, sharp sound. God she wished he would warn her before doing that! When they reached the clearing where the group had rested, she noticed that all the men were getting ready to leave. Not five minutes later they mounted the horses.

"Brodie you take the lead and I will follow." Kessan ordered and his commander obeyed.

"Why are we always at the back?" She asked him, curious. Her tone was a bit sharper than she had meant it to be, but this day was beginning to be the longest of her life. She was tired, hungry and awash with emotions. She was starting to run out of patience. She waited for him to give her an answer but the one he gave her was just as vague as all the other answer he had given her today.

"I'm the Laird." He said, simply.

"Oh of course. How stupid of me." She answered him sarcastically. Talking to him was starting to give her a headache so she gave up and settled back for the ride. She was a little more relaxed this time, but only barely. She decided to try to sleep again as Kessan had said that camp was still over an hour away. As she yawned, she wondered how he knew when he didn't even have a

watch. She closed her eyes, listening to the galloping hooves as the horses pounded the ground, taking her to a destiny she was not sure she was ready for.

Freya watched as they mounted up and left and she balled her fists up into her skirt. Oh how she wanted to scream, this was not fair. She had been following them since they had left the cave and the further on they went the more her temper threatened to boil over. Moving further into the trees so that she wasn't spotted she continued to follow them from a safe distance. She was *determined* to follow them and find out where the outcast clans were hiding. Smiling to herself, Freya could just picture the look on Kendrick's smug face as she informed him that she had been able to gain the information that he had been desperately trying to get for weeks.

The information would not be free however; she was determined to gain his help in getting Kessan back. But, before she did any of that she would kill the bitch curled up in Kessan's arms, and she would savour every moment of it.

She had almost given herself away when she'd seen the way Kessan was treating this intruder. She had wanted to jump out immediately and slit her throat but she had to stick to the plan. Her smile widened as she continued to daydream about how she was going to kill the little whore. Who did she think she was coming in here and trying to steal her future?

She realised that her horse had picked up speed, she slowed it down again pulling on the reins, making sure that she stayed well in the shadows. The last thing Freya needed was to give away her position before she had a chance to see her plan through.

Grinning again, she thought about how she would wait for the right opportunity to end the bitch's life. Her plan was to follow them back to their camp and when Ceana was alone, and there would be a time, she would strike and kill her before anyone was aware of what had happened.

They would eventually find her body and by then Freya would be on her way to her brother's castle to inform him of their victory. This was going be so much fun, she might even make her suffer a little first. By the end of it the wench would know who Kessan belonged to if it was the last thing she did!

CHAPTER 15

Kessan could not figure this woman out, one minute she was giving him hell for hurting her, the next she was making fun of him and laughing until her eyes sparkled, and then in the blink of an eye her demeanour had changed again.

He knew his answer to her question only aggravated her more, but he could not help himself, it was his way for getting back at her for calling him soft. He was nothing of the sort, and if she had ever seen him on the battlefield, he was sure she would change her mind.

It would not be long now before they made camp. Kessan had seen his sentries in the woods about a mile back guarding the perimeter; they were well hidden and it was only because they had signalled him that he knew they were there.

Ceana had not seen them, she was sound asleep, the second time on the horse she was not so fearful, but even in her sleep she had a death grip on his arm. He could not understand how anyone could be afraid of such a noble beast. *Bhaltair* had been with him since he was a lad of ten and two and had saved his life on a number of occasions.

Her fear was a strange concept, she should be more afraid of man or the death trap that she drove back home than of a horse. In the next minute, a call echoed through the air; it was the greeting of the MacDonnells. Ceana awoke suddenly. He had to tighten his arms slightly as he felt her slip in her startled reaction.

"Are ya ready lass?" He whispered into her ear.

She rubbed her eyes and looked up at him sleepily. "Ready for what?"

"To meet ya sire." He affirmed.

Saying nothing for once, Ceana straightened and peered anxiously ahead of them as they trotted down the path. He could see her scanning the crowd in front of them as they made their way deeper into the camp. She had gone rigid. Kessan knew she was nervous, the nails digging into his arms a dead giveaway.

He didn't know what to say to calm her, "it's alright lass. No one here is going to hurt ye." He soothed.

"How can you be so sure?" She asked warily.

"Trust me lass I won't let them."

Her back got a little straighter, if that was even possible, and she swallowed a nervous gulp before she replied, "alright I'm ready. Let's go meet the old bastard."

He laughed, he couldn't help it. He rarely relaxed and let his guard down in front of his men, and he noticed that quite a few eyes were on him, he didn't care. He couldn't wait for old man MacDonnell to meet his daughter. She was, after all, a chip off the old block.

❦

CEANA WAS NOT FULLY awake when he had dropped the bomb on her that they had made it to camp, but the shock announcement automatically cleared her senses. She didn't know which of the men standing in front of her was her father.

Ceana guessed, by common sense, that it would be one of the elders, but there were so many of them that she couldn't even hazard a guess as to the exact one. Even though she was nervous about meeting the man, the Archaeologist inside of her admired this moment. Each and every man in front of her resembled exactly what a highland warrior would have been had she found on a dig back home, from their dress, horses, and swords.

She knew from her studies that most Lairds from this time were gruff and unemotional, and the men standing before her definitely represented that well. They had to be as their clan's fate depended on their ability to keep them safe, and if a Laird appeared weak and unable to control even their own family members, they did not last long in such a volatile environment. She also knew from her studies how the women were treated.

The Scots were honourable people, especially towards their women folk, who were rarely abused. The few that were, were the victims of men who had no honour. However, they still had to do as they were told and they had no rights.

That didn't stop The Highland women from being tough. They had to be, the conditions didn't allow the survival of the weak. Between the elements – such as snow, rain and harsh winds during the winter –and the wars that were constantly fought, everyone that lived in the Highlands had to be.

It was time, the sooner it was done the sooner she could go home and she was determined to let the man know this. Ceana was here to help with whatever problem he had, but after it was done, she was going back to Australia! She had a life there, one she needed to get back to. She would come back to Scotland one day, but it would be the one in the 21st century and at that thought the archaeologist and historian in her died a little. This was what she'd dreamed about discovering, it was every historian and archaeologist's dream to uncover exactly what went on in the ancient civilisations and now she was experiencing it first-hand! She would make it her mission to remember every last detail.

Kessan dismounted the horse and then helped her down. Looking around she didn't see much at first, off a little to the right were about thirty tents, if you could call them that. They were all close together and a fire sat in the middle of them. She watched with wide eyes as women and children sat around the fire playing, talking and cooking.

Over the other side of the makeshift settlement there was a group of men tending to the horses that were hitched to a long makeshift hitching post. They were grooming and feeding them.

Hearing a sound coming from the bushes, she turned her head as a group of men came in from the outskirts, while an equal number walked out to where they had just come from.

Blinking, the most random thought popped into to her head, it was like the changing of the guards; she gave a soft snort, oh yeah she had finally lost it. All in all it seemed pretty cosy, and the people here obviously didn't mind it too much, many of them were laughing and talking naturally.

She wondered how much further the houses were when a cry

brought her attention back to the women and children around the campfire. There she saw a mother exit a tent with a two- or so-year old crying and then it dawned on her.

There were no houses, they were actually going to camp outside. When he said camp, she had thought he meant like an army camp or something.

"Um Kessan, where are all the houses?" She asked.

"I will explain everything soon lass. First let's introduce ya to ya father." He said, sidestepping another question. She might as well just give up and stop asking him.

"Ok first of all he is not my father. My father died. This is merely the man who sired me are we clear?" She hissed at him.

"Aye lass." He answered.

"Second of all, I am getting pretty sick to death of you avoiding my questions. Just once I would like you to stop giving me bullshit answers." She seethed.

She knew that she sounded petty but at this point in time she wasn't even certain that she wanted any kind of relationship with the man. The hurt of being rejected had returned tenfold. She turned away from Kessan, facing the men again, then one of the elders and a younger scot stepped forward to make their way to them. She stared.

So this was her father?

She made a decision to meet him half way and stepped forward herself.

She would start their relationship off with him knowing that she was equal to him, but her confidence faltered the closer she got.

Man he was tall, even for his age, and the guy beside him was just as tall, if not a fraction taller.

In addition to their height, they were both well built with muscular arms. As he loomed over her, she lost some of her nerve. She didn't feel as confident now, in fact he was starting to scare the pants off her. She fought the urge to shy away and stood her ground.

Within seconds, he was standing in front of her and the only thing that came to her mind was that he reminded her of Grizzly Adams.

He had a full head of red curly hair that reached his shoulders, his beard came half way down his chest and both his hair and his beard had two plaits running down either side.

She tilted her head to the side pondering this man; she was speechless. If she put a bandana on him and put him on a Harley, he could easily pass as a biker, she thought, biting back an hysterical laugh. She looked him up and down and then stared at his face really studying it for the first time.

Then her eyes finally locked with his and that's when she knew that this man was indeed her father, for the eyes that she stared into were the same eyes she saw every morning in the mirror.

His eyes contradicted the rest of his body; they held a youthfulness that was not evident with the rest of him. They were so sharp and clear that she knew this man still had life in him.

She stood there trying to see if he possessed any other features that she could connect to herself, and she was so entranced by the thought that she was startled when he spoke.

His brogue, which was even deeper and richer than Kessan's, rattled through her. His tone was louder and gruffer than any she had heard before.

"Hello lass. I am Laird MacDonnell. I doona ken how mooch the young lad has told ya but we are sure glad ya came." He greeted her politely.

If she wasn't so awestruck, she would have laughed. The so called 'lad' hadn't told her anything of much yet – she had a hard time connecting Kessan to the word 'lad' – but she vowed one way or another she would get him to talk. For now, she addressed the man in front of her.

"Well sir, it's not like I had a choice now, is it? But thank you anyway.

Kessan has not told me much of anything yet, apart from the fact that you are my father and you need my help." She explained a little indignantly.

"Now if someone could please tell me how I can help, I would like to get it over and done with so that I can go home." She looked her father in the eye as she said the final words.

The man in front of her didn't seem affected by her statement at all, in fact he burst out into a chuckle and slapped the back of the man standing beside him.

"Aye Hamish," he said, "she is definitely a MacDonnell alright."

"Actually, I'm a Thorne." She declared, unwilling to let them forget it.

Her last remark brought his attention back to her. Finally, she thought, I might actually get some answers. She was expecting him to start explaining things but instead he barked orders at Kessan to follow him and she could do nothing as she watched him turn around and march off with Kessan. Great, another arrogant Highlander to deal with, she thought. They hadn't gone far though when Kessan stopped and turned to her.

"Do not wander off lass." He warned.

"Aye, aye captain!" She replied giving him a salute to go with it. *Where in hell did he think she would go anyway?*

She watched them leave, feeling all kinds of emotions running through her mind. She was angry, scared, hurt and intrigued all at once.

"Looks like something out of *Braveheart* doesn't it?" She heard behind her.

She jumped, she had forgotten about her sister.

"Damn it Bata! How many times have I told you not to sneak up on me like that. I swear you do it on purpose!" She fumed.

Katie laughed, "it's not my fault you're deaf. By the way, who was that?" She asked.

Surprised that Katie had not heard any of the exchange, she turned to face her, suddenly glad that she was here, glad that she wasn't alone. She had been so caught up in the moment that she hadn't stopped to see where her sister was.

"Are you kidding me, didn't you hear who he was?" She asked.

"No, I only just got here when they left, and I only caught the order he gave to Kessan. Oh my God," she babbled, "did you hear how loud he was? I swear I don't know how they have stayed hidden for so long or how any of them have any hearing left." She joked.

Ceana stared at her sister, wishing she could share her innocent enthusiasm.

"So, Cee who was he?" Katie pressed.

She didn't answer straight away, but then bowed her head. "My father, Laird MacDonnell himself."

Katie froze, and her mouth dropped open as she processed what Ceana had just said. "Holy cow Cee, what the hell happened to you? I think the growth gene skipped you somehow. Did you see how big he was?"

She looked at her sister shocked. Was that all she could say?

"What?" Katie saw her look and shrugged her shoulders, "it's true!"

Ceana just shook her head. "I tell you that man is my real father, the one who abandoned me and that is all you have to say?"

Katie laughed, "come on Cee you must admit he is a mammoth. I don't know why you're so serious. Look on the bright side, you can now get the answers you have been looking for and as a bonus think of the story you will be able to tell your children." She reasoned as she put her arm around Ceana.

She hadn't really thought about it like that. All she had really been thinking about was meeting the man who had given her up. "I suppose when you look at it like that, Ok I will try and look on the bright side. Let's just hope that whatever they need my help with doesn't take too long and we can get back to our normal boring lives."

She heard someone clear their throat behind her, she thought it must have been Brodie or one of Kessan's other men coming to make sure that she hadn't run off, she wouldn't put it past Kessan to have a man follow her. When she turned around, she came face to chest with the man who had been with her father.

"There has to be something in the water here that makes all you men so huge." The words flew out of her mouth before she could stop them and she heard Katie snigger.

The man in front of her was as tall if not taller than Kessan, he had broad shoulders and legs the size of tree trunks. Now *he* was what she expected a Scottish man to look like, he wore a tartan like most men here, and a white shirt of some kind.

She looked up to his face and studied it closely making sure to catalogue each feature so that she could use it in the descriptions of Scottish warriors in her report when she got home.

That was if she ever got home. His hair reached his shoulders, much like all the other Highlanders. Two braids ran either side of his head.

The colour was a cross between red and brown. The blonde streaks throughout told her that he spent a lot of time in the sun. His face though, unlike the elder Highlander's, was clean-shaven, and quite handsome. Turning her attention to his eyes, she noticed that they were as emerald green as her own, and it was then she noticed his mouth twitch into a half smile, but he still didn't say anything.

"I'm sorry." She apologised. "I did not mean to be so rude." She said as she stuck out her hand to him as a peace offering. She let out a sigh of relief when he took it. She thanked her lucky stars that he didn't find her scrutiny offensive. "Hi." She offered, "I guess you know who I am. This buffoon here is my sister Katie."

She saw Katie give him a little wave and he nodded his greeting to her. He stood there in the same stance that Kessan often used, and it dawned on her that most of the men around here appeared edgy, as if they expected trouble. As she quickly glanced around the camp, she noticed that there was not one single male just sitting down or relaxing. They all seemed to be preparing for something. The man in front of her seemed anxious. His eyes were darting around, looking at the forest on the edge of the camp. He didn't look at her again until she started talking.

"What can I do for you Mr...?" She realised she couldn't remember what her father had called him.

"Please call me Hamish," he offered, smiling at her, and then rather shyly, added, "I just wanted to thank ya for coming to help us. I haven't seen Da this happy in years."

Da? She trembled as she realised the implications of what that meant. She should have picked it; the eyes should have given it away instantly and now that she was aware of who he was she could see the resemblance. He may have been taller but he was the same build as her father, with the same rusty hair, the only difference was that he spoke in a softer tone of voice than MacDonnell.

"You're my brother aren't you?" She said faintly as she remembered Kessan mentioning something about a brother back home.

He nodded confirming her question, she suddenly felt overwhelmed. She had to sit down, "Jesus, how many more surprises are there?" she asked. "I wish someone would just explain to me what is going on." She fumed. She found a boulder nearby and flopped down onto it, resting her head against her knees as she sat.

With her head still on her knees, she asked in a small voice. "Are you younger or older than me?"

"I am older by two years." He answered patiently.

Her sister had been silent for which she had been grateful, she smiled into her hands. "You hear that Katie. You got your wish, there is finally someone older than me who can now boss me around." She joked weakly. She hadn't lifted her head during any of this. Ceana was still feeling off-balance and incredibly exhausted. Thankfully, Katie saved her from having to keep up any kind of conversation while she came to terms with her new family.

"It's nice to meet you Hamish." Katie smiled, "and it's about time Cee, now you will know how Tris and I feel when Ham here starts telling you what you can and can't do." She teased.

"Did you just call me a pig?" Hamish asked confusion on his face.

Both Ceana and Katie looked at him, surely he wasn't serious?

Then she chuckled at the mistake. "No she didn't. The thing is, at home we all have what we call a nickname. Nicknames are given to family members or friends that are close to us and you, MacDonnell, were just given one."

She jumped off the rock. It was time to go and find Kessan and find out once and for all what was going on. "Where did they all go?" She asked Hamish.

Hamish pointed her in the right direction. She thanked him and left him and Katie discussing, well she couldn't remember what they were discussing, her mind was on all the things she had to ask Kessan. Walking through the tents to the far edge of the camp, she made her way to the area that Hamish had pointed her to. Once there she noticed a large rock that reached up to her waist and the top of it was flat, all the men were standing around the rock looking down at something on top. It did not take long to find Kessan right in the centre of them all embroiled in a heated discussion with the older Laird and several other men.

She cleared her throat. They all turned and looked at her.

"Kessan," she ventured. "I think it's about time I find out what's going on, don't you?" She asked. She was not leaving here without the information. If she had to throw a tantrum in order to gain it, she would.

"Aye lass." He said quietly indicating to others that whatever they'd been discussing was over.

He signalled her to come to him and when she was close he picked her up, placed her on top of the rock, and then leaned back against it beside her legs. This was where they stayed for the next hour while he explained about that the war she had been reading about in her books was really happening and that she was the key to stopping it. It all came back to her then, the names that she had read in her studies and all the times that she knew something was off about them but could not put her finger on it. Was it real, could she really believe that she was in 12th century Scotland? She sat in silence for a while. It was a lot to take in. Finally, she asked the one question she had wanted answers to all her life.

"Ok so explain to me why my father sent me away, instead of trying to protect me?"

Kessan shook his head almost apologetically. "I wish I could lass but that is something ya going to have to discuss with ya Da."

She sat there for another minute and pondered what he had told her. She still wasn't sure she believed the whole thing. It was like an extended version of her dream. It was too surreal. Her mind kept trying to come up with a plausible explanation but at the moment nothing was even coming close. She needed time to think, to absorb everything that had just been revealed. Jumping down from the rock she asked Kessan to give her a moment. What she needed to do was find her sister. Katie was the only one that knew her for who she was, and right now she needed to talk her.

"Are ya alright lass?" He asked gently, concerned.

"I'm not quite sure yet" she answered truthfully, her voice still trembled despite her efforts to put on a brave face, but she was so full of emotion, she could not hide it in front of the Highlander. "I just need some time."

He nodded. "I will be around lass, when ya need me."

With that she walked away. She was almost back to her sister and Hamish when she noticed a path that looked as if it led to water. Hamish saw her and she gave him a nod to let him know that she would be fine. She truly did love this place and as she walked down a narrow path lined with trees and heather, her mind raced with everything that she had been told and the people she had met. She could not believe it and she had an older brother to boot.

She knew she was going to have to talk to her father at some point but right now, she needed to wrap her head around her life.

She could see the path opening up and once she reached the end it was like walking into heaven. She was again awestruck at the beauty of this place. She had thought the other glen was beautiful but it had nothing on this one. This one had a little lake, which was nestled in the middle of small cliffs covered in moss.

At the top of the cliffs, the trees appeared as if they were trying to reach the heavens. Off to her right were two tiny waterfalls that cascaded from small openings at the top of the cliff and they were running into the small pool at the bottom. The smell was heaven. It was so lush and fragrant from the purple heather that laced the outer edges of the pool that she relaxed instantly. She knew that, just like her waterfall at home, here was a place that she could work out all of her troubles. She inhaled deeply and closed her eyes, just listening to the cascading water. She was so lost in her thoughts that she didn't notice a figure coming up behind her and, before she knew what was happening, there was a knife at her throat.

CHAPTER 16

Her eyes flew open and she stiffened as a harsh female voice whispered furiously in her ear. "Ya little whore. How dare ye try and steal him from me. Ya should have stayed in whatever hole ya crawled out of." The blade felt cold against her skin and she fought to stay calm. Was she talking about Kessan?

"I'm sure if you let me go we can work something out." Ceana reasoned, trying to control the fear in her voice, the last thing she wanted her attacker to know was how scared she was.

"Well ain't ya a smart bitch, ya should be thankin' me." The voice mocked. She could feel the woman's hot breath against her neck and she shivered.

"Thanking you for what, holding a knife at my throat?" She asked, confused.

"Nay, thankin' me for saving ya from my brother because if he gets a hold of ya, ya gonna wish ya *were* dead." The woman hissed and the knife bit into her neck.

Ceana felt an evil presence creep up her spine, and she knew without a doubt that this woman was deranged. She reminded her of the soul sucking serpents from the demonic movies she watched. Her mind lost focus as she realised just how many horror movies she loved. She really should cut back. Her mind came back to the present as she felt something warm trickle down her skin. A panic rose in her as she realised she was bleeding. She had been too lost in herself to take Kessan's warnings seriously and now suddenly that danger had become all too real.

She forced herself to concentrate on her breathing. *Don't show fear,* she reminded herself. This woman was insane; and who the hell was her brother, what had she ever done to him? She had no idea what the woman was going on about, and right now, she didn't really care. When the woman had first put the knife to her throat, her first instinct had been to panic but many years of martial arts had taught her that, if you let fear rule you, the harder it is to stay focused and the better your chances are of losing. She knew that she had to keep this woman, whomever she was, talking until someone noticed she was missing or until she had the chance to kick her arse once the knife wasn't so uncomfortably close to her throat. This Scottish woman was about to get a taste of the 21st century. She braced herself, just waiting, hoping that the woman would make a mistake.

"But do no' worry about my brother, lass, I am going to kill ya myself. Kessan belongs to me." She cooed, bring her face closer to Ceana's. Her breath smelt terrible and so did she – the woman mustn't have had a wash for days. Ceana tried to control the urge to gag at the stench that was radiating from the woman, not wanting to bump the steel biting into her. *Focus.* She told herself.

"And how do you propose you are going to get away with that?" She tried to keep her talking. "It's not like you can just stroll out of here after you kill me. You're surrounded by highlanders!"

"Oh lass, I'll be long gone before they find ya body."

"They will still come after you." She said as icy fear gripped her heart, wishing desperately that she could somehow call out to the army of men she knew to be just metres away.

"Nay that is where ya wrong, I am going to make it look like an accident." The voice said with confidence as she suddenly gripped her tighter and forced her to walk with her, pulling her backward.

She snorted, "and how are you going to do that might I ask, it's not like I'm dumb enough to fall on a knife and slit my own throat now is it?"

"Has anyone ever told you that you have a smart mouth?" Her attacker asked. At any other time, Ceana would have laughed, she was told that quite often.

"I was thinkin' more of a drowning." The voice cackled in a harsh evil tone that sent chills through her body.

Drowning? Ok this was getting serious, in the corner of her eye she eyed the river of water behind her and felt a flicker of alarm, she hadn't thought of that. She had to act quickly. They were now right near the water's edge. She knew she had to do something and fast, the water was likely freezing and the shock would be enough to take her breath away. That would be all the time her attacker would need. If she managed to force her head under water, she would not have a hope in hell of calling for help. Her best bet was to get the woman mad enough to make a mistake.

She tried to keep her voice steady, "so, what now, you're going to kill me just because Kessan likes me better than you? Perhaps if you had taken a bath occasionally or were better looking he would not have gone looking for someone else." She knew that she had to make her angry enough to make a mistake, of course it could go the other way in which case she would be cutting her own throat, in a manner of speaking.

"Ya a smart mouthed bitch aren't ya? Well we will see how smart ya are when ya mouth is full of water." The foul woman mocked as she gripped Ceana's head.

She briefly closed her eyes, steeling herself for the battle that was to come. She was not going to die here like this! She had just found her father, her brother. She had her PhD to finish. She would be damned if she would let some crazy arse woman kill her because of a jealous rage.

"You know," Ceana said, "even if you do kill me, Kessan still won't come back to you. You obviously couldn't keep him happy in the first place! I can tell you now, I know how to make him happy. I've made him happy more than once."

The woman was now in such a rage that she could feel the grip on her hair start to loosen and the knife was no longer pressed so snuggly against her neck. It was now or never. Ceana kept prodding her, hoping to distract her more.

"So what is your name?" Ceana asked calmly, disarming her with a sudden change in topic.

"As if I would tell ya that." The assailant scoffed.

"Why? It's not like I'm going to live." She baited.

The assailant paused before answering her, "I suppose ya right. It's Freya." She sneered. "Now ya ken the name of the woman who is going to end ya worthless life. Not that it will do ya much good." She continued.

Ceana was surprised at how easily the information came. "Well I just wanted to know the name of the woman I'm going to kill!"

Ceana taunted, throwing her own words back at her. And with that, she used a move that her martial arts teacher had taught her. It was commonly used when a dirt bag tried to grab a woman from behind. She grabbed the hand holding the knife and twisted it to an angle that made Freya scream out in pain. Once she had dropped the knife, she flipped her over her shoulder until she was face first in the dirt with her arm twisted behind her. Placing her foot in the small of her back, she turned to call for Kessan, only to find him standing on the edge of the glen glaring at her.

"Well it's about time!" She retorted.

AFTER CEANA LEFT, Kessan went for a walk to check the boundaries. He needed to come up with a way to get his sister back. MacDonnell wanted to storm the castle and fight them all, but Kessan knew that Kendrick had become too powerful and they would lose more men and possibly get his sister killed. He would not allow that to happen, nay, he would do this alone. It didn't take him long to check on his men, so he headed back to camp. He started making his way back to the elders but changed his mind and headed over to where Katie and Hamish were. He wanted to make sure Ceana was Ok. He looked around the camp to see if he could find her. She was nowhere to be found.

"Where is Cee?" He asked curiously.

Both of them looked up at him at the same time.

"She went down there." Katie replied, pointing towards the glen.

"How long ago, lass?" He asked worried. Something didn't feel right.

"I would say about ten to fifteen minutes ago." She answered.

"Did anyone go with her?" He snapped, looking around the clearing to see if any of his men were missing.

He directed this question at Hamish. Even though the camp was safe, they still needed to take precautions. MacDonnell had told him that McKenzie had almost found the camp twice in the last two weeks.

"Come on Kessan, Ceana is a big girl," Katie scoffed at him. "She doesn't need an escort to follow...."

He did not wait for her to finish, he needed to see Ceana.

Despite the reassurances of the others, he couldn't shake the feeling that something was wrong. He took off in a run towards the glen. He was aware of footsteps behind him and he assumed Hamish had followed him but didn't stop to look. As they neared the clearing, he stopped and listened to see if there was any danger. He could hear two female voices, Cee's and, someone… familiar?

He signalled everyone else to be silent as they edged their way towards the clearing. He would never forget the sight that met him when he got to the edge of the clearing. Freya had a knife to Ceana's throat. Her other hand had a firm grip on her hair tilting her head back at a horribly awkward angle so that she could get a clean cut.

As he stood still assessing the situation, he realised that Ceana was antagonising Freya. He could hear her mocking the madwoman as she was dragged back towards the water. He balled his fists, that damn woman! Freya was going to pay for this. The sight of her threatening Ceana sent a rage through him like no other he had felt before. He was going to kill the bloody woman with his bare hands. Ceana was never going to be left alone again. The woman had no sense at all, didn't she know better than to antagonise the person who had a knife to her throat?

He could see the small line of blood running down her neck where the knife must have torn her skin and the rage inside him intensified. He clenched his fists tighter preparing for a fight. He had to go and help her before she was killed. Turning around he saw that Hamish, MacDonnell, Katie, Camden and a number of his men had followed his sudden dash for the glen. He signalled them to start spreading themselves out around the glen, he was hoping that, if he could draw Freya's attention away from Ceana and onto him, one of the men might be able to sneak up on her from behind and take her down. He was just getting ready to step out, when he felt a hand on his arm.

"Kessan you need to give her time. Trust me. She knows what she's doing." Katie said.

He looked down at Katie his mind working overtime trying to figure out what to do.

"You have to trust her Kessan. My sister has had some experience with situations like this." She pleaded.

Her comment brought back the day at the beach, when her ex had attacked her, and he realised that she was not as fragile as he first thought.

Looking down at her sister he nodded, "fine but she doesn't have long before I go in."

Katie nodded.

"Are ya mad, she is going to get herself killed." MacDonnell protested, his eyes never leaving his daughter.

Before Kessan could answer MacDonnell, Ceana suddenly moved, and his eyes widened as he watched Ceana disarm and disable Freya faster than he would have imagined possible. A wave of emotions hit him. Disbelief, relief and a little bit of pride rushed through him knowing that all the men had just witnessed Ceana's ability. Katie was the only one standing there with a smile from ear to ear, while the rest of them looked shocked. He wondered if this was how he looked the first time he had seen her do that.

"See. Told ya!" Katie said with satisfaction. Kessan entered the clearing and stood there waiting for Ceana to notice him. He was trying to calm his racing heart and his anger before he faced the two women. It didn't take her long to realise he was there, and the greeting she gave him was one he was not expecting, he thought she would be relieved when she saw help had arrived, but in true Cee spirit, she was mad.

She turned to him, and snapped, "well it's about time."

CEANA WAS PISSED. She had been through hell today and all she had wanted was some time to herself, and then this crazy bitch had come along. Now everyone was here, her sister had come running up to her, soon followed by Kessan and the rest of them. She had an audience.

"I told them that you could handle it. After all she is much smaller than the creep that attacked you." Katie boasted.

Kessan was standing behind Katie, his arms folded across his chest, his face showing no emotion, as usual, he looked as though he didn't have a worry in the world.

"Well, I guess that answers the question of whether ya can look after yaself." He said in a strangely calm tone.

He was angry all right, one thing she had learnt during their time together was that the calmer his voice and the more controlled his moves, the angrier he was. Well she had news for him! He may be angry but she was furious.

"I told you, I could but as usual you wouldn't listen!" She yelled at him. She was dimly aware of the others as they took up the same stance as Kessan, surrounding her in a circle. They were all glaring at her as if she had done something wrong. That was enough! she had had enough of the macho bullshit for one day.

"Oh come on, surely you have seen a 'lass' fight before." She said acerbically "I was *never* in danger. I had it under control the whole time." She said as she yanked Freya to her feet.

"Never in danger? Never in danger! Do ya ken who this person is?" Her father asked angrily, pointing to the woman who had just tried to kill her.

Who the hell did he think he was reprimanding her? She couldn't take it anymore, she didn't care how big or scary he was, it was time to for him to realise that he had no control over her or her life. She started shouting back at him with as much contempt in her voice as she could muster.

"As a matter of fact *Father*." She spat the word out as if it was a dirty word. "She was more than happy to fill me in on her sordid love affair with McKinnon over there. Oh and that she is the sister of the man who is going to make me die slowly. Have I forgotten anything?" She asked sarcastically

She had thrown the old man off-kilter; she wasn't sure if it was because she had shouted at him or if it was the fact she had called him father, even though it was said with such disdain. The man just stared at her, mouth agape before he cracked a smile and started to chuckle. Soon the others joined in. She certainly hadn't expected that reaction and even Hamish was looking at him as if he had lost his marbles.

"Oh, I pity McKenzie, he will never ken what hit him." Her father said after the laughter died down.

He strode out of the clearing and back towards camp chuckling all the while and leaving her to face Kessan, who hadn't taken his eyes off her the whole time. She could hear Freya trying to get his attention. "Kessan ya cannot be believing this whore, she is only trying to make me out to be the bad guy so that she can have ya all to herself. I only came here to warn ya about Kendrick and she attacked me. She's crazy I tell ya, she's obsessed with ye." She lied pathetically.

Ceana snorted. "Yeah right, nice try psycho. For all I care you can have him," she shot back, still angry and not sure whether she should be feeling humiliated at being laughed at, she didn't mean it of course. But, there was no way she was going to let either of them see how much she loved him. She was just about to give her more of a mouthful when Kessan finally spoke.

"Start explaining yaself lass." He demanded, she turned to face him, thinking that he was talking to Freya, but he was looking directly at her. He had to be kidding, he had better not be talking to her and yet, there he was still standing in front of them looking at her. He was angry, his expression was still blank, but the tone of his voice gave him away. Oh it was on.

"Me explain? How about you start explaining yourself buster! The only reason I was in the situation in the first place was because you are apparently so good in bed that it sends women around the bend." She fumed at him.

"Around the bend?" A confused voice came from behind them.

She turned around to face the man who had asked the question, she was not surprised to see it was Brodie, Kessan's main man.

"You know," she waved her hand dismissively, "crazy, cuckoo, two sandwiches short of a picnic..."

But he just looked at her before shaking his head, "You sure do have a weird way of saying things lass."

She turned back to Kessan. "So are there any other crazy ex-girlfriends in your past that I can expect to try and kill me anytime soon?" She fumed at him. Distracted by her annoyance with Kessan, Ceana did not realise that she had relaxed her hold on Freya and before she could stop her, Freya twisted out of her grip and broke free bolting into the forest, screaming vengeance on Ceana.

"Go," Kessan shouted at his men.

"Don't bother." She snapped angrily, "she will probably go back to her brother and tell her we are here. Besides, isn't that what we want? Wouldn't we be better off coming up with a plan of attack than following a woman who can't tell us anything we don't already know?"

She could see the tic starting in the side of his jaw. "Don't worry, if all goes well you will get to kill someone today, or tomorrow." She said as she walked past him and tapped him on the cheek. She continued past the men remaining in the glen towards the camp aware of the eyes on her, hearing some of the men snigger.

"Ya need someone with ya at all times when ya leave the camp from now on lass." Kessan cautioned.

"Yeah, yeah whatever." She replied without turning around.

§

WHAT WAS he going to do with her? Didn't she get the gravity of the situation they were in? He shook his head. To his annoyance, he could hear Caelan chuckling to himself, "She sure is a handful Kessan, are ye sure ye'r up for the challenge?" His brother grinned at him. Kessan glared back at him as he made his way back to camp, unwilling to let her out of his sight. It was time to come up with a plan. Freya was probably on her way back to Kendrick to let him know where they were. It wouldn't be long before their time was up. Time was also running out for his sister, he would have to go and get her before Kendrick attacked, otherwise she would be used as bait and nothing would stop Kendrick from killing her if he needed to. Kessan just hoped that he had not done it already and that he could get in the keep and save his sister before anyone at the camp knew he was gone, the last thing he needed was for anyone to find out what he had planned. His sister was his responsibility and he would be damned if he would leave her in the hands of that monster. But he didn't need anyone following him either, be damned if he was going to let anyone else get hurt. It was his duty to protect the clan and that was exactly what he would do

CHAPTER 17

Kendrick could not believe that the bastards had gotten away again. It was time to talk to Thora, perhaps the three days and nights without food in his dungeon will have softened her attitude towards helping him. He had tried everything and nothing seemed to be working, she would not tell him what her brother was planning.

"Tavis bring me the McKinnon lass." He seethed.

"Aye Kendrick."

The double doors opened and his sister entered, he was sitting in his chair in front of the hearth in the main hall. She walked down the steps into the room. She looked as though she had been in a fight. There was dirt on her face and her hair in disarray. "Freya, where have you been?" He snapped. He had no patience to deal with her dramatics today.

She looked at him, eyes sparkling with excitement. "I found them Kendrick, I found the camp. I almost killed the little bitch, but the men came and helped before I could. I'm lucky that I got out of there alive, but I still found them and I could take ya back." She replied breathlessly, her voice eager.

He narrowed his eyes, the stupid, lovesick woman had almost ruined his plan, "Did ya tell the lass who ya were?" He whispered dangerously. He watched as she took a step back.

Freya hesitated, "aye, but I dinna mean to, she tricked it out of me!"

Kendrick was furious, "How could ya, do ya ken what ya have

done?" He screamed. She trembled, clearly not getting the response she'd been hoping for. She was afraid, he could see it, but he did not care. He could feel the dark magic rising up inside. Its tentacles were wrapping around him and the voices were whispering, urging him to kill her. The rage that ripped through his body was uncontrollable.

"You stupid woman! How am I going to get to the lass now? They will never leave her alone again." He hissed in a low scornful voice as he walked slowly towards her.

"I'm sorry Kendrick, I didn't think, I was only trying to help." She pleaded. She was still backing up, she had placed her hand out in front of her as if trying to stop his advance.

He glared at his wretched sister, "Nay you were only worried about helping yourself. Now I will have to kill them all, Kessan included." He said, dismissively.

Freya lunged at him, grabbing him by his collar, screaming, "Ya promised he would no' be harmed. How could ya lie?"

He gripped her arm and held her back, "he chose his destiny, he could have had it all, power and fear. But he chose death instead." He said with finality.

Freya shook him and started pounding his chest. "You, you MONSTER!" She wailed and the darkness in Kendrick snapped. He swung around, grabbed her by the neck and lifted her high off her feet.

"Ya dare to insult me!" He roared, "I have given ye everything and this is how ye repay me?" He could hear her gasping for breath and she was trying to say something. He pulled her close so that he could hear her.

"Please Kendrick," she croaked, "I am sorry. I beg your forgiveness, please." Her frightened eyes bore into his, eyes that used to hold compassion, but were now nothing but cold slits.

He could have easily let her go but instead, he decided it was time to show them what he was capable of.

"Begging does not suit ya sister. Think of this as your last act of loyalty towards your brother." It was said with such coldness. There was no humanity left in him, all he could feel was power and he loved it.

Her eyes widened with realisation and she shook her head vigorously, tears streaming down her face. He took a moment's pause, he should have felt some remorse for what he was about to do, but there was nothing inside him anymore, nothing but darkness.

He began to squeeze and Freya's eyes bulged. Then, suddenly, he twisted his hand slightly to the left and, like a twig, her neck snapped. He looked at the limp body hanging in his hands. The power inside of him surged to life. He never felt more powerful or alive than he did at this moment. He could only imagine what it was going to feel like when he killed McKinnon's whore. He threw his sister's lifeless body to the ground stepped over it and made his way back to his chair, signalling for one of his men to take the body away.

"What do ya want me to do with it?" Davey asked eyeing the corpse with a renewed sense of fear for his Laird.

"Burn it for all I care, just get rid of her." He said disdainfully.

The man grabbed his dead sister's body by the hair and dragged her out of the castle. It was time to talk to the McKinnon lass.

THORA WAS PETRIFIED. She had been stuck in the dungeon for days now with no food or water. The hunger didn't bother her too much. It was the waiting that terrified her. The dungeon was not a nice place to be, it was dark and the only light that came into the cell at all came weakly from the torches mounted on the wall further down the hall. It didn't help, she spent most of the time lying on her cot, if you could call it that. She flinched as she heard another rat scurry across the floor underneath her. The smell of putrid blood and unemptied chamber pots reached her nose. It had taken her weeks to get a handle on the smell, but not before she lost weight, she had continually thrown up every time the stench reached her nose.

She could hear the groans of the injured men around her and it killed her that she couldn't do anything to help them. She had tried talking to them in the first week, but she had learnt quickly that it only gave McKenzie another avenue to torture her. He had caught her talking to the man diagonally from her the second night here and he had him nearly beaten to death right outside her cell. He had then warned her that if she tried talking to anyone other than him he would kill the next one and his death would be on her hands. Over the weeks many had tried to talk to her, but had given up when she hadn't replied. She would not be responsible for another man's death. Until McKenzie had what he wanted she would remain alone in her misery. McKenzie wanted information from her, information that she didn't have. She could see that his patience was wearing thin. He had stormed the castle looking for Kessan and demanding to know where he had gone. As far as she knew he had been in the field with his men practicing.

"Stop lying!" He had shouted at her. She could not figure out why he was so angry with Kessan. She had originally thought it was because he had sent Freya home. She knew better now though. He had then captured her and exiled the rest of the castle, she had watched on in horror as some of her clans-people were murdered right in front of her eyes as a message for Kessan. Kendrick had taken her back to his castle and thrown her in the dungeon.

"Why are you doing this?" She had asked.

"Because your dear brother has betrayed me and, and when he comes to rescue ya, I plan to kill him for it." He said with an unnatural amount of pleasure.

"Kessan would never walk willingly into a trap." She said as calmly as she could manage, praying that she was right.

"I wouldn't count on that if I were you, dear Thora." He had mocked, before slamming the door shut.

Not knowing what was happening was worse than torture and Thora felt sick to her stomach at what could be happening to people she loved. If only she knew what was happening behind that door. She prayed that Kessan would realise what he was up against and stay away but she knew that was not going to happen. Kessan would never leave her here. From what she could make out, it sounded like Kessan had chosen a side in the war and Kendrick wasn't happy. Thank God he had not been swayed to Kendrick's side! It was time that they all stood up and defeated this madman.

She knew that it would have been a hard decision for Kessan, he and Kendrick had grown up together and their history was long and Kessan had vowed to stay out of it. But, from what she had seen, any evidence of the old Kendrick was gone, instead, what lay in his place was cold, dark and terrifying. She didn't want to die here, she still had so much to do with her life. She had not shared her dreams with anybody but she wanted to travel, she wanted to see lands beyond her home and she wanted adventure. Now the chance for that was slowly slipping away. She would not give up without a fight!

She heard someone coming down the stairs that led to her cell, she was terrified but she knew that they would get pleasure from her fear, and she would not give them that. She stood up, defiantly.

"Come on lass, time to go." A voice said, a little softer and less cruel than Kendrick's but still with a hint of menace.

It was Tavis. Earlier in the week she had tried to appeal to his good side; they had known each other since they were kids, but he had crossed over to Kendrick's influence, drawn to the idea of the power and riches that Kendrick had promised him. He unlocked her cell and she followed him through the castle. Castle Eilean Donan was on the Loch Duich and the only way in was over a bridge. It was surrounded by water so there was no way out. Unlike her home on the Isle of Sky, Kendrick's castle no longer had any warmth about it. She remembered coming here as a kid, when Kendrick's mother was alive. This place used to be so full of love and laughter and the walls appeared to glow with warmth that made anyone who came here feel like they were at home. How different it was now; it was cold and dark, even the servants scurried about fearfully, always seeming afraid of something. Aye, the boy she knew growing up no longer existed and what stood in his place was controlled by pure darkness.

She could hear raised voices as they came to the hall. They had just rounded the last corner that would bring them into the hall when Tavis stopped suddenly, gripping her arm so that she could not run. Freya was with Kendrick and they were arguing about Kessan, she listened intently, waiting to find out if he was still alive, but she could not quite make out anything clearly enough from where they were standing. She leaned closer to the door trying to make them out, she could see them now as well as hear them, and in a split second she regretted her decision. She watched in horror as Kendrick killed his own sister, he just picked her up and snapped her neck, but what he did after made her sick to her stomach. He just tossed her away as if she was nothing more than a bag of rotten food.

Fear returned to her stronger than before, her legs were shaking so badly that she wasn't sure she would be able to stand in front of him. If he could do that to his own sister, she didn't stand a hope in hell. She wanted to run, but her feet wouldn't move, she just stood there helplessly as one of Kendrick's men dragged Freya's limp body out of the castle, right past her and Tavis. She covered her mouth with her free hand as she gagged, Freya's eyes stared up to heaven, lifeless, the tears she had been crying still fresh on her cheeks. Was this how she was going to spend her last moments, praying for someone to come and save her? She took a step back and tried to reef her arm free, but Tavis was stronger and he dragged her down the steps into the room. Kendrick turned to face her with eyes that were empty and she truly believed that his soul was just as void. Aye, there was no humanity left in him now.

"Start talking, Thora, my patience is wearing thin." Kendrick said, bringing her out of her musing, his eyes were so cold.

Thora had never felt so afraid, he was looking at her with such intensity and such hatred that she knew if she said the wrong thing she would certainly meet her death.

"I'm sorry Kendrick but I really do not ken where my brother and the lass are. I told you…"

Before Thora could finish, Kendrick let out a roar that was so loud and unhuman her words became stuck in her throat. He strode right up to her, placing his face so close that she could feel his hot breath against her cheek. He stared at her silently for about a minute, before he backhanded her so hard across the face that it knocked her off her feet. Her head hit the ground with such force that the world around her lurched and swam in her vision. Her eyes could not focus and tears sprung to them. She blinked rapidly trying to clear the fuzziness, she tried to stand, but before she could, he was upon her. He grabbed a fistful of her hair and reefed her up so quickly and violently she had to hold back a scream. She would die before she showed this bastard how much he was hurting her. She was after all a McKinnon.

"Start talking lass," his menacing voice demanded again, "or is it that, perhaps you *want* to die?"

Thora tried to clear her throat. All she wanted to do was kick, bite and punch this man but from the account she witnessed between him and his sister, she knew that angering him any more would only result in ensuring her a quick death. She only hoped that he still had use for her, long enough for her to escape or be rescued.

"I'm sorry," she choked out. "I cannot give ya the answers I doona have!"

This was it, the moment of truth, she was either going to die or he was going to let her go, she said her final prayers and waited for him to decide which it was going to be.

Kendrick glared at her, "Get this wench out of my sight 'afore I kill her!" He screamed at his men before turning back to her, an evil, terrible smile on his face.

"She might not be able to tell me anything, but it doesn't matter. Kessan will come to get her and he can watch me kill her right in front of him." He mocked and his dark eyes glittered with eager amusement.

He laughed and Thora's blood ran cold. He released her hair and tossed her roughly before Tavis' feet. Tavis grabbed her, yanking her up by her arm practically dragging her back to her cell. She struggled feebly but it was no use, there was no way she was getting out of his grip. Hearing Kendrick's last comment echo through her mind sent shivers up her spine. She had to escape and find her brother before he found her. Kendrick was right, she knew Kessan would come for her, and if he did, he would seal both their fates.

CHAPTER 18

She was at her wits end, *again*! Kessan was nowhere to be found, no one had seen him in a day and a half, his men knew where he was but nobody was bloody talking! To top it off, Duncan, Brodie and Caelan were avoiding her. They really must think she was stupid. How could she not know something was up? Kessan had not left her side since Freya's attack and now, all of a sudden, he was nowhere to be found, and come to think of it neither was Camden or William. She had not seen the two young warriors, who were usually not far from camp, in at least a day. In fact, they had disappeared around the same time as Kessan. It was time to try another tactic. She had to be crafty if she wanted to get answers.

She knew exactly who to ask. There was one person here that would know exactly what was going on, Caelan. She knew that there was no way he would tell her openly and she would bet her bottom dollar that Kessan had left strict instructions with him not to. She would have to be as underhanded as they were, and that was where her dear little sister came into play. Katie was down at the glen cleaning up. She started down there and as she expected, one of the men started following. Kessan's orders again she assumed. It didn't really bother her because she knew they would give her a modicum of privacy down there. These Highlanders were in for a rude shock. She was no simpering Miss. This little black duck wasn't going to sit around and wait for Kessan to be killed. She found her sister lying beside the pools staring up at the blue sky.

"Bata I need to talk to you." She said seriously.

Katie sat up with a jolt, her hand to her heart. Any other time she would have found it amusing. It wasn't often that she could scare her sister. But right now, she didn't particularly find anything funny.

"Damn it Cee you frightened me. What are you doing sneaking up on a person like that?"

She looked at her sister incredulously.

"You're one to talk. Only yesterday you scared the bejesus out of me. I was just returning the favour." She said, "Besides I was not sneaking, Duncan heard me coming a mile away." She pointed out, nodding at the warrior standing some distance back.

Her sister looked towards the warrior for confirmation and when he nodded, she poked her tongue at him and turned back to her.

"Sorry I was just a million miles away. What's up?"

"If you wouldn't mind Duncan, can we have a bit of privacy?" She asked.

"Aye lass, but I will no' be far. Just yell if ya need me." He responded with a respectful nod.

She nodded her thanks and watched him leave. Once she was sure he was out of earshot she turned back to her sister.

"I need your help, none of these louts will tell me where Kessan is and I have a serious feeling that he is in trouble. We both know that there is only one person here who Kessan would have trusted with the information, but he will not talk to me. I'm sure if you asked nicely…" She said, leaving the rest of the sentence unfinished. Katie understood, and frowned.

"What makes you so sure?" Bata asked.

"I'm not, but you have to try. Go and bat your eyelashes at him and give him your puppy dog eyes, or something. I'm sure you can find some way to pry the information out of him. Please Bata, I'm desperate. What if something has happened to him?" She begged.

Her sister thought it over for a minute.

"Come on Bata you owe me." She tried a plea.

Finally, her sister looked at her and nodded.

"Ok I will give it a go, but I'm not promising anything. And if we do find something out you have to promise me that you will not go off half-cocked!"

"Deal." She said quickly. She reached over and gave her sister a hug, and she found herself thankful, once more, that Katie was here. She talked to her sister a little longer, before she headed back to camp. Maybe this might just work. She just hoped Bata found out where he went before it was too late.

A short while later, she saw Katie pull Caelan just off towards the side of the camp where they could talk in private. She could still see them from where she was standing. Ceana knew she should turn her back or walk away but she was too anxious. She knew her sister would be furious for spying on her but she couldn't help it. She watched as Katie worked her magic but she could tell by the look on Caelan's face that he wasn't happy with whatever she was saying. Man, she really could make a man squirm. It was times like this that she was reminded again how much her little sister had grown up. She was so focused on her sister and Caelan that she didn't hear Hamish come up beside her.

"Lass, do ya mind if I sit down with ya?" He asked, almost shyly.

Ceana gave a start; she looked up at him and nodded. She noticed that he was still a little uneasy around her, and yet he was fine around Katie. She couldn't blame him though. It wasn't like she had been overly nice to him. In fact, she had been nothing but a bitch. It was just too much, this man was her older brother, by blood no less and yet she knew nothing about him. That was not his fault and it wasn't like she had tried to get know him. She guessed now was as good a time as any. It couldn't have been any easier for him either, she relented.

As he sat down, she realised that she really did want to get to know him. She wanted to know if they were alike in any way. Even though she was close to Katie and Tristan they never really shared any traits.

"Hamish do you not have a family of your own?" She asked, wondering about him for the first time.

She could tell she had taken him by surprise with her question, but he still answered it.

"Nay lass I am still on my own. I have no' met the right lass yet." He said hesitantly.

She turned her head and really looked at him. For the first time she noticed how handsome he was.

"So why are ya sitting here all alone lass?" He questioned her.

"I am just sitting here thinking and waiting for Bata." She told him.

"Bata?" He asked quizzically. She was starting to get used to the people staring at her as though she had lost her mind. She smiled at him and explained about the nicknames that they had for each other.

"And apparently Bata has given you the nickname of Ham." She informed him.

She saw him smile to himself.

"I have gotten to ken ya sister over the last couple of days and I am glad that ya have had a wonderful family to love ya over the years." He said. "When ya went forward and were lost to time, it was one thing that we prayed for."

She noted that there was a slight wistfulness to his voice and it occurred to her that while she had had her siblings, he had only their father and their lives hadn't exactly been peaceful.

"I'm sorry that I haven't really talked to you much or gotten to know you. I know it's not your fault that I was sent away. But I want you to know that I am really glad that I have another brother, one who is older than me. It's just that this is all new to me and it will take me a little time to adjust, but I promise that by the end of it you will be sick of having a nagging little sister." She said giving him a teasing smile. It was then that she realised she really meant what she had said. She really did want the same relationship with him that she had with Katie and Tristan.

He smiled back at her. She was just about to ask him a few more questions when she noticed Katie and Caelan walking towards them. Caelan did not look happy, and his next question confirmed it.

"How do ya ken Kessan is in danger?" He snapped, his expression a mix of worry, uncertainty and anger. It was the first time she had ever seen him angry. He usually spoke in a calm tone, much like Katie, but looking at him now she was left with no doubt that he was every bit a Highlander as the men surrounding them.

"I cannot explain it. I have always just known things like this and usually my gut feeling is right. Look, I just know that whatever it is he thinks he is doing, he cannot do it alone, he is going to get himself killed. We have to help him, Caelan." She pleaded.

He stood there staring at her. He was clearly torn between telling her and keeping his promise to his brother but, in the end, his concern for his brother won.

"He has gone to McKenzie's keep to rescue Thora." He whispered.

She was dumbfounded. Out of all the scenarios that he could

have come up with, she was not expecting that one. But she should have, she knew how much Thora meant to her brothers, and of course he would see it as his duty to help her. She did not think that any of them would be stupid enough to try and rescue her from the keep, especially with only two men as back up.

"Man you Highlanders really do think you are invincible, don't you?" She fumed. "Are you all raised thinking that you cannot die? God save me from Highlanders and their ridiculous notions!" She raged as she stood up. She stormed off cursing men and their stupidity. She was determined to find the man herself and give him what for. He couldn't just take off and get himself killed without sparing a thought for the people who loved him. Granted she hadn't told him she loved him yet, but still. He could have at least considered her when he made the decision. She stormed right past her father and all his men and she was just about to head out into the forest when someone stopped her.

"Lass ya cannot go out there by yourself looking for him, especially not on foot, ya will not last long." She wasn't sure who had stopped her.

Ceana turned around to face her brother and saw that Caelan, Brodie, Camden and her father were all standing there looking at her. She shot Caelan a look that was heated, she could have fried him on the spot.

"Well I guess you had better hurry up or just point me in the right direction. Either way with or without you, I am going to find him!"

"I'll go with ya lass." Her father said as he stepped forward. It surprised her. She thought he'd be the last one to help. She was expecting him to order her to stay in the camp.

"We can only take a few men though; we still have to leave some behind to guard the camp." He cautioned.

She nodded letting him know that she was grateful for any help.

"Hamish, Caelan and Duncan get ready to ride out." He ordered.

No one questioned his authority. They all just did as he asked. Within five minutes they were mounted up and leaving the camp. She was sitting in front of Hamish and she willed them to hurry, she had a sinking feeling that they were already too late to stop him.

❧❦❧

KESSAN GAVE the signal for his men to stop, they had been riding hard for three days and finally they could see the castle in the distance. Kessan had come up with a way of getting in without being detected. For any other person, it would have been near impossible, however growing up with Kendrick, Kessan knew all the secret ways of getting in and out of the holding. Often as boys they would run through the tunnels that led from various parts of the castle to the hills they were in now. The tunnels had been built under the water surrounding the castle as way out in the event of an attack. He was just hoping that Kendrick had forgotten about them. There were four in total, one led to the kitchens, another to the hall, the third went to the master bedroom and the last, which was the one he wanted, ran right into the dungeons – built to smuggle prisoners in and out unseen. Each of them led to different points in the surrounding area. This plan had to work.

Kessan could see Kendrick's men up on the barracks, waiting for anyone to approach the castle. Hopefully this was where his sister was being kept. He would not be given a second chance to find her if she wasn't here. He gave the signal to go forward. It was time. If they stayed out here any longer, the better chance they had of being discovered. Kessan led his men a mile back down the trail away from where they had tethered the horses. There, in the thicket half-hidden by overgrown shrubbery, was the entrance that would lead to the dungeon. He instinctively knew it was the right entrance, the old abandoned dungeons had been their favourite place to play as children and it looked neglected and forgotten.

Entering the cold damp tunnel, they walked another mile in the dark passageway, it looked like his luck was holding out. No torches lit the path, it was full of cobwebs and stank of the rotten flesh of long-dead animals. It seemed as though they had not been used for many years. In his thirst for power, Kendrick had clearly forgotten about the tunnels – but still they had to be cautious. They continued deeper into the tunnel as rats scurried past them, twittering and splashing in the darkness. They let their eyes adjust and went by feel, too afraid to light a torch without knowing whether someone *was* down here.

They finally reached the secret door that would open into the dungeon. It was made of stone of course, hidden so well it looked like part of the wall. Kessan used most of his strength to open it, it hadn't been opened in years. Peering into the dimly lit corridor he was sickened. The sounds that greeted him filled his stomach with a gnawing fear as they spoke of unspeakable things. All around him, the prisoners moaned in pain, chains rattled, and rats skittered; and the stench here had grown much stronger than that that had followed them in the tunnel.

He turned to his men, "Camden, ye come with me and help me search for Thora, William ye can wait here, when we have found her we will give the signal and then once we have her out, we will start releasing the others, aye?"

"Aye!" They repeated.

He and Camden split off, going in opposite directions searching each cell as they went. He couldn't believe what he was seeing. The men and women down here had been tortured, some within an inch of their lives. The dungeon was built in such a way it made it difficult to talk to the other prisoners without being heard. It was designed in a circular style where all the cells were placed in every second space on the inside and the first space on the outer part so no two cells were facing each other. In addition, there was a tunnel that led out from the main stairwell which contained more cells with the same spacing design. It was a brilliant idea for keeping prisoners unaware of what was going on, however, with over fifty cells to check it made it hard to find one prisoner, especially when they were all full. Some even held more than one occupant. There were too many to save now, they would have to come back for them. Many of them would not be able to walk on their own.

He kept checking as he suppressed his growing rage. He hated leaving anyone behind but it had to be done. The smell of dried blood and the stench of rotting flesh burnt the hairs on his nose. He was praying that none of these poor wretches were his sister and a renewed sense of hatred for what his old friend had become surfaced inside him. He had reached the last cell on his side without any sign of her when the low signal came from the other side. Someone had found something! He abandoned his search and moved over to where Camden was standing, staring with a shocked expression at the cell in front of him. He had found her. She was here. Bracing himself, hoping against all hope that she was okay, he leaned against the bars and looked into the dimly lit cell, where he saw his

sister huddled on a makeshift cot on the floor. Dirty, thin and ragged, Thora was staring up at them with such fear in her eyes that it broke his heart.

THORA WAS LAYING on her bed staring at the ceiling of the old dungeon. It was not like anyone could sleep in a place like this; the moans and smell of the other prisoners assaulting both ears and nose with no refuge. She curled up tighter, her stomach cramping from not having had any decent food for days, but it was nothing to the pain that

was radiating through her skull. How were they going to defeat him now? She knew that Kessan and the MacDonnell Laird had faith in this lass, but she wasn't so sure anymore. Kendrick's powers had grown stronger.

What could the lass do that seasoned warriors couldn't?

The magic within him was too great.

She believed the best thing for everyone to do was to try and leave the Highlands as soon as they could, there was no hope of escaping the determined monster that Kendrick had become. But she knew it was wishful thinking, most of the Highlanders would die trying to save their homes, evident in the cells around her. She started to cry softly. She couldn't help it, she had tried to stay strong but, laying here in her own little hell, it seemed hopeless.

Just then there was a slight noise from outside of her cell. Instantly alarmed that she hadn't heard her tormentors approach, she looked up in horror as she saw the outline of two men standing there. The pathetically weak light was behind them and she couldn't see their faces. She shrank back in fear. What were they going to do to her now? If only there was a way for her to escape. She would not make it easy for them, they would have to come in and drag her off the bed, they were going to kill her anyway so what did it matter if she fought? She would show them that nothing could breakdown the pride of a McKinnon. She waited, preparing herself for the onslaught to come, but the men just stood there. It had felt like time stood still, but she knew it had only been seconds. What were they waiting for? Then a voice came out of the darkness; a voice that made her both happy and terrified at the same time.

"Thora lass, can ya hear me? How bad are ya hurt? Come on

lass talk to me!" Kessan's familiar voice whispered urgently, heavy with emotion.

Thora stood up as quickly as her weary, shaky body allowed and went to the bars. The movement made her head spin but she didn't care, Kessan had really come for her!

"Kessan, what are ya doing here?" She cried, hope and fear pulsing through her. "Ya must go. Kendrick is out of his mind and the magic has taken over him. He is no' the Kendrick we knew!" She paused for a minute to gather herself. Even though Freya was a nasty woman, no one deserved to die the way she had and she knew that at one-time Kessan had felt something for her.

"Freya is dead, Kessan. He killed her, snapped her neck, I saw the whole thing." She whimpered. She could see still see the way Freya's empty dead eyes had looked into her as her body had been dragged past her. Overwhelmed with fear, shock, hunger and relief at seeing a comforting face, she burst into tears, she couldn't stop them. She could hear Camden working on the locks and the minute the door swung open, she collapsed into Kessan's arms and sobbed. He held her tightly, letting her release the terror of the last few days.

She heard him give his men orders to go and check that they were still alone. She was thankful that he was not stupid enough to come on his own. They had to get out of here now before they were discovered. If they were caught, they were in a world of trouble.

"Kessan, we have to go, we have to leave now. Kendrick will kill ya if he finds ya here." She said urgently, looking up at him, trying to get him to understand.

"It will be alright lass; we will be out of here afore he kens you're even gone." He reassured her as they turned to leave.

"Ya really should have listened to ya sister McKinnon!" A harsh voice rang out. Her eyes widened and, clutching on to her brother's arm, she bit back a scream of frustration and despair. They had been so close.

CHAPTER 19

He felt his sister go stiff in his arms as she tightened her grip and a terrified shudder ran through her body. He bent to whisper into her ear.

"Stay behind me and get ready to move."

He pushed her behind him as he turned around to face his enemy. He folded his arms across his chest, giving the appearance that he was calm. Keeping his voice strong to hide the rising panic building inside him, he faced his enemy. "Ah Kendrick, what brings ye down here to the lower levels? Did ya come to torture some more people? Or did ya come to help me escape?"

"Aren't we the funny man today. Hand over ya sister and ya sword Kessan!" He hissed.

Kessan stood his ground. He could hear Thora whimpering behind him and he could only imagine what she'd been through. Was he crazy, did he really think he was going to fold that easily?

"Nay." He said loudly, firmly, watching his men behind Kendrick.

But before he knew what was happening to shout out a warning, Kendrick turned around and drove his sword into the silently approaching Camden's chest.

"No!" He choked out before he could stop himself. How had Kendrick known he was there? He had been so quiet. He stared open mouthed in horror as the loyal young warrior fell to his knees, blood already pooling at the side of his mouth.

"I'm sorry, Laird." Camden whispered before he fell forward, collapsing on the ground.

Pure rage washed over him and he moved to rush at the bastard, preparing to strike him down where he stood, when his sister's hand grabbed his arm. He seethed and it took all he had, but he stopped and looked down at Thora.

"Nay, Kessan that is exactly what he wants ya to do." She reasoned, pleading with him.

She was right. They were dealing with a madman. A madman with dark magic at his beck and call. He had to calm himself, he couldn't think clearly with anger clouding his judgement. That's what Kendrick wanted.

"I see that killing a man has become easier for ya to do." He said icily, as he glared at the man who was his former friend.

A sound erupted from the man in front of him, a sound that was so dark and evil that in that minute Kessan knew Thora was right. The Kendrick he had grown up with was gone. For the first time since entering the castle, he was truly afraid.

Kendrick scoffed, "Ya really have gone soft. This is war and men die in wars all the time, ya should know that by now, only the strongest warriors will survive."

Kessan shook his head. "This is not a war, Kendrick, it is one man trying to control everyone else, ya are no better than the Sassenachs who try the same thing." Kendrick fumed. One thing hadn't changed – his pride.

"Come on, how about you take on a real man and see how well ya fare." He taunted.

Before he knew what was happening Kendrick was behind him. With unnaturally rapid movements, Kendrick grabbed Thora before he could protect her. The man moved faster than was humanly possible.

Kendrick sneered an evil, twisted grin as he held Thora in his clutches, "Now let's try this again shall we, pass over ya sword Kessan or I will slit her throat!"

Now the dungeon's one source of light was shining on Thora and he was finally able to get a good look at her, the entire left side of her face was a deep purple colour. Her lip was split and there was a deep gash just below her hairline, along with a gash above her left eye. It took every ounce of control he had to stop himself going after the bastard. There was no doubt in his mind now that Thora would die if he made any kind of move to disarm him.

Not seeing any other option that wouldn't result in their deaths anyway, Kessan pulled out his sword and reluctantly acquiesced his stance, buying them time. His only hope now was that William had gotten out alive.

"Tavis, Niall." Kendrick barked and grinned triumphantly at Kessan.

Kessan could only stare in horror as two of McKenzie's men dragged William around the corner bloodied and beaten. It had gone from bad to worse and he had few options remaining. Regretting that he hadn't organised an army he recognised that he had drastically underestimated his old friend's capability. His stubbornness was about to get them all killed. He had to do something; he couldn't stand by and watch another of his men die in front of him, because of him. Kessan placed his sword on the ground, stepped back and waited.

"You win, here is my sword. There is no need to kill another man. Ya have what ya want." He said, kicking his sword towards Kendrick. Thora shouted at him to pick it up. Kendrick ripped her head back so violently Kessan heard it crack. Holding his breath, he waited to see if he had snapped her neck. He exhaled the minute he heard her whimper.

"Ya have what ya want Kendrick, ya can let the two of them go, I will no' fight ya!" He pleaded quietly.

Kendrick's men dragged William back out and he had no idea what they were going to do but to ask would be sealing his death.

"What about Thora?" he asked, realising that if he didn't get her out now she would most likely die.

"Come on McKinnon, ya don't really think I would let the only leverage I have go now do ya?"

More men had come down to the dungeon, standing around Kendrick, waiting for his orders. Kessan felt beaten, how could he have been so stupid? He should have waited and not gone off without more planning. He hadn't realised just how bad Kendrick had gotten and now he had not only put himself and his sister in danger, but he had also endangered the people that would come and save him. He only hoped that Caelan had not told Ceana about his plan.

Arms gripped him tightly as McKenzie's men dragged him back

into Thora's cell. He half-hoped that they would simply throw them in there and leave them to starve. But Kendrick was smart, he knew not to underestimate Kessan's strength as Kessan had underestimated his own and he was not taking any chances with him.

Kendrick's men pushed him roughly against the stone wall and shackled him by his wrists just far enough above his head so that there was no chance of being comfortable or of escaping. He remained silent, thanking the gods for a small mercy as his sister was brought into the cell with him. Kendrick strode up to him so that they were almost nose to nose – cockier now that Kessan was in his grasp.

"Let me give you a little taste of what will happen if ya try to escape again." Kendrick whispered coldly.

He then turned around and hit Thora so hard against the side of her head that it flung her across the room. Kessan heard her head hit the hard, stone ground with a sickening thud. She didn't move. She just lay there on the floor bleeding and unconscious.

Kessan let out a scream of rage and tried to break the shackles but they would not budge.

"Ya bastard, you will pay for that!" He roared. He looked helplessly over at his unconscious sister, praying that she was not dead.

"You had better kill me now Kendrick, because if you let me live I will make you sorry you ever touched her!" He spat.

Kendrick smiled at him, "Och McKinnon, I doona plan to kill ya, no I have bigger plans in store for ya. Ya see, I plan to use ya to lure that bitch out. I ken she is the only one who can destroy me."

Kessan's blood ran cold, so that was what the bastard had planned. First, he'd used Thora as bait for him and now he was using him to lure Ceana here, playing their weaknesses against them. He was once again thankful that pigheaded Ceana didn't ken what he'd been up to.

"You're out of luck Kendrick. She doesn't even ken where I am." He said, defiantly.

"She mightn't, but I'm sure little brother does, and when ya doona come back, he will come looking for ya. When he does she will be with him, and ye are going to watch her die slowly afore I kill ya. Once you two are gone there will be no one powerful enough to stop me." He laughed.

Kessan slumped in his shackles, God he hoped he was wrong. Caelan had better keep Ceana away from here. But he knew that it was unlikely. Kendrick was right. As soon as they'd realised he'd been gone too long, he knew that they would come for him, just as he would do for them. He only hoped that they were smarter than he had been and brought an army with them. He had sorely underestimated the power that had a hold of his old childhood friend. Old man MacDonnell had better be right about Ceana being able to defeat him, because if she couldn't kill Kendrick, MacDonnell had just killed his own daughter.

"Now, let's see if we can't make ya life a living hell while we wait." Kendrick hissed in pleasure. Kessan saw a flicker of darkness cross over Kendrick eyes, a darkness that clearly was not human and it truly terrified him. Kessan was sure that what or who stood in front of him was no longer human. He just prayed that they all got out of this alive. He hung there in silence, waiting with rising trepidation as Kendrick stuck his dirk into the flame of his torch. As he turned around and walked over to him, he saw dark shadows pass over them once more. "What are ya?" Kessan whispered.

"Ya worst nightmare." Kendrick whispered back, as he slowly pushed the hot blade of the dirk deeply into Kessan's side. It seared through his flesh and his body trembled; it was all he could do not to scream as immense pain radiated up through his entire body. But Kessan made no sound. Kendrick then pulled the knife out just as slowly, twisting it inch by inch as it moved within his skin, warm blood following its trail. Kessan tried to block it out, tried to focus on anything else but the pain, he would not give Kendrick the satisfaction of seeing him beaten, so summoning as much of his warrior training as he could, he prepared himself.

Kendrick merely grinned, "I see it's gonna take a lot more before you break. But break ya will and I will hear ye scream for mercy before the night is through."

His reply came out short and sharp, "That will never happen." He vowed, in between rapid breaths.

"We will see about that." He promised as he stuck the knife into his other side, repeating the process. As his body shook, Kessan realised that if any man could break him, it was the one standing in front of him. Any ounce of humanity had been completely wiped away and he knew that he was going to endure a lot more before help arrived, if it ever did. He needed to remain strong

CEANA WAS BEYOND FRUSTRATED. They had been waiting in the forest not far from the castle for over an hour now. They had been a day and half behind Kessan so they knew they had to hurry and the urgency only increased when they had found William about two miles down the track. That was as far as he had made it before he collapsed. He was in bad shape. The only thing that he had been able to tell them when he came to was that Camden was dead and McKenzie had captured Kessan. That lunatic had Kessan and Thora and God knows what was happening to them, and here they were just sitting out in the woods cooling their heels!

She'd had enough of waiting. It was time to take action. She stood up. "We have to do something." She said to MacDonnell. "What is Caelan waiting for?" She didn't understand how he could be so patient knowing that both his brother and sister were in there.

"Come on lass ya have to be patient, he is trying to find a way into the castle without being seen." MacDonnell reasoned.

She snorted, "Yeah like that's going to happen. This whole area is wide open. We may as well just stand up and wave."

Her father gave her that now familiar look again, the one that wondered if she had lost her mind, and perhaps she had. She knew better than anyone that getting themselves captured would not help them, especially Kessan and Thora, but this waiting was killing her.

"Look," her father said gently, "I ken ya wanna save them lass, I do too. But we have to wait for the signal and do this right."

She sighed; she knew he was right but the waiting was torture. She needed something to take her mind off of what was happening. She guessed now was as good a time as any to find out about her past. Here went nothing.

"Um, may I ask you something?" She said clearing her throat nervously.

He turned around to look at her, "Aye." He said cautiously.

She closed her eyes and exhaled. "Why did you send me away?" Her voice sounded like that of a lost child, even to her own ears. "Is it because you didn't want me anymore? I'm not sorry that you did, I have had a wonderful life. I just need to know why." There it was, out in the open, and she couldn't take it back. She was finally going to get an answer to the questions that had tormented her over the years. She just wasn't sure she was ready to hear the truth. It was too late to back out now and she waited nervously for him to answer. She was staring at the ground, just wishing it would open up and swallow her. He was taking his time in answering her. Perhaps he was trying to figure out what lies to tell her? But when she looked up at him she saw that he was just sitting there staring at her with a look of horror on his face.

"Oh lass, is that what ya have been thinking all these years? Ya Ma and I loved ya dearly and that *was* the reason I sent ya away. Ya Ma she was killed only days before I sent ya through and then I found out that McKenzie was coming after ya too, so I did what I had to do. Ya were only meant to go a little forward in time, but a mistake was made and you were sent much further. I have spent every day since trying to find ya." His voice trembled with emotion.

"Oh!" She whispered, not sure how to react. It wasn't quite the answer she had been expecting.

"I am really sorry, lass, that it took so long, but ya have to believe me when I say that we did not do it because ya were unloved." He said earnestly, bringing her back from her thoughts.

She nodded numbly letting him know that she understood, but deep down she wasn't sure she understood anything anymore. She didn't know how she felt, all she had ever known had been turned upside down in the last couple of days. Her emotions were all over the place, changing from happiness, to sadness, to wonder. She would never get used to this magic stuff. Her brain had been having trouble comprehending what was going on from the moment she woke up in the cave. And coming to terms with being in another century was a hard thing to swallow. The archaeologist in her believed in science, things you could prove, and she had grown up in a time where things like magic and time travel were nothing but fairy tales that parents told their children. However, the historian in her loved the fact that the magic really did exist, and had simply been forgotten, it was like finding out that Santa Clause really did exist.

She suddenly needed to move. Standing up she placed a reassuring hand on her father's shoulder before walking away, needing to be with her own thoughts.

She wandered around the area, trying to piece together her life, her mind was racing with all the possibilities. As she tried to imagine the life she had missed out on, she wasn't really paying attention to where she was walking.

She realised she had strayed too far and she was just about to turn around and go back to MacDonnell when she saw what looked like the entrance to a cave, only smaller. It could have been something out of an *Indiana Jones* movie.

It was overgrown and hidden beneath the brush so well that she had almost missed it. Was *this* a way into the castle? It could probably lead to nowhere but then again it might not, it may be their way in! She felt breathless, she had to find out. She wondered if she should tell her father where she was going but she knew that he would only try and stop her. She took one more look at him to make sure he was busy and then she ducked in, making her way down the long corridor. The tunnels were dark and they smelled terrible, old and musty with aromas she didn't want to identify, but at least she could still see somewhat.

She had only gone about five hundred metres into the tunnel when someone grabbed her from behind. But before she could scream, her father's angry voice penetrated her ears.

"What are ya thinking lass? Why dinna ya come and get me?" He barked.

"Shhh keep your voice down, before you get us caught," she ordered.

"Donna be changing the subject lass," he once again barked, his anger raising his voice.

She knew the only way that she was going to get him to be quiet was to answer him. "Because I knew you would try and stop me, but I have to do this." She pleaded. "Please help me, you owe me this." She knew it was a low blow bringing up their past but at the moment she would use any tactic she could to gain his help and it worked.

His face sagged, "Fine lass I will help, but ye are to do as I say, understood." He waited for her to agree before he continued, "I sent my men around to tell Caelan about the tunnels and they will meet us inside."

"Thank you," she replied, grateful that something was finally going to be done, "shall we see where this tunnel leads?" she asked.

He nodded a terse nod instantly wary and alert in their surroundings. They hadn't gone far when, all of sudden, the tunnel ended and they were standing in front of a stone wall. It appeared to be a dead end. They looked at each other, confused. Then, with anger and helplessness rising in her, she began pressing all over the wall, trying to find a way out of the tunnels. She was starting to feel helpless again, until her father tapped her on the shoulder and pointed up. Above them was what looked like a trapdoor. Reaching up, her father slowly pushed it open enough so that they could climb up, while holding a finger to his lips, reminding her to remain silent. *Well, duh,* she thought, as she climbed.

When they emerged, they noticed that they were standing in the middle of the buttery, at least that's what she assumed it was. She edged her way over to the door and cracked it open just wide enough so that they could get a view of the courtyard. Night was starting to fall and mercifully the courtyard was empty apart from a few guards standing up on the barracks facing the opposite way. It made sense that they didn't need anyone on guard in the courtyard, no one could get in here without being seen and, obviously, no one knew about the tunnels; he would have had them guarded as well.

"Where would the jail be?" She whispered. At the confused look on his face, she remembered that in this time they were called dungeons not jails. "Sorry where would the dungeon be?" She corrected herself.

Understanding flashed on the old man's face, "Aye, I have been here once when Kendrick's father was alive and the entrance should be just opposite us."

Ceana looked out across the courtyard and tried to locate the entrance. It was hard to see at first but then the outline of an opening in the wall became clear. Ok they were going to have to make a run for it to avoid being seen.

"Ok old man, are you ready?" She smiled at him, softening the remark.

"Aye lassie. Make sure ya keep up with me." Before she could say any more he was gone, stealthily making his way across the courtyard. She followed him. Again amazed at the agility of these Highlanders. They were so big and brawny that you wouldn't expect them to be so stealthy. They kept to the shadows until they finally reached the steps that descended down into the dungeon. With each step she took, it eerily felt more and more like they were descending into the underworld and, when they reached the bottom, she was sure that they had reached hell.

Every cell was full of men who had been tortured and she prayed that they found Kessan in better shape. Her father let out soft whistles, whistles that she recognised as the signals of his clan as they made their way around. But there was no reply and she didn't know if it was a good sign or a bad one. She felt panic rise through her, what if they were too late? What if he was already dead? Then relief almost overwhelmed her as she heard it. Through the darkness a faint reply sounded, it was the sweetest sound she had ever heard. They hurried over to the cell it was coming from but it wasn't Kessan, instead they found a woman pressed up against the bars barely conscious.

"Och lass, what have they done to ya?" Her father whispered in a horrified voice.

Ceana looked over at her father with questioning eyes.

"Aye it is the McKinnon lass." He acknowledged.

She looked back at the young girl. This poor wretch was Kessan's sister? Her stomach lurched, the girl's face was battered and bruised and one eye was closed from the swelling. Her lips were puffed up, bleeding and blackened and dark stains coated her shredded dress and face. What monster could have done this? She felt the young girl grab her shirt through the bars and tug. She was trying to say something. Ceana leaned closer so that she could hear. "Help him." She rasped.

Had she heard right? But where was he? "Where is he Thora?" She asked softly, trying to remain calm. This was the stuff of true horror, she felt herself detach from the safety of her 21st century world as she comprehended the terrible reality of the situation.

"Here." Thora croaked before she dropped back to the cot, weak and exhausted. Unable to see what she was indicating, Ceana strode over to the opposite wall and grabbed a torch that had been placed there, still lit. She shone the torch into the cell, but nothing could have prepared her for the horror that greeted her. She drew in her breath sharply and tears came to her eyes. They had found him. Kessan was hanging from shackles attached to the walls. They were so tight that blood pooled around them, running in a thin line down his arms. His head lolled, unmoving, to the side. She could see that his face was as bloody and bruised as his sister's. She fought rising nausea as she realised that five horrific gashes angrily marred each side of his once beautiful body. Even from where she stood she could see that they were deep – they pulsated blood, each red inflamed and angry. Numb with shock, she hoped that infection hadn't taken hold.

As she scanned his body in the flickering light she let out a wail of horror. Protruding from his broken flesh, a long, spiked stick still sat wedged in his side. A weapon so evil, it had been designed to cause more damage when it was removed, something they would have to do before they moved him. She could only stand there and stare, her body refused to move and her father moved her gently out of the way to work on the lock until he got it open. It wasn't until she heard the lock give way and the door open that she was able to move, she knew she had to do something, he needed her now, more than ever. Ceana approached him, tapping his face, trying to get him to wake up, but he wouldn't. Oh no, she thought, numb with grief. *They were too late!* He was dead. She fell to her knees and wept.

"He's not dead, only passed out, please help him." A soft voice croaked.

She turned to look at the young girl. MacDonnell had managed to wake her up again and was giving her water.

"Are ya ok to walk lass?" He asked her. "I have to help Ceana get Kessan."

"Aye." She replied weakly.

She stood up again as her father walked towards the unconscious man. "Get ready to catch him lass."

Before she had time to ask what he meant, her father cut through the rope holding the shackles with his sword and Kessan fell forward on top of her, knocking them both to the ground. As his body hit hers, she felt the spike push further into to his shoulder. Despite the viciousness of the injury, he still did not wake up and that frightened her. Her father rushed forward and lifted him up enough to give her room to free herself from under him. She rose, sobbing in shock.

"Before we go anywhere lass we have to remove the stakes." Her father informed her, gently.

She knew he was right, but it didn't make her feel any better. She only hoped he remained unconscious. She sat down and cradled his head in her lap, and watched in horror as her father planted one booted foot gently on one side and then pulled with all his strength. The contraption came out but not before doing quite a bit of damage in the process. Kessan did not move or even flinch. She could see his chest rising and falling but it was shallow and his skin was raging with fever. If they didn't get him help soon she knew he would die. Tearing off the bottom of her shirt she made a makeshift tourniquet to stop the bleeding. Now they just had to find a way to make it hold. Her father ripped the linen from the bed and handed it to her. She twisted it into a long thin strip and wrapped it around his shoulder as best she could. They were ready to go.

Standing up they grabbed one side each and started to make their way slowly out of the dungeon. It was not easy. Kessan weighed a ton. They stopped at the top of the stairs to rest for a second and to make sure the coast was clear. When MacDonnell was certain it was clear, he gave the signal for the two women to follow him. They had just made it to the door of the buttery when one of the creepiest voices she had ever heard reached her ears.

"Well, well, well. What have we here?" The hideous voice scoffed contemptuously.

Thora screamed. Ceana knew that they were in trouble. They turned around and came face to face with the man she had been brought back here to destroy. For once in her life she felt fear like none she had ever felt before. This man was truly the devil himself, he was the stuff that nightmares were made of and they were in a world of trouble right now. Were they crazy? How the hell was she going to defeat *this* monster?

CHAPTER 20

She could not believe that they had been caught. They were so close. What were they going to do now? The others would be on their way, she had to bide time until they got here. She just hoped she didn't get them all killed before then. Here went nothing.

"So *you* are the monster destroying the Highlands?" She said, offhandedly.

"Nay my dear you have it wrong. I do not want to destroy them. I want to *rule* them." He corrected, with a wicked smile.

Was he for real? All of these people had suffered and died because one man was on a power trip. She really shouldn't have been surprised. The one thing she had learnt during her studies was that many great cities had fallen because of one man's ambitions. The only difference this time was that it affected her and people she loved.

"You know you're not going to win, right?" She taunted.

Kendrick laughed, "you ken your mother said the same thing to my father right afore my father killed her. But he showed her and while he got the pleasure out of watching her squirm, I will get the pleasure of doing what the bastard failed to will rid the world of the only weapon that can stop our power. I guess, now is as good a time as any for ya to die." He sneered.

She realised then what this monster and his family had taken from her and Kessan. They were the reason that she had been sent away, they was the reason that her mother was dead, and he was the reason that the one man she loved was in so much pain. But despite the Highlanders' misplaced faith, Ceana didn't believe that she was the one that could kill him. Maybe if they all worked together they could come up with a plan, but how was she meant to singlehandedly defeat this lunatic? A lunatic that apparently wielded some heavy-duty magic that she didn't understand or quite believe in. One way or another before she went home, she had to help these people. She had to stop the madness before any more death occurred.

"One day you will pay for what you have done." She said coldly.

"Death is a way of life. Every day people die. Only the strong survive." He acquiesced, raising a curious eyebrow at her.

"They didn't just die, you murdered them!" She screamed at him. "Mark my words you will not get away with it."

"Who's going to stop me my dear?

Ya father couldn't stop me when I killed ya mother, Kessan couldn't stop me from killing Camden and no one stopped me when I killed Kessan's parents." He laughed menacingly.

She was taken aback. Kessan had explained that their deaths were an unfortunate accident. Did he know the truth? Kessan's own best friend had killed his parents. She could not understand how anyone could do such a thing. Mel would die before she ever hurt Ceana or anyone Ceana loved. Kendrick truly was a coward.

"It should not come as a surprise. Kessan's father was starting to rally the forces against me. I needed Kessan on my side, so I did what I had to do. I killed them and made it look like an accident. Then you came along and ruined my life. Not that it matters. You are too late. The magic inside me is stronger and more powerful than it has ever been. The more the people fear me the more power I gain. So as long as they believe in me and fear me, you will have no chance of winning." He declared, dismissively, arrogantly.

"You monster!" She heard screaming from behind her.

She had been so focused on Kendrick that she didn't see Thora until it was too late. The battered woman launched herself at Kendrick punching, kicking and fighting him. Kendrick lifted her off her feet and threw her into the wall behind them. With a cry, Ceana rushed over to her. She was dazed, and barely alive. How much more could this young woman take? In true Highlander spirit, she would not give up. Ceana had to stop her when she tried to get up again.

She shook her head letting her know that it was a losing battle. Thankfully she listened and stayed put.

"Ya stupid bitch. Have ya not learned by now that ya canno' hurt me?" he hissed at her.

She was just about to answer him when a war cry filled the air. She looked up to the barracks and there stood Caelan and the rest of the MacDonnell and McKinnon clans. Many of them had their bows and arrows aimed at Kendrick, ready to fire if he made the wrong move.

"Ya really think ya can kill me that easily?" he hissed loudly enough for the surrounding men to hear.

He made as if he was about to surrender, when he stopped and faced her. The evil in his eyes made Ceana shrink back with horror. "Ya will not escape me this time lass," he rasped, and then he raced towards her at a pace that was far too unnatural for her liking with a dagger in his hands. This was it. It was as though she was watching her life in slow motion. She closed her eyes. "Tell Kessan I love him." She said loud enough for Thora to hear her and she waited for death. But it didn't come. She opened her eyes just as her father stepped in front of her and heard him groan a terrible groan as he caught Kendrick's dagger straight to his heart. Gasps rang out into the courtyard and Ceana stared down in shocked numbness.

Before the shocked group of highlanders could stop him, Kendrick spun around and disappeared with a blink. Her father fell to his knees, staring down at his chest. She quickly grabbed him and gently lowered him to the ground. Tears ran down her face as she moved his hands away.

She could see that the dagger was embedded up to its hilt, he was losing blood rapidly. Ceana didn't know what to do. Here was her father, the man who had abandoned her, she should be mad, but she couldn't be, he had done it for love, she understood that now. The danger had become very real to her very quickly in the last few minutes. She had seen in his eyes all the love a father had for his daughter as he had told her about her mother and the reasons why he had sent her through the portal. She could not hate this man, he had done what any father who loved their daughter would have done and now it was too late.

No, it was never too late to say you're sorry.

She looked down at her father, the one man in life who had literally moved heaven and earth to keep her safe. He was the least selfish person she had ever known. Everything he did he did for others, she knew that now. Tears fell faster and she could not stop them. It was too much.

"I am so sorry. I shouldn't have been so mean to you. I should have spent more time with you. I understand why you did what you did. I just want to say thank you. Please don't hate me." She begged.

"Och lass, I can never hate ya. I am just sorry that I did not have more time with ya to learn all about the family who raised such a strong-willed, fiery woman. I am proud to call ya my daughter and a MacDonnell. Always remember Ceana, no matter where ya go ya will always have the heart of a Highlander." He whispered and coughed.

His skin had become pale and clammy and his breathing was rapidly getting shallower with each breath. She had to do something. She screamed for someone to help her. She could hear people rushing towards her but all her attention was focused on her father. She had to keep him talking long enough for help to reach them.

"I don't know what to do. I can't to do this alone. I need you. Please don't die." She pleaded.

"Nay lass ya wrong, ya do not need me, ya only need to listen to ya heart. Inside you, you have the same power that ya mother had.

The power of premonition, you've had the dreams right?

The dreams you have are not regular dreams, they are telling you something. All ye need to do is listen to what they are telling ya, and listen to your heart. It will guide you down the right path. If ya do that lass, you can do anything." He encouraged weakly.

He started coughing violently, blood started running out of the side of his mouth and she knew he was dying.

"I love ya Ceana, always remember. Make sure that you and your siblings look after each other. Ya all need each other now more than ever. Look after Hamish." He coughed.

She watched him slipping away. "Please Daddy don't go, I need you." She sounded and felt like a lost child. She looked down at him just as he took his last breath and saw the light and life leave his eyes.

"No, wake up." She screamed. She began shaking him violently. She knew people were staring at her but her heart was ripping apart. Ceana could not lose another parent, she just couldn't.

She was still trying to get him to wake up when she felt two sets of hands grab her and pull her gently away. Looking up numbly, she saw Hamish and Katie sitting beside her.

Ceana could see the same pain reflected in their eyes. Katie had spent the last couple of days getting to know this man and he had treated her as if she was his own daughter. She turned to Hamish, the anguish she saw in his eyes was unbearable. This man had meant the world to him and she was all that he had left now. She threw herself into his arms. "I'm sorry, I'm so sorry. I didn't mean for him to die." She babbled as the shock reverberated through her trembling body.

Hamish gathered her into his arms and whispered hoarsely into her hair "It's ok Cee. He died a true Highlander death saving the ones he loved." He pulled Katie into their hug and the three of them stayed there huddled together in their grief until the men came to take the body.

She sat there with her brother and sister, thinking over the events of the last few days. Kessan! She suddenly thought, dazed. How could she have forgotten about him? She pulled herself out of Hamish's arms and crawled over to him. Caelan and Thora were still with him, they had him laid out flat, his breathing was shallow and he needed desperate medical attention.

"We have to get him to help now." She urged. She could not lose him too.

Caelan nodded at her, "We are going to have to stay here. We can't move him like this and the ride to the camp will only do more damage. He needs time to mend."

She nodded. Ceana knew that he was right.

"What about Kendrick's men?" She asked.

"Don't worry lass we captured those that stuck around after Kendrick left. All of the prisoners have been released. They will also need to stay here to heal, the servants are happy to finally be free of that monster and are assisting us. We are safe here Ceana. We need to get him upstairs so that the healer can work on him."

It took the men about twenty minutes to get him upstairs and settled into one of the many rooms. Men that had been badly wounded during their time here had also been moved to the bedrooms. Mercifully none of them were going to die, as long as they could keep infection away.

Thora was heading out of the room to get supplies when Ceana came in but she insisted that Thora sit down and rest. Thora had been through just as much as the rest of them. She took the list and then headed out to get the supplies. She had to do something while waiting for the men to attend to Kessan. The thought of him not making it was driving her crazy and she had to keep busy. The first one she would tend to would be Thora, she decided. The poor girl looked as though a bus had hit her.

Whilst she tended to Thora, they spent time getting to know each other. Thora was able to fill her in on what Kessan was like when he was a young boy. Their family sounded so much like hers. As they talked and treated Thora's wounds, they heard someone clear their throat behind them and she turned around to see Hamish standing behind her. He looked so sad and lost.

"Sorry to interrupt ya, lassies, but I thought ya might like to know that the healer is finished."

Ceana apologised to Thora as she dumped the rags into her lap and then she ran into the bedroom that Kessan had been moved to from the dungeon. Hamish followed her at a more sedated pace. Caelan was standing beside his bed.

"How is he?" She asked. She couldn't take her eyes off the man lying in the bed.

"He is stable at the moment. He has a bit to go yet. As long as we can keep the infection at bay, he should recover. All we can do now is wait." Caelan said.

Ceana walked over to the bed and sat in the chair beside it. She would not move from here until he woke up, she vowed.

"I swear you people need to hurry up and discover penicillin and other medical marvels. It would make your lives so much easier." She said, knowing that she would never take those things for granted again.

"I swear she says the weirdest things." Thora whispered to her brother.

Hamish looked at her and replied with a chuckle, "ya have no idea lass."

"Hey Caelan. Where is Katie?" She asked as she realised that she hadn't seen her sister since her father had died.

"She is helping with the other wounded. She wanted to give ya some space," He replied, his voice filled with love and admiration. She nodded her thanks, she will find her later. She retrieved the cloth from the bowl that was beside the bed and started pressing it gently against Kessan's battered body, trying to cool down the fever. Before the healer left she told Ceana they had to keep him covered up and the room warm. She knew better. Once she was gone, Ceana got one of the maids to put the fire out and to bring her some lukewarm water. It was going to be a long night, she could feel it. But at least they would be sleeping in proper beds.

THE NEXT MORNING, Ceana stood at the doorway just staring at him, she could not believe how pale he was, he had come so close to losing his life and that thought almost killed her. During this ordeal one thing became crystal clear. She would do anything to keep this man in her life even if it meant going up against that lunatic. She had a score to settle with the man. Ceana was going to make him pay. She just had to figure out

how to accomplish that. She felt someone approach behind her and realised that Katie had come to stand with her. Ceana looked around to see where she had come from and then shrugged her shoulders.

"I'm sorry about your father, Cee." She offered uncertainty, giving her a swift hug.

"Thanks, he was a good man." She replied and she really meant it.

Katie nodded. She looked over at the bed and tears filled her eyes.

"He is going to be ok, isn't he Cee?" She asked.

She could hear the fear in her voice. She realised that, somehow, he had become as important to her family as he was to her.

"I hope so Bata, because I can't live without him." She answered truthfully.

She walked over to the bed and stared at the man who had changed her world. Ceana could not believe how close she had come to losing him without telling him how she felt. She swore to herself that before she went anywhere he would know exactly how she felt, even if he didn't feel the same. She only had a week to figure out how to destroy Kendrick before she was sent home.

"Bata I have to figure out how to beat this guy, will you help me?" She asked.

"Of course I will Cee, but how are you going to do it?"

"I don't know yet Bata but I have a feeling I have to listen to my dreams."

Her sister looked at her puzzled.

"What is that supposed to mean?" She asked, confusion on her face.

"I'm not sure I know. It's something father told me before he died."

Ceana could see that she didn't understand, but she could not explain in words what she had just found out. Was her father right? Were her dreams really premonitions and not simply random ramblings of her unconscious mind? It made sense, many of her dreams had had relevance that eventually revealed its hand – just look at the dream that had brought Kessan to her. She just had to figure out what that meaning was before it occurred. Point in fact the man lying in a bed in front of her. Well, if they were really premonitions, it was time they started working and told her what to do about the Monster.

CHAPTER 21

"Kessan you have to take it slowly." She pleaded once more.

"Lass if I take it any slower I will be dead. I need to get my strength back." He answered irritably.

She rolled her eyes. It didn't matter if they were from the 21st century or the 12th century, men made the worst patients ever, period. She had to convince him to get back into bed. It had only been five days since he had been brought here. The first two days after their rescue attempt were touch and go as he spent most of them unconscious, running a fever. It broke on the morning of the third day. She was so relieved when she woke up to see him watching her. He thanked her for saving his life, but he then proceeded to rile at her for nearly getting herself killed in the process. She trembled as she filled him in on all that had happened and he grieved for her father with her.

Thora and Caelan were the first two to come and see him and she left them alone while they talked. Thora filled him on what had occurred to her from the day he had left her at the castle. But he was so weak that the increasing anger and rage exhausted him and by the end of their visit, he had fallen asleep. But not before he made her a promise that she would be here when he woke up. On the fourth day, he had wanted to get up and move around but his body was still weak. He could only manage a few steps before becoming short of breath, collapsing back down on the bed and she could tell that it was starting to frustrate him. He didn't like revealing his weaknesses. They took turns in making him eat regularly in order to regain his strength and at first, he could only manage small bites, but as the week went on, he improved. On the fifth day Ceana was watching him walk around the room slowly and tentatively. The longer he spent on his feet, the stronger he got but she could also see that it was taking its toll on him. He needed to rest.

They had already had dinner and everybody had gone to bed and a wicked idea sparked inside her. There was a sure-fire way to get him back to bed. It had been so long since she had felt him inside of her and considering what had happened, she needed him now more than ever.

"Kessan, if you get back in bed I will join you." She purred.

"I will be there soon lass. If ya are tired you can go on and go to bed." He snapped as he shuffled around the room, determined to get another lap in.

She laughed softly. Kessan obviously needed a little bit of help understanding what she meant. Kessan had his back to her, pacing the length of the hearth unawares that she had taken her nightie off. She walked quietly up behind him and pressed her breasts into his back.

She felt him stiffen and heard him moan, she knew she had his attention. "Come to bed and join me, you dolt." She pressed again.

He turned around and captured her mouth with his, oh it had been so long since he had kissed her like this, or had it only been days, she could not remember. Whenever this man kissed her she seemed to lose her mind, but right now that didn't matter, all she wanted was to get this man into bed.

KESSAN HAD COME CLOSE to dying.

He shuddered involuntarily remembering the first day of his torture and his determination to survive. As the time went on, his strength left him, he knew he was in trouble.

The last thing he remembered was Kendrick whispering into his ears about all the things he was going to do to Ceana when he got his hands on her, right before he stuck a stake into his shoulder. The pain had been too much and he broke, everything went black and when he came to he was in this room with Ceana in a chair beside him. Her head was on the bed, her hair tumbling around her. At first he thought he was still unconscious.

He must have stared at her for over an hour before she woke up.

He could not believe that this woman had come to his rescue and he could not help the guilt and grief that came as she had told him of the confrontation and the death of old MacDonnell. Later that day Caelan and a bruised and scarred Thora had come to see him and they filled him in on how Kendrick had admitted to killing their parents. It had knocked the wind back out of him.

The next two days he spent trying to gain his strength back, the sooner he got it back, the sooner he could go and kill the bastard. He had taken nearly everything that he loved and he would be damned if he stood by and watched as he took the one woman that he loved too. Yes, he loved her. He had allowed himself to come to the realisation the first night he was hanging in the dungeon in the belief that he was probably going to die. He kept thinking to himself that if he ever had the chance he would tell her how he felt and make sure that she knew he would be by her side for the rest of her days, even if it meant going back to her time with her. He would move heaven and earth to make that happen. He picked her up and carried her to bed, masking his pain.

"Kessan put me down. I am way too heavy. You're going to hurt yourself!" Ceana ordered, alarmed as his weak body betrayed him and he stumbled under her weight.

"Lass, it will be a cold day in hell before I cannot carry ye to our bed." He whispered huskily, pulling himself together with determination.

"My knight in shining armour." She purred.

"Nay lass I think ya have it wrong. I think *ye're* my knight in shining armour."

He saw tears spring to her eyes and fall down her cheeks, he could only imagine her pain. In just a few short days, the lass had endured burdens that would cause a lesser man to fall and yet the determination of her highlander spirit drove her forward. He leant down to her cheek and kissed them away. Then he kissed her so deeply and passionately that he felt as if he were drowning inside her. He would not lose this woman again.

DESPITE THE MIX of emotions raining down on her, she knew that if he did not make love to her soon she was going to rage. She broke their kiss.

"Kessan, please I have to feel you inside of me right now!" She begged.

Kessan stripped off his clothes and re-joined her on the bed. He gently spread her legs wide and prepared to enter her. He paused and Ceana looked up into his eyes with a questioning look. "Is everything ok?"

"Och aye lass everything is perfect." He answered with a content smile.

She was mesmerised by the look in his eyes, she knew that this time it was going to be different. She could feel him entering her slowly as they stared into each other's eyes, never breaking contact. Then he spoke.

"I love ya lass, ye are my soul and heart and I want to spend the rest of my life making ya happy." He declared, looking at her earnestly.

She melted. It felt like she had waited her whole life to hear him say those words. She planted her legs on the bed and thrust herself up so that his manhood impaled her. She could feel him right to the entry of her womb, renewed strength filled her with an energy she had never felt before and it felt as if they were one.

Complete.

Whole.

"Kessan, I love you so much. I have loved you since our first encounter in the woods. But even before that, you have been in my dreams for as long as I can remember."

They made love and before Kessan's body finally gave way to fatigue, he again reminded her how much he loved her. Before he drifted off, he asked her what she had meant by the comment about her dreams. She promised that she would tell him all about it in the morning. It was a promise she would not keep.

CEANA WAS STANDING in the car park of the Firefly Hideaway. Katie was kneeling behind her crying, but she could not see why. She was focused on the man in front of her, Kendrick. It didn't make sense. How had he made it to her time? In fact, when had she come home?

"I told ya lass, I am too powerful for ya to stop. The magic in me is too

strong for anyone to stop."

"We'll see about that. You're in my world now Kendrick." She was reminded of the comment about people's fear fuelling his power.

Ceana leapt forward and rammed the dagger deep into his heart. She watched as his body turned to ash and floated away on the afternoon breeze.

CEANA WOKE UP IN A SWEAT. It had been so long since she had had a dream as clear as this that she instinctively knew it was a premonition now that she had a word for it. It was still early in the morning as the sun had not risen. There was no chance of sleep now. The dream had shaken her. Why would she have dreamt that Kendrick was in the twenty-first century? It didn't make any sense. How was killing Kendrick in the 21st century any different to killing him here? She lay there going over it in her mind before it finally came to her. Of course! She was such an idiot, she should have seen it sooner.

Ceana flew out of bed waking Kessan in the process.

"Cee is everything alright?" He asked sleepily.

She spun around, "I'm sorry, I didn't mean to wake you." She put on a smile to hide her emotions. "Yes, everything is fine. I just need to go to the bathroom. Like right now." She said, squirming to make it more believable.

He eyed her for a moment, until he finally nodded and closed his eyes. She smiled, she had learnt that if you don't want a man to keep questioning you about what you are doing, tell him you need to go to the bathroom and they quickly forget all about interrogating you. She waited for a few moments until she thought he was asleep, got dressed as quietly as possible, and left to find her sister.

They had a lot to do in only a short time. She ran through it in her head as she looked for Katie. First, they had to go to the camp and find the druid that had brought them back in time. He had been at the camp with her father waiting for her to arrive.

He never really said much to her, other than filling in some of the details, but he was always watching her. He could send a message to Kendrick without anyone finding out and convince her sister that what she was doing was right. If she had understood her dream's message, they had to lure him back to the 21st century in order to kill him.

CHAPTER 22

It was time for them to go. Ceana hated lying to Kessan but she knew that if she told him what they were doing he would insist he come along. There was no way she would risk his life again and he wasn't strong enough for a battle. This was something she had to do on her own. Something she was born to do. They had found the druid and explained what they needed of him. They needed Kendrick there at the right time. They only had two days to make it to the cave before the portal closed for another six months. They needed to do it now. the Highlands didn't have another six months. Kendrick's power was growing stronger with each day and soon it would be too late for everyone. They spent the day with the ones they loved – they didn't know when or if they would see each other again.

Kessan was the last person she had to see. Ceana had left him until last, she knew he was going to be the hardest to let go. Katie was with Caelan for the same purpose – their hardest goodbyes.

It was mid-afternoon. She had a couple of hours before she had to head off. They had planned to set out as soon as the sun set and they still had a lot to do. They would make it to the cave with just enough time to make it home.

She knew that it was going to be a long time, if ever, that she saw Kessan again, but this was the only way she knew how to keep him and everyone else she loved safe. Walking into the room she noticed Kessan standing at the window looking out over the countryside. He was much stronger now though his shoulder still pained him. She cleared her throat to get his attention.

"I just came up to see if you wanted anything. I will be helping Katie prepare dinner tonight so I won't be up for a while." She informed him.

She knew it was a straight out lie but it was the same one Katie had given Caelan. That way their stories matched. He turned and faced her.

"There are cooks for that lass, ya doona have to cook here." He smiled at her.

"You forget, Kessan. Where I come from we prepare our own meals. It's actually something we love doing, and Katie and I want to say thank you to everyone for what they have done. So, is there anything you need?" She pressed.

"Nay lass I am fine for the moment."

Walking further into the room she stood next to him. He seemed worried about something. "What's wrong?"

Kessan looked up. "I have just been wondering what Kendrick's next move will be and how we are going defeat him. I underestimated how powerful he is." He said, the guilt clearly etched on his face.

She leaned across and kissed him. Ceana loved this man more than anything, and it was because of that love that she knew she was doing the right thing.

"Kessan, magic is only as strong as the people who believe in it. If there is no belief and no fear, magic cannot exist." She told him.

He gave her an odd look and she could see that he did not follow her logic.

After a while he said. "Well lass that is a nice concept. But ya have seen yaself that the magic does exist."

Not knowing what to say to chase his guilt away, she just nodded and kissed him once more. "I have to go and help Katie with dinner." She repeated as she walked back towards the door. When she reached it, she turned back to him.

"Kessan?" She called.

"Aye lass?"

"Please remember that I will always love you. Even through time and space. *That* is where the real magic lies." She said before quickly leaving the room. She wanted to get out of there before he could see her tears. Walking away from this man while he was like this was one of the hardest, most painful things she had ever done in her life. But she had to do it.

🙥🙞

KESSAN HAD FELT uneasy for the rest of the afternoon. Something was off. Ceana had been acting odd when she left. Her last comment worried him the most. What did she mean that she would love him through time and space? He needed to see her right now. He had to make sure that she was ok. He headed downstairs to the kitchen to find her, only she wasn't there and his unease became more urgent. He bellowed for Caelan.

Caelan came running from the other room. "What?"

"Where is Ceana?" He asked urgently.

"What do ya mean?" Caelan answered. Confusion spreading across his face. "She is in the kitchen with Katie cooking dinner."

"Nay brother, if they were in there do ya think I would be asking ya about their where aboots?"

Just then Hamish came through the front doors.

"MacDonnell have ya seen ya sister by any chance?" Kessan questioned him.

"Aye Ceana and Katie were entering the buttery about an hour ago, discussing what they needed for dinner."

His panic rose. He knew that Ceana had found the tunnel the night they had saved him. Surely she wasn't stupid enough to go after Kendrick alone, but this was Ceana they were talking about and he had learnt never to underestimate her. He rushed past Hamish and out the door. He was hoping he was wrong, but somehow he knew that when he opened the doors to the buttery he would not find them. He was right. His heart was racing and fear was taking over, where would they have gone? Then their last conversation replayed itself in his head and it all made sense. He froze as his blood ran cold.

They were going back to their time! And they were going to take Kendrick with them. But how? He had to find the druid. "Where is Fer Doirich?" He commanded.

"He left about an hour ago; said that he had to go and tend some business at Clan McLean." Hamish replied.

Kessan let out a string of curses as he ran to the stable. His sides were killing him but he didn't care. He ordered the stable boy to ready his horse and with a sinking heart he noticed that three horses were gone. They must have at least an hour's advantage on them. He raged once more.

"Kessan, what is going on?" Caelan asked.

"I do not ken yet, but I have a growing suspicion that Ceana is planning to lure Kendrick into her time to kill him." He voiced his fears.

"Surely the lass is not that daft?" Hamish replied incredulously.

"Aye I believe she is. She is a stubborn mule, if she thinks it will work, she will try it." He answered gruffly.

Without needing to be told, Caelan and Hamish mounted their own horses and all three men rode hard and fast, hoping that they would get there in time. As it was, time was running out, and if they didn't get there soon they would not be able to stop them.

She walked into the cave with her sister and the druid.

"Are you sure this is going to work, Cee?" Katie asked nervously

"No not really." She answered truthfully. "But we have to give it a go. Just stick to the plan and hopefully we will get out of this alive." She just hoped that she was right.

Then, out of the darkness behind them, they heard an evil laugh and they turned to see that Kendrick had indeed followed them to the cave, he had fallen for their trap. She had hoped that he would be watching the castle and made no effort to conceal their escape. Now came the hard part. They needed to get him into the circle, so the druid could send them to the 21st century.

She grabbed Katie's hand and slowly walked to the centre of the room.

"Well here I am, Kendrick, come and get me!" She taunted as she watched him inch closer to them.

"Och I am going to enjoy making ya suffer until your last dying breath." He hissed.

She watched as he drew closer to her. Mind on the single task of destroying her, he hadn't noticed the druid position himself at the altar, sketching in the symbols. She tightened her grip on Katie's hand so that when they went through the portal they could make a run for it together. The two of them had been through the portal already; they knew what to expect, this would give them the advantage.

They only had about ten more minutes before the portal closed for six months, it had taken them longer than they expected to get here and, if the druid didn't hurry up, they would run out of time. They had hoped to have time to get back but that was no longer an option. Maybe one day they would see the men they loved again, but for now just knowing they were safe would have to be enough. She thought of Kessan and how mad he was going to be. She just hoped that he understood why she had to do this.

Fer Doirich gave her the signal that he was ready to etch the last symbol.

"Well it's about time you put your money where your mouth is!" She beckoned.

Suddenly, a commotion came from outside.

Kendrick heard it too. In a panic, he rushed to grab her before anyone came in, but she grabbed him.

"Do it now!" Ceana shouted at the druid as he put the last symbol on the column. The vortex started up around them and, like last time, the wind got faster, and faster. She knew what was going to happen next but she could hear Kendrick screaming that he was going to make her pay. Ceana no longer cared. She only had eyes for the man who had just entered the cave. Right before she lost her sight, she saw Kessan fall to his knees and she could still hear his war cry as the sounds of the cave faded away and were replaced with those she had grown up with.

CHAPTER 23

Ceana's eyesight was returning and she could still feel Katie holding her hand. As soon as they could they had to make their way up to the car park. Had it worked? She spun to see the 12th century Laird blinking and stumbling about, stunned and confused. It had. She felt relieved. But it wouldn't be long until his eyesight also returned and it wouldn't be long before he found his feet again.

They needed to make a move now so that they stayed ahead of him. She turned to her sister urgently, "Run Katie. Remember do not stop until you are inside." She pleaded, hoping her sister would obey despite what might happen. They both set off in a sprint. Kendrick let out a roar and started after them. They knew he was fast, but he was also at a disadvantage.

This was their home turf. He didn't know the shortcuts, they did. They ran together and were able to stay ahead of him, but only just.

"Ya will never out run me, ya little bitch!" He roared.

Her heart pounded, and her chest burned but she did not stop or slow down. They were close now. Either way this would be the end. Katie kept up the pace as they ran through the forest towards home. She followed glad that Katie had listened to her.

It was not long before they reached the car park. Looking around she tried to gauge how many people were at the cabins. Thankfully there were no cars but their own parked there.

If they were lucky there would not be anyone there. She only hoped that Tris had taken this day as an opportunity to go surfing.

She stopped and waited, breathing heavily from exertion. Quicker than she had expected, Kendrick caught up with her and lunged before she could move out of his way. His body hit her so hard that he slammed her into the ground and knocked the remaining wind out of her. She heard Katie scream her name and she came rushing back to help. Katie jumped on his back and started hitting him.

"Noooo," she tried to scream. "Katie! Run! Get inside!" She wheezed horrified.

Kendrick let out a roar and stood up throwing her sister off his back. Katie tumbled back into the garden, winded but she seemed ok. Pulling herself to her feet she was just in time to duck Kendrick's fist. She rushed forward and kicked him hard, and felt her foot connect with his stomach. He doubled over and coughed but he was still standing.

He grinned evilly at her. "Come on lass, ya will have to do better than that." He mocked.

Ceana hated his voice. She was just about to kick him in the head when a shout from her right caught her attention. It was just enough of a lapse to give him time to knock her off her feet. She landed so hard on the ground that every muscle in her body screamed in agony. Through the haze of pain she could hear someone shouting. When she looked up she saw Marcus bolting towards them. The anger in his eyes warned her that he was about to do something stupid. She tried to warn him, but she couldn't choke the words out, her breath escaping her and she could only watch as Marcus delivered a punch to Kendrick's head. She noticed that the hit affected Kendrick more than anything else she had witnessed. She also noticed that he was not anywhere near as fast. His strength was also different. It was working, she realised. He was losing his powers.

That didn't help Marcus. "Ya stupid Sassenach I hope ya said ya prayers today." Kendrick raged.

She watched in horror as Kendrick pulled out a dirk, her father's dirk to be exact – the bastard must have stolen it in the escape – and thrust it deep into Marcus' stomach. Marcus backed up, staggered, turned to face her and said her name as he collapsed on the ground.

Crying his name in shock, Katie rushed to his side and pulled the knife out. She applied pressure to the wound, but Ceana knew that he wasn't going to make it. This was the part of her dream that didn't make sense, she hadn't seen the victim. She knew now that this was where it ended. She walked over to the where Marcus lay and picked up the knife, and walked straight up to Kendrick

"This is for all the people I love you bastard!" She hissed.

"What are ya going to do with that, lass? Ya ken that I cannot be killed by now, the magic is too strong." He mocked, drawing closer to her, unfazed by her threats. "Besides, ya are a woman, from the 21st century no less you do not have it in ye to kill a man!"

They would be the last words he ever spoke. She drove the knife deep into his chest, put her face right up to his and whispered.

"That's where you're wrong McKenzie. Your magic has no power here. No one believes in it, and if no one believes, it can't exist. I may be from the 21st century, but I will always be a Highlander at heart."

She watched coldly as the realisation of his death entered his eyes and he fell to his knees screaming. She stared, surprised, as a dark cloud left him, floating away and dissipating on the evening breeze – the dark magic *had* left the Highlands, forever. She looked down to see a soulless man lying there looking with empty eyes up at the sky. She felt nothing. She would deal with it later.

Shaking herself out of her reverie she turned around and rushed over to where Marcus and Katie were. Using Marcus' phone, Katie had called the ambulance but they both knew that he wasn't going to make it. She sat opposite Katie and took his head in her hands. She placed it on her lap and looked down at him. She ran her hand across his forehead, smoothing his hair down as she tried to comfort him

"Just hold on Marcus the ambulance is on its way." She soothed, choking down a sob. "You can't die yet. You promised me that you would take me out to dinner." She reminded him.

Marcus gave a soft, pained laugh. "Come on Cee, I know that you do not love me the way I love you. I just wish that I could have been the man that you were looking for." He coughed.

She could see he was fading fast and she leant down and kissed him. As she lifted her head she could see the surprise in his beautiful blue eyes, eyes that were starting to dim. "You're wrong about one thing, Marcus, you are my hero. I have always loved you and I will always love you until the end of time."

And he died, there in her arms with a small smile on his face. Ceana's head fell onto his chest and she cried, she cried so hard. It was all too much she was so sick of losing people. What was the point of it all, why did Marcus have to die? All he ever wanted in life was to have fun.

That was how Tristan found them.

TWO YEARS HAD PASSED and she was still here, a few things had changed but she had gone back to her life. After Marcus' and Kendrick's death, the police had taken their statements. Eventually, it was put down to a robbery gone wrong. Over the coming months, Ceana and Katie explained everything that had happened to Tristan and he vowed that he would stand up for people who had to deal with power hungry dictators. He joined the army not long after and he was just getting ready to go back to Afghanistan for his second call of duty. They hated saying goodbye and worried when he was gone but they knew it was something he had to do. Marcus' death had hit him harder than anyone else knew and in the years that followed, Ceana could only watch and support him as best she could as he slowly changed.

For a year after the incident, she had waited for Kessan to come back through the portal and tell her it was ok, but he hadn't come. It had been just over two years and there was still no sign of them. Something must have gone wrong, or perhaps he had decided that she was just not worth the trouble. Nevertheless, for the last two years, on the equinox, whenever she had heard a thunderstorm she hoped with all her heart that it was Kessan. But nothing changed. It had now reached a point that she no longer waited for him – thunderstorms were just thunderstorms. Perhaps it was for the best, they were from two different times after all.

Katie was just as heartbroken. For months, she listened as Katie cried herself to sleep, missing Caelan and not understanding why he too hadn't come for her. Meanwhile, Ceana had gone back to university and finished her degree. She was now a fully-fledged archaeologist and Katie had decided to go to med school. She wanted to know how to save people. She believed that if she had done so before, she might have been able to save Marcus or MacDonnell.

They were still running the Firefly lodge. It was their home and the last connection they had to their parents. They had hired more people to help them especially now, this time of year was their busiest. They were at ninety-eight percent capacity and it would be like this for the next month.

"Hey Cee seeing as I leave tomorrow, can we have spaghetti bolognaise for dinner tonight?" Tristan asked as he approached her at her desk.

He knew she hated that meal, but she relented. It was his last night and she would have it just for him.

"Sure Tris, whatever you like." She said, somewhat distracted.

Tristan walked up and gave her a big hug and kiss. "Have I told you lately that you are the best sister a guy could have?" Despite his grief over losing Marcus, he had just as equally become a doting brother. So much so that it was almost stifling, but she understood. Life was just too short.

"Hey, what about me?" Katie asked indignantly as she entered the room.

"I had no choice with you squirt, but of course you're fantastic. You are *my* twin after all." He joked.

Katie poked her tongue out at Tristan and then the bantering started. She was pulled from her musings when the phone started ringing and she shook her head at her siblings who were still going at it when she went to answer the phone.

"Hey Cee, I was just wondering what you were doing tonight?" It was Mel. Mel had been her rock since they'd returned. When she had gotten home, she had filled her in on her adventure and then she cried for hours, while Mel cried with her.

"Nothing. Why?" She asked

"No reason I just thought I might pop up for a visit and I just wanted to make sure you were home."

"Yeah I will be here."

They continued to talk and Mel was telling her about a client that had come in today. The client was an old man who came to her every year and, instead of cash payment, he brought her an old coin from his coin collection. Apparently, the old duck had proposed to her today. She burst out laughing and started teasing Mel about accepting his proposal. She had her back to the door and only faintly heard the doorbell chime. She knew that Katie would have heard it and let her deal with the new arrival. She would just act like she was on the phone to another customer. But, as silence stretched on, her customer service persona took over and she looked up irritated that Katie hadn't acknowledged the guests.

She noticed that Katie had indeed entered, but that she had stopped dead in her tracks. Distracted she realised that Mel was saying something, but she paid her no mind. What the heck was wrong with Katie? Had she suddenly forgotten how to do her job? Irritated, she turned to face the front door but, when her eyes hit the door, she dropped the phone receiver in shock. Her mouth opened in stunned silence.

Before her stood Kessan, every bit as gorgeous as she remembered. Caelan not far behind him. Never taking her eyes from him, she picked the phone back up and told Mel she would have to call her back.

"Hello lass." He simply said.

She didn't know what to say.

Clearly it wasn't the reaction he'd been hoping for and he started babbling nervously running a hand through his hair. "Sorry it took so long for us to get back. After you went through the portal all hell broke loose, Kendrick's men started the war and before we could come and get ya we had to make sure the Highlands were safe. Och and they'd kidnapped the Druid. It took us near on over a year to finally find him and it was only after everything finally settled down enough that we were able to come and get ya lass. Did ya miss me?" He asked, hesitantly.

"Did I miss you? Did I miss you? What kind of dumbass questions is that?" She yelled. Ceana knew she was starting to screech, but she couldn't believe the lout would even ask her such a question. She was just about to give him what for when she was interrupted.

"Mama, Mama." Cara squealed as she come running out of the kitchen right around the desk to the entryway where she stopped dead in her tracks. She tilted her head right back so that she could look at the massive stranger standing in front of her. Most kids would have gone running the opposite way, but not Cara. She simply put out her arms and demanded up.

She watched as Kessan picked her up. "Now lassie what seems to be the problem?" He asked

"I want Mama."

"Well wee one, where would your Mama be lass?"

Cara giggled, "What's so funny?" Kessan asked her.

Again Cara giggled.

Ceana watched in amusement as Kessan really looked at her for the first time. Walking around the desk she took her nearly two-year-old so that he wouldn't drop her as the cogs turned. Kessan paled.

Placing Cara back on the ground, she turned to Kessan and started to speak. But, just then Tristan came rushing into the reception area chasing Camden at the same time Katie had finally processed the moment and had run and thrown herself into Caelan's arms.

"Now see lass that is how ya were supposed to greet me." Kessan told her finally, still staring down at her child.

She just looked at him and shook her head. Then all of a sudden, a high-pitched squeal rent the air. Cara started jumping up and down demanding to be picked up again. Kessan obliged. Once she was higher up, Cara turned in his arms to face Ceana, folded her arms across her chest and demanded.

"Mama, tell Cam NO!" Cara wailed, pulling her pigtail for emphasis. Ceana turned around to tell her son to stop it. Kessan grabbed her. "There's another one lass?" He asked, looking a little green. Picking up her son, she handed him to Kessan.

Then, in her best Scottish brogue, she answered him, "Aye laddie, ya have twins." And a fascinating mix of horror, shock and pride danced across Kessan's face as Caelan boomed with laughter. She then leant forward and kissed him "Welcome home daddy. We've been waiting for you."

EPILOGUE

Scotland, two years later

Ceana was pacing in front of the hearth. She could not believe it was almost Christmas again. She was running through all the things that she had to finish when she felt someone come up behind her.

It was her husband. He placed his arms around her waist and rested his chin on her head, "What's wrong lass?" he asked. Ceana could hear the concern in his voice and she was once again reminded of why she loved this man so much. Turning around she laid her head on his chest and answered.

"It's nothing of great importance I'm just worried that Mel and Tristan will not like it here."

This was the first time Mel and her brother were coming to the Highlands. Kessan and Ceana had been home plenty of times in the years but this was the first time they had been able to come here. Tristan was finally back from his last post and she had missed him so much. She didn't have to worry about missing out on their lives. She knew she could go home and visit every six months – that was more than some families living in the same century did.

Caelan had decided to stay in the 21st century with Katie and run the Firefly Hideaway. They made sure to visit each other at least once a year, twice if possible. She sighed, she had a lot to be nervous about, not only was this the first time that Mel and Tristan were coming, it was also the first time that they would meet Hamish and they would all finally get to be together as a family. Hamish was curious to meet Tristan, a brother of the 21st century. Hamish had already become an important part of Ceana's life and, through her stories; he learnt to love Katie and Tristan as if they were his own brother and sister. Katie of course was over the moon, she loved Hamish just as equally. But Tristan had yet to meet him and she was not sure how *he* would feel. Her brother had changed over the years. She'd gradually noticed it after Marcus' death, and Katie had mentioned that it was getting worse the last time she was here. Even though he still treated them all the same and loved them with all his heart; he had lost the youthfulness he once had. With each tour, more of his youthfulness disappeared. She didn't want him to feel as though Hamish had replaced him in anyway, she still needed Tristan as much as ever.

"Lass, it will all be fine ya will see." He comforted.

Ceana looked up into his eyes and saw all the love he had for her. She loved this man more than her own life, and the last two years had been more than she could have hoped for. Leaning in she kissed him passionately showing him just how much she loved him.

"Do ya think we have time to make love before the others arrive, husband of mine?" She purred.

She had started picking up some of their language habits since being here, but she was happy to note that her husband had picked up a few of his own.

"I bloody hope so." He said as he grinned at her.

Chuckling she began to lift up his shirt, when a familiar voice bellowed through the castle.

"Cee, get your butt down here and give me a hug! This is no way to leave your guests waiting. Oh and bring a stiff drink with you, that was the most intense experience of my life."

She heard Kessan mumble a curse under his breath. Leaning forwards, she gave him one last kiss. "Later I promise." She winked.

She headed out of the room and once she was at the top of the stairs she couldn't contain her excitement any longer. She bolted down and practically threw herself into her brother's arms. "Oh Tris, I am so glad that you're here and that you made it safely!"

"So am I Cee, so am I." He whispered faintly into her hair, hugging her tightly.

She didn't know if she was meant to hear that or not so she let it go, she wriggled her way out of his embrace so that she could get a good look at him. Something was different. Her brother had changed. There was a rigidity about him that hadn't been there the last time she seen him. On the outside, he appeared to be the same, fun loving and mischievous, but something was missing. She knew him like no-one other than Katie. He was holding something back. She would have to remember to ask him about it later. She needed to make sure he was okay. Something was still haunting him. Leaning forward she gave him another hug just as Mel came bursting through the door. Hamish in tow. Mel seemed to be telling him off for the way he had manhandled her on the horse.

Tristan gave a small chuckle, and whispered to Ceana, "I think our brother there has got a thing for Mel, should we warn him about her bossiness, or should we let him find out the hard….?"

He didn't get to finish, instead his reply was replaced with an oomph as Ceana thumped him in the midsection.

Then she realised what he had said. "Are you truly ok that he wants to be part of the family?"

Tristan looked down at her, shocked. "Cee, were you really worried about that? You should have known better. This man is part of you, part of our family and besides, it might be nice having another male to help deal with you three. I've been outnumbered for way too long although he looks as though he might need a few pointers in how to handle you 21st century gals."

Kessan had heard what he had said and burst out laughing. Ceana looked at the both of them and then back at Hamish. "Actually, I think it might do Hamish good. I would say he has finally met his match."

They turned to watch the show. Mel was facing Hamish now and her eyes were flashing daggers as they stood toe to toe. Hamish informed her that here, in the Highlands, she would have to follow his rules for her own safety and that, if she didn't, he would have to show her how a good woman behaved both in and outside of the bedroom. Mel began to sputter. She was at a loss for words. This was the first time Ceana had seen her like this, but then she remembered how she was with Kessan those first few weeks and it all made sense. Perhaps she should tell him to go easy on her, but in that moment he looked up at her over Mel's head and winked, she was floored and snorted back a giggle, Hamish was doing it on purpose.

"I think he likes her." She said in an off-note to her husband and brother.

"Don't even think about it." They said in unison.

"But..."

"But nothing Cee, they will work it out on their own." Tristan said.

"Hey guys, what are we talking about?" Katie said as she entered the room. Ceana turned to see Katie standing behind her with six-month-old Marcus in her arms. This was the first time she had seen her new nephew.

She reached out and Katie passed her the little boy. She gave him a big hug as her two four-and-a-half-year-old terrors came running down the hall and threw themselves into their uncle's arms.

"Uncle Tris!" They screamed together. He caught them mid jump and swung them around.

"Oh my lord, look how much you two rug rats have grown." They both giggled and then proceeded to tell their uncle all about what had happened since the last time he had seen them.

"Oh and guess what uncle Tris?" Cara said pulling on his shirt trying to get his attention.

Yes munchkin?"

"We are going to have another sister or brother."

They all looked at Kessan and Ceana waiting for a confirmation. "It's true we only just found out this morning, although it was supposed to be a surprise." She said pointedly, looking at her children. They all said their congratulations, greeted each other excitedly and made their way to the dining room. The rest of the night was amazing and Ceana wondered why she had ever been so worried.

Giving Ceana an excuse, he made his escape to the ramparts where he sat staring out at the night sky.

He couldn't get over the view here, the night sky was like twinkling diamonds, and with the lack of pollution from the city lights he could see for miles.

As Tristan stood there staring out at the stars, his mind drifted to those who were up in the heavens. He wondered if Marcus and his team were looking down on him, proud of the man he was trying to be.

"I promise I will get justice for you." He whispered up to the sky, hoping that somewhere up there someone heard him.

Now all he had to do was head home and chase the ghost who had been haunting his nightmares.

Tristan was brought out of his musing when he felt someone grab his arm.

Normally he would not have been so jumpy, but because of where his mind had just wondered he was on guard more than usual.

This caused his instinct to act first, grabbing his knife from his boot, Tristan grabbed the intruder and swung them around until he had his knife at their throat.

A small squeak escaped his victim's mouth, bringing his thoughts back to the present.

He was such an idiot.

Tristan looked down into the face of his captive and it was then he noticed his victim was a beautiful young woman.

Her beauty caught him off guard, so he didn't let her go right away, instead he drunk in all of her features.

She had long jet-black hair, with a gold rope braided into parts of it, and the eyes that were staring up at him were a deep ocean blue, so crystal clear he could see right into her soul.

She was wearing a dress of the same colour with a gold trim sewn around the edges. She looked like a princess out of a fairy tale.

The idea that she was from a fairy tale had him believing in magic, and with the conversation from earlier today still fresh in his mind, he decided he needed to taste her.

He could not help himself if he tried, with no other thought he lowered his dagger and leant forward to kiss her.

She tasted of honey and lemon, mixed with a touch of ginger. It was intoxicating.

He wanted nothing more than to devour her.

Thankfully, Tristan had been able to control himself, for some unknown reason he instinctively knew that if he did taste her once more, he would never let her go.

He knew in his heart that this slip of a woman could make a man fall in love with her so quickly he wouldn't even see it coming.

Tristan knew he was being fanciful; he didn't even know who this woman was. She had not been at dinner tonight, he would have remembered that, so she could not be family.

In that moment Tristan realised what he was trying to do. He was trying to find a way for him to see her again. He could not allow that to happen, his life was not his own at the moment and it would not be fair to drag someone's into, no matter how tempting they were.

Tristan loosened his grip on her and slowly allowed her to gain her balance again.

After making sure that she was stable on her feet he offered her an apology.

"I am sorry for scaring you. I hope you are alright." Tristan had half expected her to run away from him scared.

But she didn't, she simply looked at him and shook her head.

Tristan wasn't sure if she was telling him the truth, but he had no other choice but to believe her, he just didn't know enough about this woman to determine otherwise.

Besides he had already accosted her body tonight, he did not want to accost her honour as well by calling her a liar. Highlanders seemed to be rather touchy about that he had noticed earlier.

Tristan waited a minute more for her to say something, but her perfume was starting to distract him. He needed to get out of her as quickly as possible.

The last thing he needed while he was here was to form attachments. He would not be staying, and it wouldn't be fair to lead the young lady on.

Women in this time were different from those at home. In this time the women expected marriage.

And that was something he could not give.

Deciding that it was time for him to get the hell out of here, before his mind decided marriage was a good thing he started to walk around her but before he could his eyes became trapped by hers.

Tristan's breath caught in his chest, all the light and goodness that shone from them squeezed at his heart. It was the same feeling he used to get from the innocent of his niece and nephew. It was a feeling he had been missing and he knew that he needed to feel that goodness again, even if only for a minute.

Without giving it another thought, Tristan grabbed the beautiful young woman, bent forward and placed a gentle kiss on her beautiful lips.

He had only meant for it to be fleeting, but when she yielded to him a possessiveness like nothing he had felt before rushed over him, making him breathless, making him want to claim every part of her body and soul.

He had never reacted to anyone this intensely before and Tristan knew that he should stop before things got out hand, he could already feel his resolve slipping.

When she wrapped her arms around him and moaned it was like having a cold bucket of water thrown on him.

Tristan released her and stepped back, regretting instantly the loss of her. It was a shame, because he knew in a heartbeat that if he had meet her at a different time in his life, he would have jumped at the chance to get to know her and he never would have let her go.

But his life was not his own and he could not in good faith drag her into the turmoil that was his life.

With a that in mind Tristan used what vestige of restraint he had to remember that he had been raised a gentleman.

Making sure not to touch any part of her body, least he lose his resolve, Tristan bowed slightly before offering, "well, then beautiful lady. I apologise once more for ruddiness. I hope you will forgive me for attacking you. Now that I have done the damage I have I will leave you to your night walk."

Tristan didn't wait around to hear her reply or see her reaction to his words, he simply walked away without even looking back.

It was what needed to be done, now all he had to do was work out a way to remove her scent from his memory.

THORA'S HEART was racing she had never been kissed before and being kissed by him was the most extraordinary thing she had ever experienced. She had only come downstairs for some fresh air. She had not

been feeling well for the last couple of days and was on bed rest, but now she was feeling better. Tomorrow was a big day for her, she would meet the rest of Ceana's family, but for tonight she just wanted the peace and

solace that she got from looking at the stars. Instead she had found him. She had never met anyone like him and she swore to herself that she would find out more about him.

❧

Upstairs Kessan and Ceana were preparing for bed. Kessan was watching her brush her hair, she was smiling and appeared to be so happy. "What are ya thinking lass?" he asked.

She placed the brush on the vanity and turned around. "I was just thinking to myself how I got to be so lucky. I always thought that I was the luckiest girl on Earth to have the family I did, even though I didn't think my real family wanted me, and to have the most loyal and beautiful best friend. And then I came here and found Hamish. My brother."

Ceana started to walk towards him; she climbed up the bed and straddled him. She kept on talking as she pulled her nightgown off over her head, "But the one thing that makes me the luckiest girl on the planet is you." She said with sly grin.

"Nay lass I think you have it all wrong. I am the luckiest man alive to have found you."

Ceana laughed, "It might have taken you long enough, but I'm just glad that you finally did find me and bring me home, it didn't matter how happy I was, no matter what happened in my life, my dream had shown me that, as long as you were not in my life, I would always be missing a piece of my heart. Even though I do not quite possess the heart of a Highlander, it has always belonged to one."

Kessan grabbed Ceana and rolled over on top of her, "nay lass there ya are wrong, ye do possess the heart of a Highlander."

At the questioning look in her eyes, he entered her slowly while answering.

"Mine!"

AFTERWORD

Dear Readers,

I hope that you enjoyed reading my first published book. I have many more to come. Firstly, throughout this novel I have used quite a few Scottish words that may have thrown a few of you. Therefore, to help you understand the characters more, and where they come from, I am adding a list of Scottish words and their meanings below. I will also add the calculations for the timeline. This will allow you, my readers, the chance to enjoy the storyline and the characters in their entirety

DICTIONARY OF SCOTTISH WORDS.

- Aboot: About
- Afore: Before
- Ailleagan meinn: Mine
- Aye: Yes
- Bairn: Baby
- Bhaltair (Kessan's Horse): Strong Fighter
- Buttery: Building that was like an old fashion pantry.
- Chit: Woman
- Dirk: Dagger
- Doona: Don't
- Heather: Purple flower found throughout Scotland
- Keep: Village
- Ken: Know
- Reivers: Thieves
- Sassenach: Englishmen
- Trews: Jeans
- Tryst: Meeting